Praise for *The Hourglass Door*

"I never imagined the adventure I'd find when I opened *The Hourglass Door*. Abby and Dante's world is intoxicating and I didn't want to leave. . . . Mangum's book flowed smoothly and effortlessly and led me through a tale I'll not soon forget."
—www.teensreadtoo.com, 5-star rating, Gold Star Award

"The perfect romance!"
—Ally Condie, author of *Being Sixteen*

"What's not to love? A mysterious, gorgeous Italian who recites poetry? I'm so there."
—Becca Wilhite, author of *My Ridiculous, Romantic Obsessions*

THE GOLDEN SPIRAL

Also by Lisa Mangum

The Hourglass Door

THE GOLDEN SPIRAL

A Novel by

LISA MANGUM

First printing in hardbound 2010
First printing in paperbound 2011

Library of Congress Cataloging-in-Publication Data

Mangum, Lisa.
The golden spiral / Lisa Mangum.
p. cm.
Summary: When Dante, a Master of Time, is sent into the past to find Zo, Tony, and V, Abby knows that he will need her help to prevent the trio from destroying time itself, but soon things start to change as Zo targets Abby's past.
ISBN 978-1-60641-635-8 (hardbound : alk. paper)
ISBN 978-1-60908-070-9 (paperbound)
1. Fantasy fiction, American. [1. Time travel—Fiction. 2. High schools—Fiction. 3. Schools—Fiction. 4. Interpersonal relations—Fiction. 5. Good and evil—Fiction.] I. Title.
PZ7.M31266537Fol 2010
[Fic]—dc22 2010003447

Printed in the United States of America
Publishers Printing

10 9 8 7 6 5 4 3 2 1

For Tracy

Roll the Bones—track 2

PROLOGUE

The middle passage. He's been here before. Once, long ago—no, wait . . . not so long ago. He shakes his head. It's hard to remember anything, swallowed up in this narrow throat of darkness.

A flash of white obscures his vision and he remembers.

A girl. Brown hair, brown eyes, a mouth sculpted to smile. He sees worry and fear in her eyes. And something else. A locket is fastened securely around her neck like a collar. Or a noose. He knows this girl. He struggles with his memory, forcing it to offer up a name.

Abby. Of course. Heat like a dying sun scorches through him at the thought of her name, turning the white flash red.

As the redness bleeds into black, he draws a trembling hand across his eyes. He made promises to the girl. To find. To bind. Promises he intends to keep.

Another streak of white flashes through his vision. Another memory. This one of sound. *Is she yours?* A high-pitched banshee wail of music. *We'll* never *be like them ever again, and the sooner you realize that, the better off you'll be.* The quiet click of a key turning in a lock. *I couldn't have done this without you.* A low-throated laugh of success.

This time his memory is more cooperative, comfortable and familiar. His mouth is still heavy with the taste of victory. He savors the sweetness.

He remembers other encounters, other conversations with Dante, but those were the ones that counted. Had he ever truly been a threat? Or merely an annoyance? Dante had certainly done his best to stop him. Though if that was the best he had to offer, well, then there was no need to worry.

He made promises to Dante, too. Of vengeance. Of damnation. Promises he intends to keep as well.

Somewhere in the far distance he can hear footsteps. Not his. He hasn't moved in this middle passage since the door closed behind him—how long ago? He shakes his head again. It doesn't matter. All that matters now is what waits for him in the darkness.

He counts the steps, easily identifying and discarding the echoes, concentrating on the actual, individual footfalls. There. He tilts his head, listening with his whole body. A second set of footsteps rings through the stillness in a fleeting harmony. Good. Everyone is accounted for.

Words float through his mind: *The gang's all here.* Something he heard once? Something he has yet to hear?

There is no rush. He knows where they are going. Or perhaps he should say *when.*

The footsteps clatter around him; they sound like bones rattling in the wind. He knows exactly who those footsteps belong to, and he wonders why they don't take more care to disguise themselves. He wonders why they even bother walking when it's possible to slide—now *here*, now *there*—with the merest of thoughts. He considers the possibility they haven't discovered that fact yet.

He remembers the first time the door closed behind him. The stench of his branded flesh. The taste of the cold, empty air. The weight of uncertainty, of limited options. Exiled from the river of time, he was once a prisoner bound to the bank.

But now, the door has closed behind him a second time, and everything is different. He looks down at his hands, marveling that the tattooed chains encircling his wrists have turned from black to gold. They are beautiful. Like the golden torques worn by the kings of old.

He laughs a little at the thought. There is no more *old* or *new*; the words have lost their meaning. There is only *here* and *now*. There is only what he wants. There is only him in this dark place, waiting to be born again into the light. The world is waiting for him to change it like Prometheus bringing down fire from the gods.

The air around him is still cold and metallic, but now when he draws a deep breath, it turns his body into a sword, all edges and violence. This time the uncertainty is gone. This time his options are limitless.

Embraced by the river of time, he has broken the bonds of the bank forever.

He can feel the ebb and flow of the river of time *inside* him now. He can see the possibilities unfolding with every breath. The sense of freedom and power is overwhelming.

He knows the others are feeling the same thing. He knows

it will make them reckless, unpredictable. They do not have his control or his command. Without his leadership and guidance, they will squander this gift, they will waste this power. He cannot let that happen. He has plans.

He feels a grin slide across his face, and he takes a step forward.

He is surprised at how easy it is. This traveling through time. This effortless movement like flying, like dancing, like music. He is no longer afraid of what he has left behind, or of what might be waiting for him. After all, he knows what is waiting for him ahead in the darkness. The second door. The machine only works in pairs, he remembers. Two banks of the river, two doors. In one and out the other. It is an elegant design. Balanced. Complete. The symmetry of it makes him happy.

It's been a long time since he's felt this happy. He pauses. Maybe that's wrong. Maybe it'll *be* a long time until he feels this happy again. The past and future are interchangeable now; it's hard to tell the difference. He does know one thing, though: He was born for this. His previous life seems like nothing so much as a shadow by comparison. He can see from horizon to horizon; better, he can see beyond the curve now. He can hear the smallest droplet of time forming inside the roaring of the river. How had he lived without this power? This awareness?

Now that he has it, he knows he will never let it go.

He was always the brightest, deserving of their loyalty and their devotion.

He will never let those go, either.

He is drawing closer to the footsteps. He can hear voices now, though just fragmented whispers of sound.

. . . believe it . . . it's true . . . it's time . . .

With a rush, the whispers coalesce into solid sentences, individual voices: Tony and V.

He stays back a pace or two. No need to let them know he is so close. Not yet.

"I can't believe she came with him," Tony says.

V makes a noise halfway between a growl and a grunt.

"Don't get me wrong, I'm glad she did. We'd still be stuck there without her help." Tony laughs, a high note wavering on the edge of hysteria. "I guess I owe Zo an apology. I shouldn't have doubted him."

He frowns. Dissension in the ranks is not to be tolerated. Doubt is forbidden. He thought he had made that clear.

"Where is Zo, anyway?" Tony asks, looking around. "I'd have thought he'd be here by now."

V grunts again. "I'm sure he's coming. How much farther is it?"

Tony laughs. "Don't you remember?"

"I just want to go home." V sighs. "I'm tired of . . . all this."

His frown deepens. How can V be tired of this already? Things are just getting started. *He* is just getting started.

"Oh, come on," Tony chides. "Live a little. Or a lot, as the case may be." His laugh transmutes into a giggle, high and childish.

"What's wrong with you?" V asks.

"Nothing."

The lie is loud in the space between them.

He shakes his head. Lies can be useful, but they must be used correctly or else they lose their power. And this is no place for lies. The machine will destroy them, squeeze them into oblivion and leave only the truth in its place. The machine is unforgiving, unrelenting. He admires that.

He wonders if Tony knows he's lying or if he believes his own words. He wonders if it matters.

The darkness suddenly crackles into life, bright sparks flaring like stars spangled across the sky. The tiniest of golden glows blooms overhead, growing into a complex web of light laced through the shadows above Tony's head. A second web appears over V's head.

He looks up in time to see his own golden net hovering over him. Without consciously knowing how, he dampens the light. No need to announce his presence prematurely.

"That's amazing," Tony says, looking up at the golden drops. "I don't remember that from last time."

"I think it's new. Things have changed, remember."

Tony slaps V on the back. "Change is good. It's a brave new world, *amico mio*. And we will be the masters of it."

V grunts again; his shoulders hunch under a shrug.

"What? Everything is here for the taking. Don't tell me you don't want some of it." Tony rubs at the golden cuffs around his wrists and laughs.

"I can't have what I want," V says, shoving his hands into his pockets.

"That's no way to think. Listen, we'll be to the door in no time at all"—Tony giggles again, a mad light flickering in his eyes—"and you'll see. You'll feel it." He circles V, a capering jester laughing at his own unfathomable jokes.

"I already feel it." V frowns. "And I think you're feeling it too much. Stop that, Tony. You're making me nervous."

He agrees. There is a wrongness emanating from Tony. The edges of his body seem softer, thinner than before. He thinks of the word *suffused*. Of the word *bloated*. Of the word *decomposing*.

He can feel the pressure building inside Tony. After spending all those years controlling the pressure from the river, he is surprised that Tony has missed identifying something so important to his survival. He hadn't realized Tony was so weak.

He wonders if he should intervene. Warn him. But he's curious to see what they will do. How capable they are without him. He wants to know how much they need him.

"Hurry, hurry, hurry!" Tony grabs V's arm and pulls him forward. "We're late, we're late, for a very important date."

"Quit it," V barks, yanking his arm away. "Stop acting so crazy."

There is a strange note in V's voice but there is no time to identify it. The gold-flecked shadows overhead have ended suddenly in a hard edge. A solid wall rears up before them, tall as a tower, narrow, foreboding.

It is the black door.

He can see a glimmer of brass and knows that the hinges on this door only swing *in*. There are no elaborate designs on this slab of black. There is no need. No one ever expected anyone would lay eyes on this side of the machine.

He grins. He loves shattering expectations. It's important to be the first. The best.

This is the door that will lead him into a new life. He can feel the thrumming hum of energy trapped just on the other side of the door. So close. Close enough to touch. Almost. Almost.

The promise of power is screaming like a high wind through his ears. It will take only a touch to tame it, claim it for his own. The pull is insistent. Immediate. He lowers a hand he hadn't realized he'd raised.

He hears chimes ringing, a melody that is at once familiar and alien.

It is time—in more ways than one.

"We should wait for Zo," V says. "He'll want to go first."

"Who died and made him king?" Tony's words slur together in a lump of sound. They knock against the shivery chimes, a discordant clash. "I'm going to do what *I* want for a change." His laugh sounds like a seam ripping apart. "My way this time."

Tony lifts a hand, reaches for the door.

The music swells like a rising tide. The pressure gathers, thick as a storm cloud, focused as a tornado's funnel.

He thinks of the word *crescendo.* Of *corrupted.*

V takes a step back. "No, don't—"

Tony touches the door.

Cataclysmic.

A supernova of white reverses the world from dark to light in an instant. Heat floods the narrow space—a fire that doesn't burn, but one that is deadly all the same.

The golden stars over Tony's head begin to wink out one by one. The delicate web strung between them begins to sag and droop, falling, fading. In the harsh white light of destruction, Tony himself grows thinner, fainter, torn apart like a cloud in the wind.

He hears Tony scream. The laughter is ripped from his voice, and all that is left is pain. He watches Tony writhe, caught by forces he can't see, much less stop. His body begins to disappear, an emptiness that eats away at his chest before spreading out through his arms, up his neck, down his legs. He struggles, fighting against the impossible.

His mouth vanishes, and his scream is nothing more than a fading echo. The golden chains on his wrists shimmer like mirages. He is a faint outline against the burning white. For a moment, he holds his shape, and then the outline disperses like ashes.

Tony is gone, unraveled. Erased from existence.

There is no sound. Even the chimes are silent. He is alone with V. He looks at the stunned expression on V's face, follows his gaze.

There is a hole where the door used to be. A portal that empties out onto a familiar room, a familiar sight. The courtroom is empty tonight. He smiles. This time there will be no judge, no guards to watch them travel through the door. This time no one will ask him any questions.

He is glad now that he didn't intervene. If he had stopped Tony, then he would have been the one to trigger the trap. He would have been the one blasted into oblivion instead of the one to cross through the portal and step onto his homeland after more years than he cares to count.

He walks forward. He can feel the weight of V's gaze on his shoulders, equal parts surprise and fear. That is good. It's good to keep people on their toes. Prepared.

He feels he should miss Tony more than he does. Ah, well. Perhaps later. For now, V is enough. He will have to be.

"Come, Vincenzio," he says. "Let's go home."

V hesitates for a bare moment, then falls in behind him, following in his footsteps across the threshold.

A warm ripple passes over him, into him. And then he is through. He is home.

He draws in a deep breath, feeling free and whole. Turning, he looks back into the dark heart of the machine. The walls, the ceiling, the floor—everything glows with a white-hot light. As he watches, the light begins to spread deeper into the machine, moving with the speed of a wildfire and leaving behind only ash in its wake.

Though he left a warning not to follow, he secretly hopes Dante disobeyed. And if he did follow, he hopes he survives the coming onslaught.

Things are about to get interesting.

CHAPTER 1

"Is this a joke?" Jason sat down next to me on the patio steps in my backyard, a sheaf of papers in his hand. He shuffled through them, one after another, sometimes flipping a sheet upright, sometimes turning one over.

"What's wrong?" I asked, looking up and squinting against the early June afternoon sunshine. My purple Popsicle dripped a splash of grape onto my hand.

"According to these directions, this"—he pointed to a series of rectangles and squares drawn in overlapping layers—"connects to this"—he shuffled to another page, this one covered with tiny circles and ovals—"but without any apparent bolts or hinges or . . . or anything." He dropped the papers on the ground between our feet and ran his hands through his blond curls. "It doesn't make any sense."

"Um, sorry?" I offered.

"It might help if I knew what we were building. I mean, sometimes it looks like it's some kind of a house. But not like a real house—it's too narrow and long. And there seem to be too many doors. And no windows at all. It's like we just have plans for a hallway and not the rest of the house. You're not keeping something from me, are you?"

I stuck the Popsicle in my mouth, grateful for the excuse it gave me not to respond immediately. I looked at the dozen or so small flags stuck into the ground along one edge of my backyard that outlined the parameters of the project. Jason was right; it didn't seem to make any sense. What could possibly fit into a space twenty-four feet long, two feet wide, and eight feet tall?

"And if I'm reading this right, then once we're done building it, we have to burn it down. What's that all about?"

I shrugged, though I had wondered about that part of the plans myself. "It's the final step. You know—like making ceramics or forging a sword. There's always a finishing process you have to go through."

"The refiner's fire," Jason said with a nod. "That's cool. Dangerous, but cool. Maybe we'll call the fire department when we get to that part." He wrote himself a note in the margin.

I felt bad for Jason. Dante's instructions were complicated and sometimes confusing. I knew exactly what we were building, but even I couldn't see how those finely drawn lines would result in a time machine.

"And what are all these symbols?" Jason grabbed a sheet from the ground and waved it at me. "At first I thought they were just decorative, but now I think they might mean something."

I took the paper from Jason, handling it carefully with my slightly sticky fingers. "Well, this one is a spiral shell. It's called a nautilus." I traced the curved lines with my eyes, imagining

Dante's long fingers wrapped around a pen, his strong hand stroking the lines confidently onto the blank sheet. "It's an example of a natural logarithmic spiral. See, you can trace along the spiral, circling the center an infinite number of times without ever actually reaching the middle." My memory suddenly caught a fragment from the past: the feel of the night wind, the heat of Dante's eyes on me, the weight of his words on my heart. Those long-ago words slipped into my mind: *"Can you imagine it? To be forever denied the one thing you long for most of all?"*

I handed the paper back to Jason with a steady voice but a trembling hand. "The logarithmic spiral also appears in sunflowers, the nerves of the cornea, hurricane patterns, and the arms of the Milky Way. It's based on the Fibonacci sequence."

"Since when do you know so much about math?" Jason asked, bumping my shoulder so I'd know he was teasing. "I thought you were strictly a word person."

"I am." I bumped him back. "I've been studying. Is that so hard to believe? And as a word person, I know that a nautilus is also called an *argonaut*. As in 'Jason and the.' And *argonaut* is another name for an adventurer or a traveler."

"Seriously? That's cool." He leaned back on the steps and stretched his legs out on the grass, studying the nautilus sketch. The sun lined his body with golden light. "I still don't get why we have to carve it on what appears to be the front door of this crazy house."

I bit my lip. I wanted to tell him the truth—*because it's a mathematically perfect representation for traveling through time*—but I knew I couldn't.

I had shown the complete blueprints of Dante's design only to Jason. He was my muscle on the project and needed to know as much as I could tell him, which admittedly wasn't much. I had told my parents about the project, but in very general terms—I couldn't very well build something in the backyard without their permission. Hannah knew the basics too, but that was more because she was a nosy little sister and I figured it was safer to tell her *something,* if only to prevent her from snooping around, looking for answers on her own.

All of them believed it was a rather offbeat school project for a rather offbeat school.

"It's just something I have to do for my scholarship application for Emery," I said, hating that I could hear the lie in my voice. I hated even more knowing that I didn't have a choice. It was too dangerous to tell Jason the truth. "They wanted to see how I would approach a seemingly impossible project."

"And your approach is to rope me into doing your homework for you?" Jason grinned.

"No, my approach is to delegate the task to a qualified, talented individual and then supervise his work. That shows serious leadership ability, which is a very important and desirable quality, you know."

"So is honesty," Jason retorted.

I flinched inwardly. "I'm also being resourceful and creative. Besides, it's not like anyone from Emery is going to come check up on my work. I'm just supposed to send them pictures of the finished piece along with a written report of what I learned from the process. It's an exercise in creative, out-of-the-box thinking. A kind of organic experiment. You know—the journey is more important than the destination and all that."

That was less of a lie than the rest. I knew that the journey to finish the time machine would be as important as the destination, if not more so. I tried not to think about what it would mean if I actually succeeded in following Dante's plans. "I'm glad that Mom and Dad will let us use the backyard," I finished.

Jason sighed. "*I'm* glad all I had to do for my scholarship was fill out an application. That took me a half hour; building this will take us weeks. Literally." He tapped a page that detailed the step-by-step assembly instructions, annotated with specific dates and times. Start to finish, it would take eight weeks exactly. As if that weren't bad enough, the plans specified that we had to start on the first day of a season, and since we had missed the first day of spring, I had to cool my heels, waiting for the first day of summer. I was trying to be productive with my time—studying, reading, researching, anything to help the time pass faster—but every day seemed to be traveling at a slow crawl.

"Yeah, well, Emery is a very exclusive college. They don't let just anyone in."

"They let *you* in." Jason bumped me again. His grin was all teeth and teasing.

"Then that must mean I'm not just anyone." I tossed my hair back over my shoulder and gave him my most haughty supermodel smile. "I'm Abigail Edmunds and I'm going to change the world."

"I don't doubt it," Jason said softly. A wistful look crossed his face, flashing through his eyes so quickly I almost missed it.

My heart stuttered. I thought we'd been over this. We'd tried the boyfriend-girlfriend thing and it hadn't worked. At least, it hadn't worked for me. And besides, I knew Jason and Natalie were still together because Nat had told me he'd already planned to take her out to dinner after graduation tomorrow.

I was saved from having to say anything because Jason, ruffling through the papers, handed me another sheet.

"Look at the detail on this one. It's incredible."

I licked the last of my Popsicle and swallowed hard. A heart filled the entire page, drawn in solid black lines. Thinner lines crossed the surface, connecting to each other in a tight, interlocking web. The patterns seemed alive, twisting and twining around each other until it was impossible to tell where one line started and another line ended. A host of endless Möbius strips of ink. Two hinges were inked along one side of the heart.

I recognized the image immediately. How could I not, when the physical version of it hung on a chain around my neck? After that terrible night almost three weeks ago when the Dungeon had burned to the ground, I had taken to wearing high-collared shirts to hide the scars around my throat. My neck still bore the imprint of the chains that had been flash-burned onto my skin when the black door had disintegrated on the bank.

Dante had given me that locket—the key to his heart—

and I couldn't bear not to have it close to my own heart. I never took it off. Not to shower, not to sleep. Never.

"It's beautiful," I managed. My fingers twitched, itching to touch the solid lump of silver under my shirt. I shoved my hand under my leg.

"It looks like the locket Dante gave you before—"

"What?" I interrupted, a little sharply. I'd been so careful to erase any remnant of Dante's name from the copy of the blueprints I'd shown Jason. The originals were locked away, safe in my desk drawer.

"Oh, sorry." Jason winced. "Natalie said I shouldn't bring him up."

"No, it's just—"

"You don't like talking about him," Jason finished. "I understand."

"No, it's just that—"

"He broke your heart and left without even saying goodbye."

"No, he didn't," I protested automatically.

"What? He didn't break your heart, or he didn't skip town the first chance he got?"

I shut my mouth, trying to keep my emotions in check. "That's not fair," I finally said. "You weren't there. You don't know what happened."

"Because you won't tell me."

"What's with the third degree all of a sudden?" I asked, surprised at the bitterness in Jason's voice.

"We're friends, right?"

I nodded, strangely cautious.

"Well, as your friend, I'm worried about you." He shifted a little closer to me. "Look at it from my point of view. We break up, and you start dating Dante."

I opened my mouth, but Jason overrode my feeble attempts at an explanation.

"Which I was fine with. I could see he made you happy, which is all I ever wanted for you. And I'm happy with Natalie, so it all worked out, right?"

I closed my mouth and looked down at my hands. I didn't deserve such a good friend.

"But then it all went wrong. The next thing I know, you almost die in a fire at the Dungeon and have to spend days and days in the hospital. Leo and Dante seem to disappear overnight. Valerie is in a mental hospital, of all places. Everything is different."

"Not everything," I said, willing my voice to remain light. "I'm still the same old Abby."

Jason looked at me seriously. "No. You're not. That's my point. There's something different about you, and all I can think is that when Dante left, he broke your heart, and now you're in denial, hoping he'll come back one day."

I couldn't help myself—I reached up and touched the locket at my throat. Tears burned the backs of my eyes and a sour taste coated my throat. Dante *had* left me, but not like Jason imagined. I had worked so hard not to think about it. Now suddenly I remembered so clearly stepping away from Dante, releasing him so he could follow after Zo before the door of time closed forever. I remembered how the flat light of the bank seemed to part around him as he turned away from me. I felt again the music ringing deep in my bones, the song of time as it spilled out of the doorway, drawing Dante like a moth to a flame. I heard the echo of destruction as the black door dissolved into white light.

"He's gone, Abby," Jason said quietly, sliding his arm around my shoulder and leaning his head against mine. "And he's not coming back."

I closed my eyes, and for one small flash of time I wondered if Jason was right. It had been weeks, and if Dante had survived the passage through the door a second time, then he, like Zo, was now a master of time. He could go anywhere and any *when* he wanted. And if that was the case, then why hadn't he come back to me, if only to let me know he was okay? Deep down I knew he would come if he could, but since he hadn't, I feared that it was because he *couldn't.* I worried that something had happened to him somewhere along the river of time. What if he had never made it past the door? What if he was trapped somewhere on the bank, or lost in time? What if he'd already confronted Zo . . . and lost? What if I never found out what happened to him? What if he *was* gone forever?

"Hey, Abby, I'm sorry," Jason said. "I didn't mean to make you cry."

I rubbed at my eyes, surprised to feel the tears flowing down my cheeks and soaking into Jason's shirt. Dante's locket felt like a rock chained around my neck.

"You're wrong," I insisted, my low voice muffled by Jason's shoulder. "He *didn't* break my heart, and he *is* coming back to me. He promised."

Jason was quiet for a long time, rubbing his hand up and

down my back until my tears dried and my breath stopped hiccuping in my chest.

"Do you feel better?" he asked me, brushing my hair away from my face.

I nodded, swiping my sleeve across my eyes. Oddly enough, I did feel better. It was like the tears had washed away three weeks' worth of worry and fear and in their place was a clean and clear resolve. I would follow my heart; I would trust my instincts.

Dante had left me the blueprints for a reason. He had seen something in the river that made him decide to give them to me. He had trusted me to make the right choices, even difficult choices, and I didn't want to let him down.

It was simple: If Dante couldn't come to me, then I would go to him. And that meant finishing the time machine no matter what.

"Thanks, Jason," I said, sitting up straight and squeezing his forearm.

"For what?"

"For being a good friend. For helping. For everything."

"Well, in that case . . ." He grinned and wiped the last trace of a tear from my face. "I'll only charge you *half* the going rate."

"The going rate for what?"

"For doing your homework." He laughed.

"Brat." I scowled at him and slapped at his shoulder. "And you're doing this for free, remember?"

He shrugged easily. "As long as you're paying for the materials, I'm okay with that. Do you know how much"—he consulted the paperwork—"'a beam of black walnut wood, turned by hand, and inscribed with a needle-pointed awl' costs?"

"I don't even know what a needle-pointed awl is."

"Me neither, but it sounds expensive." He stood up, pulling me to my feet with him. "According to the plans, we'll need to start actual construction on the first day of summer—that's what? two weeks from today? Will you have everything ready by then?"

"Two weeks and two days, but who's counting, right? And yes, I'll be ready," I said, crossing my fingers behind my back.

"Even the needle-pointed awl?"

"Especially that."

"Okay, then." He tapped the papers into a neat square and handed them back to me. "I hope you know what you're doing."

I watched Jason head for home, a spring in his step, and heard the faint whistle of a random tune trailing after him.

I looked again at the small orange flags fluttering on the lawn and thought about how much time two weeks really was. And how fast it could disappear. "I hope so too," I murmured.

The moon was lost behind the clouds, and I could smell the coming storm in the hot breeze blowing past my open window. I sat on my window seat and propped a pillow behind my back. Crossing my feet against the wall, I pulled a brush through my wet hair. After dinner, I'd watched some TV with Hannah, then headed upstairs for a bath before bed.

I loved late-night summer storms. There was something soothing about being inside while a storm raged outside. A feeling of being protected, safe against the raw power of nature. Lightning raced ahead on the horizon; thunder grumbled in the distance, petulant at being left behind. The humid air was heavy with rain.

My cell phone rang. I slipped it off my desk and flipped it on.

"Are you watching?" Natalie asked.

"Absolutely."

A silver flicker sliced through the shadows. Natalie and I *ooh*ed at the same time.

"That was a nice one," she said.

"Very." I shifted the phone to my other ear. "Where are you?"

"Family room. What about you?"

"Window seat."

"Excellent vantage point. You'll have to tell me what I'm missing."

I grinned. "How long have we been watching storms together?" I asked.

Natalie laughed. "How did this tradition even get started? Do you remember?"

"Of course I do. I was sleeping over at your place and we were staying up late watching old Hitchcock movies when a storm hit. We turned off the TV and ended up watching the weather instead."

"That's right. Ugh, weather watchers—does that make us nerds or what?"

"I'll take the 'or what' category."

"You would."

"Hey, that sounds vaguely like an insult."

"It is." She laughed again. "Kidding!"

I shook my head and grinned. "I know, I know." Raindrops started to fall, invisible in the darkness, but loud against the leaves and the side of the house. "It's starting to rain here—what about you?"

"Yep. Just now. I wish it wasn't the middle of the night. I would love to go play in the rain."

"And risk catching a cold before graduation? Are you crazy?"

She sighed and her voice turned serious. "I can't believe it's tomorrow." She sounded sad. "One last time together before we all go our separate ways."

"What are you talking about? You and Jason are going to school together."

"I know, but you're going somewhere else, and Valerie . . ." Natalie's voice trailed off. I heard the thunder outside my window echoing through the phone. "I guess I just thought things would be different, that's all."

I leaned my head back against the wall, a fine rain touching my face with mist. "Have you been to see her?" I asked quietly.

"Not yet." She hesitated. "Does that make me a bad friend?"

"No. I haven't seen her yet either."

"But you had a good reason—you were in the hospital."

"Still."

"Are you okay now?" Natalie asked. "I mean, things were a little crazy there, weren't they?"

"I'm fine," I said, pretty sure it was the truth. And if not, pretty sure it would be soon enough. The orange flags flickered in the lightning like individual flames. I shivered and rested my hand against the scars on my throat, memories filling me at the touch. Memories I wasn't sure I wanted to face tonight.

I heard Natalie yawn.

"It's late," I said, grateful for the easy out. "I'll see you tomorrow, okay?"

"What about the storm?"

"It'll be fine without us," I said. "Besides, there'll always be another one."

I hung up the phone, but I didn't leave the window seat right away. Instead, I closed the window and watched the raindrops as they traveled down the glass, each one making tiny, individual tracks. Some drops ran in a straight line; others meandered in wandering trails before being swallowed up in the wake of another drop. The rain fell and the water continued to branch out into countless rivers, endlessly moving, endlessly flowing.

I closed my eyes and thought about promises and possibilities.

I couldn't tell how long I listened to the rain before I fell asleep.

CHAPTER 2

The bank was barren, like always. The vast, flat landscape stretched into infinity, and the omnipresent gray light hung like a miasma over the ground. I didn't belong here. Nothing did. The bank was outside of time. A dead place. A terrible place.

And it was impossible that I was here at all. Panic settled over me like a shroud. I didn't remember traveling here: no counting, no concentration, no thinning of the edges of reality. Regardless of how I had gotten here, though, I knew the only way home was to find the river. But I had no sense of direction here, no idea which way to go. And even if I did find the river, even if I returned to my own time, I knew I would bring some of the bank's timelessness with me. And with both Dante and Leo gone, who could free me from that prison? No one.

I closed my eyes, dread weighing down my limbs like chains. I couldn't have moved if I had wanted to. But it didn't matter. I was trapped.

I realized I was crouching, my arms wrapped around my

knees, my back curved like a half shell. I drew in a deep breath, the taste of a scream filling my mouth—

And that was when I knew.

This was a dream—one of nightmarish proportions, certainly, but still it was just a dream. Or almost. I'd had one of these kinds of dreams before, when I'd stood on the near side of the dream landscape, eavesdropping on Dante and Zo as I peeked in on the bank without actually traveling there. Now that I was paying attention, I could feel the difference. There was less pressure, less sense of otherworldliness. I could breathe freely, without a kiss from anyone to protect me. My eyes didn't hurt as much from the severe lack of landscape or from the false light that hovered eternally somewhere between dusk and dawn.

This was a dream. And I had nothing to fear from dreams.

I stood up, straight and tall—

And space bent around me like I was the event horizon of a black hole.

The sudden curvature almost drove me to my knees again. The light snuffed out—my ears rang with sound, a note that was less a shivering chime and more a knelling bell—and the gray was stripped away into black.

I hadn't thought the bank could get any worse. Standing on shaking legs, looking up into the dead black void that used to be the sky, I knew that not only could things get worse—they already had.

Wakeupwakeupwakeup, I ordered myself in one long command. Squeezing my eyes shut, I held my breath and counted to ten. *Wake. Up. Now!*

I opened my eyes, but nothing had changed. At least not that I could see. But now there were voices drifting on a nonexistent wind. Wild, indecipherable sounds. Strings of vowels and guttural consonants that made the hair on my arms stand up with animalistic adrenaline.

. . . here . . . she's here . . .

I turned in a tight circle, trying to follow the thread of sound in the emptiness around me. Useless—the words were everywhere, sometimes a whisper, sometimes a shout, like a horde of night-flying moths blinded by light.

. . . not . . . go . . . stay . . . never . . .

. . . save . . . go . . . She's here! . . .

I didn't want to be here. The voices wanted me to go and I wanted nothing more than to obey. But where could I go? How? I looked around desperately, but all I saw was more of the same—emptiness. Sheer, vast emptiness.

. . . too late . . . always too late . . .

I imagined myself back in my own bed, safe under the covers. Then I pinched my arm hard enough to raise a welt. I dug my fingernails deep into my sweaty palms. Why wouldn't I wake up?

The voices increased in volume, layering and overlapping in intensity. I couldn't tell how many there were—two, three? More? I tried to listen, tried to pick apart the individual voices, but they were too interwoven, shuffled like playing cards in a deck.

I closed my eyes so I could concentrate. I pressed my hands to my ears, trying to strain the noise through my fingers. I felt the air warp, almost like it was bending around me, enclosing me in a column. In the shelter of the curve, I heard one voice clear and sharp.

Don't move.

I knew that voice. I heard it in my dreams and longed to hear it in person once again. Velvet, warmed with the unmistakable tones of Italy. Dante's voice.

I opened my eyes, sure that I would see him standing next to me, his lips curving in a small smile and his gray eyes swallowing me whole. I could almost smell the musky sweet fragrance of his skin. I turned my head, but the voice spoke again, low and insistent.

No. Don't move. Dante's plea came to me tied on a thread of a whisper. *Don't go. Not yet.*

"Dante?" I called out, hoping against hope that he was somehow close, could somehow talk to me. "Are you there?"

I'm here.

I felt his voice resonate in my body; I could almost feel his hands pressed against mine.

"Where are you? Why can't I see you?" I risked a glance around, but all I saw was the black sky above me and the black bank at my feet.

Things are . . . different—

"I noticed." I clung to the sound of his voice, hungry for more. But all I had were fragments, crumbs and sips instead of the feast I wanted.

. . . he's unpredictable . . .

"Who? Zo? What's going on?" I shifted, and the protected pocket of air shimmered. Dante's voice stuttered and skipped like a lost radio signal.

I didn't expect . . . dead . . . death . . . gone . . .

Quickly, I moved back to my original position, searching for that sweet spot of sound. "I need answers, Dante. Can you hear me?"

I felt him draw in a deep, shuddering breath. *I can hear you. But I can't see you. I can't see anything. It's dark. And cold.*

"What happened? Did you make it through the door?"

I . . . don't know. I don't think so.

"What about the others? Did you catch up to Zo?" My breath tasted like hope.

No. He's gone. They're both gone.

"Both?"

V and Zo. I don't know where they are. Wherever I am, Tony is with me.

Hope transformed into surprise.

Though he's not well. I don't know how long he will last—

A scream ripped through the air. A dark, throaty roar that sounded as black as the ruined sky above me. The sound tapered off, only to resume a jagged breath later with another scream.

"Dante!"

I'm here, Abby, he said. *I'm here. I'm all right. It's not me. It's Tony. He's not . . . I don't know what's happening to him.*

I clenched my hands into fists, helpless in the face of the frustration I heard in his voice. I couldn't see him; I couldn't help him. I couldn't do anything.

I can't touch him. He just . . . slides through my fingers. It's like he's disappearing. Dante's voice held a complex mix of confusion, fear, and awe.

"Where are you?" I asked again.

I don't know. It feels confined, though. I don't dare leave Tony to explore too much.

I wanted to reach through to wherever he was and pull him to safety. But I feared he was beyond where I could go.

Where are you? Dante asked.

"I'm sort of on the bank—"

What? No, you shouldn't be there. Go back. Go home.

"Wait, no, I'm not actually here. I fell asleep and I'm still dreaming. I think."

I slowly lifted my hand, my ears attuned to the slightest sound around me. If I paid attention, I could hold on to the thin thread that connected us. I took that as a good sign. I touched the ripples in front of me with my fingertip. The air flexed, but it didn't stop shimmering. I took that as a better sign. Pressing my palm flat against the curved wall of air, I dared to push out. The ripples converged, sliding over my hand like a glove.

"Dante," I whispered. "Are you still there?"

Always.

I extended my arm fully, holding my breath, anticipating a pain that didn't come.

What are you doing?

"I'm trying something. Is anything happening on your end? Can you see me? Feel me?"

No. It's still dark and—wait, I think I see something. A light. Faint, but . . . Is that you?

I felt the touch of his hands on mine, though it felt like a ghost.

It is you!

I grinned and wiggled my fingers in Dante's hand, delighted to hear his low chuckle in response.

If you're dreaming, how are you doing this?

"I don't know," I admitted. "I've only dreamed my way here once before, remember? I'm figuring this out as I go."

There was a pause, then, *I'm glad you're here, Abby. Wherever here is. I almost don't dare ask how it is possible in case this doesn't happen again. In case this is the only time we have left.*

I felt the pressure of his hand around mine increase in a tight squeeze.

"Don't talk like that," I said. "I'm here now; I can come again. And we'll figure out where you are and how to get you home." My fingers prickled with impending numbness. I withdrew my arm from the shimmering air and rubbed my hands together until they were warm again. A pang of longing went through me. Already I missed the feel of his hand in mine. "Tell me what happened. What's the last thing you remember?"

The door closed behind me, and I started walking. I don't know for how long. But all at once I saw a net of stars above me.

"Stars?"

That's what they looked like. But almost as soon as they appeared, I heard a noise. A scream. I started to run.

I could hear the tension in Dante's voice as he related the events.

I thought it was Zo, and if it was, then I wanted to be there. I didn't want to lose him—I couldn't. The tension fell into frustration. *It was so dark, though. And I wasn't fast enough. I saw something up ahead.*

"What? What was it?"

Dante continued as though he hadn't heard me; maybe he hadn't. *A halo of white fire sped toward me out of the darkness. I thought at first that I had reached the other side, that what I was seeing was sunlight through the open door. But this light burned everything it touched—the walls, the ceiling, the entire machine—even me.*

"It burned you?"

It burned everything. Dante's voice sounded strained, feathered with panic at the edges. *When it reached me . . . I didn't have anywhere to go. I couldn't escape it. The light*—he made a strangled noise like a growl. *I felt myself . . . fading, dissolving. Then the light passed over me—through me—and then . . . darkness.*

A tremor shook me, so violent it made my teeth click together. I wrapped my arms around my chest. I could imagine Dante's wall of light so clearly because I had seen it as well. But from the other side. I had the scars on my throat as a reminder of what had happened in that moment of destruction.

In my memory, I was on the desolate bank, alone except for the black hourglass door that had shut behind Dante. As I replayed that moment, I saw again the door disintegrating in a flare of white light.

"Dante," I whispered, "do you know how long you have been—wherever you are?"

He paused, then said, *No. I can't sense the river at all. There is just me and Tony and the darkness. All the stars are gone, too.*

"It's been almost three weeks." I closed my eyes against the thought of Dante wrapped in unending darkness for so long. I took a deep breath and said the impossible. "You never made it out the door. I think you're still there somehow."

What? I'm still in the time machine?

"I think so."

Dante was quiet for a long time. So long, I started to wonder if we had lost our tenuous connection.

But if the time machine is gone—if the door is destroyed—then how can I leave?

"I don't know," I said, hating how often I found myself saying those words. "But there's got to be a way."

Tony screamed again, a piercing howl that brought sudden tears to my eyes. The cry seemed to take a long time to fade away. Even still, I could hear a low moan bubbling continuously in my inner ear. What had happened to Tony to cause such agony? And—I almost didn't dare think it—would it happen to Dante too?

He must have been thinking along the same lines because his next words were low and fierce.

Hurry, Abby. Please.

"I will," I said. "I'll figure something out. Promise me you'll hold on, that you'll be here when I come back."

Silence.

"Dante? Answer me!"

And then I felt his presence next to me so powerfully that my body trembled in anticipation. He was clearly still somewhere else and I was still in my dream, but suddenly the barriers between us were as thin as smoke.

I felt the ghost of his hands slide up my arms, my shoulders, to the curve of my neck.

"Dante, do you promise?"

Yes. The word rolled through me like thunder. I felt his lips touch mine in a kiss so lightning-fast it left the ends of my hair crackling.

Sound washed over me, the roar of a flood overrunning its banks—

And then he was gone.

I shivered with the loss, feeling a tingling numbness where he had touched me.

My thoughts felt equally numb, sluggish and leaden. These kinds of dreams were exhausting, but I knew I'd need to have more of them if I wanted any chance of solving the riddle of how to free someone from a prison that didn't exist.

I wasn't even sure how I had the dreams in the first place. Was it something I did before falling asleep? Something I ate? Maybe they couldn't be controlled at all, and I was simply at the whim of an unknown power.

No. I refused to believe that. There had to be a way to control my dreams. A way to access this shadow side of the bank. A way to reach Dante before it was too late.

The dark sky seemed to lower over me, the weight of it making my shoulders hunch as though under an unseen burden. The bank felt unstable beneath my feet, sliding and shifting. I imagined a quicksand pit opening up and dragging me down, or a bottomless sinkhole with sheer walls like a throat, gulping me whole.

Stop it, I commanded, giving myself a little shake. *You don't have time for this.*

I took a last look around the bank. This place had taken so

much from me—it would not take Dante from me without a fight. I kicked down at the ground with my heel, daring it to make the first move.

It was long past time to wake up and leave this horrible in-between place—not quite the bank, not quite a dream. If Dante was caught in the limbo between doors, then it meant only one thing.

I had work to do.

CHAPTER 3

The knock on my door sounded like thunder to my tender hearing.

"Abby? Are you up yet?" Mom's voice slipped through the crack in the door.

"Yeah," I managed to croak. I checked the clock by my bed: 10:14. Later than I thought. What had I been dreaming about? Had Dante been there? My mind still rang with fragmented sounds of tolling bells, whispered voices, and wild screams.

"Good. Listen, I've got to run some errands; Hannah's coming with me. Dad's mowing the lawn if you need him. Oh, and Jason is here to see you."

"Okay," I called to Mom as I struggled to find my footing in the world of the awake. "I'll be right down." Rolling out of bed, I managed to exchange my pajamas for some sweats and a T-shirt.

As I reached for the doorknob, a sudden flash of light across my vision stripped away my sight, turning the world into a stark black-and-white outline. Except everything was switched, like the negative of a photograph. A raw shot of pain tracked fire along my nerves, ending in a knot between my shoulders. I closed my eyes as a wave of dizziness hit me, rocking through my stomach and making me nauseated. Needles of cold pricked at my wrists, turning my fingers numb. I shook them hard, trying to force some circulation back into them.

As quickly as it had hit, the contraction of pain disappeared and my vision returned to normal. I wiped the sweat from my forehead with hands that wouldn't stop shaking.

In some ways it was like those white flashes I'd had a few months ago when I'd been out of sync with the flow of time. But this was worse. Much worse.

I didn't know exactly what was going on. But I knew it was something bad.

Jason was waiting for me in the front room. He had made himself comfortable on the couch, piling the throw pillows to one side so he could lean back against the cushions with ease. It was his favorite spot to relax, and seeing him there—just as I had seen him there countless times before—evoked a sudden sense of déjà vu. There was something so *right* about seeing him there, and yet, something so *wrong* as well that I almost missed the last step on the stairs and had to grab at the banister to steady myself.

Jason leaned forward, one hand out to catch me even though I was too far away. "Are you okay, Abby? You look terrible."

I offered up a weak smile. "Gee, thanks." The world

continued to tilt around me in a rolling circle. I made my way into the front room and sat down heavily next to Jason on the couch. I leaned against the mounded pillows, hoping they would offer some stability for my spinning vision.

Jason brushed the hair away from my face, his touch tender and cool. "Do you want me to get you a glass of water or something?"

I shook my head and then wished I hadn't. "Just . . . give me a minute." Breathing deeply, I counted my heartbeats, concentrating on keeping them even and steady. The world finally began to settle down and play nice.

"What are you doing here?" I asked, wincing a little at the harsh undertone to my words.

Jason didn't seem to notice. He leaned back and reached his arm around my shoulder. "Do I need a reason to visit my best girl on graduation day?"

A thin whine of panic sounded deep in my ear. I wasn't Jason's best girl anymore. I hadn't been for some time now. Why would he think I was?

"Uh, I guess not," I stammered, trying to catch hold of my fluttering thoughts. "It's hard to believe it's already graduation, huh? Who would have thought we'd make it?" I grimaced; my words sounded lame even to me.

But Jason still didn't notice. "I always knew you'd be top of the class. Abby Edmunds, valedictorian. It has a nice ring to it, don't you think?" Jason traced his fingertips across the back of my hand, resting lightly on my wrist. He was sitting so close—almost too close.

The panic rose from a whine to a howl. I tried to shift away just a little, but the pillows were in the way.

"What are you talking about? I'm not valedictorian."

Jason's smile was indulgent and teasing. "It's okay if you want to brag about it. Top marks. Every college fighting over you. Speaking of which, have you picked one yet?"

"Emery," I said automatically. It was hard to concentrate; the edges of my vision kept blurring into a blue-white haze. "I'm going to Emery College."

"Really?" Jason frowned. "When did that happen? Last night you were looking at USC."

"USC didn't want me." The sting of rejection was all but gone, but in its place was something worse: doubt and confusion. I remembered getting the rejection letter; I still had the letter. Didn't I? And what did Jason mean about "last night"? I hadn't seen Jason since yesterday afternoon. Had I? My thoughts seemed to be fracturing along major logic lines, my memories sliding and colliding into new configurations.

"Since when?" Jason laughed. "Your acceptance letter came weeks ago. Nat and I are just trying to tag along as best we can."

The blue-white haze hardened into a ring of ice, chilling my blood. The longer this conversation went on, the more things were wrong with it.

"At least you and Natalie are still together," I said, unsettled by the sense of wrongness that filled the room.

Jason looked at me so strangely, I actually glanced over my shoulder to see if he was looking at someone else.

"What?" I asked.

"I'm not dating Natalie. *We're* dating. In fact, we're going out tonight to celebrate. Seven o'clock at that new barbecue place you wanted to try—the Devil's Pit—remember?"

The edges of my vision rippled as the world did its horrible inside-out trick and another wave of white-hot pain contracted through me. I clenched my teeth around a gasp to prevent it from escaping.

"I don't feel so good," I managed to say. I actually felt worse than that, but there was no point in trying to articulate the details. When your whole body felt on fire, what was one more flame?

"You don't have to be sorry for being sick. Are you okay? Do you think you'll make it to graduation?"

"Yeah, I think so." I didn't dare nod; my headache had sprouted spikes.

"Listen, we don't have to go out tonight. Why don't we just do pizza and a movie instead?"

I couldn't believe we were having this conversation. Jason and I hadn't had a pizza-and-movie date since before we had broken up on Valentine's Day. Jason should be dating Natalie—not me. Jason was *not* my boyfriend; didn't he know that?

I had that sudden sense of false déjà vu again. I felt like I was standing still and the whole world had picked up, turned 180 degrees, and dropped down again. Everything was still there—just *wrong*. Everything had just . . . *changed*.

The panic in my chest exploded into full-blown terror. Pain twisted through me and a drizzle of cold seeped into my fingers and toes.

I faced Jason and set my jaw. "Kiss me," I said, though I feared it sounded like a dare.

He blinked once in surprise, but clearly I didn't need to ask him twice. Jason slipped his hand around the back of my neck and leaned close. His lips met mine and I felt a slightly electric ripple pass through me. But not a good kind of electricity, not like when Dante kissed me. This was more of the knife-in-the-toaster kind of shock. A buzzing burr that made me want to flinch.

Jason finally noticed. He broke off the kiss and backed away from me. A shadow of confusion turned his hazel eyes the color of desert sand, and his voice, when he spoke, was as dry and dusty. "Okay, that was weird."

"You're telling me," I said. I lifted the back of my hand to my mouth, barely resisting the urge to wipe it against my lips. Instead I let my fingers rest on the locket around my throat, drawing strength from the familiar shape and weight of Dante's silver heart. At least that hadn't changed.

"What was that all about?" Jason said. "You kissed me like I was your brother."

His words summoned two quick memories—our first kiss last January, then the February breakup—flashing back-to-back so fast they felt like a double punch to my gut. He wouldn't have said that on purpose; it wasn't like him to be deliberately mean. And I doubted that he was simply pretending those two pivotal events in our relationship had never happened.

No, this was something else. Something worse.

Zo had made it through the door where Dante hadn't. And that meant that Zo was running unchecked, imposing his will on the river, on the past.

Jason didn't remember those events happening because they had *never happened.* Jason remembered something different, a different past. One in which our first kiss had been fireworks for both of us, one where he and I were still dating, one where he still loved me—and not Natalie.

Things had changed—the evidence was sitting right next to me on the couch. Dante had said changes would be like rocks in the river, polluting the flow of time, creating dangerous ripples, undertows, riptides. I had known the changes were coming. I just hadn't thought they would start so soon. Or hit so close to home. This was the first ripple in the river, and I knew it wouldn't be the last.

If only I'd had some way to prepare, a hint of what was coming . . . I grimaced. Was that what the white flash had been about this morning? A signal that time was reversing and changing direction? If so, then maybe I had my own painful warning system in place, though I wasn't looking forward to feeling like I'd been turned inside out every time a ripple of change reached me.

I realized I'd been sitting in silence for so long that the awkwardness in the room had turned palpable.

"Sorry," I said, trying for a smile to break the tension. It didn't work. I felt my heart constrict a little, and I dug my fingernails into my palms. "Could I have that glass of water now?"

Jason stood up from the couch without a glance at me or a single word. He returned from the kitchen and handed me a glass, careful not to let our fingers touch.

I noticed he didn't sit back down next to me, but instead

stood a pace or two away, his fingers tapping his leg, his body already tense and turned toward the front door.

I drained the glass dry in three long swallows, the water tasting like sand in my throat. Jason didn't deserve to be caught up in this mess. Breaking his heart once had been bad enough. I really didn't want to do it again.

Maybe I could change things on my end, set things right again. Maybe I could toss this particular rock out of the river.

"Thanks for your help, Jason. I'm feeling a lot better." A small truth. "Let's still go out tonight, but . . . maybe I should meet you at the restaurant, okay?"

"All right," Jason said after a moment's hesitation. "Are you sure you're okay?"

I wrapped my hands around the empty glass and nodded; I didn't dare meet his eyes in case he saw right through me.

"Okay." He took a step toward me, and paused. "If you're sure."

"I'm fine."

"Okay," he said again. "Well. I'll see you later, then."

"See you."

I waited until he'd closed the door behind him before I set the glass on the coffee table and went back upstairs to grab my cell phone off my desk.

"Natalie? Hey, can you do me a favor tonight?"

It had been surprisingly hard to convince Natalie to come to the Devil's Pit. She kept saying she didn't want to be a third wheel on my date with Jason. I kept trying to convince her that it would be fine. I finally had to promise to buy her dessert in order to get her to say yes. I hung up the phone and sighed. Here was more proof that things were out of whack. Normally Natalie would not have thought twice about coming along; we'd done enough as a group that no one ever felt like a third wheel. And since when had Natalie obsessed about dessert that much? She enjoyed a slice of New York cheesecake as much as the next person, but to hold out for it? No, that wasn't like Natalie at all.

I went back downstairs and fell face first onto the couch, closing my eyes against the cushions. Playing matchmaker and fixing things might prove harder than I'd anticipated.

I heard the garage door rise with a growling hum. Great. Either Dad was done with the lawn, or Mom and Hannah were home. Or both. I wasn't sure I wanted to deal with either possibility.

"I'm all done with the lawn," I heard Dad say, followed by the sound of a kiss.

"Thank you, dear," Mom said. "What are all those orange flags for?"

"I don't know. They were in the lawn. Whoops—were you marking out some new flower beds or something?"

"No, I didn't put them out there. Maybe Abby knows what they're for."

I heard the clatter of thin metal sticks falling on the counter and I looked up in shock. Those were the flags designating the dimensions of the door. If Dad had gathered them up, then that meant he didn't remember they were mine. That wasn't good. What else didn't he remember? What else was different? The ripples of change were sweeping over my family too. What if everyone had changed but me? The thought made me dizzy.

"Is she home?" Dad asked.

"She better be." Mom raised her voice. "Abby? Where are you?"

I sat up and turned in time to see Hannah run through the kitchen door, pause on the first step to glare at me, and then head up the stairs. I sighed a little in relief. I didn't know why she was mad at me, but I didn't care. It was typical Hannah behavior and that was good enough for me.

"I'm in here," I called back.

"What's going on?" Mom said, stepping into the front room. "Why aren't you dressed yet? We have to leave by noon."

"Graduation isn't until three; we have plenty of time."

Mom shook her head. "I can't believe you forgot already. The principal specifically asked everyone who was on the program to be there at one. How would it look if the valedictorian showed up late to her own graduation?"

I bit down hard on my lip. There it was again—valedictorian. The changes in the river were starting to feel more widespread. More out of control. I just hoped they weren't permanent.

"Oh, right," I said, trying to cover my distress. "Sorry. It'll just take me a minute."

"Hurry, please. Hannah's not happy at having to spend extra time at the school." Mom walked back into the kitchen, and I heard her open the fridge and ask Dad if he wanted a quick bite before we had to leave.

"Sorry my graduation is an inconvenience for her," I muttered, pushing myself off the couch and heading upstairs.

I indulged myself for a moment, imagining how it would feel to have really been named valedictorian of the school. Yes, my grades were good, but they weren't perfect. And although I had done a lot of extracurricular activities over the years, they certainly didn't add up enough to warrant valedictorian status. I had been too scattered, interested in too many things, to really have excelled in any one particular arena at school.

But could it have been different? Could *I* have been different? The kind of girl who set a goal to be valedictorian and then followed through on it, no matter what distractions came my way? Maybe. It certainly felt good to think about myself that way.

I closed my bedroom door behind me. I had planned to wear my favorite red blouse and a denim skirt underneath my graduation robes, something comfortable and not too fancy, but if I had to stand in as valedictorian, then I figured I'd better wear something more formal. I stepped out of my clothes and into a summer dress with sling-back shoes. It was a quick change, but it would have to do. The clock by my bed warned that it was almost noon. We'd have to leave in a few minutes.

My gaze fell on my desk, where, locked in the drawer, lay the biggest secret I'd ever kept. Those blueprints represented a goal that would require my complete attention. Build it, or don't build it—there was no middle ground. No room for error or excuses. Once I started, I'd have to see it through to the end. No matter what. Was I up to the task? I hoped so.

Unlocking my desk drawer, I pulled out the binder where I kept Dante's original blueprints. I had a backup copy of the plans, of course, but seeing his handwriting—the small hook he added to his lowercase "t"s—always made me feel connected to him. Like he was still close to me—close enough to communicate with me. I brushed my fingers over the cover of the binder. Close enough to touch.

I remembered the strange, ghostly touch of his hands on my hands, my arms. The touch of his lips against mine. It had been a dream—more than a dream—but that had been the best part of it for sure.

Taped to the top of the binder was the tiny slip of paper from my fortune cookie: "Remember June 4th. Great things are in store for you."

I thought back to my date with Dante where I had cracked open that cookie. That had been the night I had first dreamed my way to the bank, the night Zo and Dante had discussed the fact that I could somehow summon the black hourglass door that led back to their home, more than five hundred years in the past.

I nibbled on the edge of my fingernail, an itch of worry just out of reach. That had also been the conversation where Zo had mentioned two people from Dante's past: Orlando and Sofia. Orlando was Dante's older brother, though I knew him as Leo. And as Leo, he had lived those five hundred years instead of skipping them like Dante had. But I had never found out who Sofia was.

Was she Dante's sister? A girlfriend? Someone else altogether? I had asked Dante about her once, but he hadn't answered my question, more concerned with the events on the bank and the threat Zo posed to us both.

I returned the plans to my desk drawer. As I turned the small key in the lock, a bolt of pain skewered through my stomach, and I doubled over, gasping as unexpected heat flared in my brain. The world around me reversed to black and white, the shadows as thin and sharp as the light. The air around me felt as viscous as blood.

Oh, no, I thought. *Not again. Not now.*

The flash was there and gone in a heartbeat. My vision stabilized; relief filled me. Maybe whatever changed this time would be small, localized.

A small bell chimed from my computer, alerting me to an incoming e-mail message. I forced my hand to stop trembling and reached for the mouse. Clicking on the small yellow envelope in the corner of the screen left me exhausted. If these changes in the river were going to be a regular occurrence—and I fervently hoped they were not—then I was going to have to build up my stamina.

The e-mail opened and I read the words on the screen. But they didn't make any sense.

Dear Ms. Edmunds,

We regret to inform you that your application to Emery College has been declined.

Sincerely,

Mr. Wilson Cooke

I read them again, baffled. I recognized all the individual words and I knew what they all meant, but somehow, when they were arranged in just that order, it was like trying to read hieroglyphics.

Emery didn't want me? Impossible. I had an e-mail from one Mr. Wilson Cooke that said yes, they did. I had spent months planning my life at Emery, visiting the Web site every day, clicking on every link, reading every post, until I knew it top to bottom. And now this?

"It's impossible," I whispered if only to hear myself say it out loud, as though that would make it easier to understand, easier to believe.

"Abby!" Mom knocked on my door. "C'mon, sweetie, it's time to go."

"Just a second," I called back, my attention divided. I grabbed for my phone even as I read the e-mail a third time. I had programmed Dr. Cooke's phone number into my phone the same day I'd received my acceptance e-mail, so it was only moments before the dial tone turned into a ring. I bit my fingernail.

"Don't be long," Mom said.

"Okay." I bounced my knee, keeping time with my agitation. "Answer already," I muttered into the ringing phone. Yes, it was graduation day, but it was also a Friday. Surely someone would still be on campus.

"Good afternoon, Dr. Cooke's office. How may I help you?" A woman's voice answered in the neutral tones of secretaries everywhere.

"Yes, hello," I said. "I'd like to speak with Dr. Cooke, please."

"He is unavailable at the moment. Is there something I can help you with?"

"Maybe. I think there might be a mistake on my admission and—"

"Oh, no worries." The neutral tone warmed up and I heard the distant click of fingernails clattering over a keyboard. "I'd be happy to look up your file and see what's going on. What was your name again?"

"It's Abby. Abby Edmunds."

Another knock sounded on my door—a hard bang that told me Mom had sent Dad to collect me. Sure enough, I heard his voice call out, "Let's go, Abs! We don't want to be late."

And I didn't want to be denied admission to Emery. I covered up the mouthpiece. "Just a sec!"

"Everything okay?"

"Yeah, Dad, I'll be right there."

The secretary made a confused "humph" sound on the phone, pulling my attention to a point.

"What? What is it? Did you find it?"

"How do you spell your last name, again?"

My anxiety rose with each letter I listed. This couldn't be happening. I scrolled through my inbox, looking for my original acceptance e-mail. Where was it? *May. April.* It had to be here. I had kept it; I knew I had. *March. February.* When I hit the e-mails dated January, I stopped.

"I found your file, but . . ." The secretary paused.

The edges of my vision rippled and I closed my eyes. *No, oh, no, please, no . . .*

"But it's . . . *not* on the acceptance list." She paused again. "I'm so sorry."

My hand began trembling again, but not from shock this time. I felt a thread of rage wind its way through my fingers, pulling them into a fist. This was Zo's handiwork; it had him written all over it. First Jason and Natalie, then this valedictorian business, now Emery. I supposed it made sense that Zo would attack my life first, if only because I had been a thorn in his side, defying him every chance I got. But why did it have to hurt so much?

"Oh. Okay." Numbness spread through me like cracks through ice. Even my voice felt brittle. "Thanks for checking."

"Would you like to leave a message for Dr. Cooke?"

"No," I said, turning off my computer. "No, thanks. I'm sorry to have bothered you. I have to go."

I set the phone down. I was not going to cry. There would be too many questions if I went downstairs all splotchy and red. Questions I didn't want to answer; questions I couldn't answer. I took a deep breath. *This isn't real. It's just Zo. This isn't the way it's supposed to be,* I told myself. *This isn't real.* But the pain was real. So was the uncertainty.

I looked at my bedroom door, closed and quiet. On the other side waited my family, ready to celebrate my graduation as valedictorian. And Jason, my boyfriend who still loved me. And a whole reality that was already drifting and dividing into wrongness.

Standing up from my desk, I crossed to the door. Until Zo

was stopped, my life wouldn't return to normal. Until then, there was nothing to do but face the changes the best I could. I took another deep breath, then opened the door and walked through.

CHAPTER 4

I spent the entire graduation ceremony on edge, waiting for another wave of pain to hit me, for some other part of my life to spiral into unexpected change.

I managed to stumble through a speech I didn't remember writing. I barely heard them call my name. My diploma felt like plastic in my hands. The photographer's flash was pure white and I broke out in a cold sweat at the temporary blindness. It seemed like everyone wanted to hug me—Mom, Dad, Hannah, Jason, Natalie—but I felt like a mannequin in their arms, detached and unnatural. My arms ached to embrace the one person who wasn't there. The one person who would understand what I was going through.

My thoughts were filled with Dante. Our brief encounter last night had been over all too soon and had left me with more questions than I could possibly answer. Was my suspicion correct that he was trapped? And if so, was there a way to free him? And if not, what would happen to him? I feared his fate would be the same as Tony's; I couldn't bear to think of Dante screaming in pain the way Tony had.

I preferred to think of him standing tall and strong, his hands twined with mine, his gray eyes alight in anticipation of a long conversation with me, a warm smile at one of my silly jokes. My fingers brushed against the curve of the locket at my throat. I chose to remember the times he had held me close to his heart, made promises to remember me, told me he loved me.

I suspected my memories were going to be important in the coming days. I had to remember what had really happened—I had to hold on to the truth of the past—so I could identify the changes that were occurring and guard the river as best as I could until Dante could join me. I had to stand immovable against the constantly changing river of time that flowed around me. I hoped I was up to the task.

I heard my name being called for the second time. "What?" I swam up out of the depths of my own thoughts. "I'm sorry, what did you say?"

Mom sighed in exasperation. "Honestly, Abby. Is it too much to ask you to pay a little attention?"

"Sorry, Mom," I said, straightening up and trying to smile brightly so she'd know I was being sincere. "I just have a lot on my mind. Graduation and everything, you know."

"It's a wonder you managed to graduate at all since apparently you have the attention span of a gnat," Hannah muttered.

I aimed a kick at her ankle, which she deftly avoided. Little sisters were the worst.

"Be nice," Dad chided both of us.

"Cindy!" Mom called out, standing on her toes and waving the graduation program in the air. "Cindy, over here!"

Cindy Kimball wove through the crowd, trailing Jason's younger sister, Bethany, behind her. When Cindy reached us, she threw her arms around me in a lung-crushing hug. "I'm so proud of you, Abby. Congratulations!"

"Thanks," I managed to squeak before she let me go in order to hug Mom and Dad and even Hannah. I rubbed at my chest, trying to introduce the circulation back into it. I couldn't help but smile a little, though. Cindy's enthusiasm was one of the things I loved about her.

"Isn't it exciting that Jason and Abby are going to school together?" Cindy squeezed my mom's arm. "You'd almost think we planned it that way."

Mom laughed. "Now, Cindy, they seem to be doing just fine without us interfering."

"But isn't that our job? To interfere in our children's lives?" Cindy winked at me.

I saw Hannah roll her eyes; Bethany leaned over to whisper something in Hannah's ear. The two of them looked at me and laughed. I wished I could stick my tongue out at them, but Mom was watching me. Plus, now that I was officially a high-school graduate, I thought maybe I should act like one.

I did, however, want to put an end to this line of conversation. It was clear that Cindy thought I was still dating her son. And since neither Mom nor Dad had corrected her, it was safe to assume that the only person who knew the relationship was off was me. I had to get Jason and Natalie together—the sooner the better. Maybe in this version of the river Mom and Cindy still expected me and Jason to end up together, but I knew in the real world that wasn't supposed to happen. How many times was I going to have to break someone's heart?

"Where is Jason?" I asked.

Cindy looked around, unconcerned that perhaps she had misplaced one of her brood. "Oh, he's around somewhere, I suspect. He's taking you out tonight, isn't he? I heard there was a party . . ."

I swallowed, feeling the sour churn of acid in my stomach. The ripple of change was growing wider, reaching further.

"I already have plans for tonight," I started, quickly tacking on "with Jason" when I saw Cindy's eyebrows lift in an unspoken question. "Yes. I have a date with Jason tonight." The words felt wooden and clunky. I hoped they didn't sound that way to anyone else.

"Mom, can we go now?" Hannah said, shifting back and forth. "This is boring."

"It won't seem that way when it's your graduation. And no, we can't leave yet. Abby still needs to turn in her cap and gown, and the principal wanted to talk to her before we go."

"Hannah's welcome to come home with us," Cindy offered. "It's no bother."

"If you're sure—" Mom started, but by then Hannah and Bethany were already racing each other for the double doors.

"Well, I guess it's time for us to go," Cindy said, laughing. She reached over and squeezed my arm again. "Congratulations, dear. We're all so very proud of you."

Mom wrapped her arm around my shoulder in a quick hug. Dad headed out into the crowd, clearing a small pathway for us to follow.

"Do you know what the principal wants to talk about?" I asked.

Mom hesitated, then hugged my shoulder again. "No, but I'm sure it's nothing bad."

Well, that didn't help calm my fears. I felt uneasy as we left the crowded graduation ceremony for the slightly less-crowded hallway outside the principal's office.

In all my years in high school, I'd never been inside the principal's office except for the interview I'd done for the school paper. I tried to still my nerves. So much had already changed today, I hoped that what was waiting for me behind Principal Adams's door was good news.

Principal Adams's office hadn't changed much since the last time I'd been in there. He still had the same framed pictures on the wall, the same dark brown desk with a stack of bright yellow legal pads on the corner, the same chipped coffee mug next to his computer. Principal Adams himself hadn't changed much either: brown hair, brown suit, tired eyes. I breathed a small sigh of relief. With all the other changes going on around me, it was nice to find a spot that seemed untouched.

"Ah, Mr. Edmunds, Mrs. Edmunds. Thank you for coming." Principal Adams looked up as we entered and rose to shake hands with my mom. "I'm sorry this is on such short notice."

"It was no problem," Mom said, smiling.

"What's this all about?" Dad asked. I wondered the same thing.

"Please, have a seat." Principal Adams gestured to the empty chairs in front of his desk. In addition to his two standard threadbare chairs, three additional chairs crowded close by, a mismatched trio obviously pulled into the office at the last minute. It seemed he was expecting a larger crowd than the three of us. Maybe Hannah had done the right thing in escaping when she'd had the chance.

"It's good to see you again, Abby," he said, directing a smile my way. "I could not have asked for a better student—a better valedictorian. You have done the school proud."

"Thanks." I didn't know what else to say. In my real life, I didn't deserve his praise, and I felt like a fraud sitting beneath his wide smile.

"And where is Hannah?" he asked.

"She headed home with a friend," Dad said. "I thought you wanted to talk about Abby."

"I do, but I thought the whole family might have enjoyed hearing the good news together."

"Good news?" Mom asked, leaning forward in her chair.

"Oh, yes." Principal Adams glanced between my parents and me, his smile growing wider. "It is good news indeed."

I swallowed, feeling a small flicker of anticipation in my chest. After all the bad things that had happened, was it possible something good was coming my way?

"I know you applied to several schools," he said directly to me. "And I know you have had your pick of places to go." He paused, obviously savoring his next words. "In all your college shopping, did you ever consider Emery College?"

My heart almost stopped. It had only been a couple of hours since my terrible phone call to Dr. Cooke's office. I frantically tried to figure out what the right answer was to his question. Emery had declined my application, and yet that meant they *had* an application to decline. Which meant that I had, at some point in this changed past, sent them an application.

"Um, yes," I said quietly. "It sounded like a great school. I thought about going there." *But not now,* I thought. *Not until I can get my real life back on track.*

"You did?" Mom said. "I thought you wanted to go to USC."

"Well, they said yes, but—"

"USC is a fine school," Principal Adams interrupted and held up his hands in a calming gesture as though we had been arguing the fact. "But Emery is a little different."

"Like, Ivy League different?" Dad sounded worried. My family couldn't afford that kind of price tag—not then, not now.

"Better." Principal Adams beamed. "Emery College is an extremely exclusive institution and they are perhaps the most selective of all the liberal arts colleges in the country. They take only the best of the best, and they offer a single full-ride scholarship a year." His eyes danced. "Which is yours, Abby, if you want it."

"What?" The word felt like a thousand-pound weight on my tongue. I could barely get it out.

"Wait, say that again," Dad said, sitting forward.

My thoughts tumbled end over end; I tried to find a stable idea to hold on to and get my bearings. Emery had said no; now they wanted to offer me a full-ride scholarship? I didn't understand. I pressed a hand flat against my stomach, wondering if I'd missed that internal warning system that things were shifting. But there hadn't been any noticeable pain. No white flashes, no crippling nausea. I looked to my parents for help, but they looked as confused as I felt.

Principal Adams smiled a little. "I know this news is a surprise, but believe me, this is quite an honor for you, for Abby, and for the school. I'd like to introduce you to someone." He pressed a button on the phone on his desk. "Rachel, would you send him in, please?"

"Abby, what do you think? I mean, I thought you'd settled on USC. Would you like to change?" Mom touched my arm.

It was hard to get a read on what she wanted me to do. Now that things had changed, I didn't know what kind of conversations had happened before this. I didn't know if we had argued, if I'd begged and pleaded to go to USC, or if they had made the decision and insisted I obey.

Even though I didn't know what had happened in the past, I knew what I wanted to happen in my future. Emery had always been my first choice—my only choice—and if I could still go, then my decision was easy.

The door opened behind me. Principal Adams stood up, came around the desk, and held out his hand for the visitor. "Thank you for being here. I'm sorry for the wait."

"It's no problem," a deep voice replied, the trace of an accent underscoring his words.

I knew that accent. I knew that voice.

It was—I twisted in my chair—no one I knew.

He was tall, dressed in a finely tailored suit with a dark red tie knotted at his throat. He carried a black leather briefcase in one hand. A mane of dark brown hair surrounded his face. Round, wire glasses framed a pair of faded blue eyes.

Those eyes flicked a glance at me so quick it felt like a whip-kiss against my face, a strange combination of warning and welcome.

I jolted back, startled and stunned.

It was Leo.

Memories crowded behind my eyes, each one vying for attention. Leo, behind the golden-railed bar at the Dungeon, a white towel slung over his shoulder, a story in his eyes. Leo, hunched over a table in the darkness, rubbing at the faded chains on his wrists, a confession on his lips. Leo, carrying me to safety while an inferno raged behind him.

What was he doing here in Principal Adams's office? And when had he started working for Emery College?

"Mr. and Mrs. Edmunds, I'd like you to meet Mr. Casella. He's made a special trip here to talk to you and Abby about Emery College. Mr. Casella, this is the Edmunds family. And this"—he gestured to me—"is Abby."

"It's nice to meet you," Leo said in his rumbly voice as he shook hands with my parents.

I stared at the scene in equal parts amazement, surprise, and fear. My parents smiled at Leo as though they'd never seen him before. But that was impossible. They knew Leo from the

Dungeon; they knew him as Dante's guardian. He had even come to my house once.

But perhaps they simply didn't recognize him. I hadn't at first, and I had seen him more often—and more recently—than my parents had.

Mom nudged me on the shoulder, breaking into my confused thoughts, and I stood up, automatically extending my hand to Leo.

"It's nice to meet you, Abby," he said, meeting my eyes directly for the first time. "I've heard so much about you."

"Hi," I managed, wondering if I was mistaken about who was really behind the disguise.

Leo's faded blue eyes held mine for a moment. And then he smiled.

A shock of relief ran through me.

It *was* Leo. And he knew me. He *remembered* me—the real me.

Whatever Zo had changed in my life, it seemed to have bypassed my relationship with Leo. I wasn't alone anymore. I had someone I could talk to who would understand, who knew the truth. More important, I had someone who could help me rescue Dante.

"Why don't we sit down?" Principal Adams said. "I'm sure you all have a lot of questions."

More than you know, I thought. I wanted to grab Leo's arm and shake the answers out of him.

He caught my expression and a slight frown wrinkled his forehead. *Not now. Wait.* He sat in the chair across from me and set his briefcase on the floor by his feet.

"As I'm sure Principal Adams has told you, we at Emery are quite selective in our admissions." He looked at me from across the desk and a small smile hovered around his mouth. "We don't let just anyone in, you know."

I couldn't help it. I grinned; there was finally a light at the end of this long, dark tunnel.

Leo extracted a folder from his briefcase and opened it for my parents. He spread out the pages and pictures I'd seen so many times before as I wandered through the Emery College Web site, dreaming of the day I'd be walking there in person.

Mom and Dad hummed and nodded their way through Leo's introduction and explanation. I could feel their excitement growing as they considered the fact that their daughter could be granted such a gift.

"Well, it certainly sounds wonderful," Mom said.

"How did you guys find Abby?" Dad asked. "I mean, you probably had millions of applications for this scholarship."

"Well, I don't need to tell you that Abby is one in a million." Leo smiled again, and the lines around his eyes crinkled. "Seriously, though, I can tell you that I personally reviewed every application and there was indeed something special about Abby. I could tell it from the first moment."

"It all sounds perfect," I said. "I don't think I could say no."

"I thought you might say that," Leo said.

"Are you sure, honey? It's so far from home." Mom picked up a glossy photo of an ivy-covered brick building that had the words *Live without Limits* engraved in stone in front.

"USC isn't exactly in our backyard," I pointed out. "You said this would be my decision"—at least my parents had said that in the past; I hoped it was still true—"and my decision is Emery."

Mom and Dad exchanged a glance, then a smile. Then Mom laughed in delighted surprise and wrapped her hand around Dad's arm. "Can you believe it?"

Leo made a show of checking his watch as he stood up from the desk. "I'm sorry, but I have another appointment to attend to. If you'll excuse me." He reached into his jacket pocket and withdrew a card, which he handed to me. "Welcome to your future, Abby. If you have any questions, please feel free to contact me—anytime."

I glanced down at the phone number printed on the simple, white business card. Beneath the typed numbers was a handwritten addition:

Dungeon. 8:00.

I looked up, but Leo was gone.

CHAPTER 5

Mom and Dad wanted to take the whole family out to celebrate, but I managed to convince them to wait a day. I had a date with Jason that I didn't want to miss. Or rather, I had a date with Jason that I didn't want *Natalie* to miss. I wasn't sure at all that what I had in mind would work, but I had to take the chance. Leo may have come back, but Dante was still gone and Zo was still loose. I couldn't do much, but maybe I could do this.

There was a pretty big crowd at the Devil's Pit. I waited in the front, keeping one eye on my watch and the other on the door. It would be tricky to get to the Dungeon by eight if Jason and Natalie were much later. And I didn't want to miss meeting up with Leo. I still couldn't believe he had waltzed back into my life as though nothing had happened. And what was up with that whole Emery College thing? I had a lot of questions, and Leo had a lot to answer for.

Natalie pushed through the front doors and I waved at her over the crowd.

"Nat, over here."

"It's crazy tonight," she said when she reached me. "I think the whole school is here."

"Probably because it's the new place." I winced as someone with sharp elbows wriggled past me. "I miss the Dungeon," I sighed.

"Me too," Natalie said. "There was way more room. And better music." She wrinkled her nose at the heavy bass thumping through the air.

I checked my watch. "I wonder where Jason is. He's not usually this late."

"Are you sure it's okay that I'm here?" Natalie looked over her shoulder at the door. "I mean, it's your date night and everything."

"I want you to be here. We both do. It'll be fun."

Natalie twisted her mouth, unconvinced.

"There'll be cheesecake," I reminded her.

"Well . . ."

"Hi, Abby, sorry I'm late." Jason slipped up behind me and placed his hand on the small of my back. He moved in to kiss me, but at the last minute hesitated and placed a kiss on my cheek. "Hi, Natalie," he said carefully, looking at me. "Double-date night?"

Natalie's expression darkened, and I jumped in before she could say anything. "Um, no, I, uh, I invited her to come with us."

"Oh," Jason said, catching on. "Oh, okay. That's great."

"Kimball, party of two." The announcement cut into the music, crackling over the speakers.

"Party of *two*?" Natalie repeated and shook her head. "I can take a hint. Have fun—I'll catch you later."

"No, wait." I held onto her arm. I groaned inside. I hated the tension that suddenly exploded between us. It didn't use to be like this. We used to all get along just fine as one big group. "Look, I can't explain right now, but trust me. It's going to be okay. I have to go—"

"What? What about our date?" Jason asked, his eyebrows drawn down in confused frustration.

"Where are you going?" Natalie spoke at the same time.

I held up my hands, hoping I was doing the right thing.

"Last call for Kimball, party of two."

"Right here!" I called out, waving at the hostess standing at her desk. "We're coming!"

"Abby, what are you doing?" Jason asked, a sharp edge to his voice.

I met his hazel eyes. "What I have to."

The hostess reached us, smiling, with menus in her hands. "Follow me, please."

I took a step back and, at the same time, pushed Jason and Natalie closer together. "I'll talk to you guys later."

"Wait—" Jason reached for me.

But I was already gone, shoving my way toward the front doors, my heart in my throat.

I didn't dare look back.

I parked my car at the curb and jogged across the street, heading for the dark lot on the corner, chasing my shadow as the sun slowly set behind me. It wasn't quite eight o'clock yet, which was good. I'd raced from the Devil's Pit; I hadn't been to the Dungeon since the night of the fire and I wanted to be alone for my first visit back. I slipped my hand into my pocket to touch the card Leo had given me, running my fingers along the edges to the sharp corner points.

In my mind's eye I could still see the somewhat plain two-story building that had been the hub of my social life for the last few years—Leo's Dungeon—but the scorched wreckage that remained bore no resemblance to that familiar haunt. The inferno that had consumed the Dungeon had been insatiable, devouring walls, floor, and roof and melting the paved parking lot into a thick, black soup.

The lot should have been filled with cars and kids, laughter and music spilling out of the Dungeon's open doors. The Dungeon itself should have been packed as the entire senior class gathered to celebrate graduation night. But the place was deserted, destroyed. All that remained was a desolate waste-land.

I stood at the edge of the yellow caution tape that fluttered in the breeze, a poor barrier against trespassers. I smoothed the tape between my thumb and my fingers, watching the light and shadow flickering in the jumbled heaps of stone and metal at my feet. The warmth of the sun felt like flames against my back. I closed my eyes briefly, remembering the last time I had been here.

The night of the fire. My memories of that night were chaotic, just fragments of image and sound. Mostly I remem-bered Leo: the strength in his arms as he carried me to safety, the sound of his voice rumbling through his chest as he said good-bye. By the time I woke up in the hospital four days later, he was already gone. That had been the last time I'd seen him. Until today.

I opened my eyes to check the time, and a fracture of white in the field of black caught my attention. Perhaps something had survived the blaze after all.

I ducked under the tape, carefully avoiding the burnt beams and twisted metal that lay scattered on the blackened earth.

It wasn't so easy to avoid the memories that flooded through me with each step.

Here was where the Signature Wall used to stand, collecting the names of my friends in their individual scribbles and scrawls.

Here was where Leo had tended bar, and where he had offered me his famous Midnight Kiss, filled with a story and a wish.

Here was the stage where Dante had recited his poem and where Zo and his band had played "Into the River" for the first time.

Here were the stairs that led to Dante's room, where I had forced my way to the bank to save him—only to let him go.

A sliver of white glimmered like polished bone amid the wreckage of the Dungeon. I crouched down, carefully brushing away the gray ash that coated the ground.

A delicate face smiled up at me. I recognized it immediately as the porcelain ballerina from Leo's cabinet of curiosities. I was amazed that anything had survived the fire, especially something as fragile as this. I turned her over carefully in my fingers, wiping away the dust and ash from her pink skirt, frozen in mid-flare, and her tightly wound bun on the back of her head. She stood on one pointed toe, her long white arms curving in a circle above her head. Her other leg was extended, ending in a sharply pointed toe.

I felt the world tilt around me. I clearly remembered the moment when this very same ballerina had shattered into a thousand pieces. My memory called up the scene exactly: the afternoon sun slanting on the Dungeon's floor; Dante's features, drawn and tight with worry; the slight tremble in his gloved fingers as he opened the cabinet of Leo's curios; the heft of the brass hinge that he dropped into my hands. I remembered the ballerina breaking. But now it was here in my hands, whole and unbroken.

How many more fragments of displaced time would I find?

I hated this horrible double vision. I hated looking at something but seeing something else. I hated not knowing what to expect, what to remember. I hated not knowing the truth.

Anger surged through me and I wrapped my fist around the figure, feeling how fragile it was. One sharp squeeze, that was all it would take. Just one fierce twist and the ballerina would fracture into pieces, snapping her off her precariously pointed toe.

Just like my life had been fractured into pieces. If Leo hadn't opened up the Dungeon, then Zero Hour wouldn't have played there, and Zo wouldn't have gotten his claws into Valerie, and Dante wouldn't have had to save her, and I wouldn't have had to save him, and he wouldn't have left—

The soft sound of music interrupted my thoughts. Tiny,

metallic notes drifted up from the ballerina's stand. I glanced down in surprise. I hadn't known it was a music box. The dancer pivoted on her toe, turning in a tight circle.

"I'm glad she survived," a voice said from behind me. "She was always one of my favorites."

I turned, the ballerina cradled in my hand. "Leo!"

He had exchanged his suit and power tie for his more familiar white shirt and slacks. His once silver-white hair was still dark brown, though the glasses were gone. He smiled at me, and in the transition time of twilight, he looked so much like Dante—although a slightly older Dante—that I had to stop and catch my breath.

"I'm glad you came," Leo said.

"Like I had a choice. Where have you been? Do you know what's going on? Things are changing and it's bad—"

"Slow down. One question at a time, please."

I took a deep breath and focused my energy on the most important question.

"Have you seen Dante? I think he's somewhere on the bank."

Leo seemed surprised. "If he has been there, I haven't seen him. He's free of the bank now, remember? He doesn't have to go there if he doesn't want to."

I shook my head before Leo stopped speaking. "He's trapped somewhere. He said the door—I don't know—collapsed around him before he could get out. I think he's still inside."

"Inside the time machine? That's impossible."

"I don't think that word has much meaning anymore," I said dryly.

Leo was silent a moment, his eyes unfocused in thought. "You spoke to Dante? When?"

"Last night. I was on the bank and I heard his voice. But I didn't see him." I wondered if I should mention his kiss, but decided against it. Some things were better kept private.

Leo frowned. "You were on the bank last night? By yourself?"

I shook my head. "I wasn't there exactly. It was more like a dream—"

"The bank is dangerous. You shouldn't have been there."

"Believe me, I didn't intend to go."

"Something changed on the bank last night. The sky turned black. That's never happened before."

"I know. But what about Dante?" I looked at Leo, feeling frustrated and maybe a little desperate. "He's not on the bank, he's not in the river, and he's not with Zo. Where else could he be?"

"But if he is trapped in the machine, and the machine is gone . . ." Leo trailed off in thought. "Where *is* he, exactly?"

"You don't know? I thought you knew all about the door and how it worked."

"I know a lot, but not everything. This is new territory for me too."

"So, what do we do?"

Leo looked at me with sadness in his eyes. "We'll have to wait. Until we know more, learn more, there isn't much else we can do. But we're not going to leave him, Abby. I promise."

I looked down at the ballerina in my hands. I knew how she felt: fragile and alone, teetering on a point. I knew I had made the right choice in letting Dante go, even though it had been a hard choice, but now I wondered if I was partly to blame for the danger he was in. The thought twisted in my heart like a knife.

"Why did *you* leave me?" I didn't mean for the pain I felt to come through so clearly. Once I'd started, though, I couldn't stop. "You just vanished. Do you know what it's like to wait for someone who isn't coming back? It was bad enough to know that Dante was gone, but I was counting on you still being there. Then you were gone too."

Leo's face crumpled. *"Ti chiedo perdono, mia donna di luce. Mi dispiace di averti causato pena."*

"I don't want your apologies," I said, recognizing some of the words from Dante's brief lessons in Italian. "I want an explanation."

"Would you believe me if I told you I left to make it easier for you?"

"Easier? Nothing about this has been easy."

Leo exhaled slowly, and the lines around his eyes and mouth seemed to deepen, aging him as he stood there. "You're the only one who knows my story," he said quietly, not looking at me. "You know I've lived a long life—a life of sacrifice. I don't say that for sympathy or to make myself into some kind of martyr. I say it because it's the truth. My life has been a constant series of good-byes. I can settle down in a place for only so long before I have to say good-bye. When I moved here and built the Dungeon, I did so with the knowledge that eventually I would have to leave it all behind. I've gotten very good at leaving. Maybe too good."

He stooped and gathered up a handful of ashes and dust, letting the gray shadows slip through his fingers.

"When the Dungeon burned, I knew it was time to leave. I couldn't stay."

"But why not? You knew I needed your help."

"If I had stayed, there would have been questions. Awkward questions. How would I have explained Dante's absence? What would I have done about the Dungeon? Rebuilt it? It's difficult enough to hold down a regular nine-to-five job with my . . . condition. I lost my home. And it's not like I have family I could stay with." Leo shook his head. "My life here was over, I could see that clearly."

"So where did you go?"

A ghost of a smile appeared on his weary face. "Nowhere."

I drew my eyebrows together in confusion.

The smile solidified. "I packed up; I told everyone I was moving away. I had to appear to leave, but I never left you, *mia donna di luce*. I couldn't." He looked out over the quiet houses. A soft breeze ruffled his hair. "I stayed on the bank for as long as I could. When I'd come back, I was careful to stay hidden, isolated. I had time; I could wait."

"What were you waiting for?" My voice was low, weighed down by the magnitude of Leo's actions.

"You." His voice caught on the word. "I knew that eventually the time would come when you'd need my help. And then last night, things changed."

"Everything's changed," I murmured. "And I don't know how to fix it."

"That's why I came back. Whatever is happening, it's too much for one person to handle alone. I'm here to help."

"How?"

"However you need me to." He squared his shoulders, lifting his chin. Then he bowed low, his hand over his heart. *"Faró quello che desidera, donna mia."*

Even though I didn't understand the words, the message was clear. The air was thick with expectation and I was reminded that long ago, in his other life, Leo had been a soldier and a warrior. He had been a hero.

He remained still, waiting for me to respond.

Time seemed to slow and thicken like it did when I was with Dante. I was acutely aware of the breeze slipping past, of the crunch of dirt beneath my feet. I took a step toward him, touched his shoulder. "Thank you, Leo. I will honor your vow." I wasn't sure where the words came from, but they felt like the right ones to say.

He stayed motionless for another moment, then straightened quickly. He moved his fingers from his heart to his lips and then held out his hand to me, palm up.

The gesture felt formal, almost as though it had been rehearsed from a long-ago ritual. I placed my hand atop his. Again, it felt like the right thing to do.

"Grazie," he said simply.

"Prego," I replied, a little surprised at how easily the Italian came to me.

Leo smiled then, a complex emotion crossing his face. It looked like pride, but with a touch of sadness beneath.

I withdrew my hand and closed my fingers. I wasn't quite ready to let go of the warmth of his touch. The entire moment had felt strangely familiar, like waking up from a dream you can almost remember, but as soon as you try, it's gone.

I tried to marshal my thoughts back in line. "So what was all that business with Emery?" I asked. "If you never really left, I guess that means you don't really work for the college, does it? And why didn't my parents recognize you?"

"No one expects to see someone they're not looking for," Leo said. "A fast dye job, some reading glasses, and a nice suit are usually enough for a quick meeting. I said I worked for the college; they expected to see someone from the college. As a result, they didn't see *me*."

"It seems like a lot of work for you to do."

"After what happened last night, I knew I needed to get in touch with you as soon as possible. I knew you would be at graduation and I thought it would be the best way to reach you. I called Principal Adams this morning, told him the story of the scholarship to Emery, and asked if he could arrange a meeting."

"So, that's all it was—just a story? I don't really have a scholarship?"

"I told the truth. There is a scholarship, and it's yours if you want it."

"In my real life—the life I had yesterday—I had earned a place at Emery fair and square, but this morning I found out that they had rejected my application. And then you showed up." I shook my head. "It's all so messed up. It's all happening so fast. I don't know what to believe anymore."

Leo caught my gaze and held it. "I know things are bad right now. I know it's hard to see the end. But believe me—we can fix this. We will. You, me, and Dante—we will. Can you believe that? Can you hold on?"

Hold on. I had made Dante promise me the same thing at the end of my dream. I looked up at Leo. With his dark hair, he looked so much like Dante it made my heart constrict. I felt a tingling in the palm of my right hand and I squeezed my fingers into a tight fist.

I felt like all I had were my memories of what I knew to be true. I would be strong and hold on until I could find a way to fix things, return them to the way they were supposed to be.

"Yes," I said. "I will."

Leo nodded solemnly. "Good. Then what would you like me to do first?"

Leo and I talked for another hour, trying to figure out a plan of action, but without knowing exactly where Dante was or what exactly was happening to him, it was hard to settle on something that would work. Finally, I asked Leo to go back to the bank and make sure—doubly sure—that Dante wasn't there. It was all I could think of to do. Leo wasn't happy about it, but in the end he agreed. I assured him I would be fine while he was gone, but once he had left and I was alone in the broken ruins of the Dungeon, I wondered if I had told him the truth.

Fine was such a noncommittal response, a word that covered a host of emotions and meanings. It was the best I could hope for under the circumstances.

I turned the ballerina on her music-box stand, the notes filling my hands like fine grains of sand. But once they slipped away and I was left standing in silence, I realized how hard it was to hold onto anything anymore.

CHAPTER 6

"You're sure you want to go by yourself?" Mom asked me the next afternoon. She had parked the car in the small lot, but left the engine running. She touched my arm as I stole a glance at the building in front of us and read again the sign posted in the immaculate lawn: James E. Hart Memorial Hospital.

The building didn't look like a hospital. In fact, it looked more like a bed-and-breakfast with its brightly painted shutters and gingerbread trim around the eaves. A flower bed lined the cobblestone walkway, and a white wicker patio set sat empty beneath a tall oak tree. It looked so normal it gave me the creeps.

I took a deep breath and unfastened my seat belt. "I'd like to see her alone. I'll be okay," I said, hoping it was true.

"Call me when you're done?"

I nodded and opened the car door. I waited until Mom had driven away before I turned and walked up the short path to the front entrance.

The woman who opened the door was dressed in pastel

hospital scrubs; her shoes were somewhere between sneakers and slippers. She wore a small plastic name tag that read "Dr. Blair." She smiled brightly at me. "You must be Abby," she said, stepping aside so I could come inside. "Dr. Hamilton said you would be coming by today." She closed the door and looked at me expectantly.

"Oh, sorry," I said, fumbling in my purse for the note from Dr. J. Hamilton's office granting me permission for a one-hour visit with Valerie. Since when did friends need a doctor's note to visit? It sounded like the setup to a very bad joke with a worse punch line: When that friend was in a mental institution.

I handed the note to Dr. Blair, feeling awkward and uncomfortable and hating every moment of it.

She briefly glanced at the note before tucking it into her pocket. "Right this way, please."

I followed her into a side room that had been decorated more like a parlor than an office. Instead of hard plastic chairs along the wall there was a cozy love seat draped with blankets and covered with pillows. Dr. Blair sat down behind a desk and adjusted the lace tablecloth, moving the vase of fresh flowers to the other corner of the desk so we could see each other more easily. She turned on the stereo, and soft music floated into the room from hidden speakers.

I felt the hairs on my arms prickle with unease. Why couldn't it just have been a hospital? I could have handled a hospital. I didn't know what to make of this strange hybrid of hospital and hotel.

Dr. Blair clasped her hands on the desk and smiled at me.

I felt strangely like I'd been called to the principal's office. I sat on the edge of the love seat, tense and ready to bolt out of the door if given the chance.

"Abby, there are a few general rules here at James E. Hart Memorial Hospital."

I nodded, gripping my purse tighter in my hands. I just wanted to see Valerie. Why couldn't she take me to my friend, already?

"First, you should know that our guests—we refer to them as 'guests' and never as 'patients'—are here because they need a safe place to rest and recover from whatever traumatic event brought them here. We do all we can to make their stay with us as comfortable as possible. So while you are here visiting, we ask that you speak quietly, move slowly, and that, at all times, you exude an aura of peace."

I blinked. How, exactly, was I supposed to do that? I didn't dare ask.

"Second," Dr. Blair continued, "we ask that you don't interact with anyone other than the guest you are here to visit. I know it may be tempting to smile or say hello to the guests you see in the common area or the yard, but for your own safety it is best if you avoid any unnecessary contact."

I swallowed. What kind of place was this? How could Valerie's parents stand to keep her here?

"And lastly, we forbid any kind of electronic devices on the premises." She held out her hand. It took me a moment to realize what she wanted.

"Oh, of course," I said, opening my purse and handing over my cell phone.

"And since you will be visiting with Valerie today, I'm afraid I will also have to ask for your watch."

I glanced at the gold watch on my wrist. I'd gotten the watch for my last birthday, and I'd worn it today specifically because I'd hoped it would remind Valerie of her life before all this happened.

"We have learned that with Valerie it is best not to take any kind of timekeeping device into her room. No watches, no clocks. You understand."

Actually, I might be the only one who did understand. I obediently unclasped my watch and handed it over as well.

Dr. Blair swiftly locked my watch and my phone into the drawer and then brushed her hands together briskly. I wondered if her smile was permanently fixed on her face.

"Now, then, shall we go visit your friend?"

I nodded and followed her out of the room, trying my best to exude an aura of peace.

Valerie's room was on the second floor and, thankfully, we didn't pass any other staff or guests on our short journey down the hall and up the stairs. I didn't want to accidentally make eye contact with anyone I wasn't supposed to.

"Now, then, Abby, you may visit for one hour. If you wish to leave early, simply say so and I'll escort you out."

"But Dr. Hamilton said I'd be able to see Valerie alone," I said.

"Oh, yes, that's true. But we watch and record everything that goes on with our guests." Dr. Blair pointed up at the black dome attached to the ceiling. "It's just one more way we make them feel safe and secure here at James E. Hart Memorial Hospital. Now, are you ready for your visit?"

Dr. Blair didn't wait for me to answer, instead reaching past me to open the door to Valerie's room. I stepped inside, feeling cautious and shy. For one crazy moment, I felt like I was meeting a blind date.

Then I heard the door close—and lock—behind me. My mouth was dry and I felt my hands tingle with fearful anticipation.

"Valerie?" I whispered.

She sat in one of the two chairs that had been arranged next to the window, the pale drapes parted to let in the morning sunlight. I tried not to notice the diamond pattern of reinforced glass on the window or the fact that the chairs were made of molded plastic so there were no sharp edges or any way to take them apart. A faded bedspread covered the twin bed pushed into the corner. Two dolls lay propped up on the pillows.

Along one wall was an open closet filled with hangers of identical fluffy white bathrobes and folded stacks of gray sweatpants and loose shirts. My heart sank at the sight of Valerie sitting passively by the window, wearing a pair of those sweatpants and a plain white T-shirt. Her hair was still short and black, the same as the last time I'd seen her, on the night of the Spring Fling all those weeks ago; the nurses here must be keeping it trimmed. Her face was free of any makeup or expression. Her vacant eyes stared without blinking.

The Valerie I knew, who loved the latest fashions and the

brightest colors, wouldn't have been caught dead in such bland and shapeless clothes.

But that was the whole point, wasn't it? She hadn't died that horrible night on the bank—she'd simply lost her mind.

And it was my fault.

If I hadn't asked Dante to take me to the bank, then Tony wouldn't have seen the bridge and the door and then Zo wouldn't have taken Valerie away and then she wouldn't be here in this horrible place under the care of the unsettling Dr. Blair.

I sat down in the chair across from Valerie and her distant eyes, my legs suddenly unable to support my weight. I reached out and touched the white plastic name band that overlaid the black chains tattooed around her wrists. Somehow the sight of that black-and-white combination made the whole thing real. I swallowed hard and felt a hiccup in my chest.

Was I a bad friend if I wondered whether perhaps death would have been a kinder fate than being locked up in this place?

"You're not a bad friend," Valerie said. "And I'm glad I'm not dead."

"What?" I didn't think I'd spoken my thoughts out loud.

"I'm glad I'm here at the James E. Hart Memorial Hospital. They take good care of me." She finally turned to look at me and there, deep in her shadowed eyes, was a flicker of light, but if it was of lucidity, I couldn't tell.

"It's good to see you, Valerie," I said. My voice sounded funny to my ears, muffled by my pounding heartbeat. "I've missed you."

She didn't say anything for a long time, and I squirmed a little under her gaze.

I saw a flash of color on the wall behind her. "Did you draw that?" I asked, pointing over her shoulder.

Valerie didn't look where I pointed, but simply nodded. "I like drawing pictures. They help me see what's real."

"What's it a picture of?" I stood up from my chair and took the few steps to her bedside.

Heavy crayon strokes and shapes covered the paper taped to the wall. A line of neon green for the grass, a ball of yellow for the sun, three triangles stacked on a stump for a tree. Standing next to the tree was a man-shaped shadow with dark hair curling up from the head like smoke. The only feature on the blank face was a razor-sharp grin.

My heart stuttered. "Who is this?" I asked, though I feared I knew the answer. I knew that grin.

Valerie joined me. "He watches over me," she said. "He keeps me safe from prowlers and predators." She suddenly looked down. "Would you like to play with my dollies?" She plucked the two dolls from the bedspread and sat on the edge of the bed. "They don't like me having my dollies, but they don't like me *not* having my dollies more." Her smile didn't look quite right. I couldn't help but think of the bared fangs on a rabid wolf. "They haven't learned yet that I always get what I want."

I swallowed and nodded cautiously, sitting next to her on the bed. "I'd love to play with you."

"Good. I'll be the Pirate King." She held up one figure. The doll had dark hair fringed with white and a wide, predatory smile beneath coal-black button eyes. For all that it was a simple rag doll, it looked eerily like Zo. I could see where Valerie had drawn chains around the doll's wrists with a yellow marker. I wondered about the chains, though—why were they gold instead of black? Maybe yellow was the only color she'd had access to.

"And you can be the River Policeman." Valerie handed me the second doll and I felt a flush of surprise. This doll also had dark hair and yellow chains inked around his wrists, but his button eyes were silver and his smile was small and secretive. He wore a long blue coat with a sheriff's star drawn on the lapel. I half smiled at the thought of Dante as a policeman, patrolling the river, on the prowl for lawbreakers.

Then I remembered the ghostly feel of his hand holding tight to mine and the whisper of his voice, *Hurry, Abby. Please.*

"What should we play?" I asked, my mouth dry and my mind rough with unwelcome thoughts.

"Oh, I know a lot of good stories. They're in my head all the time now, but sometimes the endings change when I'm not looking. Stories can be tricky that way. You have to watch them carefully all the time or else they'll catch you and you'll never get away." She clapped her hands in delight. "I know! Let's play the story of how the brave Pirate King escaped from the bad River Policeman." She leaned forward conspiratorially. "This is one of my favorites."

"I don't know that story," I said, glancing between the Zo and Dante dolls. I knew, with a sinking feeling in my heart, that this story was not going to be one of *my* favorites.

"Of course you don't, darling," Valerie scoffed, and for a

moment she sounded like her old self. I glanced up in hopeful surprise, but her eyes held a hard edge of anger. "Don't be stupid. I haven't told it to you yet."

"Oh," I murmured, my heart quiet. "Right."

"The story starts with a gunshot." Valerie slapped her hands together with a bang and I jumped, making the bed bounce a little.

"It's not a real gun, silly," she said, giggling. "It's just the sound I hear in my head when I tell this story. Sometimes it sounds like a door closing and a key turning in a lock. Do you know what that sounds like?"

I nodded. The echo of the door closing behind Dante rang in my ears every moment of every day.

"Then the story sounds like footsteps—running from the beginning straight to the end. It's a fast story, so I hope you can keep up." She tapped her toes on the floor, the bottoms of her slippers rasping like sandpaper.

"The Pirate King likes to run too." She moved the doll's legs up and down on her knees. "He likes to run through grass and across fields and over bridges. But mostly he likes to run through puddles. He likes to see the splash and the ripples. He even likes to run on the deck of his boat. He built a boat, you know—a fast boat—and sails it up and down the river. His boat is so fast that nothing can stop him. He knows that for a fact so he stands at the front of his boat and laughs into the wind."

She tilted the doll's head back with her fingers and laughed. I felt a sick twist in the pit of my stomach as Zo's laugh filled the room.

"But one day, when the Pirate King was standing high on the crow's nest looking up at the stars, he saw a strange sight. A River Policeman was sailing behind him in a dinky old dinghy."

She held a doll in each hand so they were face-to-face.

"'Stop!' the River Policeman shouted.

"The Pirate King just laughed into the wind. 'You can't stop me. I am too fast for you.'

"'I'll follow you wherever you go,' the River Policeman said. 'You won't get away from me.'

"'Full speed ahead!' the Pirate King shouted to his crew." Valerie paused, looking at me with her head tilted to one side. "I think every pirate ship needs a crew, don't you? I don't have any other dolls yet, so you'll just have to imagine the other pirates."

It was all too easy to imagine Tony and V as rag dolls with matching black button eyes, following in Zo's footsteps. I tasted acid in the back of my throat. But Tony wasn't with Zo, I reminded myself. He was with Dante somewhere in the dark place between doors, disappearing with each successive scream. I dragged my thoughts back to Valerie's story. As unsettling as her words were, I preferred them to thinking about the alternative.

"The Pirate King orders the crew to sail faster and faster, and it seems impossible, but the River Policeman keeps up with them. In fact, it starts to look like he's gaining on them, that he'll catch the Pirate King and his crew."

Valerie chased one doll with the other up and down her lap.

"The Pirate King can't let that happen. He knows the River Policeman would take him away in chains and wouldn't let him run free through the grass and the fields and the puddles anymore. So the Pirate King orders his crew to stop and make a stand."

She paused. I held my breath for the next part of the story.

"The River Policeman climbed aboard the pirate ship and cornered the Pirate King's crew. But it was a trap! The Pirate King was smarter and stronger and faster than anybody could have imagined. They fought and fought until the river turned black with blood and the stars fell from the sky."

The two dolls wrestled on Valerie's lap while she growled and grunted deep in her throat.

"But just when it looked like the River Policeman was going to win—surprise!"

Suddenly, she reached out and tore away the policeman's eyes, the silver buttons as small and thin as dimes in her hand.

"'I'm blind,' the River Policeman shouted. He tried to cry, but since he didn't have any eyes, how could he have any tears?"

She threw the ruined doll on the floor by her feet and lifted the Pirate King high above her head in victory. "And so the Pirate King and his crew sailed away, off on another adventure, and they left the River Policeman on the riverbank, blind and bleeding and helpless."

She lowered the Pirate King doll and looked at it fondly. "I love stories with happy endings, don't you?" She looked at me with a huge smile. "What was your favorite part?"

She didn't let me answer, which was good since the only

word I could think of was *no.* Just—*no.* A unilateral negation of everything that was happening.

"My favorite part is the ending. When the story is in my head, I can see all the endings. And they all end the same way—with a kiss between the king and his queen." She lifted the Pirate King doll up and kissed the painted mouth with a loud, smacking sound. "I can't wait," she sighed and tucked the doll into her arms, rocking it like a small child.

I picked up the blinded doll from the floor with shaking hands. I didn't want the story to be true, but parts of it were horribly easy to recognize and identify. Was the Pirate King really so strong? Had he really left the River Policeman for dead? Was that why I couldn't reach Dante? Was the darkness beyond the bank . . . death? I felt a chill lift the hairs on my arms.

My mouth filled with dust. I didn't want to be here. I had known it was going to be hard to see Valerie like this, but I didn't think it was going to be *this* hard. I wanted my friend back, the one I'd known since third grade, the one I'd told my secrets to during late-night sleepovers, the one I'd grown up with. I didn't know this person sitting across from me.

I wanted to leave and was ready to say so when Valerie leaned close and touched my knee.

"I knew you were coming, darling," she said. The childish lilt to her voice had fled and she sounded like the Valerie I remembered. A flicker of almost familiar light touched the corners of her eyes. "I told him so when he came to see me. He said he hoped you would. He wants to see you, but he said you're a hard woman to reach." She held up one of her chained wrists, and the light in her eyes grew brighter.

"He knows exactly who you are. He wanted me to give you a message. He wanted me to tell you that this is only the beginning. That he's in charge of the river now. That his gifts are stronger now. That you can't stop him."

I looked at the Pirate King doll propped up in her lap, then at the crumpled River Policeman in my hand. Maybe I couldn't stop him. But I knew I had to try.

"Riddle me this," Valerie said suddenly, wrapping her fingers around my wrist and turning my hand up. She opened my fist as easily as peeling an orange.

"Made of steel or hair, it can be snapped like a finger or picked like a string. It will stay closed to any but its partner, though it will always open for skeletons. What is it?"

As she spoke, she traced a series of letters on the flat of my palm with her fingertip. It was an old game we'd played as kids. A silent and secret method of communication. The goal was to pose a riddle while writing something completely different from what you were saying; the winner was the one who could answer the riddle *and* recite the secret message correctly.

I watched her finger move fast and sure, tracing out each individual letter; her nail felt like a needle against my skin.

When she finished, she closed my hand around the words she'd written and met my eyes.

"Do you understand?" she asked me.

I nodded, my heart beating hard and fast. "I understand perfectly." If Valerie was somewhere in there, trying to communicate with me, then I hoped she would recognize the words and finish the game.

"Then speak the words and answer," she responded.

"It's a lock," I said, recognizing one of our first riddles. "A lock made of steel, or a lock of hair. It can be snapped closed, or picked open. It prefers its own key, though a skeleton key can open anything."

Valerie nodded, a wise and slightly sad smile on her face. "You win." Then the light faded from her eyes. "Oh, he will be so mad." She cupped her hands over her mouth and giggled like a child. "But first he will have to find me." She darted from the bed to the open closet, crouching down in the corner behind the bathrobes. Covering her eyes with her hands, she started counting. "One. Two. Three. Ready or not, here I come." But she didn't move or uncover her eyes. "I said—ready or not, here I come!"

I slowly stood up and backed away until my heels hit the closed door. Seeing her like this was bad enough, but having caught a glimpse of my old friend trapped inside made it worse. I couldn't stay here anymore. Pressing my closed fist to my chest, I reached behind me, fumbling for the doorknob. I didn't find one, though, and realized that I wasn't particularly surprised. This place was more of a prison than a hospital. Why would they want to give the inmates a way to leave their rooms?

"Dr. Blair," I said. "I'm ready to leave."

The door opened behind me and Dr. Blair stood in the hallway as though she had expected my call.

"And did we have a nice visit?" she asked, clasping her hands in front of her like a schoolteacher.

I nodded; I didn't dare trust myself to speak. Behind me I could hear Valerie's voice, high and quick: "Four. Five. Six. Ready or not, ready or not."

"Oh, good. If you'd like to follow me, I'll show you out."

Dr. Blair led me to her office, returned my phone and watch, and then walked me to the front door. I could feel her eyes on me, watching, while I dialed Mom's number. She might still have been watching a few minutes later as I climbed into the car and we drove away; I wasn't brave enough to look back at the James E. Hart Memorial Hospital.

The whole drive home I kept my fist closed around the words Valerie had written on my palm like they were a handful of diamonds. No, they were better than diamonds; I suspected they might be the key to everything.

F-I-X I-T. Y-O-U C-A-N F-I-X I-T.

CHAPTER 7

There was another message waiting for me when I got home. A sticky note slapped to my bedroom door bore Hannah's unmistakable touch:

Dearest Abby,
Call Natalie.
Love,
Your personal answering service

I plucked the note from the door and walked down the hall to Hannah's room. "Hannah, when did Natalie call?"

"When you were gone," she said from behind a book. The title on the spine read *The Once and Future King* and the cover had an elaborate painting of King Arthur wielding Excalibur.

"Ha, ha," I said dryly. "When—exactly?"

"I don't know. Ten minutes ago. Maybe twenty."

"Did she say anything?"

Hannah sighed and let the book drop onto her stomach. "I sort of thought 'Call Natalie' would be enough, but I guess not." She cleared her throat. "Natalie said, and I quote, 'Is

Abby there?' And then I said, 'No, she's not. Can I take a message?' And then *she* said, 'No, just have her call me, okay?' And then I said—"

"Okay, okay, I get it."

"I would have written it down, but the note was a little small, and—"

"Yeah, I get it. Thanks for the message."

"I'll bill you later." Hannah disappeared behind her book again, effectively dismissing me from her presence.

Returning to my room, I slouched into the window seat and fished out my cell phone.

Natalie picked up on the third ring.

"Hey, I'm back," I said. "What's up?"

"When I agreed to meet you at that restaurant, I didn't know you were setting me up on a date. And with Jason, of all people!"

"What's wrong with Jason?"

"Nothing. He's nice. It's just—I wasn't expecting it, that's all."

"What did you guys do?"

"It was dinner, Abby. We ate, then he took me home."

"What did you talk about?"

"I don't know—stuff. What's with the Spanish Inquisition routine? You could have stayed with us, you know. Where did you run off to, anyway?"

"Did you have fun?" I dodged her question with one of my own.

"I guess." Natalie sighed; I heard her shift her phone to her other ear. "I don't understand why you did it, though. I mean, aren't you guys dating?"

Now it was my turn to shift the phone, stalling for time. "It's complicated," I said finally.

"Wait, you're breaking up with him?" Natalie's voice hit a high note of disbelief.

"I didn't say that!"

"Yeah, but since when has your relationship with Jason been 'complicated'?"

Since time fractured and I woke up in a different present and I would do anything to get my life back on track. "It's just—it hasn't all been peaches and cream lately."

"So? Most people would love to have a boyfriend like Jason."

"Would you?"

"Would I what?"

"Would you want Jason to be your boyfriend?"

"Okay, this is officially the strangest phone call I've had in a long time. Are you offering to, what, *loan* me Jason? He's not a sweater, you know."

"No, no, that's not what I meant." This wasn't going the way I'd planned at all. "I was just wondering if, you know, if the circumstances were different, if maybe you could see yourself with a guy like Jason."

"So you *are* going to break up with him."

I couldn't bring myself to deny it outright.

Natalie must have heard the hesitation because when she spoke, her voice shook with hard emotion. "You're going to break up with Jason, and you want to let him down easy by handing him off to me? Okay, I'm hanging up now."

"No, wait! Please—" The past had changed, but I hoped it hadn't changed so much as to make my next words a lie. "I've seen how you look at him." I could hear Natalie breathing on the other end, so I forged ahead into the unknown. "I've seen how you light up when he comes into the room. How you smile, and then look around to make sure no one saw you."

"How . . . ?" Natalie's breath hiccupped a little and I closed my eyes in relief. She was still listening—and what was more, she wasn't denying it.

"It's okay, Nat," I said. "I haven't told anyone."

A sigh threaded its way through the phone.

"Would you do me a favor?" I asked after a pause. "Would you consider going out with Jason if he asked you?"

"He won't ask."

"But you want him to."

I barely heard the word—"Yes."

"That's good to hear," I said.

"You're not mad?"

"Hard to believe, but no, I'm not mad. You were right before. I'm not sure I see a future together with Jason, so it would make me happy to know that you guys might have a chance to be happy together."

Natalie was quiet for a long moment. "Are you dating someone else?"

I closed my eyes, Dante's face instantly forming in my memory. "Don't say anything, okay? I should tell Jason on my own."

"Abby! When did this happen? Who is it? Details, please, I need details."

I had to remind myself that in this present, not only did my friends not know I was dating Dante, they didn't even know he existed. The thought made me unbearably sad and lonely.

"You'll love him. I know you will," I said, rushing on before Natalie could articulate a protest at my dodging her demands. "Listen, Nat, I've gotta go. I'm sorry. We'll talk more later, okay?"

I hung up and let my head fall back against the wall. I felt terrible for cutting Natalie off like that, but my emotions were running too close to the surface and I feared I'd lose control if I tried to explain my relationship with Dante.

Why did relationships have to be so complicated, anyway?

Valerie had told me I could fix it, and I felt like I had started the process, at least as far as Natalie and Jason were concerned. But they were the least of my worries. How could I fix what was happening to Dante? How, when I couldn't even talk to him except in my dreams?

I wished I could just pick up the phone and call Dante as easily as I could Natalie. I wanted to hear his voice again, his laugh. I wanted to watch his eyes capture the light of the setting sun, turning them to mercury. I wanted to tell him what was going on, ask his advice.

I was grateful Leo had come back to help; just knowing he was close by had alleviated some of my stress. But talking to Leo wasn't the same as talking to Dante. I knew Leo would be willing to answer my questions and offer suggestions, but my relationship with Leo, while it certainly went beyond acquaintance, still wasn't quite to the level of good friends. I felt like there was mutual respect between us, but there was something else, too. Something that sometimes felt distant and businesslike. And other times . . .

"Mia donna di luce," I murmured, remembering how Leo had offered me his pledge. It sounded a little cheesy, but the memory of his actions reminded me of a knight and his lady.

With Dante, though, I didn't have any question about what was between us or what we shared. With Dante, I felt like part of a team. We were *together.* And when we were together, I felt more like myself. He brought out the best in me. I felt braver and stronger knowing he was on my side. I knew I could count on him. Beyond that, I knew he knew he could count on me.

He was counting on me right now. And I didn't know how to help him.

That wasn't entirely true, I realized. I had promised to return to him again, and even if I didn't have any answers yet, I could still let him know he wasn't alone. He wasn't forgotten.

But how could I get to the dream-side of the bank? It was the middle of the afternoon; I wasn't tired enough to fall asleep. And even if I could pull the covers over my head and sleep, I didn't have any guarantee that my dream would take me where I wanted to go.

There had to be another way. Once before I had traveled to the bank deliberately, and I'd already been to the dream-side twice. If I could combine the two experiences, then there might be a chance of success. The worst that could happen was that I would miss the safety of the dream and land squarely on the actual bank. I hesitated; if that happened, I might not make it back. But if I did end up on the bank, Leo could find me. He could bring me back. And the best that could happen was that I would find a way to reach Dante. Was he worth the risk?

There was only one answer to that question.

I slipped out of the window seat and crossed to my bed. There was no time like the present, and if I was going to try the impossible, I might as well be comfortable.

Lacing my fingers across my chest, I settled back into my pillows, exhaling in one breath. I closed my eyes, trying to tap into my memory from that night in the Dungeon when I'd counted my way to the bank.

Butterflies beat a slow rhythm in the pit of my stomach. I squelched the fear I felt building and concentrated instead on forcing my surroundings to thin, to shift from *here* to *there*. I needed to slide between. I needed to get close enough to the bank and yet still be able to stop short.

Was it even possible?

Or was I fooling myself into thinking that I had the ability to do what no one else seemed to be able to do?

Lying in bed, I centered my thoughts on Dante. He was the difference. I wanted to be where he was, and he most certainly wasn't on the bank. With my eyes closed, I traced the letters of his name in my mind. The tall, straight back of the D, and the convex curve, so smooth and graceful. The pyramid point of the A, angular and precise, and the steady crossbeam that connected the slanted sides. The twin pillars of the N, with a slope sliding between them. The balanced T. And finally the three prongs of the E—like a brass hinge covered in symbols: a shell curling on itself; a half-sun, half-moon; a rising scale.

The pivoting hinge of the black hourglass door.

I drew in a quick breath and held it, tasting the delicate air under my tongue and in the soft tissue of my throat.

A shiver moved deep in my bones, as though a chime had been struck far away and the reverberations had reached me before the sound had.

I could feel the world around me slow, bending and twisting before drawing to a point, waiting for me to take the next step.

This was the moment. It was my choice. Would I go forward and risk it all, or would I withdraw?

In that still moment, I heard laughter in the distance. Wild, unfettered laughter, as though I had arrived too late to hear the punch line of the greatest joke ever told. The laughter grew louder, stretching out longer and longer. I stepped forward, following the sound like a thread strung through a labyrinth. As I drew closer and closer to the source, it became easier for me to count my heartbeats, the rhythm of my breathing. I fixed my destination firmly in my mind. I fixed the image of Dante in my heart. I summoned my memories of how the bank had looked the last time I'd visited it in my dream. I would find my way there. I had to. I focused on my counting, on capturing that feeling of dreaming, on following that laughter.

Silence enveloped me between one breath and the next, and I jerked back, startled. At the same time, my surroundings shifted, tilting on an axis like a twisted kaleidoscope. Watching in amazement, I saw the walls of my room fracture and fade into the wide-open spaces of the bank. A black sky replaced my ceiling and the black ground rose to meet my feet.

For the first time, I looked around the bank in delighted surprise. I had done it. I had wanted to end up on the dream-side of the bank, and here I was. Now that I had done it once, I knew I could do it again. And now that I was here, I didn't want to waste any time.

"Dante! I'm here. I came back."

The silence stretched out, thick and oppressive. I looked around for him even though I knew I wouldn't be able to see him. He had to be here; he'd made me a promise.

Abby? Is that really you? I must be dreaming.

It felt so good to have his voice wash over me again, I almost didn't notice how frail and hollow it sounded. "No, I'm the one who's dreaming. I'm getting good at it, too." I grinned. "I made it back on my first try."

How long has it been?

"Not long. Only two days. I told you I'd be back."

Two days? Impossible. It's been longer. It has to be. I've been counting . . . He sounded disoriented, distracted.

"Oh, Dante," I murmured, my heart afire with sympathy. I reached out my hand through the rippling air around me, pushing my arm in up to my elbow, hoping we could connect like we had before.

Almost immediately, I felt Dante's ghostly hand grab mine and squeeze tight. He lifted my hand to his face; I could feel the contours of his cheek and the hard edge of his jaw. Stubble scraped along my palm as he turned to press a kiss on the inside of my wrist. An electric tingle shivered through my arm and around to the back of my neck.

You taste like light, he said, his voice filled with awe and longing.

The electricity I felt shot from my neck down my spine. The air that had been shimmering silver flashed gold.

Will you stay?

"For as long as I can."

Good. He kissed my wrist again, adding another one to the curve of my palm as he slipped my hand from his face. He didn't let me go, but held my hand between both of his.

"Tell me what's been happening," I said, feeling a little breathless as his thumbs gently stroked small circles on the back of my hand. "Has anything changed where you are?"

Only Tony. He's . . . less. And sometimes he wanders away. I have to follow him; I don't want to lose touch with him. Dante paused. *At least he's stopped screaming.*

"Does he know what happened? Can you talk to him?"

No. He can't talk anymore. Dante's voice sounded strained.

"Why not?"

Dante paused before saying simply, *Parts of him have been disappearing.*

He didn't say anything else; I was relieved. I didn't want to have to hear the words that would make it true. I remembered that night so long ago when Zero Hour had played at the Dungeon. I could picture Tony's bright, quick smile. It was impossible to think it was gone. Worse to think that the rest of him would follow into darkness. I felt sick to my stomach.

"What about you? Are you okay?"

I think so. It's hard to tell. The darkness . . . I can't get away from it. It makes it hard to think.

The pressure on my hand increased and I felt my fingers start to go numb. "I have good news," I said, hoping to give Dante something else to focus on. "Leo's back."

I didn't know he was gone.

I heard him muttering numbers under his breath, counting.

"A lot has happened since you left." I told him briefly about the changes I'd started to see rippling down the river. "But I think I might have started to set things right—at least with Natalie and Jason. And if Leo can help me straighten things out with Emery, I think things will be okay."

It sounds like you've been busy.

I paused. "I'm worried about Valerie, though."

What happened to her?

There was no nice way to say it, so I blurted out the words. "She cracked mentally on the bank. Now she's in a hospital. I'm worried that she won't get better."

I'm so sorry, Abby. I tried—

"It's not your fault," I said quickly. "It happened as soon as Zo took her to the bank. There was nothing either one of us could do at that point."

I wish I could be there to help you now.

"I'm just trying to do my best. It'll be good when we get you out of there. Then we can be one step ahead instead of running to catch up."

Dante was silent; I would have thought he had gone except for the constant pressure on my hand. Coldness encased me all the way to my wrist. I didn't want to lose touch with Dante, but I wondered how much longer I could last.

I've been looking around—if you can call it that. There's nothing here, Abby. No door, no light, nothing. It's like I've gone blind. I didn't think I'd ever say this, but being here is worse than being on the bank. And as long as I'm here, I can't do anything to help. I can't stop Zo. I can't even stop what's happening to Tony. It's horrible. Death would be a mercy.

"Don't talk like that. We'll find a way to get you home."

What if what is happening to Tony starts happening to me?

"It won't. I won't let it."

How can you change it?

"I don't know, but I'm here, aren't I? We're together—at least in a small way." I flexed my fingers in his grasp. The coldness flowed up my arm, almost to my elbow. My teeth started to chatter and I repressed a full-body shiver. "And together we can do anything, right? Even the impossible. Even this."

When Dante finally spoke, his voice sounded stronger, more aware and alert. *Do you know how remarkable you are, Abby?*

A blush warmed my cheeks. "I'm not that special. I'm just me."

You're more than you think you are. You're brave and determined. You make it easy to believe in you. Whatever happens, you have risked much to bring light to my darkness, and your courage is a gift I will never be able to repay—no matter how long I live. Dante moved my hand in his, quickly pressing it flat against his chest, then lifting it to his mouth. He breathed a kiss over my fingertips; his lips felt like fire on my iced skin. Lowering my hand, he placed his palm over mine. *My life is in your hands. I know you will keep it safe.*

My memory flashed back to Leo, standing in the wasteland of the Dungeon, offering me the same gesture.

I felt a little dizzy and light-headed, the edges of the dream starting to fray. My heart sped up; I wasn't ready to go yet. I still had more I wanted to say, more I wanted to hear.

You're leaving, aren't you? Dante said, resigned and rueful.

"I don't want to," I said. "But I'm not sure I have much choice. I don't know what the rules are for this."

I do. Do what you have to do. Change what needs to be changed. Come back when you can, he said.

And then I woke up, thrown back to awareness like a rock through a window.

I sat upright and opened my eyes all in one motion. I rubbed my hands over my arms, afraid I would see the black shadow of frostbite on my skin, but instead, there was the faintest tinge of gold on my fingertips, as though I'd touched something covered with paper-thin gold leaf, or caught a falling star.

Yes, our conversation had been brief, but we'd had one. I'd made it to the dream-side of the bank without dreaming. And Dante wasn't lost to me yet.

No matter how you looked at it, I counted that as a victory.

I grabbed a notebook from my desk and wrote down everything I could remember about how I was able to reach Dante and what we had talked about. For good measure, I wrote down Valerie's story of the Pirate King and the River Policeman. As I read over the accounts a second time, I noticed again the similarities, the places where reality and dream and story touched and overlapped.

The River Policeman in Valerie's story had been blinded, cast into darkness. Those were the same words Dante had used about himself. I doubted it was a coincidence. It was clear that Valerie not only still had ties to Zo—he had come to visit her, a thought that made the hairs on the back of my neck stand up—but she also had access to the world of the bank and river.

Do what you have to do.

I knew what I needed to do, though the thought filled me with dread.

I had to visit Valerie again.

CHAPTER 8

Dr. Blair was not happy to see me first thing Monday morning. She held out her hand silently for my phone; I had known better than to wear my watch this time.

"I was not aware that Dr. Hamilton had approved another visit for you."

"He hasn't," I admitted. "But I really need to see Valerie right away. Please."

"Valerie has been a . . . difficult guest since your last visit."

"I'm sorry," I said, trying to exude an aura of peace, but obviously failing since Dr. Blair frowned and made a "humph" sound.

"It's against policy to allow visitors without a note."

"I know, and I wouldn't ask if it wasn't important."

Dr. Blair turned my phone over and over in her hands. I noticed she had painted her fingernails a baby-pink hue, though the shade was almost the same color as her flesh and the effect was just this side of creepy.

"Do you think this is funny?" she asked abruptly, setting my phone down on her desk. "Did the two of you plan this during your last visit? This is a hospital. We do not welcome pranks here."

I blinked. "I'm sorry, I don't know what you're talking about. This isn't a joke."

"Valerie knew you were coming today. She told me this morning what time you would be arriving. She even drew a picture and *ordered* me to give it to you. She'll be impossible if I *don't* give it to you, so . . . here." Dr. Blair's lips twisted in a frown as she handed me a sheet of white paper.

A bright yellow sun filled one corner, the fat rays pointing out in ruler-straight lines. A brown scribble bisected the paper, and standing on the uneven horizon was a black stick figure with brown hair and a large, toothy grin. The figure wore a blue shirt and shorts. The word *Abby* hovered around the figure's head with an arrow pointing at its body.

We both looked down at my dark blue shirt, and I brushed self-consciously at the unraveling hem of my shorts. "I haven't seen her or spoken to her since Saturday. I swear."

"Then how do you explain that?" Dr. Blair pointed to the picture in my hand. "And what does the note mean?"

An additional message was written in a small, cramped hand in the corner: "The bearer of this letter has acted under my orders and for the good of the State." Valerie had signed her name, complete with her trademark heart over the "i."

"I don't know. It probably doesn't mean anything," I lied. I recognized the wording from *The Three Musketeers.* That had been us, once—me, Natalie, and Valerie. Not so much anymore.

I knew that trying to explain anything to Dr. Blair would

take too long, time I didn't have. "I really need to talk to my friend. Could I please see her? Just ten minutes. Please?"

After a long moment, Dr. Blair finally pushed my phone into her desk drawer and locked it with one of the small keys on her key ring. "You may have ten minutes with her."

I folded the picture of me and slipped it into my purse before falling into step behind Dr. Blair. I suspected I might need longer than ten minutes with Valerie to get the answers to my many questions, but I knew Dr. Blair could easily have turned me away, denying me any time at all. I would take what I could get and be happy about it. I had only a few minutes, so I'd need to use them wisely. I might only have the chance to ask Valerie one question—which one should it be?

Instead of leading me up the stairs to Valerie's room, Dr. Blair turned left and walked toward a small room tucked away at the far end of the hallway.

"Valerie is in a heightened state of anxiety at the moment, so may I remind you to stay calm. Do not aggravate her or upset her in any way. I would hate to have to revoke your visiting privileges."

"I'll be careful," I said.

Dr. Blair weighed me with her gaze, then *humphed* again before opening the door for me.

I stepped inside and looked around in surprise. The small room was actually a brightly lit conservatory, filled with an array of startlingly green plants. The windows were still scored with protective diamond panels, but the sunlight pouring in was warm and golden. The sound of an unseen waterfall gurgled nearby. A small bird chirped.

The door closed and locked behind me. I walked around a large potted plant. The leaves brushed against my arm and I jerked away at their cold touch. Hesitantly, I rubbed a leaf between my fingers. It felt waxy and slick. The whole plant was plastic; all the plants were plastic.

Following the sound of the water, I moved deeper into the room. I found Valerie sitting on the edge of a wide stone fountain. Instead of the traditional carvings of flowers or animals or people, this fountain was a basic gray pillar rising up from a curved basin. Dressed in her standard white bathrobe over a T-shirt and sweats, Valerie leaned over to trail her fingers in the basin. Her hand came up dry, and I realized there wasn't any water in the fountain, just the sound of running water.

Was anything in this place real?

"Hi, Valerie," I said with a small wave. "Remember me?"

She turned to me and her whole face lit up. Running to me, she threw her arms around me in a wild hug. "Abby! You're here! I knew you'd come!" Just as quickly, her face fell into shadow. "But, oh, you shouldn't be here. He won't be happy." She jammed the end of the bathrobe belt into her mouth, sucking and chewing. Her eyes darted from side to side. "Oh, no, no, he won't be happy at all."

"Do you mean Zo? Why won't Zo be happy?"

Valerie shrieked and covered my mouth with her hands. "Don't say his name. You're not allowed to say his name."

Startled by her sudden movement, I took a step back. "Okay," I mumbled, gently pulling her hands away. "Okay, I'm sorry, I won't." I grimaced. We'd only been together a few moments and already I had upset her. Dr. Blair would be furious.

Still holding Valerie's hand, I pointed back to the stone fountain. "I'd like to talk to you for a minute. Can we sit down?"

Valerie looked from me to the fountain and back again. "What do you want to talk about?" she asked hesitantly.

I sat down on the edge. The stone was cool against the backs of my legs. The endless sound of the invisible waterfall was oddly soothing, like a long-ago lullaby.

Now that the moment was here, I wondered if I had made a mistake in coming. I took a deep breath; it was time to find out. "I'd like to hear another story."

Her eyes widened in excitement. "I *love* stories!" Valerie scurried to my side, crossing her legs beneath her and holding the toes of her scuffed slippers. "I know a lot of stories."

"I know. That's why I came to see you today. I was hoping you could tell me another story about . . . about the River Policeman." I watched her eyes, hoping to see that faint glimmer of her old self beneath the surface, but she wouldn't meet my gaze.

"No, the best stories are about the Pirate King. Can't I tell you one of *those?*"

"Maybe later," I hedged. I did want to hear more about Zo—a lot more—but I had only so much time today and Dante couldn't wait. "But I really, really like the River Policeman. Don't you know another one about him?"

Valerie nibbled at her fingernail, twisting her lips in thought. "Well, I know one. But I don't know if it's a good story to tell." She looked around the room as though something lurked behind the plastic leaves. "It's a dark story."

"Dark how? Like, scary—with monsters and things?"

She laughed, the sound like a chittering bird. "Silly girl, monsters aren't scary."

"What makes it scary, then?"

Valerie finally met my eyes, her blue gaze steady. "It's not scary. It's *dark.* It's dark where the River Policeman is. Dark and cold." She crossed her arms and rubbed her shoulders, pretending to shiver, even though she sat in a slant of sun.

My breath slipped out with my words. "Where is the River Policeman? Do you know?"

Valerie half closed her eyes and tilted her head to the side as though she was listening to more than the babbling waterfall. "He is nowhere. He is everywhere. He is in between. He doesn't like it. The darkness presses on him and it hurts."

I bit at my lip. I heard again the sound of screaming coming at me from the darkness between the doors.

"He thinks a lot about how much it hurts. It's hard to think, but thinking is all he can do while he waits for the darkness to eat him alive. He knows that once it has finished nibbling at its prisoner, it will come for him."

The prisoner is Tony. She's talking about Tony.

"The Policeman knows he doesn't have much time left. The thought makes him laugh and laugh and laugh. But there is no one to hear him laughing."

I heard him, I thought. *It was his laughter that drew me to the dream-side of the bank.*

"The Policeman is smart, though. Smart and brave. He will need to be brave to face what waits for him in the darkness."

"What's that?" I asked. I realized I was touching Dante's

locket, unaware that my hand had moved to my throat. "Is there something else in the darkness?"

Valerie's eyes snapped open and she frowned. "Stop interrupting the story."

I swallowed and looked down. "Sorry. Go on."

"He has a choice to make. He can wait for the darkness to crush him. Or he can escape. It will mean leaving behind the prisoner, and the River Policeman is not sure he can do that. After all, he has never left a man behind before. But it's not like the prisoner will mind."

I knew that was true enough. From my conversation with Dante, it didn't sound like Tony was going to mind much of anything for much longer. I risked speaking again. "How can the Policeman escape?" Like Tony, I didn't have much time left either. Dr. Blair would be back any minute, but I couldn't leave before hearing the end of this story.

Valerie paused, frowning at me. "If you can't stay still, then I can't tell you the story."

"I'll be quiet," I promised, drawing an X over my heart and holding up my finger.

"Cross your heart, hope to die. Stick a needle in your eye," Valerie chanted, but the words sounded more like a threat in her eerie monotone than they did in the familiar cadence of a childhood rhyme.

I didn't dare say another word; I could barely breathe.

Valerie regarded me in silence, the sound of running water in the background reminding me how fast time was slipping away.

"Now I don't remember where the story is. It's so dark, it's easy to get lost in it." She closed her eyes, her hands clutching the hem of her bathrobe. "Oh, there it is. You thought you could get away, but I found you." Opening her eyes, she smiled and straightened her spine, settling into her pose on the stone like a regal queen granting an audience. "The River Policeman has decided to escape. No matter what. He has to get away from the darkness. He has to join the girl he loves. He has to make sure the darkness doesn't get *her*."

Words clogged my throat—*That's me. I'm the girl. Is the darkness coming for me?*—but I stayed still. I didn't want to rush Valerie and make her mad.

"He stands on what is left of his feet, reaches out into the darkness with what is left of his hands. He is blind in the night so he must search by touch."

I rubbed my palms together, remembering Dante's ghostly touch and the strength in his hand as he wrapped his fingers around mine, the fire of his lips on my skin.

"He is looking, he is looking, and . . . ah-ha, he is *finding*. There is a way out of the darkness. A way back to the girl of his heart."

How? I felt my mouth shape the word, but I held my breath instead of giving it life.

The message must have been clear, because Valerie nodded sagely and answered. "How does anyone go from place to place? Through the door."

"But there *isn't* a door," I blurted out, unable to stay silent another moment. "Dante said he looked, but there wasn't a door!"

Valerie slouched out of her pose and rolled her eyes. She

blew out her breath in exasperation. "Well, duh, darling. Of course the *old* door isn't there. He wants to go someplace new, right? So he'll have to go through a *new* door."

The change in her posture and in the tone of her voice was so sudden it made me blink. For a moment, I could have sworn that the old, friendly Valerie sat next to me. The next moment, though, she was gone, and the light I saw flickering in her eyes was unfamiliar.

Then her words caught up with me. "A new door?" I repeated, a flurry of thoughts cascading in my mind. Was it possible? The blueprints Dante had given me were for a door that would open onto the bank—that was what it was designed to do. But could those plans be changed, twisted somehow, to open into the dark space where Dante was trapped? *Change what needs to be changed.*

Changed how? What would be the key that would unlock the blueprint and turn it from a time machine into something else? I didn't know. But I was willing to bet Dante did.

Valerie had said it herself—Dante had found a way out of the darkness, a way back to me.

"Thank you, Valerie," I said, reaching over to give her a hug. "That was the best story I've heard in a long time."

She rested her head on my shoulder and sighed in contentment. "I always feel better when I can tell my stories. They don't make so much noise in my head and then I can listen to the river better."

The door to the conservatory opened and I heard the mouse-squeak sound of Dr. Blair's hospital shoes on the tile. My time was up, but I had one more question.

"Valerie, how did you know I was coming today?"

"I drew you a picture. Didn't the lady doctor show it to you?"

I started to withdraw the paper from my purse. "She showed me this—"

"No, no, no, don't take it out!" Valerie pushed at my hands, her fingers fluttering like startled birds. "He's not supposed to know you have it."

"Why not?"

"Why do you think? Because if he did, he would steal it from you and then he would have the power—not you. And you'll need the power. The *picture* is power."

"What about the note?" I asked. "Why did you write me that note?"

"To give you permission. So you could do what you needed to do without fear." She looked from side to side, her forehead wrinkled in paranoia. "But don't tell anyone, okay?"

I mimed drawing a zipper across my lips, turning the key, and tossing it away.

Valerie pretended to catch the key, slipping it into the pocket of her bathrobe. She looked even more troubled than before. "Keys are important. You shouldn't just throw them away. You might need that one day. When you do, you can come back to see me and I'll give it to you, okay?"

I nodded, my eyes darting to her pocket, strangely unsettled by her words. I'd have to think about them later, though. Right now, I had to focus on Dante. He needed me more than I needed a cartoon picture and a pretend key.

Dr. Blair emerged from the plastic foliage and folded her arms across her chest. "And how are we doing?" she asked.

Valerie sprang up from the fountain and danced over to Dr. Blair. She pirouetted on the balls of her feet, turning in small circles around where Dr. Blair stood. While she danced, she cupped her hands around her mouth and spoke into the hollow like it was an intercom. "Dr. Blair. Dr. Blair. Dr. J. Hamilton. Dr. J. Hamilton."

"Thank you for letting me visit," I said to the doctor. Standing up, I slipped the strap of my purse over my shoulder, Valerie's picture tucked inside. "Could I come back? Maybe in a few days?"

Dr. Blair thinned her lips and pointedly didn't look at her patient. "Perhaps. I'll discuss it with Dr. Hamilton."

Valerie continued to dance, humming the same three rising notes in an endless loop. I recognized them as the opening tones of "Into the River," and a shiver drew a shadow over my thoughts.

Valerie sidled up to me and shot a venomous glance at Dr. Blair, who was standing motionless, waiting for me to leave. "They are always watching me, you know. Always. Even when they don't think they are. But they can't watch me when I'm sleeping. That's when I'm free to go sailing with my Pirate King." She sighed with longing. "Such sweet dreams. I hope you have sweet dreams, too, Abby." She kissed my cheek, then drifted away from me past Dr. Blair, past the neon green plastic trees, until the scuff of her soft, slippered feet was swallowed up in the sound of the invisible river that filled the room.

CHAPTER 9

I climbed into my car, my nerves humming with plans. There was so much to do. *Hang on, Dante,* I thought. *I know what to do. We can do this.*

I made a series of quick calls. First, I called Leo at the number he'd left for me on his card to make arrangements to meet for—I checked the clock in my car—a late lunch (Helen's—two o'clock). Then I called Natalie to see what her plans were for the day (nothing much, maybe some shopping or watching a movie). Finally, I called Jason. I told him I was sorry for bailing on him at the Devil's Pit and promised I would make it up to him. I made sure to mention that while I had to take care of some stuff today, I knew for a fact that Natalie was free and that if the two of them wanted to do something—say, go to the movies?—I'd love to catch up with them later.

I hung up before Jason could ask too many questions. I could only hope that he would take the hint and call Natalie. It was the best I could do under the circumstances.

I sped home and was in my room at my desk in ten minutes flat. With swift and sure motions, I unlocked the drawer and wrapped my hand around the binder containing the copy of Dante's blueprints.

The world flashed black to white and back again. I had time to think, *Oh, no, not again,* before the shock made my knees buckle and I dropped hard into the chair. A sour churning bubbled in my stomach and I tasted the hot green sting of nausea. I rubbed at my eyes, trying to scrub color back into my world.

I was really starting to hate Zo's interference with the river.

Wiping a layer of cold sweat off my forehead, I blinked until my vision slowly returned. The nearby clock warned that it was almost two o'clock. My heart hardened like a rock. It was bad enough that the changes in the river made me feel like vomiting, but now it appeared I was losing time, too.

I grabbed the binder and leaned forward, ready to stand up, when the second binder—the one containing the original plans—caught my eye. The fortune cookie slip that I had taped to the outside bore a new message, a different message: "The eyes may lie, but the heart is always true."

The rock in my chest cracked and tumbled into the pit of my stomach, threatening to pull all my bones with it.

"No, no, oh, no, not this. Not now. Anything but this . . ."

I clutched the binder to my chest as though I could ward off the changes with my body and protect what was inside by mere contact.

The clock ticked past two o'clock.

I shoved both binders into my bag and ran.

But I feared I was already too late.

When I walked into Helen's fifteen minutes later, Leo was waiting for me in a corner booth.

"It's good to see you, Abby," he said, standing up by the edge of the table. "I took the liberty of ordering; I hope you don't mind." He gestured to two plates, one with a turkey club sandwich, the other piled high with the pale green lettuce of a chef's salad.

"Sorry I'm late," I said. I immediately grabbed a glass of ice water and drank it without stopping or sitting down. The water seemed to help clean out my system, washing away the residual effects of a changing reality.

"Is everything all right?"

"Probably not." Grimacing, I slid onto the bench, pushing my bag ahead of me. I hadn't dared look inside the binders. Not yet. "Nice glasses," I noted.

Leo touched the wire frames, needlessly readjusting them. He was back in his Emery College "disguise," wearing the same suit from graduation day. His hair wasn't quite as dark as before; I could see the silver threads starting to reappear at the temples.

"I thought it best since we were going to meet in public."

I looked around the nearly empty café. There wasn't much of a lunch rush at Helen's. "Um, I don't think we're in any danger of eavesdroppers."

"I've learned it's always better to be safe."

Considering he had lived more than five hundred years without anyone discovering his secret, he had a point. Being careful was all well and good, but I had more important things to talk about.

"I looked for him," Leo said before I could start. "But, as I told you before, he's not there."

"I know. I talked to him Saturday night." I lifted Leo's glass of water and drank that one, too.

Leo raised an eyebrow.

"But thanks for looking," I added hastily, wiping the ice off my lips and offering Leo a quick smile in apology. "The good news is that he's okay for now, but the better news is that I think I know what to do. How to bring him home. You're the only person I can talk to about this who won't think I'm crazy."

"I've never thought you were crazy. Tell me what you need to."

I quickly recounted Valerie's two stories of the Pirate King and the River Policeman, as well as my two conversations with Dante. Leo listened intently without interrupting. When I mentioned that Tony was with Dante—and that he was rapidly disappearing—Leo's brows drew down in sharp slants. When I added that Dante feared he would be next, a dark flush crept up Leo's neck.

"Valerie said the River Policeman could escape through a new door. That's the key, don't you see? If Dante is going to leave that in-between space, he certainly can't open a door he built from the inside. There's nothing there. So it has to be a door that someone else builds for him. And that someone is me." Digging in my bag, I pulled out the binder containing the copy of the blueprints, setting it down carefully in front of me.

I pressed my palms flat against the outside. "It has to be me. I'm the only one who has the plans."

"You what?" The dark flush raced from Leo's neck all the way to his hairline.

I sat back, startled at his reaction. "The plans. For the door. I have them. Dante gave them to me. Before he left." My words tripped over themselves in an effort to explain.

Leo placed his hand on the tabletop; I could see the slightest tremble in his fingers. "So that's what he asked me to deliver. And why he wouldn't tell me what it was." He flicked a masked glance at me. "If I had known . . ."

I forged ahead, though I was curious as to how Leo had planned to finish that statement. "Dante said there was a fail-safe built into the door—a trap. Tony must have activated it when he touched the door. Since Dante left me the same blueprints for the same door, I thought perhaps the same fail-safe is written in my version of the plans. If we can figure it out, then maybe we can figure out how to reverse it or modify it or something and build a door that he can use."

Leo shook his head, his focus still elsewhere. "Not like this. It's too soon." His low voice sparked a shiver at the base of my spine. I didn't think he had intended for me to hear those last few words.

"But there's a problem."

Leo's attention snapped back to me. "Just one?"

I squared the binder with my fingers. "Zo is changing things." I felt a shudder ripple through me when I said his name. I remembered the last time I'd said his name and felt again the pressure of Valerie's hand on my mouth, silencing me.

"I know," Leo said. "And that is a big problem—"

I held up my hand to cut him off. "And I can tell when he does."

Leo looked at me with concern, the lines around his eyes and mouth deepening.

"Even though it makes me feel like throwing up and my vision goes all weird, that's not the problem. The problem is that when I touched the binder, it happened again."

Leo paused before speaking carefully. "So those are *not* the plans Dante left you?"

I bobbed my head in a maybe-yes, maybe-no gesture. "I don't know. I hope so, but so many other things have been changing, it's hard to know. Leo, everything hinges on these blueprints. If they're different, or wrong, then I can't build the door that will release Dante. And if he stays there much longer—if the darkness comes for him—" My voice caught on a jagged exhale.

Leo reached out his hand, resting it next to mine on the binder. "We both know you won't let that happen."

"But what if the blueprints have changed?"

"Let's find out if they have." Leo slipped the binder from beneath my hand and opened it to the first page.

"That's the copy I made. But I brought the originals, too, just in case."

I pushed the plates, silverware, and empty glasses to one side of the table to make room. Pulling the second binder from my bag, I touched the changed fortune-cookie message like a talisman. I hoped and prayed that those stark red letters were all that had changed.

They weren't.

I knew it the moment I opened the book.

The first page was supposed to be the schedule where Dante had meticulously outlined the precise times of when to start each phase of the building.

This page was blank.

"No, no, no," I murmured in one long breath, heavy fear filling my bones with lead. I quickly fanned through the rest of the papers. Front to back; back to front. All blank. Every single page. All of Dante's delicate drawings were gone. Erased. Lost.

I closed my eyes against the sight of so many smooth, white pages.

What was I going to do now?

"Abby, what is it? Talk to me. Tell me what's wrong."

Leo's voice seemed to come from far away. I opened my eyes in time to see him remove his glasses, folding them into his suit pocket. He leaned over the table closer to me. He looked so much like Dante that I felt tears burn my eyes. It wasn't fair. I had figured it out; I was so close. I was going to fix it. And now it was over before it could begin. Without any kind of plans to follow, there was no way I could build the door. I was going to lose Dante to the ravenous darkness.

I turned the binder so Leo could see the unbroken expanses of white.

A frown creased his forehead. He looked down at the binder in front of him and then back at mine. "I don't understand. I thought you said this one was a copy."

"It is." I dropped my head in my hands, massaging my temples in a feeble attempt to ward off a headache.

"If the original is blank, then where did these plans come from?"

My head shot up. "What plans?" I pushed aside the blank binder and grabbed the one from Leo's hands. There on the first page was the schedule I had expected to see. Turning page after page, I saw each one was filled to the edges with Dante's drawings and notes. There were the sketches of the nautilus, the hinge mechanism, my locket. There were the lists of supplies and directions. Everything was right where it was supposed to be. Even better, everything was *right*.

My headache disappeared and a grin crossed my face. I laughed in surprise. "Leo, *these* are the plans! The right ones. They didn't change!" I ruffled the pages again, inhaling the sweet scent of copied ink. "They're still here."

Leo didn't seem to share my enthusiasm. He pulled the blank binder toward him, idly flipping through the paper. His mouth thinned to a straight line as he reached the end of the stack.

"What? What's wrong now?"

"I'm just wondering why the *original* changed, but the *copy* didn't."

I leaned back against the booth, tilting the binder toward me so I could continue to browse in comfort. "Does it matter?" I asked, grinning. "We have the plans. We can do what we need to do."

"I think it matters a great deal." Leo reached over and plucked the copy from my hands. He closed the binder, set it aside, then laced his fingers together on the tabletop. "You say you can tell when Zo has changed something. But here is an example of something that *should* have changed, but didn't. If we can figure out *why,* maybe we can predict it. Control it."

I couldn't tell if the flutter in my stomach was from hearing Zo's name or from the idea that we might have found a way to neutralize his power, maybe even strike back at him.

We were both quiet for a time, thinking. The waitress stopped by the table, cleared away our untouched plates, and left behind a slip of a bill.

I rattled the remains of the melting ice cubes in my glass. The sound reminded me of the invisible water fountain at James E. Hart Memorial Hospital. The memory of sitting with Valerie sparked an idea. I dug into my bag again, withdrawing the picture Valerie had drawn of me. Smoothing it out on the table, I studied it for a moment before saying quietly, "The *picture* is power."

"What did you say?" Leo asked.

The small ember of an idea flared into life. "Maybe," I started, "maybe it's like a photograph. You know—if I take a picture of you, then even though you get older, the picture stays the same."

Leo raised an eyebrow, a half smile curving his mouth.

"Okay, maybe that was a bad example," I said, matching his smile. "But the idea is sound: the person—the original—changes." I tapped my chest with my finger. "But the photograph—the copy—stays the same." I pointed to the picture Valerie had drawn of me.

Leo nodded thoughtfully. "It makes sense."

I shook my head. "Maybe that helps to explain why the copy of the plans didn't change, but I'm not sure it helps us figure out how to prevent changes from happening in the future. I mean, it's not like I can go around making copies of everything I want to stay the same. There has to be another way to fix in place what we want to *stay* in place."

A light glimmered in Leo's eyes, turning them the shade of bright sky instead of faded denim, and his half smile widened into a full-fledged grin.

"What? What did I say?"

"There *is* a way to make a copy of what you want *and* fix it in place."

"There is? How?"

Leo tapped the edge of Valerie's crayon drawing. "You said it yourself. By taking a picture of it."

My eyebrows drew together in confusion and disbelief. "You think if I take a picture of something, then Zo won't be able to change it? Could it really be that easy? If it's true, then I'm willing to try it." I pulled out my phone and aimed the built-in camera at Leo.

He threw up his hand, shielding his face. "No, wait. Don't test it on me; there's no point. Since I'm outside the river, Zo's changes don't affect me." He lowered his hand and met my eyes. "But I think we're on the right track, though I doubt if it'll be that simple. I think if you want to *fix* the image, then it can't be digital."

I lowered my phone. "Why not? How else do you take a picture?"

Laughing a little under his breath, Leo shook his head. "Sometimes I forget how young you really are."

"Hey—"

"I meant no disrespect, Abby. Truly. It's just that for decades before the advent of digital photography, people took pictures the old-fashioned way—with actual film."

"I know that," I said, rolling my eyes. "Fine. We can use film. Do you have a camera we can use?"

"Not anymore. But I know where we can get one."

"Excellent! Let's go." I gathered up my binders and put them back in my bag.

"There's a small problem. It's not enough to just pick up a camera—we could do that almost anywhere. We'll need access to a darkroom as well."

I sat back, feeling the hard edge of disappointment hit me.

Leo continued. "My friend owns a camera shop, and she opens the darkroom on the weekends."

"What? It's Monday! I can't wait all week."

"I'll see what I can do, but you may not have a choice."

I pulled my bag closer to my side, resting a protective hand over the contents. They were safe, which meant Dante was safe—or would be soon—but there were other people in my life who were still in danger, still subject to Zo's whims of change. The sooner I could fix them in place, the better I would feel. "Promise me you'll call me the minute you find out about the camera and the darkroom, okay?"

"Lo prometto," he said in Italian. "And promise me that you'll keep that copy of the plans safe."

I remembered all the times Dante had made promises to

me and how he had always kept his word. Now it was my turn to return the favor. I would do what I had to do. Even if it meant waiting.

"*Lo prometto,*" I repeated.

Leo nodded, accepting my promise, and smiled tenderly. "I know this isn't what you want to hear, Abby, but go home. You've done some amazing work in just a few days. If we have to follow those plans, then we won't be able to even start building the door until the first day of summer. Try to relax this evening. Go out with your friends. Get a good night's sleep. Things will look better in the morning. They always do."

CHAPTER 10

I took Leo's advice about going out with my friends and called Natalie that evening. After the day's roller coaster of emotion, I was thrilled to hear that something had actually gone as planned. She was out with Jason. They'd gone to the movies and were on their way to the Sugar Shoppe for some ice cream, and would I like to meet them there?

A chance for a normal night with my friends? Count me in.

I hadn't spent much time with Jason since graduation morning, and I wondered how things would be between us. He greeted me with a hug, but I could tell he was still feeling a little distant. I realized I didn't mind so much. Letting him go was going to be a lot less painful than breaking his heart.

The three of us shared a triple-decker banana split with five different kinds of ice cream and four different toppings. We talked and laughed and, for a time, I was able to set aside the problems plaguing me. At one point in the evening, I looked across the table at Jason laughing at something Natalie had said. I thought about what Leo had said about photographs and

I took a mental picture of the moment, enjoying the way the light turned Jason's eyes golden as he watched Natalie scoop up a spoonful of whipped cream and chocolate sauce. I recognized the strangeness of the moment, for sure, but it felt like old times. Almost. For that night, at least, it was enough.

Once I got home, however, I ignored Leo's advice about getting a good night's sleep. I wanted to see Dante again. So I climbed into bed, slowed my breathing, and thought about the points and curves of Dante's name. I thought about the sweep of his dark hair falling over his gray eyes. I conjured up his smile, the way a shadow would appear along his collarbone when he tilted his head. I traced in my mind the arch of his eyebrows, the line of his jaw, the tapering ends of his fingers. I welcomed the darkness of sleep that enveloped me, still listening for the echo of his voice.

I opened my eyes to darkness. The clock on my bedside table shimmered 3:40 A.M. What was I doing awake? I remembered dreaming—something about a ferret? a Ferris wheel? Certainly not Dante, which frustrated me.

And then . . . something woke me up.

I stretched my toes to the edges of my bed and held my breath as though that would help me hear better. The darkness blanketed me, weighted down with silence. I heard the quiet creaks as the house settled and sighed. I propped myself up on my elbows, listening. Straining to see through the shadows in my room, I peered at the curtains shrouding my window. Had they moved? Or was it simply a trick of the moonlight?

I leaned against my headboard, pulling my knees to my chest. The logical part of my brain coolly observed that no one could get into my room from the window; I was on the second floor. But such solid logic seemed paper-thin against the onslaught of instinctive panic that covered me as completely as my blankets did.

There. It had happened again. I was sure of it. Moonlight didn't *breathe*. And I was positive I could hear someone breathing. Someone besides me.

I pulled my sheet to my neck, the material as taut as my nerves. What should I do? Should I scream? Grab my phone and call 911? Call Leo? Pretend to go back to sleep and hope that whoever it was would just go away?

I told my brain to tell my hand to reach for the phone, but it didn't seem like any part of me was willing to do anything but freeze in unexpected fear. All my focus was pinpointed on the spot where the curtains split, and my imagination shifted into high gear. Any second now, whoever was behind those curtains would slip a hand between the panels, curl his bone-white fingers around the fabric, and then, with a menacing nonchalance, he would pull back the curtain and step into my room, right next to my bed.

Against my better judgment, I closed my eyes. I didn't want to see whatever it was that was going to happen next. And yet, I could already see it happening, could already hear his breathing quicken the closer he got to me, could already hear his voice as he said my name—

"Abby."

I bit down on a scream. I pushed myself as far back against my headboard as I could go. My eyes flew open.

But no one was there. No creepy killer stood over me, razor-sharp teeth bared in a snarl. No annoying little sister crouched by my bed, laughing at a hysterical practical joke. Nothing moved. The curtains hung still and heavy. Even the shadows seemed to have paused in their nightly wanderings.

I was alone in my room. And everything was just as it was supposed to be.

No, not quite everything.

With my senses heightened by the adrenaline shot, I saw that on the corner of my desk there was a square-shaped box that hadn't been there before. I spent a good long time studying my room, making sure that the curtains had stopped breathing and were behaving again, before I slipped out from beneath the covers.

Slowly, as though crossing a minefield, I tiptoed across the floor to my desk. I reached out a hand and switched on the desk lamp, blinking in the sudden flood of light. Spinning around, I looked again in every corner of the room, only daring to breathe when I confirmed that yes, I was alone.

Alone with a mysterious, brightly wrapped box, complete with a bow.

Smaller than a shoe box, the package was covered in a thick material—a brocade of shimmering yellow and gold—instead of traditional wrapping paper. Patterns had been woven into the fabric with gold thread, thin spirals connecting to nodes that were scattered in a haphazard fashion across the entire surface. The box was almost a perfect cube, a little wider than it was tall, but with the gold bow on top, the measurements just about evened out.

It was beautiful and carried the unmistakable aura of a homemade gift. But it still made me uneasy. The yellow wasn't the sunlit sheen of summer; it was the pale shade of thick pus. The woven gold strands looked more like tiny chains binding the box closed than the sparkling trail of falling stars I suspected they were meant to represent. And for some reason, the bow made me think of a hangman's noose.

I sat down at the desk, my eyes never leaving the box. Where had it come from? Had Mom left it here earlier today and I'd missed seeing it when I fell into bed after my ice-cream feast? Or had a mysterious stranger really managed to slip into my second-story window in order to leave me . . . what? A present? A threat?

I leaned close, but the box didn't seem to be ticking. Then again, I supposed real-life bombs weren't like in the movies with their loud ticking clocks, counting down on a large LED readout nestled in a snarl of multicolored wires. There was a strange, faint odor—a sharp, bitter smell that made my nose itch.

Did I dare open it? I rested my hand on the desk next to the box, pressing my palm against the wood and feeling the clammy cold of my sweat pressing back.

Tucked into one of the curves of the bow was a small note about the size of a business card. I carefully extracted it from the curls, tweezing it between my fingernails, and let it fall to the desk. The card, too, appeared homemade, one edge tapering off as though the person had been in a hurry to cut it to size and misjudged the dimensions. But what demanded my attention were the three small letters written on the card: A. B. E.

It seemed so obvious that the gift was for me—it was in my room, after all—but somehow seeing my initials on the card made it real in a way it hadn't been before.

I touched the edge of the card and pushed it away from me. I wanted whoever had made the box appear to make it disappear so I didn't have to make the decision of whether or not to open it. I didn't want this gift—whatever it was. I knew, deep down in my bones and my belly, that whatever the box held was bad. And yet I kept sitting at the desk, staring at my initials on the card. I knew I should leave it alone, but I couldn't seem to stop myself from reaching out and brushing a finger along the tail end of the ribbon.

The gift was for me. Given to me by someone who knew my name. My *whole* name, including my middle name. That narrowed the list down dramatically. Obviously my parents hadn't left me this. Dad couldn't tie a fancy bow to save his life, and Mom always seemed to use an entire roll of tape to get the edges squared up. And just as obviously it wasn't from Jason or Natalie or Valerie.

So who else knew my middle name?

Dante did.

But he had more pressing matters on his mind than sending me presents. He was suffocating in darkness somewhere on the far side of the bank.

Was it possible Zo had left this for me? He was traveling

through time, and I had no idea what the rules were about that. Could he have dropped into the river—into my room—left the box, and then dropped out again?

My eyes flicked to the curtains, which were thankfully still not breathing. Had it been a dream? Or had it been real? Did it matter? The memory of my name echoed in my mind—someone had said it. Thinking back, I tried to recall exactly what I'd heard.

"Abby." A deep voice—masculine? Yes. A hint of an Italian accent? Maybe.

I didn't want a gift from Zo, but what other explanation could there be? I picked at my curiosity like the rough edges of a scab, at once awful and irresistible. There was only one way to find out for sure.

I pulled on a curl, and the bow deflated into a mass of golden material spooling around the lid and dripping down the sides.

I told myself I could still stop, still leave the lid closed, but I knew I wouldn't. I had made my choice to see what was inside.

Taking a deep breath, I swept the bow aside and lifted the lid of the box. The brocade was as thick as it had looked and the fabric felt soft under my fingers, soft and a little spongy, the texture of bruised flesh. My stomach turned thinking of the comparison and I almost dropped the lid.

Then I looked inside the box and I did drop the lid.

In the bottom of the box lay a severed rag doll's head on a bed of black velvet. Her brown hair tumbled around her painted face, which was still smiling, unaware of the violence that had been done to her. Where her painted brown eyes should have been, two coal-black button eyes had been inexpertly sewn on instead; one looked askance to the left while the other looked directly at me. Directly into me.

A note was pinned to her torn throat: *I'm watching over you, Abby. Always.*

An ice-cold wave washed through me, followed immediately by a tsunami of hot nausea that flooded my stomach with acid. My peripheral vision shimmered like white lightning in the desert and I staggered out of the desk chair, stumbling to the bathroom.

Not bothering with the lights, I collapsed to my knees in front of the toilet and felt the sour sting of vomit surging up my throat. I retched until nothing was left. Dizzy, I lay on the bathroom floor, wrapping my arms around my knees and trying to force my uneven breathing into stability.

My thoughts were in as much turmoil as my stomach was.

The doll in the box—it had been *my* doll.

Immediately, in my memory, I was four years old again, tucked into bed with the blankets drawn all the way up to my chin. Dad sat on the edge of my bed, brushing back my hair, telling me a nonsense story about a dancing rabbit, trying to convince me that it was okay to go to sleep.

But I knew better. We had recently moved into a new house in a new town, and my four-year-old self *knew* there were creatures in the night, terrible creatures with flat, staring eyes and too many fingers and toes and elbows. Creatures that were waiting for me to close my eyes so they could slither out of the cracks like smoke and perch on the rail of my bed to stare at me while I slept. They were just scouts, after all. Spies for the *real* monsters that had started haunting my dreams.

That night, Mom had come in with a special surprise. She had made a rag doll for me—beautiful brown hair, soft brown eyes, a red smile, and real blush on the cheeks. The doll wore a pink jumpsuit and had a silver cape attached to her shoulders. On her chest was a shield with the letters L and A intertwined in black ink.

Mom sat next to Dad and gave me the doll.

"She looks like me!" I said, hugging her to my chest.

"She should," Mom said. "She's a superhero like you. Her name is Little Abby and she's here to help protect you while you sleep."

"I don't know. She's so little. What if she gets hurt?" I frowned, unwilling to subject my new doll to the terrors in the night.

"She's only little when you're awake," Mom said, winking at Dad. "When you are asleep, she grows to be ten feet tall. Plus, she is as fast as lightning. And she can't get hurt—see this cape? It protects her like a shield. And you know the best part?"

I shook my head, already feeling calmer just holding the doll in my hands.

Mom leaned down to whisper, "She can see in the dark. So it's okay to fall asleep, sweetie. Little Abby is watching over you. Always."

That night was the first time in a long time that I had fallen asleep without any trouble. And as long as I had Little Abby with me, the nightmares stayed away.

Always. Always. Always.

My four-year-old self drifted away until just my seventeen-year-old self was left, lying on the floor of my bathroom, crying in the dark.

Little Abby had always protected me, just like my mom had promised. At least, until I was nine years old and we had gone camping with the Kimballs. Of course, my nightmares had long since ceased, but I still secretly slept with Little Abby, and I still secretly felt braver when she was with me at night. It was on that trip that somehow Little Abby had gone missing, vanishing into thin air. That was the same trip when Jason had taught me to be brave all by myself with a simple counting trick that always seemed to work. Still, I missed Little Abby and mourned her loss for weeks.

I hadn't seen her since I was nine years old—until tonight.

Until I lifted the lid on that horrible box and saw her face looking back at me.

I squeezed my eyes shut, trying to erase the image from my mind, but all I managed to do was squeeze more tears out and down my cheeks. Well, at least I knew for sure who had sent the box to me. This was Zo's work through and through. And the implications of that made me shiver uncontrollably. With Dante trapped, Zo was free to impose his will on the river of time. And the fragment of my childhood tucked into that box made it perfectly clear that Zo was interested in imposing his will on *my* past.

I'm watching you, Abby. Always.

A torch of hate flared to life, blinding me. Zo had waded into my past and stolen part of me, only to taunt me with it, laughing at me from beyond the bank. How dare he? He thought he knew me, but he had no idea what I was capable of. Burning with sudden purpose, I pushed myself to my feet, unwilling to let Zo's threat remain in my room, my house, my life for one more moment.

The box was still where I had left it, the lid upside down on the floor. I gathered up the slithery gold ribbon and stuffed it inside the box, hiding those polished black button eyes. Then I snatched up the lid from the floor and slammed it into place on the box, resisting the urge to wipe my fingers on the edge of my T-shirt.

The thought of carrying the box all the way downstairs in my bare hands made my flesh crawl, so I grabbed a shirt from the hamper and wrapped it around the box. I made my way downstairs, quick, silent, and furious. Easing open the back door, I stepped out onto the patio.

The air held a slight predawn chill, and I inhaled deeply. The silver wind chimes shivered in the cool breeze, murmuring musically behind me. I had no idea if what I had in mind would work or not, but I suspected I could *make* it work. I had done it before, after all. And apparently the barriers between me and the bank were thinning.

Looking up at the still-dark sky, I spent a moment counting the stars, counting the spaces between the stars, counting my breaths as I focused all my concentration to a single sharp point. I felt the edges of myself thin, the boundaries between here and there soften into smoke. The familiar vise tightened around my lungs; the buzz of dark silence began burrowing into my inner ear. But I had no intention of going to the bank.

I wasn't even trying to reach the dream-side of the bank. No, I simply wanted to send a message to a place where I knew it would reach Zo wherever he was. And with a mental shout, I sent the words winging away into the void.

Are you watching, Zo?

Then I snapped back to myself, gasping in a harsh breath, feeling my ears pop as sound returned full force.

I set down my bundle and dragged Dad's charcoal grill to the center of the patio, wincing as the stuck wheels scraped against the concrete. I hinged back the lid and dumped Zo's gift out of my shirt and onto the grill. Padding around the corner of the house, I quickly gathered up my supplies and returned with a half-full bottle of lighter fluid in one hand and a box of matches in the other.

Setting the matches down, I drenched the box with lighter fluid, the acrid stench making my eyes water. The yellow brocade soaked up the fluid until the fabric looked nearly black in the shell of the grill. When the bottle was empty, I turned the garden hose on, waiting until the water began dribbling out of the nozzle before I picked up the box of matches.

I touched the first match head to the rough striking strip on the side of the box and paused. I knew that crossing Zo could prove dangerous to both me and Dante. But Zo had to learn that I could be just as dangerous.

I struck the match.

Zo's box flared up in an instant inferno, the flames devouring the fabric. The brocade retreated in huge swaths, shrinking, melting, leaving behind only blackness streaked with red.

The golden threads flared into brief life as each knot blazed like a small supernova.

I took a step back from the crackling heat and watched the smoke begin to spiral up into the air. The gray smoke was almost invisible against the gray sky, and yet the trailing wisps seemed to form patterns that I could almost recognize. A message I could almost read—a prayer, a wish, a warning.

I don't know how long I stood there, watching the shifting patterns in the sky, but when I finally drew in a deep breath, I could taste the scratch of smoke in my mouth and feel the sting of tears in my eyes. Zo's box had collapsed into ash, taking all my hot anger with it. Exhausted, I swiped a trembling hand across my forehead.

Dawn began stretching awake, long fingers of light reaching to push aside the stars. My thoughts returned to my childhood doll, now gone for good in her own small funeral pyre.

Good-bye, Little Abby, I thought with a pang. *Thank you for being my warrior . . . and my friend. I'm sorry you got caught up in this mess.*

Stooping, I picked up the garden hose and directed the stream of water into the bottom of the grill, soaking the remains of the box until it was a soggy black-and-gray lump. Then I turned off the water and closed the lid to the grill. I would clean the rest of it later.

"Abby?" My dad's voice came from the doorway behind me. "Everything okay?"

I turned around and dropped the hose at my feet. "Yeah, everything's fine." I glanced at the closed lid, hoping I had told the truth.

Dad tightened the belt of his bathrobe and stepped out on the porch in his slippers. "Good. I heard someone banging around out here. I didn't think it would be you." He wrapped me in a hug and rubbed his hands over my arms. "You feel a little chilled. How long have you been out here?"

"Not long," I said, feeling myself relax into the protection of his arms.

"What are you doing, anyway? Is something the matter?"

"No, everything's okay. I just had some old stuff I needed to get rid of."

"And you had to do it in the middle of the night?" Dad asked.

"I guess I didn't think about the time."

"You couldn't just throw the stuff away? You had to fire up the grill?"

"Oh, um, it's just . . . I didn't want anyone to see me," I stammered. "You know. Because it was private."

"Oh, I see how it is. Keeping secrets from your old man. I get it." Dad ruffled my hair. "What was it? Old love letters? Incriminating photographs?" He wiggled his eyebrows like Groucho Marx and I laughed. Dad always managed to make things better; I loved that about him. Grinning, I kissed his cheek, leaving behind a black smudge from my nose.

"I must look a mess," I said. I rubbed at my eyes, feeling the hours of missed sleep starting to catch up to me. My hand came away streaked with soot.

"Ah, you'll always be pretty as a princess to me, sweetie." Dad kissed the top of my head. "But you might want to get cleaned up before Hannah comes down. If she sees you like this, she'll never let you live it down." He released me and stepped over to the grill. He slapped the lid with the flat of his hand. "Tell you what—you go on upstairs and I'll make breakfast this morning before I go to work. What are you in the mood for? Grilled pancakes? Flambéed French toast? Cereal shish kebabs?"

I laughed again. In the middle of the night, Zo's threats and warnings had been scary, but now, with dawn on the horizon, his efforts seemed a little sad and small. Was that really the best he could do?

"See you in a bit, Dad," I said before heading back to my bedroom. I had every intention of hitting the shower and washing away the soot from my hands and the shadows from my mind, but once I closed the door behind me, I fell into bed and pulled the covers back over me.

I was asleep before the summer sun spilled over my windowsill.

CHAPTER 11

Darkness had fallen on the bank. Instead of the omnipresent flat gray light, the bank was cloaked with a thick black veil that stretched across the horizon and curved overhead like a closed eyelid.

I hadn't expected to be here. When I had tried before, nothing had happened, and yet, this time, when I wasn't thinking about it, I made it here. Would I ever learn the rules of the bank? Then again, did I really want to?

I looked around, wondering if I had made it to where Dante was, but everything looked the same. No, not quite. The bank was vast, but something was different this time. There were feelings in the void that drifted around me like unmoored ghosts.

Anger, grumbling like an awakening volcano. It tasted like red.

Hostility, cracking like knuckles. A flash of pain.

Hate.

Of all the times I had been to the bank—real or dreamed—this was the worst. This was bad.

I risked speaking. "Dante?"

The horizon line rippled. I rubbed at my eyes, sure it was a mirage. Nothing ever changed on the bank; that was the whole point. But that wasn't true anymore, was it? I looked up involuntarily. The black sky seemed even lower, even closer. I swallowed. What other impossible things were going to change in this impossible place?

As I watched, the ripple bubbled up into a fat blister, a wavering sunrise of light pushing against the oppressive night. But it was unlike any sunrise I'd ever seen before. Instead of stretching a gentle pink across a pale blue sky, this light boiled and churned, straining to break free from the bank's flat two-dimensionality. My heart dropped in my chest, beating fast and hard in the veins at my temples, my wrists, my knees. I didn't want to be anywhere nearby when that white hellfire light cracked through the black.

Distances were deceiving on the bank, so it was hard to tell exactly how far away the blister of light was. From where I stood, though, it looked to have swollen to the size of a small car.

The growing light demanded my attention and I watched the blister, now the size of a small building, fill with electric fire. The edges boiled and sizzled. The flickering light in the middle seemed to paint patterns, swirling into intricate pathways that looked almost familiar. Mesmerized, I let my focus soften, my eyes captured by the hypnotic rhythms.

"What is it?" I was barely aware of my words, barely heard them in my own ears. I wasn't really expecting an answer, but a voice sounded low in my ear anyway.

Change . . .

But it wasn't Dante's strong and comforting voice that reached me through the veil of my dream. It was Zo's voice: sly, confident, and unmistakable.

Are you watching, Abby?

The blister blossomed into a dome the size of a sun, blinding white like a hole cut into the black of the bank.

"What's happening? Are you doing this?"

I'm so glad to see you again, Zo said, his voice filling first one ear, then the other. *I was worried that we'd lose touch, what with you being where you are, and me being—well, wherever I want to be.* His low-throated laugh sounded like an earthquake.

"Stop it!" I ordered the voice, pressing my hands to my ears.

Oh, but I'm just getting started.

"What have you done?"

Silly question, my sweet. It's what I am *doing that you should be worried about.*

"I'm not scared of you," I bluffed.

My ears rang with sudden, dreadful silence.

I lowered my hands, surprised to find traces of tears on my cheeks.

And then the blister on the horizon burst open in an explosion of boiling light.

The shifting, swirling fire shot upward like a fountain. At the apex of the column, the light began to bend, curving into a mushroom cloud as white and empty as the blackness it penetrated. Wherever the two touched, the edge glittered with golden stars.

I expected a rush of sound—the sonic boom after a bomb—but there was nothing except my ragged exhale and low moan.

And then the landscape of the bank buckled as waves rippled just below the surface. Lumps became hills became mounds became mountains. The earthquake raced toward me, silent, destructive, deadly.

Instinct screamed at me to turn and run, to *move,* but it was too late.

Cracks fractured around my feet, thin lines that widened as they raced outward to meet each other in a tightly woven spiderweb. When the lines collided, the web broke open and chunks of land fell into a deep chasm as black as the sky above me.

The aftershocks continued to crash into each other, creating larger ripples, which created even larger cracks. And as each crack broke open, more and more of the bank fell away into darkness.

The bank was disintegrating before my eyes.

But thankfully, not from beneath my feet. The patch of land where I stood remained intact, a small island of safety. My screaming instinct quieted; there was no point in running if there was no place to run to. I wrapped my arms around my chest, frozen with fear and confusion. Was I still just dreaming, or was this actually happening?

Eventually the ripples lessened, stilled, smoothed out into oblivion, and I was left standing on a scrap of stability. The chasm around me felt as wide and as deep as the Grand Canyon. I didn't dare look down, afraid that whirling vertigo would pull me down with it. I still felt the tattered remains of the dream state wrapped around me, a gentle fog that softened the edges of the harsh black-and-white world. I almost took a breath.

And then the mushroom cloud of light imploded, folding in on itself to form a single point on the jagged horizon. Surrounded by thick blackness, the spot looked like an eye frosted with milk-white blindness, an eye fixed directly on me.

I began to shake.

The light changed again, but this time, instead of blossoming upward, it descended into a waterfall of flame, bleeding down into the blackness of the chasm that stretched between me and the shattered horizon line.

It happened so fast. One moment the light was *there*—in the distance—and then it was *here,* rushing past my feet in a churning, frothing river of silver and white, the sharp peaks of the waves glittering like broken glass.

The wild river parted around my small island, dividing and rejoining in the blink of an eye.

It wasn't just a river, though. It was *the* river.

As before when I had gazed into the endlessly changing, endlessly flowing river of time, I could see images flashing past.

A girl, standing on her toes, her hand on the frame of an open wooden door. Her head swinging right, then left, looking, searching.

The river shifted and I peered over her shoulder, catching a glimpse of the darkness of an underground prison. I blinked, and she was washed away from sight. I wondered who she was looking for, or who she was running from.

Another image rose to the surface: A man cresting a hill in the distance. A tall man, but lost in a shadowy fog. I recognized him, but I didn't know how or from where. He opened his mouth, and the river poured into him, drowning out his words, dripping from his eyes in tears that fell like stars.

The river tore the image to pieces, fragmenting only to reassemble into a scene that stopped my heart in my chest. Dante stood on the burned wreckage of the Dungeon, his boots coated with a fine layer of gray ash, the same color as his eyes. The light from the setting sun rested on his shoulders like a coat. Seeing him was like a balm to my fevered mind. His eyes met mine, and I could have sworn that in that moment, he saw me—really *saw* me—even through the ripples of the river and the cocoon of my dream.

Almost immediately Dante was pulled apart by a whirlpool of time and I cried out with the loss.

Zo's voice slithered back into my ear. *Do you like what you see?*

The river boiled around my feet, the silver stream filled with jumbled images. A collection of flashes of me appeared, each one layered on top of the next like a giant, personalized flipbook: walking to school with Hannah, watching movies with Jason, laughing at a joke with Valerie, listening to Leo's story of the Midnight Kiss, dancing at the Dungeon with Dante, studying with Natalie. My life frothed around my feet as wildly as the swirling river did. I felt dizzy, disoriented. Which one was the real me?

Time was running free and loose, unchained from its moorings, carving a new path through old land.

I took a deep breath, hoping this was still just a dream. But then why couldn't I wake up?

This was Zo's doing. He'd admitted as much. But what could he have done that would have completely redirected the river?

As soon as I thought the question, though, I knew I didn't want to know the answer. Only something catastrophic could result in this kind of devastation, this kind of wholesale *change.* He'd threatened to kill da Vinci—had he succeeded? Or had he struck closer to home? Was I here because he was somehow targeting me?

I had had enough. I was sure that, even in a dream, the key to getting home was to go through the river. Surely the shock of the transition would be enough to wake me up. At least, I hoped that would be all it would do.

As much as I didn't want to leave the safety of my small island, I also didn't want to stay here another moment.

"I'm leaving, Zo," I called out into the void. "You can't keep me here any longer."

I swallowed my fear and stepped off into the river.

And I started awake, my body sheathed in sweat and my heart snapping like a flag in the wind. My mouth felt lined with cotton and I swallowed, hoping to clear it out enough to cough. I folded my legs against my chest, wrapping my arms around my knees and burrowing my face into the deeper darkness of my own body. I braced myself for the inevitable wave of black-and-white flashes that accompanied the changes to the river. I expected the pain would match the severity of what I had seen firsthand; I wasn't disappointed.

Hot needles pierced the soles of my feet, injecting liquid fire into my veins. Lava bubbled up my curved legs, pooling in my stomach. Steam cooked my heart. Sweat beaded on my forehead and dripped into my hair, mingling with the tears that dribbled from my eyes. I tightened my grip on my limbs, biting down on the agony until my scream softened to a whimper. I prayed that the darkness sweeping toward me was unconsciousness.

Dante's locket around my neck burned like the cold fire from a distant star.

I'd never felt so alone in my life.

Zo's voice pierced through the tattered remains of my dream, his words lingering in the still air of my room. *But sweet Abby, I am with you . . . always.*

Some distant time later, I woke again. This time to the smell of bacon. My mind slowly shook off the rust of unconsciousness, piecing together fragmented memories into some kind of cohesive whole. That's right. Dad was making breakfast. I could do with a hot meal to help banish the cold stone that seemed to be lodged in my chest.

I crawled out of bed, straightening my back first and then stretching each individual limb. Residual heat seemed to crackle along my bones—one last needle-shot of pain before sloughing off into a flash of numbness. I shook out my hands, flexing my fingers.

I swung back my curtains, disoriented to see the sun so high in the sky. The darkness of the bank and the following hours of oblivion had thrown off my timing.

Whatever Zo had done was done. I'd seen the redirected river; I'd felt the repercussions of pain. Now it was time to see what I could do to fix it.

The house was strangely quiet as I went downstairs to the kitchen. I thought for sure Hannah would have been up and running around. Maybe she was at McKenna's or next door with Bethany.

Rounding the corner, I saw Mom at the counter, slicing tomatoes. She wore a navy blue suit with a string of bone-white pearls around her throat. Her normally curly hair was pulled back into a tight bun. She looked tired, and a little pinched around her eyes and mouth.

"Mom?" I said, my voice croaking from disuse. My mind felt foggy, sluggish. Where was Dad? He was supposed to be cooking breakfast.

She looked up and laid down her knife. "Abby! What happened to you?"

I turned my hands over, only distantly surprised to see my fingernails were still black with soot. After all, I was still wearing the T-shirt and shorts I'd fallen asleep in oh so long ago. A scratch I hadn't noticed before ran along the side of my index finger.

Mom came around the island, grabbing a dish towel from the sink on her way. Her high heels clicked on the floor.

I frowned. Since when did Mom wear heels in the middle of a summer day?

"Here." Mom gently pushed my shoulder until I allowed my knees to buckle enough that I could sit down at the kitchen table. She wiped at my face with the towel, the roughness oddly soothing. If I closed my eyes, I could imagine I was six years old, coming in from a hard day of play and having Mom help me wash up for dinner.

"What have you been doing?" Mom asked. "Is everything okay?"

I didn't have the faintest idea of how to respond.

Luckily, Mom didn't seem to notice my dilemma but simply added to her list of questions. "What are you still doing in your pajamas? I came home from work special so we could have lunch together. Mr. Jacobson had some last-minute reports he needed me to do, so I left later than I planned. I'm making BLTs, though. Does that sound good? Are you hungry?"

I blinked slowly, trying to keep up with the flow of her words. Some of them made sense, but not all of them. "Mr. Jacobson?" I asked. "Reports?"

Mom balled the towel in her hands and sighed. "We've been over this before, Abby. I know you don't like him, but he was hiring. And I needed the work."

"That's why you're all dressed up. You've been at work."

Mom sat down in the chair next to me and covered my hand with her own. A worried line appeared between her eyes. "Are you sure you're okay? You don't seem like yourself. Are you feeling sick?" She pressed the back of her hand against my forehead before moving it to check my face.

"Does Dad know you're working?" I asked. The idea felt slippery in my mind; I was having trouble hanging on to it. I kept coming back to the fact that he was supposed to be here. In the kitchen. Cooking breakfast.

Mom jolted back as though I'd slapped her. Red spots appeared high on her cheeks, and her mouth thinned into a slash of cracked lipstick.

"What? What did I say?" I searched Mom's face for a hint, but all I saw was the black anger in her eyes.

"Your *father* most certainly knows I'm working. His *lawyer* made sure I didn't have a choice."

"His lawyer?" I repeated in a squeak.

Mom sighed, and the anger drained out of her eyes, replaced by the sheen of tears. "Oh, Abby, I know the divorce was hard on you. But I thought we were past this. I thought you had come to accept the way things are."

I felt the blood throb in my temples as a headache pounded into life. "You're . . . you and Dad . . . you're divorced?" My lips were numb. "Since when?" I asked reflexively.

But I knew the answer already: since Zo had redirected the river. Whatever he had done in the past—in *my* past, specifically—this was the cataclysmic result of his work. The river had been redirected, and now not only were my parents divorced but they apparently hated each other, too.

I shook my head as though I could turn this new truth into the lie I wanted it to be.

"But . . . but what about Hannah?"

Mom tilted her head, a puzzled look on her face. "Who's Hannah?"

CHAPTER 12

I ran. I ran up the stairs, taking them two at a time. Slamming open the door to Hannah's bedroom, I stopped in shock, staring at the neatly made-up queen bed covered with a sandy brown comforter and matching pillows, at the low dresser and mirror in matching oak.

I shook my head in denial. Where was Hannah's frilly daybed with her white curtains and pink pillows? What had happened to her casual clutter scattered over the dresser? Where was her Snoopy lamp that Dad had brought home the day she'd been born? Where were the shelves and shelves of the books she loved so much?

I turned away and tried to push past Mom, who had followed me up the stairs. She grabbed my arms, holding me in place.

"What's going on? Talk to me, please."

"It looks like a hotel!" I accused. "You turned Hannah's room into a *guest* room."

"I don't understand. Who is this Hannah you keep talking about?"

"She's my sister!" I shouted. Tears streamed down my face. "She's your daughter. You and Dad aren't supposed to be divorced. You aren't supposed to hate each other. You're supposed to have another daughter. We're supposed to be a family!"

Mom's face turned white. "Abby, stop. You're scaring me—"

"This is all wrong. This isn't how it's supposed to be."

"Calm down—"

"I have to fix it," I said, though, even as I did, I wondered how I could. Where was I supposed to start? This was more than just playing matchmaker with Jason and Natalie; how was I supposed to bring Hannah back if she had never existed in the first place?

"Let's go sit down and talk about this," Mom said, her voice striving to be soothing, but I heard her anxiety and fear. "It'll be okay, I promise. Just . . . let's just go sit down."

I let Mom lead me back down the stairs to the front room. Now that I knew what to look for, I could see the evidence all around me. The large family portraits that used to hang above the couch had been replaced with smaller snapshots of just me and Mom lined up in a short row on the fireplace mantel. There were the two of us at Disneyland. There we were in front of a Christmas tree. There was me in my graduation cap and gown, standing alone.

No pictures of Dad. Nothing that even hinted at Hannah's presence.

A howling wind blew through the empty cavity of my chest. I couldn't stop crying, but I didn't want to. Half of my family had just disappeared. They'd been erased from my life, but I still held a lifetime of memories of them in my heart. I was divided; I couldn't reconcile what was inside of me with what was all around me. My life was spiraling out of control, and the more I tried to hold on, the more it felt like it was slipping through my fingers.

I heard again Zo's voice from the dream-side of the bank: *It's what I* am *doing that you should be worried about.*

For as many lies as Zo had told, he had told me the truth about that.

"I have to go," I said, blindly turning to the door. "I can't stay here right now."

"Abby, wait—"

But I was already gone.

I ran out the front door, pounding down the steps and across the lawn. Counting my footsteps gave me something else to concentrate on—*forty-two, forty-three.* A thousand thoughts and a million memories batted around my head, each one demanding entrance to my brain—*sixty-five, sixty-six*—but I didn't dare let my mind wander too far. *Seventy-eight, seventy-nine*—and I was at Jason's door.

I banged on the heavy wood, calling Jason's name.

But Jason didn't answer. No one answered.

That was when I finally saw the wooden plaque hanging above the door frame: *The Birds' Nest. Welcome, Friends!* Cartoon birds flew around the edges of the plaque—red and blue and green—with flowers in their beaks.

I moved my fist from the door to my mouth, biting down hard on my knuckles. Who were the Birds, and why were they living in Jason's house? The Kimball family had lived here for almost my entire life—and yet now some other family lived here. Backing away slowly, I shook my head. If the Kimballs hadn't ever moved in, then I'd never met Jason. Was it possible? Looking at the painted birds circling above the door, I knew it was more than possible, it had actually happened.

No Dad. No Hannah. No Jason.

I hardly recognized my life anymore.

I turned around and, for the third time that morning, I ran.

It sounded like noise at first. It was only when I slowed my frantic steps that I realized where I was—the edge of Phillips Park—and what I was hearing—music. Specifically, the distinct music of an acoustic guitar.

A stitch threaded needles of pain up and down my sides, my legs. I pressed my hand against the throbbing ache and bent forward, gulping down as much air as I could. How had I gotten so far, so fast? The only memory I seemed to have left was of running: the methodic movement of one step after another, the rise and fall of my chest. As horribly as my chest hurt, though, my bare feet hurt worse. I looked down, only distantly surprised to see them covered in scratches. I glanced over my shoulder at the trail I'd left behind, my footprints outlined in pale pink blood.

The park was crowded with kids running, laughing, and playing. A pack of moms pushed strollers weighed down with sleeping babies. A soccer game was under way out on the far side of the playground. Wincing, I limped onto the park's wide lawn and grimaced in relief at the cool touch of the grass on my battered feet.

The music grew louder, the notes tugging at me, demanding attention.

It was a song I almost recognized. A light, dancing refrain that brought to mind swift, high-moving clouds and fizzing bubbles.

A memory engulfed me: the summer before high school. Sitting on the back porch with Natalie and Valerie, toasting our future with Valerie's own blend of Sprite, ginger ale, and lemonade. The hot August sun beat down on us, rippling the edges of the cement with heat waves. The three of us linked pinkies and vowed that our friendship would survive the unpredictable years ahead of us. No matter what.

The taste of the sticky sweetness of my drink was as vivid now as it had been then. And my fingers felt the remembered heat of a joined promise.

The song suddenly changed, the notes sliding into another key, picking up speed before developing into a dark intimacy that was as beautiful as it was unsettling.

The memory dissipated like smoke, leaving me feeling strangely blank and empty. It seemed to take a moment for my senses to catch up with me.

When they did, they brought with them a cold certainty. Only one person played music like that. The kind of music that reached inside your soul and *twisted.*

Zo.

He was here. In the park. I knew it.

A darkness as thick as coal shadowed my vision, stained

my heart with black anger. I cocked my head to the side, straining to listen for the invisible trail of his music in the air.

The music led me to a small grove of trees. I cautiously parted the branches to peek through the leaves. The park included a small meditation area with a few scattered benches and a statue of a child reaching up, a butterfly poised on his fingertips. I had always thought the boy was letting the butterfly go, but in my black mood, I wondered if he was simply going to catch and crush it instead.

I walked forward, taking slow, careful steps. A figure sat on one of the benches. He was curled over a guitar, fingers idly strumming the taut strings. The bright sky lit the scene with a friendly, soft glow that seemed out of place against the emotions running through me.

Zo looked up and met my eyes across the slim distance between us. My bones twisted like a groan. I hadn't been face-to-face with Zo since he had slipped into the dark embrace of the time machine's door, his laugh trailing behind him like a shadow.

"Abby," he said in delight, strumming a chord on his guitar. "I'm so glad to see you. I wondered when you'd finally stop by. And look at that—right on time." He smiled thinly and the chord changed to a minor key.

I didn't want to admit it, but time had been kind to Zo. His once-narrow face looked full—relaxed, even—and his dark eyes seemed larger, brighter. A light flush touched his cheeks. Excitement fairly crackled off him, as though he'd just found the missing piece of a puzzle. He rose, set down his guitar, and held out his hand to me.

My eyes immediately fixed on the gold chains around his wrist. Those were new. They reminded me of the yellow chains around the wrists of the Pirate King doll. I hated to think that Zo had been visiting Valerie, showing off his new power.

Heat blazed through me and the faces of my father and sister flashed across my eyes. I welcomed the pain in my heart. My family was fractured, lost, and my friends were trapped. And the man responsible for all of it was in front of me.

A red veil fell over my eyes and I crossed the distance between us at a dead run. My hand curled into a claw and I reached out to slash my nails across his face. I wanted to dig deep. I wanted to feel him bleed.

Zo caught my wrist, stopping my momentum cold.

My nail touched his skin, close enough to make a dent, but not to cut. I tried to extend my fingers, but his pain was just out of my reach.

"Come now, my sweet, there's no need to be rude." Zo squeezed my wrist and gestured with the long fingers of his free hand to the bench beside him. "There are things we need to talk about. We might as well be comfortable."

"I don't have anything to say to you," I snarled.

Zo shrugged, pulling my attention to his face. His smile widened into a grin—the sharp, tight grin I still saw sometimes in my nightmares—and I shook my head.

"I take that back. I do have something to say: Go to hell."

"Been there and back," he said easily. "I think I'll stay here instead." Zo watched me with his dark eyes, his stance deceptively casual, but this close to him, I could see the lines of strain in his shoulders. The tightness continued up his throat, strangling him with tension.

I wondered if being near me made him uncomfortable, even caused him pain. The thought made me happy.

"Do you treat all your friends like this?" he finally asked, releasing my wrist and taking a step back.

"You're not my friend," I snapped, rubbing at my wrist. His hand had left a ring of red on my skin.

"I'd like to be."

I stared at him in horror. "Are you crazy? After what you've done?"

"And what have I done—exactly?" Zo sat down. Leaning back into the bench, he spread his arms wide and kicked out his long legs, heels thunking to the ground.

"Let me count." I flung up a finger for each point. "You stabbed Dante. You made Jason break up with me. You burned down the Dungeon. You stole my best friend and drove her crazy—literally! Your lies ruined Leo's life—and Dante's." Tears burned my eyes, but I didn't let them fall. "And more recently, my parents are divorced because of you. And Hannah—she doesn't even exist anymore! You are nobody's friend."

Zo regarded me for a moment, his eyes thoughtful and still. He was quiet for a long time before he spoke. "I must thank you, Abby."

"For what?" It was perhaps the last thing I expected him to say.

"Perspective. When you opened the door for me, you may not have known you were granting me such a gift, but you were. And now, here, on the other side of time, I realize what an invaluable gift it really is."

I opened my mouth to say something when Zo held up his hand.

"Tell me, if events had not unfolded the way they had, would you be happier?"

"Yes!" I said, my memories twisted around the past. "Everyone would have been happier."

Zo tilted his head, the white tips of his dark hair as pointed as teeth. "Do you really believe that? You'd rather have your old life back, including those scheduled Friday night dates with Jason and your future rolling out ahead of you like a flat road through the desert? And you can honestly say that you'd be happier without Dante in your life?"

"I'd be happier with my family back!"

"Even if that meant you'd never have met Dante?"

Zo's questions landed like so many rocks in a pond; the ripples sent me reeling.

He didn't give me a chance to recover or respond. "Yes, I stabbed Dante, but he survived—as I knew he would. And yes, I'm sure it hurt to break up with Jason, but then you were free to pursue a relationship with Dante, weren't you? Perspective changes things, doesn't it?"

"You ruined everything," I repeated automatically. "You destroyed everyone's life—Valerie's, Dante's, mine, my family's. I wish I had never met you."

"I could arrange that," Zo said quietly.

"Don't joke about that, it's not funny."

"You know I'm not joking. You know what I'm capable of.

What all of us who went through that door a second time are capable of. So I have to ask myself, if you truly wish we'd never met, why haven't you asked Dante to change things? He would do it; he'd do anything for you. Even if it meant endangering the river, or his own life."

My mouth went dry. Dante's life was already in danger, trapped as he was in the darkness. I shook my head. "No. He wouldn't do that. And I wouldn't ask him to."

"Then why don't you ask me?"

My legs wobbled beneath me. I groped for the bench, collapsing onto the seat, not even caring that I was close enough to Zo to touch. "You wouldn't . . ."

"That's not the point. The point is that I could. You seem to think that Dante and Leo are the only people with answers to your questions. You forget that they are not the only people with experience. With power."

"I don't want your help," I managed. "I don't want anything from you. Ever."

"I noticed." Zo's voice hardened. "I go to all that trouble to give you a gift, and you refuse it. I wrapped that box myself, you know. I wanted to give you something you'd remember. It wasn't easy to get, either. You're a hard woman to shop for."

"That was no gift," I spat back. "That was a warning, and we both know it."

"And then to taunt me with it?" Zo clicked his tongue in disapproval, ignoring my words. "That borders on cruel."

"You erased my sister! You destroyed my family!"

Zo looked at me with false sympathy in his eyes. "What happened to your family happened because of you. You *made* me do it. I wouldn't have had to change the river if you hadn't defied me. This is *your* fault."

"That's a lie. You've always done whatever you wanted. You can't blame this on me."

Zo shrugged. "Perhaps next time you'll be more considerate of my feelings."

"There isn't going to be a next time," I said.

I could see him out of the corner of my eye as I looked straight ahead, leaning forward slightly so the edge of the bench dug into the back of my legs. A tense silence filled the space between us.

"What do you want, Zo?"

"What does anyone want, Abby?" he countered. "To be loved. Peace on earth. The winning lottery numbers."

I shook my head in disgust. "No one could love you."

"Valerie does," he said with a grin.

I couldn't take it anymore. I stood up from the bench, wound tight with a rage that filled me to my core. "Stay away from me, Zo. Stay away from me, my family, and my friends."

Zo frowned at me, his eyes tight. "I can't do that."

"Why not?"

He stood up next to me, so close that I could feel the heat from his body.

I took a step back, but his hand shot out and grabbed me by the back of my neck. I tried to twist away, but he held me tight, pulling me even closer to him.

With his other hand, he brushed the locket around my neck, tracing the shape but never touching my skin. "Because I need you, Abby. I always have."

I broke out of his grip, but he reached out and caught my hand before I could escape. Without letting go of my gaze, he bent his head and lifted my hand to his lips. "I can see why Dante was able to snare you so easily. It makes me wish I'd met you first. Things might have been very different."

I yanked my hand away as though I'd been burned. I backed away from him—one step, then two—slowly increasing the distance between us, my eyes never leaving his, my hand never leaving the locket at my throat.

Zo watched me go, a smile on his lips.

I turned and walked toward the opening in the trees that would lead me back to the heart of the park.

Behind me, the first notes of another melody lifted on the breeze.

My walk turned into a run. And I ran until I couldn't hear it anymore—not the music or Zo's mocking laughter.

CHAPTER 13

When Natalie opened the door, she was on the phone. "Oh, wait, she just showed up." She mouthed the words *It's your mom* and moved to hand the phone to me.

I shook my head vigorously, waving my hands in front of me. I wasn't ready to talk to my mom just yet. I knew I wouldn't be able to answer her questions and I feared I would just make things worse.

Natalie slanted a disapproving look at me, then returned to her conversation. "Uh, can she call you back? . . . No, no, she's okay. . . . I will. Uh-huh. I will. Okay. 'Bye."

The instant Natalie hung up the phone, my words spilled out in a rush. "You know me, right? You remember me, and we're friends, right?"

She looked at me strangely, and for a moment my heart stopped. "Of course I know you. And, yes, we're friends."

I rushed forward and wrapped Natalie in a hug. "Thank you," I said. "Thank you for still being you."

Natalie patted me on the back. "Uh, you're welcome. I guess. Abby, what's going on? Your mom said you ran off—"

"I know. Listen, I can explain—well, not easily, it's complicated—but I'll try." I peered past Natalie's shoulder into her family room. "Is anyone else home?"

Natalie shook her head. "Robert's off on a camping trip with the Scouts and Mom and Dad are visiting Grandma for the week."

I sighed in relief. I was still shaken by my conversation with Zo; I wasn't sure I was up to talking to anyone other than Natalie at the moment. "Can I use your shower?"

Natalie stepped back from the door, pulling me inside with her. "I thought you'd never ask," she said, wrinkling her nose. "You look terrible. How long have you been in those clothes?"

"It feels like forever." I picked at my T-shirt sleeve and frowned at the smell. I followed Natalie downstairs to her room. "I really appreciate this."

She waved off my thanks, pointing to her bathroom. "Go. Clean up."

I started to close the bathroom door behind me when Natalie called my name.

"I told your mom I'd drive you back home. Don't be long, okay?"

I nodded. Closing the door behind me, I leaned my back against the wall. I could feel the burdens piling up on my shoulders. There were so many loose ends that demanded my attention. Dante was trapped in the darkness, and I couldn't even start building the door that would free him for another week at least. Leo thought he knew how to help me stabilize the timeline and reduce the effects of the changing river, but not until this weekend. And now with Zo's latest strike at my past and my present, I feared I was too late to fix anything. I shuddered, remembering my conversation with Zo and the feel of his lips on my wrist and how his black eyes had laughed at me.

Turning on the shower, I peeled off my clothes, stiff with sleep and sweat, and tossed them into the corner.

The hot water hit me like a fist, coating me in a sheet of fire. I hissed as my skin turned red; the steam rose in clouds around me. I ducked my head under the streaming water, letting the flow cover me like a baptism.

I leaned my head against the shower wall, the water washing over my back in waves. Breathing deeply of the steam, I closed my eyes and, finally, after days and nights of unrelenting heartache, I gave myself permission to let go.

The tears I'd held back for so long rose like a flood.

I cried for Dante, trapped. For my parents, unfairly divided. For my sister, lost before her time. For Jason, and our missed possibilities.

I cried until the stone wall that had been guarding my heart cracked open and crumbled to dust.

I cried until all my anguish, all my anger, all my pain had drained out of me and flowed away beneath my feet.

When I was sure that the water on my face was only the shower and no longer mixed with my tears, I twisted the knob all the way to cold. I gasped; the shock to my system was electric and exhilarating. The edges of my vision turned blue. I shut off the shower and stepped out onto the mat. The bathroom was still warm, almost humid, and I stood for a moment, dripping and shivering inside a cocoon of lingering steam.

I felt cleansed inside and out. The hot water had washed me clean; the cold tears had scoured my soul raw. I had passed through the fire of anger and been quenched in the water of anguish.

My resolve hardened into a solid blade of steel. Zo could do what he wanted, but I was not going to let anyone but me decide the outcome of my life anymore. I would take back what belonged to me—my life, my love, my family. I would find it and fix it and protect it. No one was going to take it away from me again.

I felt reborn.

I felt ready to face the unknown again.

And this time, I was going to win.

Natalie pulled into the nearly empty parking lot of Helen's Café.

I looked around in surprise. "I thought you were taking me home."

"I am," Natalie said. "But first we're going to Helen's. You need to eat and then you're going to tell me everything that's going on."

I swallowed, then nodded. The idea of telling someone the whole crazy story was oddly terrifying and comforting at the same time. Natalie was the only link I had left to the way my life was supposed to be. What if I told her the truth and she laughed at me? I didn't know what I'd do if she didn't believe me.

It wasn't until we had settled into our booth by the front window, ordered lunch, and waited until our plates had arrived that I heard it.

Can you see . . .

The whisper sailed by on the breath of a breeze. I waved my hand past my ear as though brushing away a fly.

Dante . . . stop . . .

I frowned, looking around to see who might have said Dante's name. Helen's Café would hardly be considered crowded: just Natalie and me, an older couple tucked into a back corner booth, and a young guy in a green army jacket, hunched over his plate. The sidewalk outside had more people.

"Abby? Hello? Are you listening?"

I yanked my wandering attention back to Natalie. "What? Oh, sorry. Yes, I'm . . ."

In the way . . .

"Did you hear that?" I asked, rubbing at my ear. A buzzing sounded deep in my ear; it felt like the vibrations of a dentist's drill.

"I heard me," Natalie said with a fleeting smile. "It's okay, Abby. You don't want to talk about it until we eat. I get it."

"No, it's not that." I frowned.

Do something . . .

"There! Did you hear that?" I half stood in the booth, scanning the café as though I could spot the sound as it traveled to my ear. My gaze snagged on the guy at the next table over. There was something almost familiar about him . . .

Natalie followed my gaze. "Do you know him?"

I waved my hand to erase her words. "Hang on." I tilted my head and closed my eyes as though that would help me listen. It must have worked because as soon as I focused on that elusive whisper, I found it.

Sound crashed over me, close and hot, and I heard Zo's voice speaking clearly. *I'm impressed . . . I didn't think you could keep up.*

And then it was gone, the sound whipped away on the tail end of an invisible sigh.

The silence that followed in its wake left me cold and disoriented. Natalie's hand on my arm felt like a sun-baked brick, hot and scratchy.

"Seriously, Abby, what's wrong? You're scaring me."

Zo's name stuck in my throat, only the "o" sound escaped in a round exhalation. I had left him in the park just hours ago, but now somehow he was here, whispering in my head, his voice like the rough edge of a file against my mind. The sound conjured up an image of him sitting on a park bench, a guitar in his hands, and I felt goose bumps on my arms.

I could hear Zo as clearly as when I spoke with Dante on the dream-side of the bank. I feared it meant the barriers between the river and the bank were thinning, weakening. And no matter how you looked at it, that was bad.

Natalie pushed her water glass into my hand, and I instinctively wrapped my fingers around it and lifted it to my mouth. The cold sluiced through me, the ice cubes clattering against my teeth. The heat in my brain washed away but I kept swallowing until the glass was empty and I could feel a pillar of ice stretch from my throat to my belly.

I dropped the glass on the table, a few last ice cubes scattering like ghostly dice.

Natalie's face tightened with worry.

I cracked my voice out of the ice in my chest. "I'm okay. Thanks for the water."

Natalie's worry deepened into disbelief. "You're not okay. You haven't been *okay* for a while now. Start talking. We're not leaving until you tell me what is going on."

. . . *all you can do is wait* . . .

The voices were back, or maybe they'd never left. Now that I knew what to listen for—or more specifically, *who* to listen for—I could hear Zo's voice clearly all around me, drifting in and out of intensity.

You think you know what's going on, Dante. But you have no idea. Your confidence would be amusing, perhaps. If it wasn't so pathetic instead.

"Stop it," another voice said. Louder and closer than even the voices whispering in my ear.

It wasn't Natalie's voice, though. I opened my eyes to see the guy in the green jacket standing at our table, an unreadable expression flashing across his face. I knew that face. I knew that voice.

It was V.

CHAPTER 14

Stop trying to listen," V said again while all I could do was stare at him in shock and surprise.

"Who are you?" Natalie asked, frustration giving heat to her words.

"Shut up," V snapped, barely sparing a glance for Natalie. He crouched down by our table, wrapping his hands together in a knot of obvious anxiety and strain. "I know you don't have any reason to trust me, Abby, but hear me out. Please. We have to talk. It's important." He edged closer, but not too close. A thin sheen of sweat covered his forehead, darkening his hair to the blue-black of a raven's wing.

"No." It was the best I could manage past the anger blocking my throat. How could he be here—standing in front of me as though we were old friends, just wanting to visit, to chat. Like nothing had happened. But everything had changed since the last time I'd seen V—things were still changing—and seeing him now like this was more than I could bear.

"We have to talk," V said. "But not here—"

"She said no," Natalie said, shoving V hard in the shoulder. "Leave us alone."

"It's too dangerous—" The words poured out of V in a low stream of urgency. His dark eyes were ringed with a wild flicker of light. "He doesn't know I'm here, not yet, but he'll find out. He'll find me here. It's a lodestone location. We have to *go. Now.*"

"I'm not going anywhere with you," I said. I rested my hand lightly atop my table knife. I knew V was more powerful now that he'd been through the door a second time—my wrist still ached from Zo's grip—and a cut probably wouldn't slow him down, but maybe, if I surprised him, it would give us enough time to get away. I tried to catch Natalie's eye, let her know what I was thinking.

I would have to time it perfectly. I only had one chance . . .

A tremor shuddered through V's body, leaving a frozen stillness in its wake. "The streams are converging. The choices narrowing. The paths that lead away—" V's eyes flickered right and left, as though skimming a page of instructions only he could see.

I scanned the café again, scouting for the fastest route to the door. I might not have a better opportunity than right now, while he was distracted. In the instant my hand moved, V's own hand shot out and snaked the knife away from under my fingers.

I heard Natalie echo my gasp at his speed.

"And now there is only one path," V said. He stood up slowly from the table, slipping the knife into his jacket pocket.

"I'm sorry. I didn't want to have to do that, but he's coming. And you *cannot* be here when he arrives."

"Who?" Natalie demanded. "Who is coming? I don't understand—"

V merely touched two fingers to his wrist hidden beneath his jacket cuff and I knew. And worse, I knew V was right. If Zo was coming here, then I didn't want to be anywhere nearby when he arrived. I'd already met him once today and that was enough. I slid to the edge of the booth.

"C'mon, Natalie, let's go."

"What? Why?" Natalie frowned, but she followed my lead, picking up her bag and reaching inside. "Do you have cash? We can't just leave."

V reached into his pocket and grabbed a handful of bills, tossing them on the table. Then he turned and started for the front door.

Natalie paused, her hand in her bag, and then looked from V's broad back to me and back again. "Gee, thanks."

I heard a faint rustling, like leaves being tossed by a hot wind. The voices were back, but garbled, broken up and stuttering.

I'll follow you . . . I'll stop you . . .

But then, through the lumps of sound, three words rose to the surface: *She'll be mine . . .*

"Hurry up, Natalie," I whispered, feeling the room start to close around me. I had never been claustrophobic before, and now certainly wasn't the time to start.

"I'm coming, I'm coming," she said, turning me to face the

door and gently pushing on my shoulders. "Let's go, then. But I don't see what the big rush is."

V was already at the door, his hand resting on the bar, his fingers tapping a fast rhythm on the metal. As we approached, he pushed open the door and let us walk past him. He seemed to radiate a strange energy, and when I brushed against his jacket, I caught the acrid scent of burnt electricity. Like lightning had just struck—or was just about to.

"We're still too close," V said, walking across the parking lot with fast, wide strides.

I took a step after him, but Natalie grabbed my hand.

"Abby, what are you doing? You can't go with him. Let's get out of here."

I sighed. All the words were there, right there behind my teeth, words that would explain everything. But I couldn't say any of them. Not yet. Instead I said, "It's okay. I know him. Just . . . trust me, okay?"

Natalie hesitated and I took the opening. As much as I didn't want to involve her in this madness, or put her at risk, I also didn't want to go with V all alone. I squeezed her hand, offered her what I hoped was a reassuring smile, and then pulled her behind me as I followed in V's wake.

V had stopped by Natalie's car, frowning in impatience. "Open it. We have to go."

"I have a name, you know," she said.

V shook his head. "Names are dangerous. He's listening for them."

"He can hear us?" I looked around as though Zo were already standing behind me.

"Not exactly. It's more like . . . vibrations. I'll explain later."

I touched Natalie's arm. "Would you drive?"

She reached into her bag and withdrew her keys, jangling them in her fingers. She twisted her mouth. "Do I have a choice?"

"I'll make it up to you. I promise."

"Oh, I know you will," she said. "Just promise me that you'll tell me what's going on. The truth. The whole truth. Everything."

I swallowed and nodded. "Promise."

"Okay." Natalie unlocked the driver's side door and popped the locks on the other doors. "Then get in and let's go."

"About time," V muttered as he climbed into the backseat.

"Where to?" Natalie asked as I joined her in the front and she turned the key.

I glanced at V, raising an eyebrow in a silent question. The idea that Zo was listening to us made silence an attractive option.

"It doesn't matter—just someplace new. Somewhere you don't usually go. The sooner we get lost, the better."

I looked at Natalie and took a chance that this version of Natalie remembered the same things I did. "The alphabet game?"

Grinning, she nodded. "Good idea."

I breathed a sigh of relief and buckled my seat belt.

Long before any of us could drive, Natalie, Valerie, and I would ride our bikes around the neighborhood. The summer of our fifth-grade year, Natalie had become obsessed with maps and mazes. She drew up a plan of the entire neighborhood, marking the fastest routes to various destinations—the school, the church, each of our houses—often finding rarely traveled, winding back roads. That was the summer she also invented the alphabet game. We would ride our bikes to an intersection, and if the cross street started with a letter A through J, we'd turn right; K through S, we'd go straight through; and T through Z, we'd turn left. At the next street, we'd rotate the rules.

We once spent a whole Saturday playing the game until we ended up at least a half mile from home at a small place none of us had ever heard of before: Phillips Park. It turned out there was a much shorter, more direct route to the park, and once Natalie had mapped it for us, Phillips Park became our destination of choice for long summer afternoons.

Natalie stopped at the corner. "Bluebell Avenue," she read, and flipped the blinker before turning right.

We drove in silence for a while, Natalie making the turns as the game required. I tried to marshal my thoughts and questions into some kind of order. I had so many, it was hard to choose, so I started with what I thought was the most important one.

I twisted in my seat, pinning V with a hard gaze. "What are you doing here?"

He shook his head, glancing over his shoulder as though we were being followed.

"How did you find me?" I tried another one.

He pressed his lips together, clearly unwilling to answer.

"What do you want?"

At that, V's face closed with a hard snap of repressed

anger. His dark eyes seemed even darker and a flush crept up the sides of his neck.

I glanced at Natalie, who was turning left on Tulip Court, and saw a small local strip mall up ahead. I pointed to the parking lot of a tanning salon. "Pull in there."

She did, sliding her car into a space by the curb. She turned the car off and unbuckled her seat belt. I reached over and pushed the automatic locks; the resulting click sounded loud in the silent car. We both turned to V.

"We're here," I said, "at a totally random place we've never been before because you wanted to get away from Zo."

V's jaw tightened at the name, the flush spreading like a wound.

"We're as hidden as we can be, I guess. And you said we had to talk. So start talking."

V looked out the window, down and away. Tension coiled around him like a whip, taut and thick. He clenched his hands into fists and swallowed hard.

After a long silence, I spoke again. "Fine. Be that way." I turned around in my seat and rebuckled my seat belt. "Let's go, Nat. This is obviously some kind of game for him."

"No, wait—" V grabbed my shoulder.

I cocked my head to let him know I was listening.

"I'll talk."

I exchanged a glance with Natalie.

"Hey, do what you want. I'm just the driver." She shrugged. "I won't interrupt."

I turned around to face V. "Let's start with an easy one.

What did you mean when you said Helen's was a lodestone location?"

V sighed, slumping in his seat. The tension was gone, replaced by a visible weariness. "Places where you spend a lot of time are brighter, easier to see from the other side. So are places where you have strong memories or emotional ties. We are drawn to those places—like Helen's Café—because they provide the easiest access to your specific timeline."

Natalie leaned forward, but I didn't look at her. I didn't have time to answer her questions or try to explain.

"Tell me why Zo is targeting my specific timeline."

"Stop saying his name," V growled. "I told you—it's dangerous."

I remembered how upset Valerie had been when I'd said Zo's name and I felt a shiver run through me.

"Fine," I said through gritted teeth. "Tell me why *he* is targeting me specifically."

V shook his head. "He wouldn't tell me. Just that he needs you."

I wanted to slap him. Zo had said the same thing to me in the park. I'd had enough of riddles and strange Italian men with their mysterious ways and cryptic comments. I wanted answers. And I wanted them now.

"What does he want? What is he planning to do?"

"I don't know."

"Liar," I snapped. "You've been working with him. You do everything he says."

"Not anymore," V said.

I drew in a sharp breath. Zo hadn't mentioned this change. "Why should I believe you?"

V whipped his head back to me. "He ruined my life."

"Join the club."

"I suppose I deserve that," V said, "considering."

"Considering what? You've been doing *his* bidding all this time and now you want me to talk to you—to trust you—and I'm still not sure I can do either one."

"I know. It was a gamble to contact you, but the streams were pretty clear. If I wanted to see her again, I had to go through you."

"See who?"

A smile crossed his face for the first time all day and a softness entered his eyes. "Valerie."

"You want to see her again?" I asked in disbelief, hearing a soft gasp of amazement from Natalie. "After what you did to her?"

"I didn't do anything to her—"

"As I recall, *you* were the one who pushed her into the river," I pointed out.

"You know what he can do on the bank. You were there. You know. You remember."

I did remember—that loose-limbed sense of well-being, the urge of instant obedience, the gratitude at being able to serve—and I shivered a little inside.

"I didn't have a choice," V said, a muscle tightening along his jaw.

"And if you did have a choice?" I asked. "What then? What would you have done?"

"I would have gone with her." V's voice was low and confidential. "I would have taken her away from all . . . this. I would have protected her."

"The way you protected her before? You knew what kind of person you were dealing with. You knew what he was planning. You must have known there was the chance Valerie wouldn't survive—" My voice broke, but I forced myself to continue. "And now she's his—body and soul . . . and what mind she has left."

"It wasn't supposed to be like that."

"Then what was it supposed to be like? What was your big plan, if not to take her to the bank like you did?"

"The plan was always to go back. All we wanted was to go home. And he said Valerie wouldn't get hurt."

"And you believed him?" I rocked back in my seat from sheer astonishment.

"*You* went to the bank and nothing bad happened to you," he retorted. "It was a reasonable promise to believe."

"Nothing bad happened to me on the bank?" I repeated. "My whole life changed there—and not all for the better."

"But some of it did change for the better, right? It wasn't *all* bad—not like for Valerie."

"Stop saying her name." My voice shook in my throat. "You're not her friend. You don't know anything about her—"

"I know I loved her," he said quietly. "I know I would give anything to take back that moment. If it meant she would be well again . . . I'd do whatever I could to make it right."

"You couldn't have loved her. You hardly knew her," I stammered. I risked a glance at Natalie, but she was as surprised as I was by the news. The conversation had taken an unexpected turn, and I cast about for something solid to hang my swirling thoughts on. "She was his girl . . ."

"But originally she wanted *me*. Before anything else happened, she was interested in me."

I heard the fierce pride in V's voice then, the confidence and certainty. It was like a layer had been peeled away from V and I could see him with new eyes. He wasn't as charismatic as Zo. He wasn't tall or suave like Tony. And he knew it. He knew he was a rather average-looking guy, with dark hair and a build that was more stocky than stout. I had always thought of him as the thug who carried out Zo's plans. And maybe he *had* spent most of his time in the background, but Valerie hadn't seen him that way. She had seen him as the most interesting member of Zero Hour. The one she wanted to get to know better. Not Zo, with his good looks and snake-charmer's way. Not Tony, with his quick wit and ready smile. The bright star that was Valerie had been attracted to the pale moon of V. And for V, her unexpected attention must have been as surprising as waking up one morning to see the sun rising in the west.

"If you loved her," I said, "then why did you let her . . . ?" A memory of Valerie rose up in my mind—her sitting in the plastic chair next to the hospital window—and I couldn't finish.

"I hated what he did to her—"

"What you *all* did to her," I interrupted. "Zero Hour wasn't a one-man band, after all."

V grimaced. "I know. And I take full responsibility for my part in what happened. That's why I'm trying to make it right."

"Then why don't you? I thought the whole point was that

you guys could go back and change things. Make things the way you wanted them to be. Someone *else* certainly has been exercising his power, reshaping things however he wants."

V sighed and looked down at his hands. "It's not that easy—"

"Why did you bother to come to the café today?" I demanded. "You show up, spin some tale, tell me you're in love with my friend, and what? You're going to leave without giving me any answers? What was the point?"

"The point is that Zo deserves to die for what he did." The words slid from his mouth like oil. "For what he made me do." He finally looked up and met my eyes. I recoiled at the hardness I saw there, the pitilessness. "And I need your help to kill him."

CHAPTER 15

Natalie whistled low, under her breath. "Okay, this conversation is officially over. I don't have a clue what you guys are talking about, but killing someone is out of the question."

I couldn't look away from V's dark eyes. Conflicting emotions stormed through me. Instinct said no, with horror, but my anger leaped at the chance to say yes.

"I thought you guys couldn't be killed," I said slowly. "I thought that was one of the benefits of having gone through the door a second time." I nodded at the gold bands around V's wrists, winking from the dark cave of his sleeves. They were identical to the ones I'd seen wrapped around Zo's arms.

"The only person who can kill a master of time is another master of time," V said.

"So why do you need my help? You're as strong as he is. Why don't you do it yourself?"

V's mouth turned down. He leaned forward, wrapping his hands around the posts holding up the headrest. "I've tried. More than once. But every time I get close, he slips away. I need you to help me get close to him. That's all. Just a chance to get close to him."

Natalie started the car. "Seriously, guys. We're done talking about this."

"I'd be the bait?" I asked in disgust.

"*I'm* the bait," V said, shaking his head. "You'd be the trap."

"What?"

"He'll come for me, but he'll stop for you. And when he does, then you can hold him in place."

"And why would he come for you?" I asked, cautiously.

"Because he doesn't take betrayal lightly," V said, slumping back into his seat. "Especially from those he was close to."

I knew that was the truth. The last person who had betrayed Zo had been Leo, and Zo had repaid him by implicating Dante in his traitorous conspiracy and sentencing them all to a trip through time.

"He's hunting *you,* isn't he? That's why you wanted to leave Helen's. It wasn't because you were afraid for me. You were afraid for *you.*"

V looked out the window and pulled his sleeves down over his wrists. "You said I'm as strong as he is, but you're wrong. I'm not. I don't know if anyone is. Maybe if Tony was here, we'd have a chance to stop him together. But he's gone and I don't know where he is. I've tried to find him, but I can't. I'm the only one left."

I knew where Tony was, but I hesitated to tell V. There was nothing Tony could do to help. As it was, I'd be lucky to save Dante. *No,* I told myself. *Don't think that. You will save him. You will.*

"What did you do?" I asked quietly.

V shrugged. "I told him no."

"That's all?"

"That was enough." V sighed and ran his hand through his hair. "He has been targeting you—"

"Yeah, I noticed."

"—and he wanted me to do something that would hurt you. To test my loyalty, he said. I said no. I walked away."

My blood turned to ice. "Why would you do that for me? You hardly know me."

V turned his dark eyes to me. "I didn't do it for you. I did it for Valerie. She's been talking to you, hasn't she? Telling you stories?"

I nodded.

"He doesn't like anyone telling his secrets. He told me to take care of it. He said he didn't care what I did to her, just so long as she was unraveled from your timeline."

Unraveled. The word sat in my mind, refusing to be shoved aside. Several threads had already been pulled out of the tapestry of my life: Hannah, Dad, Jason. Even Dante was coming loose, fraying at the edges as the darkness between doors closed in around him. Valerie may not have been the strongest thread, but her life didn't deserve to be unraveled just because she was my friend.

When V spoke again, his voice was surprisingly gentle. "I didn't want to hurt her again. I couldn't. And now that I've walked away from Zo, he's punishing me by keeping me away from her. I can't reach her even though all I want is to see her, talk to her, tell her . . ." V met my eyes again. "Please, Abby. I can't do this alone."

I could see it so clearly then: Zo was working to isolate me. His efforts had been focused on making changes that would take people away from me, divide me from those who might help. He needed me alone and vulnerable.

He wasn't going to get it.

I reached for Natalie's hand. I still had her on my side. And Leo. And Dante—once we broke him out of prison. And with V defying Zo's wishes, it meant I still had Valerie with me. Plus, V had come looking for me, asking for my help. It was starting to look like Zo might be the one left alone and vulnerable.

Zo had been running free for too long. If V had a plan to trap him, stop him, then now might be the best time to make a stand.

"I have as much reason to hate him as you do—maybe more—so I'll make you a deal," I said slowly. "I'll do what I can to arrange a meeting between you and Valerie."

"And?" V asked, both hope and hesitation in his voice. "What do you want me to do?"

"I want you to build me a new door for the time machine."

"What? Are you crazy?"

"I have the plans. But the building schedule is on a strict timeline and I need you to figure out how to get it built now. Not in two months. Not in two weeks. *Now.*"

V shook his head. "I'm not sure that's possible—"

"Zo doesn't seem to be letting something as trivial as the impossible stop him from doing what he wants."

V flinched, his expression etched with anger.

"It's simple. You help me with the door and I'll help you with Valerie."

"And Zo," V added. "You'll get me close enough so I can kill him."

"It's in everyone's best interests for him to be stopped," I replied diplomatically. Stop him, yes. Trap him, yes. Help to kill him? As angry as I was with Zo, as sweet as my hate for him tasted, I didn't think I would be able to do that. I didn't want to be the kind of person who *could*.

A grin spread across V's face. He held out his hand to me, the gold chains bright against his flushed skin. "Deal," he said.

I slipped my hand into his, abruptly remembering Leo's hand matching mine, Dante's hand caressing mine, Zo's hand capturing mine, and I wondered if I was doing the right thing.

"Deal," I repeated.

I offered to have Natalie drop V off somewhere, but he shook his head. "I can get where I'm going easier than you can," he said as he got out of the car. "I'll be in touch."

He waited on the curb as Natalie pulled the car away. I watched him in the side mirror as he turned and began crossing the parking lot. Somewhere between the light post and the far edge of the building, he simply disappeared.

The air where he had been rippled ever so slightly—if I hadn't been watching for it, I would have missed it—and deep in my inner ear I heard the shivering chimes of time ring. The barriers between the river and the bank were thinning; there was no doubt about it.

I glanced at Natalie to see if she had noticed V's unusual departure, but she kept her eyes fixed on the road, her hands wrapped so tightly around the steering wheel that her knuckles turned white.

"Who was that guy?" she said, more of a demand than a question. When I hesitated, she whipped her head toward me. "You promised me the truth. What have you dragged me into?"

I touched Dante's locket around my neck. I was starting to wonder the same thing. Drawing in a deep breath, I tried to think of how best to answer Natalie. She'd asked for the truth, not knowing how impossible it would be to believe. But I'd made her a promise, and I needed to honor it, no matter what.

"His name is Vincenzio, but we all call him V."

"We?" Natalie asked. "Who's *we?*"

"Me. Valerie. His friends, Zo and Tony."

"The Tony who's missing and the Zo he wants to kill? Some friends."

"Well, they used to be friends."

Natalie was quietly skeptical.

I forged ahead, trying to explain. "You call him that too. You've met him before, actually."

"I've never seen him before today," Natalie protested.

"Well, see, that's the thing. It was a different you who met him."

To Natalie's credit, she didn't slam on the brakes and kick me out of the car. Instead, she said calmly, "Go on."

So I told her. Everything. I told her about the time

machine, about Zo and Tony and V and what they had done to Valerie, about Leo and the Dungeon. I told her about the river of time and the bank that paralleled it. About the door I'd opened and the choices I'd made. I told her how I fell in love with Dante.

Natalie was quiet through the whole story. She didn't look at me once but simply drove through the streets, retracing our path back home.

We pulled up in front of my house. My throat hurt from all the words that had poured out of me. I clenched and unclenched my hands in my lap, twisting my fingers into knots. Was it too much? Was it too unbelievable? Had I alienated an ally I could ill afford to lose?

Natalie finally turned to face me. Her eyes were clear and steady. "It's crazy," she said. "All of it."

I felt my heart shrivel and tighten.

"I don't know if I can believe it."

Swallowing, I waited in silent hope.

"But I've never known you to lie to me before," she continued slowly. She brushed the hair out of her eyes and shook her head. "I don't know, Abby. This . . . this is a lot to think about."

I felt tears in my eyes, grateful that Natalie hadn't rejected my story outright. The hope grew until it crowded out everything else.

"I know," I said quietly. "And it's okay if you can't believe me right now. Just promise me that you *will* think about it. And if there is any way you think you might be able to believe me, I'd really appreciate it."

"I'll try," she said.

I loved her for those two words. For taking that leap of faith and trusting that what I said was the truth. For being willing to at least hear me out.

"Thank you." I reached over and gave her a hug. "Thank you so much."

Natalie hugged me back. "No promises, but I'll try."

"Hey, I'll take it," I said with a grin.

"You owe me lunch, you know." Natalie sat back in her seat, returning my smile. "That V guy interrupted a perfectly good meal."

"I'll make it up to you," I promised. "Plus dessert."

Natalie tilted her head to the side. "So about Dante. He's real, right? I mean, you're really in love with him?"

My heart was full with too many memories and moments to detail how deeply I felt, so I simply nodded and whispered, "Yes. I am."

"When can I meet him?"

"Soon," I said, feeling the dry heat of uncertainty pass over me. "I hope."

The front door to my house opened and I saw my mom step out onto the porch. Even from the car, I could see how red her eyes were.

"Thanks again," I said to Natalie, my hand on the door handle. "For everything. I'll see you soon, okay?" I climbed out of the car and waved as Natalie drove away.

Turning toward my house, I ran up the stairs and into my mom's open arms.

As she folded me into her embrace, I was grateful that,

despite the many things that had changed in my life, there were some things that remained constant.

After a belated meal with my mom, and my constant reassurance that I was okay, that everything was fine, that I was sorry for having acted so strange and run away, I made my way up to my room, my thoughts crowded and thick. I deliberately avoided Hannah's room; I didn't think I could handle another look at the oddly sterile guest room that should have been alive with my sister's life.

Collapsing on my bed, I didn't even bother to question my next move. I knew what I wanted, or rather who I wanted.

Dante.

I didn't think it was possible to ache so deeply for another person. And as much as I wanted to see him, to touch him, I would have given anything to just hear the sound of his voice again. Was that too much to ask? Just one small breath, an exhalation, even. That's all it would take to say my name. Longing for him was a physical pain, a moving knot of nerves and raw emotion that seemed to travel at will inside me, flaring up at unexpected times. Like now.

I pressed my hands to my eyes, welcoming the darkness that rolled over me.

"Dante." I whispered his name, just to feel it on my lips. I conjured his face in my mind, just to see his smile.

I felt the world shift around me and dropped my hands in surprise. It had only taken an instant and I was on the dream-side of the bank, standing on my small island while the river churned in endless ripples and waves. The sky overhead was flat black. Out of the corners of my eyes I could see the glimmer of distant stars, though they disappeared when I looked directly at them.

My stomach dropped. Worry rubbed my mind like an itch. Usually I had come here because I had intended to. Only once before had it been a surprise. And what a surprise it had been.

But this time the transition had been almost immediate. I hadn't had to work at it at all. I hadn't been dreaming, or even sleepy. Had the barriers between my dreams and my life started to crumble as quickly as the bank was crumbling beneath my feet? I had been worried about not being able to come back. Perhaps I should have been worried about coming back too many times.

"Hello?" I whispered, wondering whose voice I would hear in reply. If I had to be here, I didn't want Zo to be with me; I wanted Dante.

You came back. His soft voice drifted from behind me, curling over my shoulder like smoke.

"Of course I came back," I said. "Did you think I wouldn't?"

I hoped you would come. I prayed to be able to talk to you one more time. But I didn't dare to believe . . . Dante's whispering voice lifted along the curve of my neck. *Oh, Abby. My angel.*

I could imagine him standing behind me, his head close to mine. I could almost feel the heat from his mouth next to my ear.

Here in the darkness, all I want to see is your face. It's so good to hear your voice and know you are close. He breathed a laugh. *I've had so many conversations with you I've lost count.*

"Oh?" I reached out my hand through the rippling air, searching for contact. "And what have we been talking about?"

He caught my hand and lifted it to his lips. *I told you about how we once walked the hills outside the villa where I grew up. It was summertime and the ground was covered with a blanket of wildflowers. I took your hand and we raced the sun over the green hills. You picked a flower for me and I tucked it into your hair. Later, we sat under the shade of a tree and you laid your head in my lap and I told you stories until you fell asleep.*

Dante's voice painted the scene so clearly that I could almost smell the heavy fragrance of flowers in my hair, on my skin.

I told you about the night I first met you and how seeing you lit up my life like the sunrise. I told you about da Vinci and his workshop. I told you my dreams—though they were all the same dream in the end.

"What dream was that?" The familiar coldness began creeping up my arm, but I simply held onto Dante's hand tighter.

This one. The one where you come to me and set me free.

"Well, I can't set you free quite yet. But I know how. I have a plan to bring you home."

Home. I hardly know what that means anymore. Dante sighed and the air around me shivered. *Is it the villa outside of Florence in the days before Orlando left for war? Is it the corner of da Vinci's studio, when I sketched alone until dawn, lost in my work? Or is it the small apartment in the Dungeon where I learned from Leo how to start a new life?*

"It's all of them," I said. "Home can be more than one place, you know. More than one time."

No, Dante said with quiet strength. *Home is wherever you are.*

A wave of warmth lifted my heart in my chest, washing through me, threatening tears.

You are my constant, Abby, Dante said, the cold from his hand flashing across my cheek as he traced the features of my face. *You are my North Star. I can always find you. No matter how dark it is, I can close my eyes and point directly to you.* His words were soft and low. *I feel like I've been cut adrift. But when I'm with you, I feel like myself again. I'm whole. I can rest. I need you, Abby,* he whispered. *I want to be where you are.*

I felt a breath of coldness against my lips the moment before he kissed me.

No matter what, he breathed into my ear, *I will find a way to come home to you.*

I twined my fingers with his, pressing my palm flat against his. "I miss you, Dante. I miss hearing your laugh. I miss turning around and seeing you standing there. I miss feeling so safe when you're with me." The tears spilled over, and with them came all the words I'd been holding in for so long. The words I couldn't say to anyone but Dante. "I've been trying to be brave and strong while you've been gone—"

You are brave—

"But it's been getting harder and harder to hold on to my memories and to what I know to be true when I feel so alone."

You're not alone. You have your family—

I interrupted him with a bitter laugh. "No, I don't. Not anymore. That's the thing. Zo has taken them. He's redirected the river and erased my dad and my sister from my life. Jason's gone too. Zo's changed everything."

Oh, Abby—

"They're gone, Dante," I whispered. "Just . . . gone. But I remember them. How is it possible that I remember someone I never met?"

I wanted more than anything to be able to feel Dante's arms around me, but though the barriers between us were thinner, they were still strong. The best I could hope for was what little we already had: our palms pressed together and the sound of his voice in my ear and his kiss.

"I told Natalie about you and the time machine and she *might* decide to believe me about the whole crazy mess—"

She's your friend. She'll believe you.

"She might, but she might not, and then what?"

Have you talked to Leo?

"Yeah, I have." I sighed. "Leo thinks he might know a way to help stop the changes to the river, but I don't know if it will work. And even if it does, I don't know if it will help bring anyone back. Dante, what if I can never get my family back? What if I've lost them forever?"

Dante squeezed my fingers so tightly that I felt the pressure despite the glove of numbness that covered my hand. *Don't say that. Don't think like that. You told me that together we could do anything—even the impossible. Well, this is just a little more impossible than it was before, but we can fix this,*

Abby. We will. Together. I promise. Don't let the darkness of doubt take hold of you. Trust me.

My tears slowed, finally stopping.

Now, tell me your idea to bring me home.

"I think if we modify the plans you left me, we can open the door to where you are and you can come home."

Dante was quiet for a long time.

He let go of my hand and I pulled it back through the veil separating us. I shook my fingers, hoping to drive some warmth back into my fingertips. Wiping away the remains of my tears from my eyes with my other hand, I breathed in his silence. I loved the stillness that surrounded him whenever he was deep in thought. It reminded me of a hunting lion: all the energy was on the inside, coiled tight, until it was time, and then suddenly he would spring into action, never looking back.

Yes, he finally said. *Yes, that could work. I think I see where to make the modifications, but you'll need help. Oh, but you said Jason was gone . . .*

"V will help me."

What?

I told him about my conversation with V and how he had chosen Valerie over Zo. "V and I made a deal. He'll help me with the door and I'm arranging for him to see Valerie again."

Can you trust him?

I thought back to the look in V's eyes when he told me he loved my friend. "Yes," I said simply, "I can. I have to."

Dante was quiet for a moment. *All right. That's good. Then here's what we need to do.*

As Dante walked me through the modifications that would

need to be made to the blueprints, I closed my eyes to help me focus on his words. I would have to remember every step, every change, and write it down the moment I could. I didn't want to make a single mistake. I didn't dare.

When he was finished, he made me repeat the steps back to him to make sure I hadn't missed anything.

Good, Dante said. *You can do this. Remember—do what you have to do. Change what has to be changed.*

"And come back when I can," I finished. "I remember. I told V we had to build this now. We can't wait until the first day of summer. We don't have time to lose. *You* don't have any time to lose."

I'll be fine, Dante said, but I heard the hesitation in his voice. *Don't worry about me.*

"I can't *not* worry about you."

You're sweet, he said with a lightheartedness I knew he didn't feel. Then he sighed. *I don't know the answer, Abby. I can't see how to get around the timeline. The schedule for building the machine is almost as important as the machine itself. The sequence is established for a reason. It's a ritual wrought with power. Maybe once you have the plans in front of you, you'll be able to see a solution. Something I can't see here in the dark.*

"I'll find a way," I said. "I won't let the darkness take you."

I know.

"I won't let Zo take you either," I added.

I know. But you don't have to worry about that. Yes, there are dangers here in the darkness, but Zo isn't one of them.

I frowned, remembering the whispered conversation I'd overheard at the café. "But I heard him talking to you . . ."

I promise you, Zo hasn't contacted me or Tony.

"Tony is still with you? That's good."

Dante hesitated, letting the silence spin out between us.

"Please tell me Tony is okay," I said quietly.

Ice lined the silence, waiting for one of us to crack it open with our words.

Tony is gone, Dante said, his voice as soft as a breeze and as quick to disappear. *At least he wasn't in pain anymore. There at the end.*

"Are you sure?" I covered my face with my hands. V's word returned to me—*unraveled*—and I shuddered. I hadn't known Tony well, but no one deserved to dissolve into darkness, lost and alone.

No. But that's what I tell myself.

I could feel the edges around me thin as I started to lose my hold on the dream. "Dante," I said, my voice suddenly fierce, "the stories you told to me under the tree? Do you remember them?"

I remember everything about you.

"The next time I see you, I want you to sit with me under a tree and I want you to tell me all your stories," I said. "Every last one."

I would love to. Dante laughed a little. *Though that might take some time.*

"Once you are out of the darkness, you can have all the time you want, forever."

Forever might not be long enough.

"Then we'll just have to see what's on the other side of forever, won't we?"

It's a date, Dante said. *And Abby?*

The dream was fading fast. I could see the outline of my bedroom door, the desk, the window, emerging through the black shadows of the dreaming bank.

I love you, Abby.

I opened my eyes, not at all surprised to find tears on my face and my hand reaching out.

"I love you too, Dante," I whispered.

CHAPTER 16

Here are the rules," I said to V, folding my hands over the binder containing the modified copy of the blueprints. It had taken me two days to annotate the plans—well, actually it had only taken me a couple of hours to mark the modifications Dante had told me to make, but it had taken me a day to get a message to V and another day waiting for him to show up. Some people had no concept of time anymore.

I had also taken the time to make a copy of the blueprints. Just in case. I didn't want to risk losing the instructions Dante had passed along to me. I had locked a set in my desk drawer and brought the second set to meet with V.

It was more crowded at the Sugar Shoppe than at Helen's Café, but, given Zo's increased attention to what V called "lodestone locations" and V's paranoia, we couldn't go there. Luckily, we were able to snag a back table, so at least we had some measure of privacy.

V leaned forward, the sleeves of his army jacket pushed up to his elbows. He wore leather cuffs around his wrists to hide the gold bands. His dark hair fell over his serious eyes as he nodded his understanding.

"First," I said, "you have to follow these plans *exactly.* No variation. No liberties. No shortcuts."

"I will."

"Second, you can't tell anyone what you're doing."

"Obviously."

"Third, once you're done, I'll arrange a visit for you with Valerie."

V's smile softened the square angles of his face. "Good."

I took a deep breath, knowing what I had to say next and wondering at what had happened in my life that had led me to be able to say such impossible words. "Last rule: you'll have to go back to March so you can start building the door on the first day of spring."

"What?" V's smile collapsed into a frown and his whole body stiffened with tension.

I looked around, for once grateful for the crowds around us. The noise was loud enough that no one was paying any attention to us. "The door *has* to be built on a strict timeline and it has to be started on the first day of a season—though, luckily, it doesn't matter which one."

"The first day of summer is coming up, why not—"

I shook my head, cutting him off. "That'll be too late. The door takes months to build and I need it done *now.*" I shrugged. "There's no other way, V. Believe me, I've looked. If you want my help, then you have to do things my way."

He leaned back against the chair and folded his arms across his chest.

"What's the problem? I thought you did this traveling thing all the time now."

"I do. But . . ."

I drew my eyebrows together in confusion. "But what?"

He sighed in obvious frustration. "Zero Hour first played at the Dungeon on January fifteenth, remember?"

"How could I forget?" I said dryly.

"That was the day our timelines intersected with yours."

"So?"

V set the edge of his hands on the table, about a foot apart. "So, we can't travel to any point between January fifteenth and the day when we went through the door the second time."

"Why not?"

"Because you won't let us."

Now it was my turn to lean back and fold my arms across my chest. "Excuse me?"

V shook his head, struggling with his words. "Okay, look." He moved his knife to the center of the table. "Here's the river, right?" He grabbed the straw from his water glass and the one from mine. Laying a straw on either side of the knife, he said, "And here's the bank." He picked up his paper napkin and tore a small circle out of it, holding it up before me. "This is you." He placed the paper circle on the knife. "And this is you on your little island that protects that portion of the river. We can move all around that island, but not right there. We can get close to you, to your specific timeline, but we can't get to any point that you're protecting." He shrugged. "I can't go back to March."

I put my head in my hands. What V said made a sort of

sense. The changes that had happened in my life had all happened before Zero Hour had entered my timeline. The events Zo had been changing had happened far back in my past, though they resulted in large changes downstream in my present. Perhaps that's what he meant when he said things would have been different if he had met me first. Perhaps if he had, he would have had access to my entire timeline, including the part of the river I was somehow protecting from his touch.

So how could I allow V access to that part of the river without opening the door to Zo as well?

I studied his makeshift diagram, trying to figure out a solution. It was hard to think. I knew from my dreaming trips that the bank was crumbling, that the river had twisted. It didn't look like the same place anymore—

And then, all at once, I saw the answer. The way out.

V looked at me with sad eyes. "I'm sorry, Abby. I wish I could help—"

I pulled out my cell phone and punched in a number.

"Who are you calling?" V asked.

"Leo," I said shortly. He picked up on the second ring.

"Abby?" he said.

"Hi, Leo." I picked up the paper island from the blade of the knife and rubbed it between my fingers. "I need you to meet me at the Sugar Shoppe in"—I checked my watch—"one hour. Can you do that?"

"Of course. Is something wrong?"

"No, nothing's wrong. I just need a favor." I snapped the phone shut and pinned V with a hard stare. "You said you would do anything to make things right."

V nodded. "If I can, I will."

"Good." I swept aside the knife and the straws with the flat of my hand. Then I pushed the binder across the table to him. "You have one hour to memorize these plans—every step. Everything."

V wrapped his thick fingers around the binder. "Then what? I told you, I can't go back to March—"

"Maybe not directly. But you *can* go to the bank. And you can take me with you."

I paced in front of V, who leaned up against a tree trunk outside of the building, the binder propped open on his bent knees. He wasn't happy about the idea of taking me to the bank, but since my answer to every one of his questions was to point to the binder and remind him that he had less than an hour left, he stopped asking questions and started studying.

Checking my watch, I scanned the parking lot. V had less than five minutes now, if Leo was on time, and he was always on time.

"This is amazing," V said, turning a page. "And you say Dante designed this?"

"Da Vinci designed it. Dante just made the modifications."

"Still." V tapped the papers with his finger. "It's incredible. It's so complicated it's a wonder it worked at all."

I stopped my pacing and slanted a look down at him. "But it did, didn't it?"

"Yeah," he said quietly. "It did. And you want me to build one for you? Why?"

I sat down next to him. The binder was open to the last page—the drawing of the heart-shaped locket. "Long story short: Dante didn't make it through the second door like you did. Building this will bring him home." I felt V's eyes on me and turned my head to meet his gaze. "You reunite me with Dante, and I'll reunite you with Valerie."

"But it's dangerous—building another machine."

"I know," I said. "But it's more dangerous not to."

V was quiet for a moment. "How do you know I won't run back to Zo and tell him what I've learned?"

I studied his dark eyes. "I don't," I said honestly. "But I trust you'll do the right thing. For Valerie's sake if not your own."

V tilted his head. Then he reached out and touched my hand. "I'm sorry," he said softly. "For everything. For bringing all this uncertainty into your life."

I smiled at him, though it felt a little crooked on my face. "You're sweet. I can see what Valerie liked about you."

"Abby?" Leo stepped up to join us in the shade of the tree. "Are you all right?"

Standing up, I brushed at my pants and dusted my hands together. "I'm great. Thanks for coming."

V closed the binder and stood by my side. "Leo." He nodded his head respectfully in greeting.

"Vincenzio," Leo replied, looking wary and confused.

"Okay, here's the plan," I said, clapping my hands together. "The three of us are going to the bank. I'll help V drop back into the river in March so he can build the door for Dante, and then you, Leo, will help me back so I don't get stuck in time. Everybody ready?"

V and Leo looked at me with alternating expressions of horror and incredulity.

Leo found his voice first. "No," he said. "That's insanity. I won't let you do this—"

V chimed in. "I've never taken anyone to the bank. What if it doesn't work?"

"Dante would never forgive me if I let you come to harm," Leo continued.

I held up my hands and both men fell silent. "You both promised you'd help me. Well, this is how you can." I lifted the binder from V's unresisting hands and wrapped my arms around it. "Now, let's stop standing around and get moving." I looked from V to Leo. "Please."

Leo sighed, frowning. "I'm not happy about this."

"I know," I said. "But it'll be over before you know it. Trust me."

"Do we have a choice?" V growled.

I smiled. "Nope."

Leo drove the three of us to the ruins of the Dungeon. As another lodestone location, I knew it was a risk going there—V worried that Zo would take note of our presence and figure out what we were doing—but the Dungeon was where I had done most of my traveling to the bank, and I hoped it would ease the transition if we at least started in a familiar place.

The yellow caution tape still roped off the area, and the twisted metal still jutted up from the ashes like teeth. I glanced at Leo, who surveyed the lot with obvious pain in his eyes. I touched his arm and smiled at him, hoping to offer some small measure of comfort.

I ducked under the tape and walked to where the bar had once been. V and Leo followed, their unhappiness as thick as the dust in the air.

"This will do," I said.

"Are you sure you know what you're doing?" V asked, walking behind me.

"No," I admitted, "but stranger things have happened."

Leo folded his arms, scowling. "Why do you have to go? Let V and me do what needs to be done, and you stay here where it's safe."

"It's not safe anywhere anymore," I said. "Besides, you can't do what I can. What I *need* to do there." I touched Leo's arm. "There's no time to try anything else. I have to do whatever it takes to set Dante free."

Leo held my gaze for a long time, and I saw a wealth of emotions run through his face. Finally, he uncrossed his arms and nodded. "For Dante," he said low.

I slipped my hand into his and held out the binder to V. "Are you ready, V?"

He took the binder and nodded.

"What do I do?" he asked me under his breath, a note of

nervousness in his voice. "Last time Zo did all the work . . ." He trailed off.

I smiled reassuringly at V. "Don't worry. All you have to do is go to the bank like you always do. I'll just be tagging along this time."

I took V's free hand with mine. Breathing deeply, I closed my eyes and thought about thinning the edges between here and there. I counted my heartbeats. I focused on the feel of my hands in Leo's and V's grip. I wanted to make it as easy for V as I could.

As I felt the pressure of V's fingers tighten around mine, I turned to him. "Oh, and remember to kiss"—the world shifted—"me," I finished.

I wondered how I had ever mistaken the dream-side of the bank for the actual bank. The pressure hit me like a rock, crushing me. My body felt tight like a knot and the vise pinched my lungs, stealing my breath. This was as bad as I remembered.

No, it was worse.

The midnight sky I'd seen in my dreams was an even darker black, oppressive and unrelenting. The crumbling bank sloughed under my feet like a shed skin.

The three of us stood on a small island in the center of the river. All around us the river bubbled and churned. I was used to seeing it flowing silver-white, filled with images and pictures, but now it was almost gray, and a murky film floated on the surface like sludge.

I freed my hands and turned V's face toward me, frantic for relief. I pulled his head down and kissed him quickly. The pressure of the bank eased up, and I relaxed as much as I ever could in that place.

"This was a bad idea," Leo said next to me, a hard pain drawing a line across his forehead. His lips thinned into a tight frown.

"Maybe, but it worked," I said with relief. "We're here on my island."

"What happened?" V asked, looking around and down at the chunk of bank beneath our feet. "The river's not supposed to be here." He pointed into the distance on his right. "It's supposed to be over there."

"Zo happened," I said shortly. I wondered if the bridge would appear like it had the last time I had been on the bank, but there was nothing to disturb the flat expanse all the way to the horizon. Maybe since the original door had been destroyed, the bridge was gone too. I wondered if that was a good or a bad thing.

"Let's hurry." A muscle jumped in Leo's jaw as he looked at the polluted river. "I don't want you to be here any longer than you absolutely have to."

I felt the same way.

"This is bad," V said. "If Zo did this . . ."

Turning to V, I took a deep breath. "You said that you were blocked from entering the river at any point since January, right? You were denied direct access to my timeline."

"Is that what this island is?" Leo asked me. "Are you protecting this part of the river?"

"I think so," I said. "That's why we had to come to the bank together." I smiled at V. "You brought me to the bank, but I brought you to my island. And now that you're here, you're part of my timeline. Do you see? This island is the key that unlocks the door to my timeline. And when you step back into the river, you should be able to access last March without any problem."

Leo placed his hand on my shoulder and turned me around. "Are you sure about this, Abby? I mean, are you sure you want to allow him access to your past like this?"

"Yes, Leo. I'm sure. I know it's a risk, but no greater than the other risks I've taken. And if I have to make hard choices, I want to make the choice that will bring Dante back to me."

Leo glanced over my shoulder at V. "What if he does something—?"

"I won't," V said, his back straight and steel in his eyes. "I promised Abby if she could get me to March, I would build her the door. We had a deal."

"It'll be okay, Leo," I said quietly. "We can trust him."

"When you go back," Leo said to V, "you'll be dealing with overlapping timelines. I don't have any idea what will happen with two of you in the river at the same time, so make sure you stay out of everyone's way—especially your own. Don't talk to anyone. Don't do anything except build the door, and don't build it where anyone will find it."

"Where do you suggest?" he asked. "It's a pretty big machine. It's not like I can work on it just anywhere."

The three of us looked at each other for a moment.

And then I asked almost casually, "Leo, did the Dungeon have a basement?"

"Yes, but—" He stopped and shook his head. "No. Not there. We'll think of somewhere else."

"Why not, Leo? It's perfect." I counted the points off on my fingers. "It'd be secluded and private. No one from Zero Hour ever went down there, did they?" I turned to V for confirmation and he shook his head. "There'd be enough space for the structure, right? And when V's done, we'll know right where the door is."

Leo frowned. "What about the noise? No matter how good you are, no one could build a machine like that without drawing some attention."

"The Dungeon was a noisy place, especially on Friday nights," I pointed out. "And what about all those days when the Dungeon was closed, or when you and Dante were on the bank? I bet there would be plenty of downtime when V could make as much noise as he wanted and no one would notice."

"What about supplies?" Leo countered. "Not only will you have to gather all the equipment and supplies, but you'll have to smuggle them into the basement without my knowledge."

"Do you still have the keys to the Dungeon?" I asked Leo.

"Of course." He reached into his pocket and withdrew a key ring, displaying the small silver keys on his palm.

"What if you gave V the key to the basement?" I asked, eyeing the keys thoughtfully. "Then he could come and go as he pleased."

"It's not a bad idea," V said. "As long as I stay out of your way, I should be able to get it done."

"But that's just the thing," Leo said, shoving the keys back into his pocket. "How can V build it in the basement if the version of me from March didn't know anything about it? I was down in the basement at least once a week. If he goes back, if he does this, I would have known about it because I would have discovered him there. There's no way around that fact."

Once again the three of us looked at each other, searching for an answer.

"You're right, Leo," I said slowly, my brain churning through options and possibilities. "You would have known about it. You'd have to in order to keep it a secret."

The blood drained from Leo's face. "No, Abby, please." His voice was ragged. "Don't ask this of me."

"What?" V asked, looking between me and Leo.

Leo spoke to V, but his eyes never left mine. "She's suggesting that when you go back, you tell me what you're doing. She's suggesting that I help you build the door. And that I keep it secret from everyone. Including Dante. Including her."

"What's wrong with that? I could use all the help I can get," V said. "And you're good at keeping secrets. What's one more?"

"Please, Leo," I said quietly, searching his face. "I know you were unhappy that Dante gave me the plans. I know you were glad to see the door destroyed and that you hate the idea of me building another one. But, don't you see? There's no other way. I'll lose him otherwise. We both will."

After a timeless moment, his shoulders curved in surrender. I saw a deep, unbearable pain cross his face as though he were aging before my eyes. But we were on the bank, and I knew such things were impossible.

"Bisogna chiudere il cerchio," he said in Italian. *"Faró quello che è necessario."*

"Was that a yes?" I asked softly.

He nodded once.

I exhaled as best I could with the pressure of the bank weighing me down. "Good. Thank you, Leo." I leaned up and kissed him gently on the cheek. "I'm sorry."

The pain I thought was gone from his face returned tenfold and my heart ached to see such anguish.

Leo fixed his gaze on V, who straightened to attention like a soldier. "When you go back, find the night of March fourth. Dante had gone to visit Abby and give her that locket. I closed the Dungeon early. Knock on the back door. I doubt I'll be glad to see you, but when you see me, tell me . . ." He swallowed and a note of emotion trembled in his voice. "Tell me that the lady of light has sent you. Tell me that it is time to honor my vow."

My mouth opened in surprise, but Leo deliberately didn't look at me.

"That should be enough to get you inside. What you do after that is up to you."

V nodded. "The lady of light sent me and it's time to honor your vow," he repeated.

Leo was all business, his words coming fast and clipped. "If you're there on the fourth, it should give you—us—plenty of time to gather the materials for the door and start construction on the twentieth. You can live in the basement; I'll bring you groceries or something so you can stay hidden." He raised an eyebrow in V's direction. "You'll be there almost two and a half months. Can you handle that?"

V squared his broad shoulders. "Absolutely. I'll be fine."

Leo looked down at me. "What about you?"

"What about me?" I replied.

"Are you ready?"

I looked from Leo to V and felt my own determination rise up like a flare. "I'm beyond ready."

Stepping back, Leo gestured to the murky river in an invitation. "The river is yours, V."

V stepped to the edge of the island and held the binder close to his chest. The space around him stilled and seemed to thicken.

I watched as a small gap appeared in the flow of the river, right beneath V's toes. It looked as narrow as a thread of black ink, but it was enough.

V stepped back into the river and vanished, the air where he'd been standing rippling ever so slightly.

I exhaled, suddenly exhausted. It was done. Now it only remained to be seen if it worked.

CHAPTER 17

I watched as the thin thread of black widened and thickened, branching back upstream into my past like an unchecked virus. I shivered at the idea.

"Will you take me home now?" I asked Leo. I was tired of being on the bank and feeling like I had to fight for every breath. And the sooner I got back, the sooner I would know if my plan had worked. And the sooner Dante would be back.

As I turned to face Leo, I swayed and my knees threatened to buckle beneath me. My eyes suddenly refused to focus.

Before I toppled over into the river, Leo swept me up in his arms, cradling me to his chest like he had done on another night, so long ago.

I felt the vibrations of his voice in his chest more than I heard his words. "Rest, Abby. Rest and know the hardest part is done."

Closing my eyes, I surrendered myself to the sound of Leo's voice and the strength of his arms.

New memories pushed into my mind, shoving out the old ones. I could almost hear them shouting at me as they were reshaped, rerouted in my brain.

I remembered the night Dante gave me my locket, but now running parallel to that was a flash of another memory—somehow not entirely mine: V standing at the back door of the Dungeon, the streetlight sparking off the gold bands around his wrists.

I remembered all the Friday nights Dante and I danced at the Dungeon, but now woven into the pulsing backbeat were other memories of V laboring away beneath my feet. The door appeared in flashes, each one revealing more and more of the final shape. There was the tall, narrow frame. There was the long, straight tunnel, like a hallway with no windows. The carvings seemed to draw themselves as my memories unspooled in new pathways: the swirling nautilus, the rising tide. Circles, crescents, and stars. The hourglass emerged from the wood in one single, curved line.

I remembered the day Dante and I went to the Dungeon and discovered the hinge had been stolen, replaced with a fake by Zo. I saw Leo standing by the door, his arms full of groceries, his eyes as ferocious as a lion's. But now I saw more: V sitting on a cot in the basement corner, a plate of food balanced on his crossed legs. A brass hinge next to his knee with a half-sun, half-moon circle already inscribed on the first prong. He leaned his head against the wall, looking out a rectangular window by the ceiling. A fading ray of sunlight touched his hair.

My memories shivered like chimes in the wind.

I remembered the night Zo came to the Dungeon looking for me—and how my whole world changed.

I remembered more: the bank, the door, saying good-bye to Dante.

And then fire consumed them all.

A hot wind blew ashes into my face. I opened my eyes, squinting in the bright light. I was lying on my side in the dirt, but I felt strangely energized, as awake and alert as if I'd slept a whole day away.

Leo knelt on the ground next to me, his hands pressed to his temples and a halo of electric blue fire fading around him like an afterglow.

I sat up and touched his arm. "Leo? Are you okay?"

He nodded and then winced. "I'd rather not do that again, if it's all the same to you."

"With luck, we won't have to."

Leo rubbed his eyes one last time and then lowered his hands. "It's strange. I have all these new memories—and I know they're new—but at the same time I know I've always had them," he said.

"I know what you mean." I put a hand to my forehead. "My head feels . . . full."

"Is this how you felt when Zo changed elements of your life?"

"Not exactly. The other times were a lot more painful. Maybe it's because I asked for it this time."

"I guess that means V did his job."

I looked around the rubble of the Dungeon. "Then where is the door?"

Leo pushed himself to his feet, dusting his hands off against his legs. The color started to return to his face. "Probably still in the basement. That's where the fire started, after all."

I paused, trying to remember if I had known that before now. My memories of that night were already fragmented, outlined mostly by color: red flames, yellow sparks, black shadows. "I thought you said Zo burned down the Dungeon," I said, frowning.

"Zo did—the first time. But you've changed things. And this time V started the fire."

"But why?" I asked, my memories fighting each other inside my mind, each one claiming to be the true one.

"Because you asked him to," Leo said quietly. He didn't look at me, but I heard the pain in his voice. "And so I let him."

"I did?" I didn't remember telling V anything of the sort. I told him to build the door, not burn down the Dungeon. But I also remembered sitting next to Jason on my back porch, watching him write a note in the margins of the plans. There had been something important about that note. Something worth remembering.

"You said the door had to be started on the first day of spring," Leo said.

"Right."

"And how long did it take V to build the door?"

"Eight weeks," I said. "The plans were very specific about the timing."

Leo smiled sadly. "So what happened eight weeks after the first day of spring?"

I thought back, counting the days, trying to line up the timeline with my spotty memory.

And then I knew.

My hand flew to my throat, clutching the locket around my neck.

Leo saw the motion and nodded. "That's right. That was the night the Dungeon burned."

"That was the same fire?" As soon as I asked the question, I answered it, the pieces clicking into place. "Of course it was. The last step in the process was burning down the door. The refiner's fire." I looked up at Leo in horror. I reached for his arm, feeling it tremble a little under my touch. "It *was* my fault the Dungeon burned down. I didn't think about that when I told V . . . Oh, Leo, I'm so sorry."

He covered my hand with his own. "It's all right, Abby. I understand. Sometimes all we can do is what has to be done. And it had to be done. *Bisogna chiudere il cerchio.*"

"You said that before. What does it mean?" I asked. "What needs to be closed?" I recognized a few of the words from Dante's lessons.

"The loop has to be closed," Leo repeated.

"I don't understand," I said. "What loop?"

"Certain things have to happen because they have already happened. And if those things don't happen one way, they have to happen another way."

I knitted my eyebrows together. "I still don't understand."

Leo patted my hand again, looking me in the eyes. "You will." He straightened his back, brushing his hands together, and somehow, in the process, let go of me altogether. "Now, shall we find the door that has cost us so much?" He offered me a gentle smile. "Shall we bring Dante home?"

I grinned in reply. "It's about time."

Leo led me across the blasted landscape to what would have been the far corner of the Dungeon's back room. He scuffed away a mound of ash and dust with the toe of his shoe. A river of dirt broke free, pouring like a waterfall over the edge, and was swallowed up by the black hole in the ground.

I coughed into my elbow, covering my nose and mouth.

Stairs led down to the underground, and Leo tapped the first step with his foot. The top crust of soot broke away, exposing the crumbling and broken stone beneath.

Leo tested his weight on the step before turning and offering me a smile. "Be careful," he said.

I nodded and followed him down. The air felt dry on my skin and still carried the faint smell of smoke. The staircase curved ever so slightly under my feet, and when I took those last few steps around the bend and saw what waited for me on the basement floor, I stopped entirely. My breath slipped out of me with an exhaled "Oh" of surprise and wonder.

There wasn't much light filtering in from above, but there was enough.

V had indeed upheld his end of the bargain. The door he had built for me towered almost to the ceiling. It wasn't as polished as Dante's door, and the carvings were not quite as intricate or precise. But the wood was as black as night, scorched from the fire that had simultaneously consumed it and completed it.

Three gaping squares ran along the edge like missing teeth in a jaw.

I hurried forward, brushing past Leo, who waited at the foot of the stairs, his face turned away.

The hinge sat next to the door, the polished brass catching the available light and making it easy to see. The binder—now tattered and worn around the edges—leaned next to it. A note had been written in the gray ash on the floor in front of the door.

Your turn.

—V

A set of footprints headed away from the door, leaving two or three imprints in the dust before disappearing midstride. Apparently V hadn't bothered to wait around once he had finished his task.

I picked up the hinge. The brass machine was just as I remembered it: the color, the designs, the weight. It even felt the same in my hands as I turned it over, smoothly pulling it open almost to its full length. The sound of metal on metal was loud in the quiet basement.

Leo gently picked up the binder from the floor. His hands shook.

I collapsed the hinge and cradled it in my arms. Returning to Leo's side, I gave him a small hug. "Thank you," I said. "I know it hasn't been easy, but I couldn't have done this without you. You've been a good friend to me. And a good brother to Dante."

Leo paused, and then inclined his head toward the free-standing door that dominated the room. "Do you need any help?"

I shook my head. "I don't think so. If V followed the plans, everything should be fine. I should be okay." I hesitated. "But, if you wouldn't mind, could you wait for me outside—just in case?"

"Of course," Leo said with a quiet dignity. "I'll wait as long as you need me to."

"Thank you," I said.

Leo stepped back and turned, one foot on the steps. "Good luck, Abby." Then he climbed the stairs to the surface, leaving me alone.

Returning to the black door, I felt a bubble of excitement and anticipation lift inside me. The last time I had stood before a door like this with a hinge in my hands, I was saying good-bye. Not this time, though. This time there would be no farewells, there would be only a welcome.

I ran my fingers over the three holes in the door, the wood surprisingly smooth and cool under my touch. My eyes followed the lines of the spirals and stars carved onto the surface. The small heart with the keyhole was missing, but I hadn't expected to see it. The key I held in my locket would only unlock the other side of the door. I focused on the sinuous curve of the two hourglass bulbs as they met in the center, separated by a narrow space.

I pressed my palm to the spot, feeling the rush of blood in my body that made my fingertips tingle. The only thing separating me from Dante now was a wooden door an inch thick.

I stepped back and extended the hinge to its full height. As the hinge clicked into place, I heard a chime deep inside my inner ear. The shivering note reverberated through me, rippling and turning on itself first in a harmony, then a melody, before rising upward on a high scale of music like a choir's shout.

Warmth wrapped around the base of my spine and I closed my eyes, acting on instinct and memory.

The hinge fit into place without protest and, as the metal met the wood, the warmth inside me licked fire along my bones. The music fell into a familiar pattern, a recognizable cadence, almost like a voice calling out. The words reached me through the music.

Love . . . always . . .

I took a deep breath, feeling the swirling energy in my body coalesce into a diamond point of light behind my heart.

Abby . . . my love . . .

Opening my eyes, I pushed the door inward with a single shove.

A wall of darkness greeted me and a gust of hard, bitter-cold air filled the room. It was the same cold that I had felt when I'd reached out to Dante through the veil of my dreams, only this time it wasn't just my hand that flashed to numbness but my entire body. I hissed in pain as a cracking cold snapped around me, icing my joints.

I managed to stumble back a few steps, but I couldn't take my eyes off the door. My heart was loud in my ears. I counted each beat, thinking how each one would bring me closer to Dante.

The darkness in the door moved, flexing and pulsing as though someone on the other side was struggling to push through, but couldn't quite break free.

This was the same devouring darkness that had unraveled Tony; I wasn't going to let it do the same to Dante. Not when he was so close.

A portion from Dante's last letter returned to me then: "Hold on to me, Abby, to my memory, to the time we spent together and the dreams of the future we shared. That way, a part of me will still be alive with you wherever—and whenever—we are."

I summoned my best memories of Dante: seeing him walking down the auditorium aisle at school with snow in his hair; hearing his voice reciting poetry—both his own and that from classic literature; his arms curving around me in a protective embrace that made me feel like I was safe enough to be my best self. I recalled the countless conversations we'd had about our lives, our dreams, and our hopes. I pulled to the forefront of my mind each and every time he said my name.

The darkness seemed to thin a little, turning a lighter shade of black.

I focused on the memories of all the times when he had helped me, from the large ones—like protecting me from Zo—to the small, almost unnoticed moments—like when he offered me his coat to keep me warm or when he opened a door for me. I matched up each memory with a time when I had been able to help him, when I had made him laugh, or relax, or feel like it was safe to confide in me.

Our lives were intertwined. I would not let the darkness take him away again.

The black bled to gray—like smoke, like ice, like air—and then it was gone.

In its place, a white flare flashed. I raised my hand to block out the light from my eyes. Distantly, I heard the sound of the door closing. When it clicked shut, I gasped, feeling the cold release its hold on me. The music in my body hit one final note and then faded away as well.

Blinking the light-blindness from my eyes, I lowered my hand.

Dante di Alessandro Casella stood before me.

Time immediately slowed, stretching and expanding around me—around us—encompassing the enormity of the moment. In that singular breath of time, I opened myself to the emotions that roared through me, welcoming the recognition that ignited a fire in my mind and gave wings to my heart. The tears I tasted on my lips were sweet with joy.

He wore the same dark jeans and heavy boots he had worn the last time I had seen him all those weeks ago.

The differences were more noticeable. His tall frame seemed thinner, leaner than before, honed like a blade that could cut shadow from bone. His shirt, once smooth and tight across his shoulders, was wrinkled and hung loose over his chest, the sleeves rolled up over his forearms. His dark hair, once bright with curls, was dull and shaggy. The planes of his face were still as familiar to me as my own, but the angles of his cheekbones were more pronounced and the muscles in his jaw tighter. His eyes were the luminous gray of rain-slicked steel, and they glimmered with the knowledge of what lay beyond the darkness and the edges of time itself.

I felt a chill drape over me. This wasn't the same Dante I had said good-bye to on the banks of the river. This man had survived the darkness and had emerged on the other side as a master of time. This man was a hunter, a predator with the taste of his quarry's blood already in his mouth. It couldn't be the same man who had told me he loved me, who had kissed me so tenderly and passionately—could it?

His hands hung by his side, and banded around his wrists were the same chains branded into his flesh that he had worn for so long, though now they had changed from matte black to shimmering gold.

I swallowed hard at the sight of him, feeling the first blushing touch of heat in the pit of my stomach. I had dreamed about Dante's hands for months. His confident hands, flipping and spinning glass bottles behind the bar of the Dungeon. His strong hands, fastening a locket around my neck. His gentle hands, writing of his love to me in a letter I had memorized by heart.

It had been the touch of his hand that had kept us connected while we had been separated by darkness and dreams.

I had imagined so many times the moment when Dante's hands would reach out to caress me again, and now that the possibility had become reality, the heat in my belly turned molten.

And when his soft, expressive mouth, able to communicate

his emotions without a single word, smiled that small smile he reserved for me, I knew that behind the predator's eyes lived Dante's tender, artistic spirit and beneath the hunter's skin beat Dante's wildly passionate heart. The chill that had frozen me in place melted and I shifted my weight forward, propelling me a step in his direction.

Dante immediately held up his hand to stop me in my tracks.

"Abby," he said, his voice raw with emotion, his eyes searching mine. He reached out his hand toward me, but stopped before he actually touched me; I could see the tremors running through his fingers. The light wreathed the gold around his wrists with a pale shimmer. "Is it really you?"

I had so many questions, but I swallowed them all. Dante's focus was so intense that I felt the pressure of it inside me. He took a step closer and the tension in the air between us changed, suddenly filling with endless potential, limitless possibilities, and unspoken promises.

Dante began to circle around me slowly, drinking in the sight of me from all angles. I shifted a little, turning slightly to keep my face toward him. I wanted to see as much of him as I could too. To be so close to him and yet no closer was agony. Once again, I shifted my weight from my heels to my toes, ready to take that final step and be in his arms.

"No," he said, his voice low in his throat. "Not yet. Wait."

I closed my eyes, all my senses attuned to tracking his progress as he stepped closer to me in an ever-tightening spiral. I could feel him behind me, the heat from his body arcing to mine like lightning. A whisper of air breathed along the back of my neck, and the hairs on the backs of my arms lifted in response. I felt him curve around my right side, and I turned my face to follow him like a flower tracking the summer sun. He passed in front of me, and I caught his familiar musky scent. I heard the rustle of his clothes as he walked slowly and deliberately around me, close enough to touch, but still a world away.

Then I felt him lean down and I heard him whisper in my ear, "*Mio angelo*. You are even more beautiful than I remember. How is that possible?"

I shivered as much from the nearness of his lips to my skin as I did from the words. The darkness behind my eyes spun and I swayed, dizzy as though I had been the one spinning instead of standing still, caught in the vortex of his desire.

Dante stood behind me, his fingers lighting on the curve of my neck, his touch as delicate as a snowflake falling and as hot as lava. I bowed my head, inhaling quickly as the heat from his touch scorched through me. I felt him gently lift the chain of my silver necklace with his thumb. He brushed the tip of his finger over the brand that remained on my skin.

"This is new," he said.

He followed the mark with his fingers as it curved around my neck and crossed the front of my collarbone. He paused for a moment, and I was sure he could feel the pounding of my heartbeat like the aftershocks of an earthquake. He slipped his hands back over my shoulders, pressing his palms flat against my shoulder blades. Then he placed a soft kiss on the nape of my neck where the clasp of the locket rested.

"I am sorry that holding my heart has brought you pain."

I opened my eyes and turned quickly in his embrace to

face him. I could see myself reflected in his dark, star-shaded eyes.

I couldn't stand it any longer; I had to touch him. I pressed my body to his, cupping his face with my hands, my palms fitting naturally along his cheeks, his jaw. "It was worth it so long as I could keep your heart safe—keep *you* safe."

Threading my fingers through his hair, I pulled him to me, finally claiming the kiss I had dreamed about since the black door had closed behind him on the bank.

I could tell he was surprised at my insistence, but only for a moment. Then his lips warmed beneath mine, shaping themselves to match mine, returning gentleness for my fierceness until I was finally convinced that he wasn't a dream, that he wasn't going to disappear into the darkness again, that the Dante I had been waiting for had truly and completely returned to me.

Pulling back a fraction of an inch, I smiled at him. "Welcome home," I said. And then I kissed him again.

CHAPTER 18

Sometime later, I slowly felt the world stop spinning and start to return to normal.

Dante still held me close, his hands locked around the small of my back and his cheek pressed against the top of my head. "*Grazie,* Abby," he whispered. "Thank you for keeping your promise."

"How could I not? I'm just following your example." I traced my fingers along the back of his neck. I loved the feel of his skin. All those months when he had held himself apart from me, afraid to touch me because he knew too much contact would upset his carefully controlled balance, and then the weeks when he'd been a voice in the darkness had been terrible. I was relieved to think that perhaps those times were behind us.

I tightened my grip. "It didn't hurt you, did it? The darkness, I mean."

A tremor ran through his body. "It didn't want to let me go," he said quietly. "Once Tony was . . ." He cleared his throat. "Once I was alone, it seemed to be worse. It was like, instead of an absence of time, there was a concentration of it. Almost like the process was accelerating." He pulled me closer. "I'd forgotten how intense it could be."

"I'm sorry about Tony," I said, trying to focus on the good memories I had of him instead of the sound of his screams. "I wish I could have saved him, too."

Dante leaned back to look at me, his eyes soft and warm.

"What?" I asked.

"Tony wasn't your friend. You barely knew him, and what you did know about him wasn't good. He brought pain into your life. And yet, you would have saved him like you saved me if you'd had the chance."

"I would have tried," I said, feeling a little embarrassed. "No one should be lost in the dark."

"I was lost," Dante said, his face serious. "There, at the end. I knew I couldn't hold out much longer, and I didn't want to go without a fight. Not when I knew you were fighting so hard to reach me."

I bit my lip, remembering Valerie's story about Dante searching in the dark. I knew now how close I had come to losing him forever.

"And then I found it. The door opened, and there you were, calling me out of the darkness into the light." He gently traced his thumb across my cheek. "You were as bright as the sun. Seeing you there—it was like I could see your soul. It was the most beautiful thing I've ever seen. You are the bravest person I know, Abigail Edmunds." Leaning down, he kissed me, gently, intensely.

I felt the heat of his body next to mine as I kissed him back.

Sometime later, lost in the sweetness of his embrace, I almost missed it when Dante said my name.

"Abby?" Dante said again.

"Mm-hmm?" I leaned back a little, opening my eyes. A thrill ran through me at the sight of him. He was still here, really here. I hoped the thought would never get old.

"Um, where are we?"

"The basement of the Dungeon."

"It looks like someone tried to burn it down."

"Someone did."

"Who?"

"This time it was V."

"What?" Dante said, gently untangling himself from my embrace and taking a step back. "What do you mean 'this time'?"

I sighed and surveyed the ruined room. "So much has happened since you've been gone, I don't even know where to begin."

"How about at the beginning?"

I looked up at him and grinned. "Once upon a time, there was a very smart man named Leonardo da Vinci and he built a time machine."

Dante didn't smile back.

"Okay, sorry." I couldn't help but be a little giddy. Dante was back. That thought filled my brain and made it hard to think about anything else.

"Abby, you said I was trapped in there for weeks. I need to

know what's been happening." Dante rested his hands on my waist, holding me away from him.

Sighing again, I ran my hands down over his shoulders and his arms. "It's a long story. I'd rather not get into it down here. Come on." I clasped his hand in mine and tugged him toward the stairs.

We'd taken only a few steps when Dante stopped in front of the door, pulling me to his side.

He tilted his head back, looking up at the towering door. A shiver flashed through his hand; I could feel the sweat break out on his skin.

"V did a good job, didn't he?" I said quietly. "It's not as good as yours, of course, but it worked."

Dante's throat moved as he swallowed hard. "It shouldn't have."

"What?"

He squeezed my hand even tighter. "See this?" He pointed to a cluster of stars in the upper right-hand corner of the frame. "This is supposed to be the constellation for Aquarius, the water-bearer, but it's missing a star in the pattern. And I don't see the balance scales of Libra anywhere."

"But what about the modifications you made? I told V exactly what you told me to do."

Dante traced the patterns with his free hand, the gold around his wrist bright against the dark wood. His eyes scanned the door as though he could read the secrets written there. "This is good here. And this." He lapsed into Italian, muttering under his breath. "But why did he do this?" His fingers jumped to another spot of stars and he exhaled in frustration, shaking his head. "A beginner's mistake."

"So, wait, if V didn't build the door correctly, why did it work?" Anger and confusion warred inside me. I had trusted V; we had a deal. Had he betrayed me? Or was it what Dante had said: a beginner's mistake? My mouth went dry at the thought that I'd blindly jumped into the unknown when so much was at stake.

"I don't know." Dante looked at me with gray eyes gone dark. "I think *you* made it work."

I shook my head. "I didn't do anything. I just wanted you back safe."

Dante glanced from me to the door. "However it happened, I'm glad you did what you did." He ran his hand down the spine of the hinge until he reached the center of the middle square. He pushed on a depression in the brass and the hinge released from the wood with a quiet click. Extracting it from the door, Dante deftly collapsed it back to its portable size. "I don't think anyone else will try to use the door, but just in case . . ." He handed me the brass machine. "I'll feel better knowing it's in good hands."

I held the hinge against my stomach, feeling the sharp edges with my fingers. I looked up at Dante's serious, shadowed eyes, and I nodded, accepting the responsibility. I had helped in the creation of this door; in a way it was as much mine as the original had been Dante's.

"I'll take good care of it," I said.

"I know you will," Dante said. Then he smiled. "Now, can

we get out of here? I can't tell you how much I want to see the sun."

"You did promise me that when you saw me, you'd sit with me under a tree and tell me all your stories."

Dante grinned. "You know I always keep my promises."

"I know you do." I reached for his hand again, and this time nothing stopped us on our way up the stairs and into the light.

"Leo?" I called as I emerged from the basement, blinking in the sunshine. "Leo, it worked!"

Leo turned at the sound of my voice, hope replacing the worry on his face. His faded blue eyes were bright with unshed tears and he crossed the broken ground in four long strides, sweeping Dante into an embrace.

I stepped back as Dante wrapped his arms around Leo's back and closed his eyes in relief. The lingering tension drained out of Dante's body as he held tight to the man he thought of as his father. I knew Leo wasn't Dante's father, but he *was* family, and that was what mattered.

I thought about my missing family—my father and my sister—and I felt tears well up in my eyes. I let them fall, brushing them away with my free hand. I wondered if I would ever be able to embrace them again, or if they would be lost to me forever. Dante was back, but we were still a long way from stopping Zo and setting to right all that he had changed.

"I'm so glad you're all right," Leo said, holding Dante at arm's length and looking him over.

Dante laughed. "I'm fine, *Papà*. I'm fine."

Leo slapped him on the back and pulled him in for one last hug. *"Benvenuto,"* he said. *"Benvenuto, caro."*

"What happened here?" Dante asked, stepping back and brushing his hand across his eyes. He looked around the wasteland. "Abby said V burned down the Dungeon?"

Leo nodded. "It's complicated."

"That's what Abby said." Dante put his arm around me, pulling me close.

I leaned against his side, grateful for his strength. The intense emotions were catching up to me and I felt a wave of exhaustion wash through me.

Dante noticed. "Perhaps we should go somewhere else to talk about it. Someplace Abby can sit down."

"Of course," Leo said, a concerned line creasing his forehead.

He led us back to his car parked beside the curb, and Dante helped me into the backseat. He slipped into the seat next to me and wrapped his hand firmly around mine.

I rested my head against his shoulder, closing my eyes as he gently brushed my hair away from my face. It felt so good to be close to him that I lost track of where we were until Leo pulled up in front of my house.

Looking out the window, I shook my head. "We should go somewhere else," I said.

Leo turned around in his seat. "There's nowhere else to go. You both need some rest and something to eat. And we need to talk about some important things—things best discussed in private."

"That's just it," I said. "If Zo is watching me, tracking me through the places I go, what better place to find me than at home? It's too dangerous." My heart sank even though I knew it was the truth. Was there no place safe for me anymore?

"Yes, it's a risk, but if we're careful, we should be fine," Leo said calmly. "There is something to be said for hiding in plain sight, after all."

I nodded reluctantly. Leo had a point, and no one knew more about hiding in plain sight than he did.

Dante and Leo followed me inside.

"Mom?" I called out. In the old days, Mom would have been home in the afternoon, but now I wasn't sure what her schedule was. As bad as it sounded, I hoped she was at work. There were too many questions I didn't want to have to answer, too many things I couldn't explain.

Luck was on my side. There was a note from my mom taped to the refrigerator: *Home late. Order pizza.*

I plucked the twenty-dollar bill from beneath a magnet for Pizza Box Delivery. Turning to Dante and Leo, I smiled. "You guys hungry?"

Twenty minutes later, the pizza was on its way, the hinge was safely hidden in my sock drawer, the binder was locked in the desk, and Dante was in the shower, his clothes already tumbling in the dryer.

I had insisted that Dante take some time to clean up. He needed to do more than wash away a layer of sweat and grime and, although it might take some time for the shadows to disappear completely from his eyes, I knew how therapeutic a hot shower could be.

I sat down across from Leo at the kitchen table.

Leo looked at me and smiled, his faded blue eyes soft and kind. "Thank you. I don't know how I can ever repay you."

I shrugged a little. "You don't have to repay me. I just was trying to do the right thing. I wanted Dante home as much as you did."

"I know, but if it weren't for you—your persistence, your courage—Dante might have been lost forever and we might never have known what happened to him." Leo drew in a deep breath. "This wasn't the first time I thought I'd lost him. Saying good-bye to him in Italy was hard enough. But that first year after he traveled through the time machine . . ." Leo shook his head. "I wondered if he would even survive those first few months. And then I wondered, if he did survive, if there would be anything left of my brother at all, or if he'd crack under the constant pressure before he could learn to control it."

"He doesn't break easily, you know," I said, glancing upward. I could hear the water of the shower running through the pipes.

"I know," Leo said, his face serious. "But he was cracking fierce."

"So what stopped him?" I asked, intrigued at this hidden chapter of Dante's past. "What happened?"

Leo smiled at me. "You happened. He met you. And you

brought him back to life. So, thank you, Abby. Thank you for bringing my brother back to me. In more ways than one."

I felt the familiar prickling in my cheeks and nose that warned of tears. I took a deep breath and rubbed my eyes. "You should tell him, you know," I said. "He should know the truth. It would mean the world to him."

Leo's smile turned sad. "I know. And perhaps someday I will. But not right now."

The doorbell rang at the same time the dryer buzzed. I pushed back from the table. "Would you mind taking Dante his clothes? I'll take care of the pizza."

Leo had gone upstairs by the time I returned to the kitchen. I set the box down on the table and headed to the cupboard for plates and glasses.

"Need any help?" Dante asked from the doorway.

I turned around and had to stifle a gasp.

Fresh from the shower and dressed in his clean clothes, he looked like a new man. His skin gleamed like polished wood, and he had slicked back his dark hair to a blunt edge at his neckline. His confidence was back as well, a certain set of his shoulders, a look in his gray eyes that spoke of control and balance.

He locked his gaze with mine and slowly walked toward me.

I caught my breath, wondering how such a beautiful man had ended up in my kitchen, let alone my life.

He stood before me and I could smell the blend of soap and laundry detergent mixed with the musky-sweet scent that I had come to associate with Dante.

His eyes never left mine as he leaned in close, closer, and his arm brushed mine as he reached past me to pluck a glass off the shelf. "Thank you for lunch," he said, stepping away with a grin just shy of wicked.

Clutching the stack of plates to my chest like a shield, I exhaled and tried to calm my racing heart. It wasn't fair that just being near him could make me weak in the knees.

I joined Dante at the table, handing out plates and pizza while Leo poured water into the glasses.

There was something soothing about the routine of a meal, and I was glad that Leo had insisted we come here. I sat down, thinking that it was good to be home, even for a short time.

As we ate, I brought Dante up to date on what had been happening, Leo chiming in as needed. It was harder than I'd thought it would be to tell the story without mentioning Zo's name. The few times I slipped up and said it out loud, I felt a shiver in the air, as though a trap was about to spring shut. I finally settled on calling him "L" for Lorenzo and hoped that Zo wasn't listening for that particular nickname.

Some of the story Dante knew from our conversations while I'd been on the dream-side of the bank, but most of it was new. He asked a few questions, but mostly he listened quietly and attentively. Some of the details were new to Leo, too, and by the time I was done explaining everything, I had drunk two glasses of water and the last slice of pizza was long gone.

Dante was still for a moment, absorbing the flow of information. He placed his hands flat on the table and then turned his eyes to me. "You are indeed a brave woman, Abby."

"I thought you said I was dangerous," I said with a wry smile. My throat felt sore from the constant talking.

"Is there a difference?"

"I guess it depends on which side you are on."

"Then I always want to be on your good side," he said. He reached for my hand, lifting it to his lips and pressing a kiss to the curve of my palm.

I felt a shimmer of electricity run through my arm.

"Your turn to talk. Tell me about these," I said, nodding at the gold bands around his wrists.

Dante looked down at his hands, turned them over. "I don't know what happened. They were black when I went in, and gold when I came out."

"L has them, you know. So does V. Did Tony?" I looked at Dante as the familiar shiver ran between us at the mention of the names. I mouthed *Sorry* and winced, reminding myself that I needed to be more careful.

Dante's mouth thinned and a shadow rimmed his eyes in black. "If he did, I never saw them."

I swallowed hard, remembering Tony's fate. I traced my fingers around the gold, interlocking loops.

"What?"

I noticed that the hair on Dante's arm stood up at my touch and I heard the quiet quiver in his voice. I smiled. Perhaps I wasn't the only one who felt weak in the knees.

"I wonder if going through the door a second time . . . reversed things."

"Because we were going back in time?"

I nodded. "What if it was more literal than anyone expected? Maybe going back was like going in reverse."

"Then shouldn't my black chains have reversed to white? Or at least silver?"

"It's just a working theory," I said with a wry smile.

"But it's a good theory," Leo said thoughtfully. "Didn't you say that when L changed things in your life, the world around you reversed for a moment from white to black?"

I nodded. "Though it hasn't happened for a little while. I wonder why. I don't suppose it's because he has decided to leave me alone."

"No, I don't think so. There is something about you that has drawn his attention," Leo said.

"Obsession is more like it," I muttered.

Leo and Dante exchanged a glance.

"Wait," I said, holding up my hands. "Do you guys know something I don't? Something about L?"

Dante shifted in his chair. Leo looked away.

"What are you not telling me? Now is not the time to hold on to our secrets." Frustration gave my words a bite, but I didn't try to soften them.

"We all know how long L can hold a grudge," Dante said quietly. "And we know how far he's willing to go to exact his revenge."

"Yeah, I know. He ruined my family and redirected the river." I looked at Dante and shook my head. "You said letting him go was our best chance to stop him, but he's doing whatever he wants with the river. How are we supposed to stop him now?"

"Yes, the majority of the river may be under his control, but V gave you a clue when he said he couldn't travel beyond the point where your timeline intersected with Zero Hour." Dante covered my hands with his. "In a way, you have already stopped him. At least a little. You are protecting a key part of the river, Abby—a part L can't see, that he can't touch directly. And the more you are able to bring under your protection, the more we can control where L goes and what he is able to do. *You* are the key to stopping him."

"How can I protect the river? It's not like I can change when I first met Zero Hour and protect more of my past."

"No," Leo interjected, "but you *can* protect your future—as well as the future of other people. Remember when we talked about fixing things in place?"

"You mean by taking pictures?" I asked.

Leo nodded. He stood up from the table. "I think it's time to put our idea to the test. May I use your phone?"

I waved to the phone on the kitchen wall but kept my attention on Dante. "So why me?" I asked him, still feeling frustrated. "I'm nobody. Why isn't he targeting you, or Leo?"

"Because neither one of us poses the kind of threat you do to his goal," Dante answered.

"What is his goal?" I asked. "V didn't seem to know. Or if he did, he wouldn't tell me."

Dante hesitated, his gray eyes dark with thought. "When you traveled to the bank today, did you notice anything different?"

"About the bank? Yeah, sure—"

"No, about how you got there. The *traveling*."

I thought back to the moment when Leo, V, and I had slipped from here to there. "It was a lot easier to reach the bank today," I said finally, knowing the truth before I said the words. "And I don't think it's because I'm getting better at it or because I had help. It's because the barriers are thinning, aren't they?"

Dante nodded, the shadows sharpening the angles of his cheekbones and the set of his jaw.

"What happens if the barriers between the river and the bank disappear entirely?" I asked, dread settling like a weight in my stomach. "What if all the walls come down?"

"The river and the bank can never mix—L was right when he called them oil and water. And if the barrier between them falls, both will be destroyed. The river will be polluted beyond saving. And the bank, instead of being a place untouched by time, will become a place corrupted by time."

"It would be chaos," I whispered.

"Worse. It would be the end of everything." Dante's face paled as he spoke. "If the barriers break, then Zo could simply dam the river wherever he wants and cut off the diseased portion of the bank and start over fresh. With a clean slate ahead of him, he could erase the world's history on a whim and rewrite the future according to his desires. Nothing would happen without his hand shaping it. Only his choices would matter. Only his vision. Time itself wouldn't even flow without his permission."

I felt a fist of ice-cold terror grip me. I didn't want to hear any more, but Dante wasn't quite done.

"Change isn't enough anymore. It's control he's after. Total and complete control."

"And it's up to me to stop him?" I asked, feeling the impossibility of the task, like being asked to hold back the tide. I hadn't realized I was crying until Dante brushed his fingers across my cheek and they came away wet.

"Leo is immune to his actions; L *can't* touch him. And I am more his equal than he'd probably like to admit; he *won't* touch me—not yet. Not until he tests my limits." Dante's voice was low but strong. "I told you once that our best chance for success against him would come from the choices you make. You made an important choice at the door. And the choices you are making now—and those you'll make in the future—can still change things."

"What if I choose the wrong thing?" I asked, my voice sounding like it belonged to someone else. "What if I just make things worse?"

"You won't," Dante said, cupping my face with his hands. "Because I believe in you." He leaned in and kissed me until my doubt and my tears were gone.

Leo cleared his throat behind us, and Dante let me go with one final brush of his lips across my cheek.

"I called my friend at the camera shop, and she's willing to help us today," Leo said, holding out the phone to me. "Call Natalie. We don't have any time to waste."

CHAPTER 19

Leo pulled up in front of the small shop at the end of the row. The building looked almost the same as the others in the strip mall: squat and square. But where the other shops were beige, brown, or gold, this one was painted black from top to bottom. Black paper covered the window next to the door, which was also dark with paint. It reminded me of Dante's black door; what waited for me behind this black door also had the potential to change my life. I couldn't decide if it was a good omen or a warning.

Dante, sitting next to me in the backseat, tensed at the sight. I reached over and wrapped my hand around his, feeling the strong bones beneath his skin lock into a fist.

Through the glare of the sun, I could just make out the two words written on a small sign in the window: *The Darkroom.*

"This is it?" I asked.

Leo nodded, stepping out of the car and opening the back door for me. Dante did the same for Natalie, who had been sitting in the front passenger seat.

"And tell me again why we're here?" she asked.

"Leo's friend works here," I said, coming around to join the three of them on the curb. "He says she can help us take some pictures." My hand instinctively connected with Dante's.

"It doesn't look like a studio," Natalie said, shading her eyes from the sun.

"It's not," Leo said, nodding to the sign. "It's a darkroom. And that's what we need."

"Is it even open?" Dante asked, glancing at me. "It doesn't look like anyone's here."

I shrugged and looked to Leo.

"The darkroom is usually open only on the weekends," he said, "but I called Lizzy and she agreed to help us as a special favor to me." Leo knocked on the door and stepped back. "I told her it was an emergency."

After a few moments, I heard a bolt being thrown back and then the door swung open. A small woman stood framed in the doorway. She wore a pair of faded jeans and a man's denim work shirt with the sleeves rolled up past her elbows. Her hands were red and weathered. Her hair was mostly hidden beneath a multicolored scarf, the patterns broken like a mosaic, though a few dark strands escaped to fall across her dark, piercing eyes.

"Elisabetta," Leo said, grinning and opening his arms to engulf her in a hug. "It's good to see you. Thank you for helping us."

"For you, Leo, it's no bother. Come in, come in," Lizzy said, gesturing for the rest of us to follow as she pulled Leo along behind her. She launched into a fast-paced Italian monologue that barely allowed room for Leo to respond.

The three of us exchanged a glance and stepped inside. I really needed Dante to teach me Italian one of these days.

As stark and plain as the outside of the building was, the inside was a riot of light and images. Black-and-white photographs of all sizes covered the walls, some as small as postage stamps, others taking up half the wall or more. One wall appeared to be devoted solely to portraits, a variety of emotions as individual as the faces they belonged to. It reminded me of the Dungeon's Signature Wall—a place where you could leave your mark on the world.

Two cloth bins stood by the door, each one filled with small, card-sized pictures. Three glass shelves jutted out from the wall and held an assortment of cameras and lenses, each one tagged with a handwritten price. There was a small, antique cash register on a table with mismatched legs in the corner. A second door was almost hidden behind stacks of prints. I suspected it led to the actual darkroom. The room felt more cozy than cluttered. I loved it immediately.

"Hey, guys," Natalie hissed, waving me and Dante over to her side while Leo and Lizzy continued their conversation. "Look at this."

On the wall was a small, delicate print about the size of my hand. The image showed a Japanese pagoda with multilayered roofs and curling edges. The beautiful building stood by the side of a lake. A cherry tree was in bloom, and a few blossoms had been captured floating away on the breeze. The picture had been printed on what looked like rice paper, making the image look more like a watercolor than a photograph. I felt a great sense of calm as I looked at the art, and I thought that if someone could capture the feeling of a haiku, this would be what it would look like. I checked the single name printed in the corner: Dahla. Even the photographer's name was lyrical and seemed to fit the image perfectly.

Next to the picture was a larger one, square like a window, showing a view of interlaced beams of steel, curving and twisting upward in a geometric pattern that dared the eye to follow the maze.

"What is it, do you think?" I asked Natalie.

"It's the Eiffel Tower," Lizzy answered, stepping up next to us. Her Italian accent had all but vanished. "My friend Angela shot this the last time she was in Paris."

"It doesn't look like the tower," Natalie said, leaning closer.

"That's because Angela stood beneath it and shot straight up. She said she felt caged in, surrounded by all that steel, and liked the idea that the only way out was through."

"Isn't that the truth," Dante murmured at my side.

I agreed, thinking about narrow hallways enclosed in darkness and doors that led elsewhere. Sometimes the only choice you had was to go through.

Lizzy folded her arms and looked up at Dante. "And where has Leo been hiding you?" she asked. "A man with your looks, your build—" She took a step back to appraise Dante. "Yes, Leo should have brought you by long ago. You will sit for a portrait for me."

"Oh, no, thank you for the offer, but—" Dante started, a faint blush staining his face.

"It wasn't an offer," Lizzy said. Then she turned to me. "You must be Abby. Leo said you had a photography emergency."

"Well, I don't know that I'd call it that, exactly," I said, feeling oddly shy around this bold woman with her declarations and unflinching gaze.

"I told Abby you could teach her how to develop film and print her own pictures," Leo said from behind Dante.

Lizzy held my eyes. "Why are you interested in learning a lost art?" She flicked her gaze to Dante and then back to me. "Haven't you heard? Digital is the new standard."

I flushed a little at her tone. "Digital won't work for the kind of pictures I want to take."

"And what kind of pictures *do* you want?"

I looked around the room at all the various images covering the walls, from the weathered face of an old man laughing, to the wide sky stretching over a midwestern plain, to a rose resting on a table, the petals veined with shadow like wood grain. "I want pictures like these. The kind that can capture a moment, make it real, make it last. I need pictures that do more than reflect. I need pictures that are truth."

Lizzy narrowed her eyes thoughtfully. Then she nodded. "She'll do," she said to Leo. "I can teach her."

I felt like I had passed a test or a ritual. Dante slipped his arm around me, pulling me against his shoulder in a hug. Now I had to hope that Leo was right and that we could fix a point and a person in time. If we could, then we could prevent future changes, future heartbreak. Maybe we could even prevent Zo from cutting off the river.

"Come with me." Lizzy turned on her heel, heading for the door that would lead deeper into the Darkroom's hidden rooms. "I hope you've all cleared your schedules. This will take some time."

Dante gave me one last hug and pressed a kiss to my temple. "Have fun," he said with a smile. "Learn what you need to. Leo and I will talk to Natalie. We'll be ready when you are."

"Wish me luck," I said. As he turned away, I rested my hand on his arm and nodded to Natalie. "Be nice, okay? Don't go overboard. I need her to believe, not be terrified."

"Go," Dante said gently. "We'll be fine. I explained it to you, and you're not terrified of me, are you?"

I let my hand linger on his gold-wrapped wrist. "Not in the slightest," I said, lifting up on my toes so I could kiss the side of his mouth.

As I followed in Lizzy's wake, I looked back over my shoulder to see Leo and Dante join Natalie by the wall of portraits.

"Natalie?" Dante said. "We need to talk."

Smiling a little, I drew in a deep breath. If Dante and Leo couldn't convince Natalie of the truth, then no one could.

Lizzy slid the door open and stepped through. She looked back at me, gesturing for me to follow.

I joined Lizzy in the darkness beyond the door.

"I'll show you the process with one of my own pictures first," Lizzy said while we walked in the dark hallway. "Then you can try it with one of yours."

I rubbed at my arms, unsettled by the closeness of the walls, the shadows thick and heavy with the smell of chemicals. We turned once, then once more, the black hallway making two ninety-degree turns before releasing us into a small room lit with a soft white light. A row of metal sinks ran along one wall with an assortment of jugs and jars lined up on a shelf directly above. Posted on the wall was a chart divided into a grid, each small box filled with either the brand and type of film or a specific time.

The room reminded me of a laboratory: neat, clean, orderly, and with a peculiar smell that made me think of metal and disinfectant.

Lizzy picked up a small silver canister about the size of a thick paperback novel. A black rubber top jutted up from the center of the canister. "This is the developing tank," Lizzy said. She produced a roll of film from the pocket of her shirt. She set both items on the counter and picked up a sealed black bag with two sleeves attached. "The tank and the film go inside the bag." Suiting action to words, Lizzy slipped her hands inside the bag. "This part is a little tricky because it's all done by touch. Use a bottle cap opener to pry off the top of the film canister. Then, you simply wind the film onto the developing spool in a tight spiral from the inside out. It only winds one way, so you'll know when you've done it right. It's important not to let the film touch anything but the reel. The spool goes into the tank, the lid is put back in place, and then you're ready to go." The bag rustled as Lizzy maneuvered the film into position.

"Will you help me with that part?" I asked, nervous. I'd never done anything like this before and already I felt out of my element.

Lizzy shook her head. "If you don't do it yourself, you'll never learn how. Don't worry, the beginning is always the hardest part. It gets easier with practice."

I swallowed, nodding and focusing on Lizzy's every move.

Withdrawing the tank from the bag, Lizzy walked over to the sink. She checked the thermometer attached to the faucet, measured out a small amount of water, consulted the chart on the wall above the sink, and then mixed in the developer powder. Pouring the mixture into the developing tank, she thrust it into my hands.

Startled, I almost dropped the tank. "What do I do?"

Lizzy covered my hands with hers and gently flipped the tank up and down. "You have to agitate the film. So keep up this pace for exactly seven minutes—no more, no less."

As I rotated the tank, Lizzy sat down on a three-legged stool by the sink.

"How do you know Leo?" she asked me, leaning her head on her palm.

It was a surprisingly tricky question to answer. What did Lizzy know about Leo? Did she remember the Dungeon? I thought through my options before settling on a fragment of the truth. "He's like family to Dante." I hoped that would provide enough answer without revealing too much.

"Dante is the good-looking boy who won't sit for me."

I smiled a little and nodded. "Dante's just a little shy sometimes."

"He's not shy," Lizzy said dryly. "A boy who looks like that has never been shy." She watched me flip the tank up and then down. "No. He's hiding something."

The tank slipped in my fingers; I almost dropped it.

"Careful. Don't ruin the film."

"Sorry."

Lizzy moved to the sink, picked up a rag, and wiped down the counter. "There's something more to that boy. He's tense. You can see it in his body. In his eyes. He has secrets."

I knew Dante's secrets. I knew his truth and his hidden heart.

"The camera eye can often see beyond the surface to the layers beneath. That's why I want to photograph him. He's layered. Complicated."

This was a dangerous conversation to pursue. I felt fiercely protective of Dante. He had been lost in the darkness for so long, and now that he'd been reborn into the light I wanted to give him time to gain his bearings. I didn't want Lizzy or anyone else poking at him, analyzing him. And if anyone was going to take his picture, it was going to be me.

"Am I done?" I asked, the muscles in my arms starting to ache.

Lizzy glanced at the clock and nodded. "Good. Now pour the developer out and rinse out the film."

I did as directed, the water running cold over my hands. "What now?" I asked eagerly. As unfamiliar as the process was, it was fascinating, and I thought that I might have found a new hobby to explore.

Lizzy grinned at my enthusiasm. "You'll want to plug your nose for this next part." She lifted a jug from the shelf and uncapped it. A stench like vinegar, but a hundred times worse, filled the room.

I gagged, my nose burning, but managed to hold the tank steady while Lizzy poured the liquid inside and plugged the lid over the film.

"It's called a 'stop bath,' and that's exactly what it does—it stops the developing agent." Lizzy tightened the cap and replaced the jug. "Important note to remember about the stop bath: Never get it in your eyes—you could go blind from it." She nodded to the tank still in my hands. "Agitate it again. One minute. Then rinse."

I felt a tickle in my throat and coughed into my elbow. "What happens if you don't put in the stop bath?"

Lizzy shrugged. "The longer the film sits in the developer, the more the silver crystals in the film react to it and the denser the film becomes. If you don't use the stop bath, or if you don't use it long enough, the film will turn completely black and you'll lose whatever image you're trying to capture." She looked at the clock again. "Rinse."

I obeyed, wincing again as the vinegar smell brought tears to my eyes.

"Almost done," Lizzy said with a smile. "Now it's time for the fixer."

I looked up in surprise. "What's it called?"

"The fixer. It stabilizes the image and removes the unexposed silver crystals from the film. It essentially *fixes* the image in place so it's safe to bring it out into the light."

A smile rose to my lips. "Of course." I could almost feel Valerie's finger writing me a secret note: *You can fix it.* And her insistence: *The picture is power.* The pieces were coming together. My smile widened. Leo was right. This was going to work, I could feel it.

Lizzy added the fixer and leveled a stern gaze at me. "Ten minutes. I'll be back." She slipped out of the room.

I claimed her vacated seat and rotated the tank. The methodical movement was soothing, like a lullaby, and I let my thoughts drift along the breathing tide of my emotions.

It was so good to have Dante back, so *right*. And seeing him with Leo made me almost feel like my life was back to normal. Almost. I couldn't forget the gaping ache in my heart for my lost father and my forgotten sister. But at least we were working toward changing that. If we could fix Natalie in place—and the more I worked with Lizzy, the more convinced I was that we *could* make it work—then we would be that much closer to not only preventing changes but possibly reversing them.

I felt protected sitting in the back room of the Darkroom. As though the uncertainty that had overcome my life had been left at the door. Here I was focused. I had a purpose, a clear goal. It felt good to be in control of something again. Even if it was just a small developing tank nestled in the palms of my hands.

I hadn't realized the time had gone by so quickly until Lizzy appeared at my side again. "Good. I think we're ready to finish it." She took the tank from my hands and peeled back the lid. She pulled a container off the shelf and poured out the fixer. I imagined I could see the liquid glittering with stripped silver. Placing the tank in the sink, she turned the water on and let the stream wash away the excess chemicals. While the river ran from the faucet, Lizzy pulled open a drawer and rummaged around until she found a handful of clips. She held them up. "For drying the film."

"Is it always this complicated?" I asked, resting my arms on the counter and flexing my empty fingers.

Lizzy laughed. "Wait until we make prints. *That's* complicated." She extracted the film from the developing tank, pulling it free from the spiral and clipping it to the hooks to dry.

"I can see why no one really does this anymore."

"It's almost a forgotten art," Lizzy admitted, sorrow shadowing her face. She hung up the wet film and withdrew a second strip of film that had started to curl along the edges. "There is more to photography than just pushing a button. You have to mix the chemicals. Follow the rules. And learning to control the light and shadow?" She sighed in appreciation. "When done correctly, it's the perfect blend of art and science. And the outcome is like nothing else in the world."

"A ritual wrought with power," I murmured, remembering Dante's words about the process of building the time machine.

Lizzy smiled and nodded. "Exactly. I knew you'd understand. Not everyone can see what a photographer sees. And I knew when I saw you that you'd have an eye for seeing the truth."

"Thank you," I said, feeling a stillness settle over me as though the turbulent river had flowed into a gentle pool, granting me a moment to breathe, to rest. "What's next?"

"Next comes the art," Lizzy said with a grin and led me into another small room where the white lightbulb had been replaced with a red one. She selected an image from the roll of film and, using the same combination of chemicals and liquids—developer, stop bath, fixer, water—she worked her magic to bring the small square of white and black to life.

I watched in fascination as she controlled the amount of light projected through the image, as she coaxed the shadows into a deeper black. Watching her move through the motions was like watching a dancer. Every action was precise and exact, but fluid and graceful. She knew when to move the paper from one chemical bath to the next without having to consult the clock, relying instead on her internal rhythms of a lifetime of working with light and shadow, liquid and time.

She slipped the paper into the developer tray and motioned for me to join her by the sink.

"This is my favorite part," she admitted in a near-whisper as though we were in church or a hospital. "The moment the image is born."

She gently rocked the tray, allowing the water to wash over the paper, and slowly, almost magically, two figures appeared from what had once been a blank, white sheet.

"Who is it?" I asked, peeking over her shoulder.

Lizzy pointed to the man on the left. "That's my father, Giovanni, the summer before he died. And that's Leo. I swear he hasn't aged a day since this photograph was taken." She clucked her tongue and shook her head. "Would you look at that? Every time I try to print this, I get those black smudges by their hands."

I studied the two men in the photograph, their arms draped across each other's shoulders. Both had similar, strong features, and if I hadn't known better, I might have guessed they were brothers. But I did know better. I knew Leo's history, and more than that, I knew what the faded bands wrapped around both men's wrists meant. Giovanni had been one of Leo's flock of time travelers.

"How long have you known Leo?" I asked.

Lizzy shrugged, lifting the paper from the sink and pressing out the excess water. She laid it on a wire rack. "It seems like I've known Leo forever. He was friends with my father for a long time. I was little when my father died, but Leo still came around the shop to visit with my mother and me, see how we were doing, bring me presents." She laughed a little. "I once thought he might marry my mother, but he never asked. He told me his heart had been pledged to another." Lizzy tilted the picture toward her. "I always wondered who she was. The woman who had captured his heart."

I wondered too. Could it be the elusive Sofia? Maybe—but at the moment, I was more curious about something else. "Your father looks so young in this picture."

Lizzy nodded. "He was only thirty-nine when he died. The doctors said it was Alzheimer's, but I don't know. One day he was here. And the next . . ."

I stared at the faces washed by the water. They both looked forward, toward the light, in a perfectly captured moment of contentment. Then the red light shimmered off the wet paper, turning the white water to blood. I shivered a little, feeling an ache of sadness for Leo and all he'd left behind. And for Giovanni, who had tried to make a new life for himself with a wife and a child. And who had lost it all to the pressures of the relentless river.

Lizzy wiped her hands on a rag by the drying rack. She tucked a stray hair back under her scarf. "Well, that's the process. What do you think? Are you ready to try it for yourself?"

I brushed away a tear, hoping Lizzy wouldn't notice, and nodded. "Absolutely."

CHAPTER 20

Lizzy led me through the twisting hallways back to the picture-filled front room. I saw Natalie sitting on the one chair in the room, her face ashen, her eyes unfocused and distant. Dante crouched by her knee, his hand gripping the armrest of the chair. Leo was standing behind them and looked up as Lizzy and I entered the room.

"How did it go?" he asked, though the same question had been on my lips as well.

"She's a natural," Lizzy said.

Leo smiled. "I knew she would be."

"Is everything okay?" I asked quickly, looking from Leo to Natalie and back again.

"Everything's fine," Dante said, standing up and brushing his hair out of his eyes.

I caught my breath at the gesture. It was one I'd seen him make countless times before, but this time it simply reminded me that he was back. He was here, with me, and I could enjoy all those small gestures I'd missed while he was gone. A warmth filled me, and it was all I could do to keep the grin off my face.

Leo crossed to the glass shelves displaying Lizzy's selection of cameras and selected a small, boxy one from the middle shelf.

"Excellent choice," Lizzy said, nodding. "The Brownies were quite popular back in the day. Easy to use and perfect for a beginner."

Turning the camera over in his hands, Leo smiled quietly. "This was always one of my favorites. Mr. Adams taught me how to use one long ago. I'm happy to see you still have one." Leo crossed the small room and handed the camera to me.

I liked how the camera felt in my hands. Solid and stable.

"We'll take it," Leo said to Lizzy, reaching into his back pocket and withdrawing his wallet.

"Oh, Leo, you know your money is no good here," Lizzy said, slapping at his hand fondly.

"So it's a negotiation, is it?" A light gleamed in Leo's blue eyes. As he drew Lizzy to the far side of the room, he caught my eye and winked.

I smiled back at him, grateful for the small amount of privacy Leo had arranged. I held the camera at waist level and looked down at the small mirror set on top of the box, happy to see how clear everything seemed through the lens.

Dante caught me framing him with the camera and he smiled and gave a half wave.

I shaded the top of the camera with my hand so I could see him better and laughed a little at his upside-down image. Natalie still sat in the chair and I stepped closer to her.

"What did you tell her?" I asked Dante in a low voice.

"The truth," he said. "She said she'd heard most of it before from you."

I squeezed his hand and then crouched down by the chair. "Natalie? Are you okay?"

She looked down at her hands in her lap, a worried line crossing her forehead. "I should say no, I'm not okay. I should say that everything I've been told is crazy. But what I am going to say is yes. Yes, I am okay."

I reached for her hand. "Do you believe me, Natalie? Do you believe *in* me?"

She raised her head and looked me in the eye. "You are my best friend. And, yes, I believe you," she said without hesitation.

I heard the trust in her voice. The faith. And I felt a swell of appreciation in my heart. "Thank you, Nat. That means more to me than you'll ever know."

My hands shook a little as I positioned the camera, focusing on Natalie's face. This was the moment. If this worked, not only would it protect Natalie from succumbing to Zo's changes, but it would open the door for me to fix all kinds of changes to the river and protect what needed to be protected.

I inhaled and summoned every ounce of energy within me, focusing it into *believing* as fiercely as I could. I thought of the images carved into the black door and how they served not only as symbols but as keys: the spiral shell, the half-sun, half-moon circle, the rising musical scale. I exhaled and felt the edges of myself thin like they did in the moments before I slipped to the dream-side of the bank. I didn't want to travel there, but I thought it might be good to be in that kind of mental state, in that in-between place.

The black sky crowded close in the corners of my eyes, the wild river flowing fast around my feet. I didn't dare let my eyes or my thoughts wander, so I concentrated on Natalie, on matching the strength of her belief with my own.

This will work. I will make *this work.* I chanted the words endlessly in my mind. Slowly, so slowly, I could feel the deep currents of the river start to change to match the rhythm of my words, shifting to accommodate my will and bending to my wishes.

Heat began a slow burn in the pit of my stomach. I felt a trickle of sweat along my scalp, down my temple, around my wrists. The shaking in my hands intensified and I bit down on my lip to keep my body in check.

I took one last breath—and then I pushed the button, capturing forever in silver and shadow the image of the Natalie-who-believed.

The camera click sounded as loud as a shout. A ripple of warmth seemed to extend from the camera, through my fingers, through my body, and out into the room. The banked fire in my body flared and then flamed into ash. I lowered my hands and looked at Dante, who looked at Leo, who looked at me.

Exhaustion overwhelmed me and I locked my knees so I wouldn't fall over. In an instant, Dante was at my side, wrapping his strong arms around me and shifting so he could keep me steady. I rested my head against the hollow of his throat, grateful for the support and safety I felt in his arms.

In the suddenly still room, Natalie asked, "So, did it work?"

I looked down at the camera cradled against my chest. It still felt warm in my hands. "I think so. I won't know for sure until I develop the picture."

"Then what are you waiting for?" A tentative smile appeared on Natalie's face. "I can't wait to see it."

"Me either," I said, enjoying the heft of the camera. It was almost the same weight as the hinge to the door. I looked up at Dante. "Would you come with me?" I asked him as I stepped out of his embrace. My knees had stopped shaking, which was a good sign. "I mean, if it's all right with Lizzy."

Lizzy and Leo had drifted closer during our conversation and she reached out to pat Dante's arm. "It's fine with me—as long as you promise to sit for me someday."

He smiled. *"Lo prometto."*

"Ah, tall, dark, and handsome—plus he speaks the mother tongue?" Lizzy raised an eyebrow at me and sighed. "If only I was a younger woman . . . Ah, well. You're a lucky girl, Abby."

"I know," I said fervently, twining my free hand around Dante's.

Lizzy pointed to the door in the back wall. "Do you remember what I taught you?"

I nodded. I couldn't wait to get back into the darkroom and transform the film into fact.

"Good. If you forget something, or run into trouble, there is an intercom button on the wall by the door. Push that and I'll either talk you through it or come in and help."

"Thanks," I said and tugged Dante toward the door.

As soon as we entered the first dark hallway, though, he

stopped in his tracks. His breath quickened, harsh and ragged. "Wait," he grunted.

I caught my breath. The hallway had made *me* feel slightly claustrophobic, and I wasn't the one who had only recently been freed from a similar dark place. "Oh, no, Dante, I shouldn't have made you come with me. We can go back. I didn't think—"

He shook his head once sharply. "Just . . . give me a moment." He closed his eyes and a shudder racked through him all the way to his fingers in my grasp. "It's just . . . dark."

"Dante—"

"No, it's fine," he said. "You asked me to come. I want to help."

Worried lines creased my forehead. "Are you sure?"

He hesitated, then nodded. He squeezed my hand tight in his. "Don't let go."

"I won't," I said, squeezing back. "Ever."

I quickened my pace, leading him through the darkness and around the corners until we reached the laboratory-like room. As soon as we saw the glow of the soft white light, Dante's breathing evened out and returned to a normal rhythm.

"You okay?" I asked as he sat down on the stool by the sink.

"I'm sorry, Abby," he said, running his hand through his slicked-back hair and dislodging a stray lock. "I didn't think it would be that bad."

"It's okay," I said, rubbing his shoulder. "After what you've been through, I'd be more surprised if you hadn't reacted to the darkness."

"I want you to be able to depend on me," he said. "I won't let it happen again."

My fingers automatically reached for the lock of his hair and tucked it back behind his ear. "I know," I said, placing a small kiss next to his ear. "Now, you rest, and I'll get to work."

I reviewed in my mind the various steps Lizzy had walked me through, and then I took a deep breath and got started.

I selected a developing tank and found a spool that would fit the film from the Brownie camera. I found myself falling into a rhythm of movement as natural as breathing. Wind the film. Mix the chemicals. Agitate. Rinse.

Dante was quiet as I worked through the process. It was nice simply to share the space with him, knowing he was close by and there if I needed him.

Stop bath. Rinse. Fixer.

This was it. The most important step. The same heat I'd felt from the camera when I took Natalie's picture seemed to permeate the developing tank in my hands. I closed my eyes and concentrated. I visualized the chemicals stripping away the silver from the film, slowly revealing a Natalie who was reversed in black and white. I imagined her face, her eyes, her smile. I focused on the idea of *fixing*. On *stability*. On being *unchangeable*.

No, not entirely unchangeable. I still wanted Natalie to be able to change and grow and become the person she wanted to be. But I wanted the changes to come about as a result of her own choices. Not because of someone else's whim or because someone else forced his will on her life.

The heat in the tank seemed to intensify. I hoped that meant that I was on the right track and that it was working.

My muscles protested the constant agitation of the tank, but I didn't dare hand it off to Dante. If there was something about me that helped protect the river and keep it stable, then I wanted that same mysterious something to help me finish Natalie's picture.

The clock finally granted me permission to stop, and I poured out the fixer with its dangerously beautiful silver crystals into the container. I set the tank down in the sink and turned on the water. I was proud to note that my hands hadn't shaken once.

Dante watched me with curious eyes, and I suspected he was taking notes, studying my every move. With his mind and skill, I wouldn't be surprised if by the next time we needed to develop a picture, he would be able to do it by himself.

I peeled back the top of the tank and hung the film up to dry in the cabinet.

"How long until it dries?" Dante asked quietly, his voice hoarse from disuse.

"Fifteen, maybe twenty minutes."

He smiled the small smile I loved so much. "Good." He opened his arms and I sank onto his lap. Wrapping his arms loosely around my waist, he let me rest my head on his shoulder.

We sat like that together in a comfortable, and comforting, silence. As often happened when we were close, I felt the time around us change its pace, slowing down a little, and I was grateful for the small moment we had to rest and reconnect.

Our breathing fell into the same even rhythm. Our heartbeats echoed each other until they sounded like one single, unbroken pulse.

After a time, Dante ran his fingertips up and down my spine. I arched my back like a cat waking from a long sleep.

"Mmm, that's nice," I said, nestling closer to him, my head fitting naturally along the curve of his neck.

He tilted his head down and the movement loosened that same unruly lock of hair; it brushed against my cheek, the ends tickling my nose. "I missed you, Abby. More than I can say."

"I'm here now. And you promised me a story, you know," I reminded him. "Maybe we can pretend we're sitting on a grassy hill underneath a tree instead of in a darkroom surrounded by chemicals. What do you say?"

He chuckled. "How can I refuse?"

"You can't," I teased. "Now, tell me a story. Tell me how you met da Vinci."

"Once upon a time," he began, his voice rumbling deep in his chest, "there was a boy. He was a very smart boy, talented and artistic—"

"I'll bet he was good with his hands," I said, capturing one of Dante's hands with my own and measuring the length of my fingers against his.

"As a matter of fact, he was. Now stop interrupting," Dante said in a teasing tone, but he didn't move his hand away from mine.

"Sorry," I said with a smile.

"So this smart and talented and artistic boy had a dream. Even though he lived in a small village, he had heard about a great man named Leonardo da Vinci. His dream was to meet the man who imagined so many wonderful and amazing things, who could paint such beautiful pictures. He thought for sure that if he could just meet da Vinci, the boy would be able to convince da Vinci to teach him all his secrets."

"I think I already know how this story ends," I said.

"Hush," Dante said, placing his finger on my mouth. "You asked for the story of how I met him, not what happened after that."

I straightened a little in Dante's lap. "Then tell me the story like it happened to you, not to someone else."

Dante was quiet, and for a moment I worried that my tone had been more bossy than I had intended and that maybe he wouldn't finish the story. Then he spoke, and his voice was softer, weighed down with memory.

"It was early spring—May, I think. I remember the sunshine was so bright that day I thought I could see stars out of the corner of my eyes. I was fifteen. Everyone in the village knew that da Vinci and his household had been visiting the Servite monks. But what not everyone knew was that the monks had offered a workshop space for da Vinci. And what even fewer people knew was that da Vinci was willing to allow someone to join his group of assistants. Someone local. And only one."

"How did you find out about it?" I asked.

"My mother's cousin was a laundress for the monastery." Dante's fingers returned to their slow journey up and down my back. "Mother knew how much it would mean to me to be able to meet him, so she convinced my father to take me to the workshop. It was a long journey, but I didn't mind. Somehow difficulties are easier to endure when you know your dream is waiting for you at the end."

I knew how that felt. I closed my eyes, listening to Dante's voice and enjoying the light touch of his fingers on my back.

"I expected to see a huge crowd at the workshop. I mean, it was the chance of a lifetime. But there were only a handful of people wandering through the courtyard, and most of them were monks hurrying to afternoon prayers."

"Were you the only one who answered the call?"

"No, there were three other boys there with me. I knew two of them—Pieter and Bernardo—from my village. The third was a stranger to me. We stood clustered in a group in a corner of the courtyard waiting for something to happen, for someone to come. More monks came and went. Hours passed and the afternoon moved toward evening. But still nothing happened. The father of the third boy finally put his hand on his son's shoulder, turning him away and saying something about wasting a whole day on nonsense.

"I didn't mind the wait. I loved watching the monks cross the stones on their well-worn paths to prayer. They were so graceful; it was like they were dancing. While I was watching them, I noticed one of the monks drop something from his robe. A shiny, silvery something that glittered. Without thinking, I darted forward, grabbing the object and turning to find the monk it belonged to. But it was no use. There were too many of them, all dressed in the same brown robes, and they all said the small object didn't belong to them."

"What was it?" I asked, lulled by the story. "The object you found?"

"It was a disc of silver about the size of my palm. It was smooth on the concave side and there was a snakeskin pattern on the curved side."

"Sounds pretty," I said, dreamily.

"My father called out to me, gesturing for me to come back, to stop bothering people. On my way back to the group, I noticed that the pillar by the corner had the same snakeskin pattern around the base. Looking closer, I also noticed that there were gaps in the pattern. Voids that were about the size and shape of the disc I held in my hand."

"Let me guess—you fit the piece into the pattern," I said.

"Do you want to tell this story?" Dante teased.

"No. But I'm right, aren't I?"

Dante laughed. "Yes, you are right. I knelt down and placed the disc into one of the openings. It fit perfectly."

"Like Cinderella's glass slipper."

"Who's Cinderella?"

"Sorry—it's an old fairy tale. I forget that your childhood stories aren't the same as mine. Go on. What happened next?"

Dante shifted me on his lap. "The next thing I remember is seeing a pair of shoes step around the pillar and stand next to me. I looked up and . . . it was him. Leonardo da Vinci. He was standing right in front of me. As though he'd been waiting for me. I stepped back in surprise."

I felt a tingle pass through me. It was strange to think that the person I was talking to had been talking directly to

Leonardo da Vinci roughly three years ago. "What did you say?" I whispered.

Dante smiled. "Nothing. I didn't know what to say. My father, of course, wouldn't stop apologizing for my actions. But then da Vinci looked right at me and said, 'Come to my studio tomorrow and I will put you to work.'"

"He picked you? Just like that?" I said, leaning back in Dante's arms in surprise.

"Just like that." Dante nodded, his pride still strong even at the memory. "Of course Pieter's father and Bernardo's father both protested, each man claiming that his son should be chosen. Da Vinci held up his hand for silence. I'll never forget his words. He said, 'You were all given the same chance. This day was your test. The monk who dropped the scale did so at my request. I was watching to see what you would do. I need someone who can wait with patience, and yet know when it is time to act without fear. Someone who is able to see patterns even when none may be obvious. Someone who can also express his own artistic viewpoint.' Then he pointed at me again. 'I want someone who will leave the world a more beautiful place than he found it.'"

"Wow," I breathed. It was no wonder da Vinci had picked Dante as one of his assistants. Dante was exactly what da Vinci was looking for.

Dante was quiet for a moment or two. "And that's the story of how I met Leonardo da Vinci."

"What would have happened to you if you hadn't gone to work for da Vinci?"

Dante shrugged. "I probably would have worked for my father as an assistant in his apothecary shop."

"That doesn't sound so bad."

"No, it wouldn't have been a bad life. But it wasn't the life I wanted."

I huffed out a half laugh. "*This* probably wasn't the life you wanted either."

"You're wrong. This is exactly what I wanted."

"It is?" I looked up at him.

He nodded somberly. "All I wanted was a life where I could learn new things. Where I could use and develop my talents. But most of all, I wanted a life that I could share with someone I could love beyond myself." His gray eyes reminded me of high, clear skies at twilight. "Then. Now. It doesn't matter, as long as I have you beside me. As long as I can be a part of your life."

"You're the best part of my life," I said, caressing his cheek. "And you always will be."

"Always?" he asked, his eyes searching mine.

"And forever," I confirmed. And then I kissed him.

CHAPTER 21

When Dante and I returned to the front room, Leo and Lizzy were nowhere to be seen. Natalie said they had left a while ago, cameras in hand, off on an impromptu photo shoot. A large book of scenic photos lay open on her lap.

I handed Natalie the print I'd made.

She held it carefully, propping the opposing corners between her palms.

The image showed Natalie sitting in the chair, looking directly into the lens. Her hair was haloed around her head like a crown. A smile lit up her face. She looked exactly like herself.

"How do you feel?" Dante asked Natalie.

"Fine, I guess." She looked down at the picture in her hands. "I mean, I don't feel any different than before. It's a good picture of me, though."

"But you still believe me, right?" I asked.

She didn't even hesitate. "Yes, I do." Then she caught herself and looked at me with wide eyes. "As soon as I said it, I knew it was the truth. That's amazing. I don't feel any doubt at all. I totally believe you."

The photo book fell to the floor with a thud as I pulled Natalie to her feet, hugging her, picture and all. I felt a laugh bubble up inside me, a gladness that made me feel as light as air. "It's better than amazing. It's wonderful. It means you're safe—and you'll stay safe. It's perfect."

"Careful, don't crumple me," Natalie said, holding the picture out of the way.

"Oh, sorry." I stepped back, but I couldn't stop smiling. "It worked. It really worked."

Natalie laughed at my enthusiasm.

"Congratulations, Abby," Dante said quietly to me.

The front door opened and Lizzy stepped through, followed by Leo, laughing at something she had said.

They saw us standing there and Leo quickly handed his camera to Lizzy. "How did it go?" he asked me before glancing at Natalie. Then he smiled. "Dare I assume it was a success?"

"A complete and total success," I said.

Lizzy walked over and looked at the picture of Natalie. "Not bad for your first try," she commented. "Very nice. I like how you captured her personality in the picture. That can be hard to do."

"Thanks." I felt a light blush creep into my cheeks. "And thank you for teaching me today. You were more help than you know. Um, Lizzy? Would you mind if we left the picture here? You know, for safekeeping?"

Now that I had protected Natalie with a picture, I wasn't sure what would happen if that picture were to be destroyed or ruined in some way. Valerie had warned me that if Zo found out about the pictures, he'd try to steal them from me, and then he would have the power. I couldn't take that risk.

"Of course," she said. "I'd be happy to keep it for you."

Natalie handed Lizzy the picture, and the small woman disappeared into the back room.

Thinking of Valerie's warning made me think of something else. I turned to Dante.

"We helped stabilize Natalie with a picture. Do you think we could do the same for Valerie?"

"I thought Valerie was . . . not well," Dante said, a question wrinkling his forehead.

Leo stepped closer. "I don't know if that's such a good idea, Abby."

"No, I don't want to take a picture of her when she's . . . in her current mental state. But both times I've gone to visit her there have been flashes of her old self. Her regular self. Maybe if I'm quick enough, I can capture that part of her and bring her back."

"Do you really think you can?" Natalie asked, hope in her voice. "That would be wonderful."

Leo shook his head sadly. "I know it's tempting, but think of the risks. We've had one success, but none of us really know what the rules are for this process. What if you miss your chance and capture her at her worst instead? Do you really want to risk that?"

I swallowed, tasting tears of frustration in my throat. "I know it's a long shot, Leo, but she's my friend." I looked to Dante. "What do you think?"

He met my eyes. "You know I'll stand behind you."

The frustration I felt evaporated in the strength of his confidence.

"She needs my help," I said to Leo. "I have to go. I have to try."

"I'm not saying you shouldn't try to help her," Leo began. "I'm just saying you should think about the consequences—" He stopped short as Lizzy returned to the room.

"Is everything all right?" she asked.

"Everything's fine," Leo said, his tone smooth and untroubled.

"You know, Leo," Dante began, "if you wanted to stay and develop the pictures you took, I could take Abby and Natalie home."

"You're welcome to stay," Lizzy said. "I'd love the company."

Leo paused, his frown turning into a polite smile so fast I doubted anyone else saw it. He looked from Dante to me and then to Lizzy. "If you're sure . . ."

"It's no bother," she said.

Leo handed over his keys to Dante, but as I gathered up my Brownie camera and headed for the door with Dante and Natalie, I didn't miss the look Leo flashed my way, a look that said *Be careful.*

I gave him a look of my own: *Trust me. I will.*

V was waiting for us outside the door.

"Abby," he said, startling me so badly I almost dropped my camera.

"What are you doing here?" I asked, my heart picking up speed. If V had found us here, did that mean Zo could too? I thought we'd been so careful at the house.

V leveled his gaze at Dante and folded his arms across his chest so his gold-banded wrists were clearly visible. "Nice to see you, Dante. You're looking well."

Dante's only response was to narrow his eyes at V.

"I know you!" Natalie said.

V flicked a disinterested glance her way. "Yeah, we've met."

"I know. I saw you play with Zero Hour at the Dungeon."

"So? What about it?" V asked her.

"It's just that I didn't remember it the other day when you found us at Helen's, but I do today. I wonder what else I'll remember," Natalie said, her voice tinged with surprise.

V shot me a confused look.

"We fixed it so the changes that are happening in the river won't affect her anymore. I guess her true memories are coming back as well." I was happily surprised by this unexpected turn of events. It gave me hope that if we could replicate the process with Valerie, we'd be able to return my friend to being the Valerie-before-Zo.

"Whatever," V said, brushing away my explanation. "I built your door. You got him back"—he jutted his jaw toward Dante, who bristled—"now it's your turn to hold up your end of our deal."

I put my hand on Dante's arm. I could feel the muscles twitch with repressed tension. "I made him a promise," I said simply.

He exhaled slowly. "Sorry. It's just that the last time I saw him, he was doing Zo's bidding."

"Yeah, well, I'm not anymore." A shade of red crept up V's neck. He turned his dark eyes on me. "Are you going to help me or not?"

"Actually," I said, trying to remain calm, "we were just going to see Valerie. You can come with us."

I was glad to see V relax a little, if only because it made Dante relax as well. Clearly the two of them couldn't both come. Not if they were both going to act like snarling alpha dogs. Plus, I doubted I could get all four of us in to see Valerie. Especially since I didn't know yet how I was going to get V past Dr. Blair.

I ground my teeth and made the hard decision.

"Dante, why don't you drop me and V off at the hospital and then you can take Natalie home."

He opened his mouth, no doubt ready with a list of reasons why he thought dropping me off with V was a bad idea, but I started walking to Leo's car before Dante had a chance to say anything.

The car ride to the hospital was stressful and uncomfortable. I didn't dare suggest that V sit up front with Dante, and yet I didn't much like the idea of V sitting with Natalie in the backseat either. So I sat in the back with V, which didn't make Dante happy, but it was the best I could do.

By the time Dante pulled up in front of the hospital, I had a tension headache and my stomach was in a knot.

Closing the door, I bent down next to the driver's side window.

"I don't like leaving you with him," Dante said under his breath.

"I'll be fine," I said, reaching in to grasp his hand. "Don't worry."

Dante squeezed my hand. "Call me the minute you're done, all right? I'll be at Natalie's house."

"I will." I leaned past him and waved at Natalie. "Thanks for watching out for him, Nat."

"Glad to help. I suspect we'll have plenty to talk about while you're gone."

Grinning, I brushed a kiss on Dante's cheek. That same stray lock had fallen free again, and I tucked it behind his ear. "Maybe I should be worried about you," I teased, feeling relieved when Dante offered up a smile.

"Good luck, Abby," he said. "Remember—do what you have to do. Just don't do anything you can't undo."

I patted my bag that held my camera. "I'll only use this if it's a sure thing."

I gave him one last kiss before he drove away, leaving me alone in the parking lot with V. He'd pulled down the sleeves of his shirt to cover his wrists.

"Is this where she is?" V's voice was a strange mix of hope and despair.

Nodding, I headed up the steps of the James E. Hart Memorial Hospital, my own heart filled with the same hope and despair.

◎

Needless to say, Dr. Blair was not happy to see us. She frowned when I asked to see Valerie. She positively scowled when I told her that V was a friend who was in town visiting for the day, and could he come with me?

After making us wait on the steps, she finally moved aside and gestured us in, directing us to her office just inside the door. I noticed that her pastel hospital scrubs were the same color as her fingernail polish—the same baby-pink flesh she'd worn the other day.

"I don't believe you," Dr. Blair said as soon as V and I had sat down on the love seat.

Next to me, V stilled immediately. His eyes darted to the door.

"Excuse me?" I asked, gripping V's arm so he wouldn't bolt.

"I don't believe that he 'just happened' to stop by to see an old friend." Dr. Blair clasped her hands together on her lace-covered desk. "You brought him here for a reason." She shifted her attention to V. "Tell me why you're really here."

"Mi dispiace. Non parlo inglese," V said.

"Yes, you do," she said almost pleasantly, brushing aside his words. "What's your interest in Valerie?"

V looked to me for help.

"We're just friends," I insisted. "Honest. We just want to visit her for a few minutes."

"Dr. Hamilton was not happy when I spoke to him about your last visit. He was very reluctant to authorize any additional visits for you."

"So does that mean he *did* authorize a visit?" I asked, smiling politely.

Dr. Blair's frown deepened. "It means he trusts me to use my best judgment when it comes to Valerie."

I was quiet, trying to exude that aura of peace Dr. Blair seemed to appreciate. I continued smiling, and waited.

She tapped her fingers together. "Who is the Pirate King?" she asked suddenly.

It took everything I had to keep the bland smile on my face and not betray the flash of panic that ran through me.

"Valerie only talks about the Pirate King when she's with you. I've asked her about him in our therapy sessions, but she refuses to tell me who he is or why he dominates her hallucinations."

"I don't know," I said and felt a muscle tick in my jaw. I knew why Valerie was fixated on the Pirate King so much, but I couldn't tell Dr. Blair that. I also knew Valerie's "hallucinations" were simply glimpses of the river, but I couldn't tell Dr. Blair that either.

Dr. Blair's lips thinned. "If I grant you a visit, do you think you could get her to talk about the Pirate King again?"

My smile wavered the tiniest bit. "I don't know. Maybe."

Dr. Blair hesitated, then leaned forward as though imparting a secret. "Valerie's psychosis is unlike any I've seen before. I've decided to feature her in my next research paper. But I need more data before I can publish my findings. And since she's no longer speaking to me . . ." She left the request unspoken, but I finished her thought anyway.

"You want me to be your spy?" I demanded, my smile vanishing for good.

"I want you to be my assistant," she clarified smoothly. "If

Valerie confides in you information that could help us help her get well, then wouldn't you want to be a part of that miracle of healing?"

Yes, I wanted Valerie to get well. And I knew if she was going to be healed, it wasn't going to be in a place like this or under the care of Dr. Blair, whose bedside manner apparently stopped at the point of publication. My frustration itched. I'd known that my visits with Valerie had been recorded—I'd been told that on my very first visit—but for some reason, I hadn't realized they were using those recordings for research. Valerie was my friend—not some bug pinned to a board to be studied and then discarded. The thought made me sick.

The camera felt like a brick in my bag. I didn't dare take it with me to see Valerie now. Not with Dr. Blair hovering over me. Even if I was able to get a picture of Valerie, Dr. Blair would want to confiscate the image for her "research," and I couldn't let that happen.

But I still needed to see her. I'd promised V.

I swallowed my outrage, my pride, and my fear, and said, "Okay. I'll help you."

Dr. Blair smiled, and I noticed her small white teeth were perfectly even. It didn't do anything to reassure me.

Valerie was in the conservatory again. The omnipresent sound of water had been replaced by a choir of songbirds. I suspected it was meant to be soothing, but it sounded more like noise than a song to me.

I gestured for V to wait by the door, and I walked past the plastic leaves so I could approach Valerie alone.

"Hi, Valerie," I said softly. "I came to visit."

She turned her back to me, folding her arms across her chest and shaking her head. "I'm not talking to you."

"Why not?"

"Don't want to," she muttered. "Don't want to hear your lies."

"I wouldn't lie to you, Valerie. We're friends, remember? And friends don't lie to each other."

"Friends don't keep secrets either." She lifted her hand and brushed tears away from her face.

"What secrets have I kept from you?" I asked, sitting down next to her on the edge of the fountain.

She twisted around and pointed a finger at the door hidden behind the grove of plastic plants. "Him! You didn't tell me you were bringing *him*." She jumped to her feet on the narrow ledge and cupped her hands around her mouth. "Come out, come out, wherever you are!"

"Valerie, get down!" I tugged at the hem of her bathrobe. "You'll fall if you're not careful."

She reached down and swatted my hand away. "You should be the one afraid of falling, not me. I know where I stand."

The plants rustled and parted as V stepped into view.

Valerie shrieked and covered her eyes with one hand. She flung out her other hand, fingers splayed. "Stop right there!"

V stopped midstep, his eyes locked on Valerie.

I could see the emotions warring on V's face: confusion, shock, and sadness. In the end, despair won out, and I watched as he stepped back, seeming to shrink a little into himself. Clearly, he had imagined a different reaction.

The air around him shimmered. He was going to jump away from this time and place, but I couldn't let him do that. How would I ever explain his disappearance to Dr. Blair? I could almost feel her leaning closer to whatever television monitor she had tuned into to watch this drama unfold. The fake birds continued tweeting their looping songs. It made me want to scream.

"V, wait!" I rushed to his side. "Just wait a minute, okay?"

"She doesn't want me here," he said, shaking his head. "I was a fool to think she would."

"No, it's fine. She just needs a minute." I tugged on his sleeve. "Come on. Come sit down."

He followed me with halting steps to the fountain. Valerie towered over us like a vengeful priestess calling down wrath from the heavens.

"Valerie," I said in as calm and reasonable a tone as I could manage. "Please sit down. V has something he wants to say to you."

"I don't have anything I want to hear from him," she said. But she did lower her hands, and her body lost some of her pent-up anger.

"He's come a long way just to see you," I continued, reaching up to take her hand in mine. "Come on. Be nice."

She trembled, cutting a glance in V's direction. "But he's not a good person," she whispered in a voice loud enough for both of us to hear.

"Yes, he is," I said, gently drawing her down from the ledge. "He's a very nice person."

Valerie frowned. "Nice people can still be not good people. You've met the lady doctor. You know."

I did know. I forced myself not to look up at the black dome eye watching our every move. "It'll just take a minute. I promise." I helped Valerie sit down next to V. "Trust me."

V inched closer to Valerie, his eyes soft. He held out his hand and waited.

She looked from his face to his hand and bit her lip, worry lines rippling across her forehead. "That's what the Pirate King wanted too. He just wanted his crew to trust him. He was going to take them to amazing places, show them amazing things." She shook her head sadly. "But they didn't trust him. They abandoned him when he needed them the most."

V curled his hand into a fist. "He asked me to hurt you. I wasn't going to do that. I couldn't." His voice dropped to a bare whisper. "I love you."

She ignored him, and I saw the hurt move across V's face.

"So he did what every good king and captain does when faced with betrayal, with *mutiny*." Valerie narrowed her eyes at V as the word twisted from her lips. "He killed them all and left them for dead."

"I'm not dead," V said.

"That's because he hasn't killed you yet," she said with a chilling calm.

He looked to me, but I shrugged helplessly. I didn't know what to say. I had hoped this reunion would be a good thing, but the conversation was quickly unraveling into madness.

"And you think you're so safe?" Valerie turned to me, her dark hair swishing around her ears as she tilted her head. "Tell me, Abby, do you miss Hannah?"

I felt dizzy. "You remember Hannah?" I asked.

"I remember everything," she said, smiling like the sphinx. "That's my job."

V stood up, his hands clenched into fists at his sides. "Do you remember this?" He pulled Valerie to her feet, wrapping his arms around her in one smooth, fast motion.

And then he kissed her.

Valerie tried to pull away, but he held her tight against him. Slowly, she relaxed into his embrace, her hands coming up to lock behind his neck.

I looked away, feeling a blush stain my face.

And that's when I saw Dr. Blair standing nearby, her hands folded passively in front of her, her face strangely slack and void of expression. The birdsong overhead suddenly cut out with a strangled chirp.

In the silence that followed, V broke off the kiss, his head whipping around to follow my stunned gaze.

Even as my blood froze in my body, even as my mind shrieked in denial, some distant part of me was grateful for small favors, glad that Valerie's eyes were still closed—her face upturned, her lips slightly parted—so that she couldn't see what I was seeing.

Dr. Blair wasn't alone.

This time she'd brought Zo.

CHAPTER 22

V disappeared in an instant, taking Valerie with him. My mouth opened in surprise, my attention divided between the rippling air that still held the afterimage of two people embracing and Zo standing in front of me, his gold-banded hands shoved into the pockets of his jeans. The handle of his guitar rose above his shoulder like the hilt of a sword, and the black leather strap crossed his chest like a royal sash.

"Hello, Abby," he said as though he had just noticed me standing there.

"What are you doing here?" I blurted. It wasn't the question I really wanted to ask, but it was the first one that came out.

"The same thing you are. I came to visit an old friend." He smiled and tossed his head so his hair flipped out of his eyes.

"You came to see Valerie?"

He laughed in honest surprise. "Not this time. I was supposed to meet V here. But he seems to have left rather unexpectedly."

I sank back on the edge of the fountain, my knees refusing

to cooperate. "But V said he . . . He said he wasn't working for you anymore."

"Of course he said that. I *told* him to say that." Zo's voice was gentle and made goose bumps lift on my arms.

"But he . . . he . . ." My thoughts spun out of my control. Had all my interactions with V been a lie, then? Every one orchestrated by Zo for his own purposes? "We had a deal." I knew it was a silly thing to latch on to, but it was the only thing I kept coming back to.

"Oh, my sweet, trusting Abby." Zo shook his head in mock remorse. He exhaled a deep sigh and turned to Dr. Blair, who was still standing motionless behind him. "Go back to your office. I'm done with you."

She turned around and shuffled to the door like a rusty robot.

"What did you do to Dr. Blair?" I didn't even try to keep the horror from my voice.

"Who?" Zo asked, looking over his shoulder. "Oh, her. I just made a few . . . modifications so she'd be more pliable to my needs."

"You changed her? But I didn't notice—" I bit off my words as Zo's attention swung back to me, a suspicion lurking in their dark depths.

I wondered why I hadn't felt that world-shifting pain warning me that Zo had changed something in the river. Was it because Dr. Blair had been his focus this time, and not me? Or were Dante's fears that the barriers were weakening justified? Were the changes becoming more commonplace, and therefore less worthy of notice? Or had Zo figured out that I was noticing in the first place and learned to disguise his touch? None of the questions made me happy.

The longer I stayed quiet, the wider Zo's smile grew, as though my silence merely confirmed something he thought he knew.

He strolled toward me. I wanted to get up and bolt for the door, but his eyes held me in place. I felt like a mouse trapped by a snake, and I didn't much care for the comparison. I remembered Dante's conviction that it would be my choices that would make the difference in stopping Zo. I had faced Zo before and survived. I could do it again. So I shoved aside the fear that threatened to well up inside me and made a choice. I would be the snake instead of the mouse. If Zo wanted to play this game, then fine, I could play it too.

Zo sat down next to me, exactly where Valerie had been a moment ago. I wondered where she'd gone. V said that he loved her. If he could still be trusted, then I hoped he had taken her someplace safe. And if he was still following Zo's orders, then I hoped he had taken her someplace where I could still find her.

Zo slung his guitar from off his back, laying it across his lap like a bared sword. "It's good to see you again, Abby. I've missed our little chats. But then, I suspect you've been busy."

"What do you want, Zo?"

"So impatient," Zo tsked. He reached out to stroke the neck of the guitar. The strings whined a little under his touch, a lost puppy begging for attention.

"Don't," I snapped. "Just . . . don't play anything, okay?"

"Impatient *and* suspicious. A bad combination." Zo tightened his hand around the instrument.

"It's not a suspicion. I know what you do with your music."

"Do you?" Zo arched an eyebrow at the same moment he strummed the guitar. "Are you sure?"

"I can guess."

Zo raised his eyebrows and inclined his head, inviting me to speak.

"We both know your music can manipulate emotions. My guess is that you've been practicing."

"Have you been spying on me?" Zo teased. "I'm flattered."

"Don't be."

Zo laughed. "It was a good guess, Abby, but not quite right. Yes, I have been practicing, and yes, I can still manipulate emotions. But now I can manipulate memories as well. And my music can do more than simply make you recall a specific memory. It can also erase it."

"So you didn't change something in the river," I said, swallowing hard, "you changed something in Dr. Blair? You erased her memory? Permanently?" If Zo was telling the truth, things were worse than I'd imagined.

He shrugged as though I'd pointed out he was wearing one black sock and one blue instead of suggesting he had tampered directly with a person's mind. "She had outlived her usefulness, so I wiped her memory. When I leave, her mind will return, but she won't remember me being here at all. She won't remember you, either, for that matter. Or anything else that happened today. And any record of Valerie will be gone as well.

I don't like to leave a trail, you know. It's too much work to clean up. It's much easier to toss out the old and start fresh."

Zo leaned forward, his mouth hovering close to my ear. "Tell me, sweet Abby. Is there a memory you wish to forget?"

"That's not possible," I said. I clutched at the edge of the fountain, feeling the rough skin of the stone, refusing to let myself contemplate an answer to Zo's question.

Zo withdrew with a smile, settling back comfortably. He smoothed his palm over the curves of the guitar, a caress of possession. "That's what I love about you, Abby. Your certainty. After everything that has happened, you can still say without hesitation what is and is not possible."

I shook my head. "Dante knows what you can do. He would have told me—"

Zo opened his mouth, but I didn't give him a chance to speak.

"Dante would have told me," I repeated. "And I trust Dante."

"Really? Are you sure?" Zo strummed a dark chord and something deep inside of me responded to the resonance. "Or do you just *remember* trusting him?"

"I know I don't trust you," I said.

Zo looked hurt. "But you should. I've been more open with you than with anyone else. I want us to be able to trust each other."

I edged away from him, shaking my head. "There's nothing you can say that will make me trust you."

"Not even if I tell you that I can restore Valerie's sanity?"

I thought of Valerie, sitting alone in her room, looking out a window that was covered with an unbreakable diamond pattern, watching and waiting for something only she could see. Waiting for her Pirate King to come save her. My heart seized up.

Zo touched the strings of his guitar again, coaxing a strange note to life.

I narrowed my eyes at him. "Don't—"

But that was the only word I managed to say before the landscape froze around me, locking me in place. The gray stone of the conservatory floor folded in on itself, turning from an ocean into a rippling wave before narrowing into a line of midnight black. At the same time, the plastic plants rushed toward me, only to flatten into two-dimensional cutout triangles atop thick brown rectangles. The diamond-pane glass dissipated as the late afternoon sunlight that poured inside seemed to grow in scope, pushing through the gray with heavy golden beams as thick as pillars. The whole thing reminded me of a child's drawing—crude and jagged around the edges.

Even Zo looked strangely flattened and outlined, a smear of green and black and gold. His guitar was disproportionately large compared to his body, the neck as thick as a tree trunk.

I stared at him in growing astonishment and horror. I'd seen him like this before. Valerie had drawn a picture of Zo—complete with his flyaway hair and his manic, wide grin—and taped it to the wall next to her bed. *He watches over me,* she had said. *He keeps me safe from prowlers and predators.*

She couldn't see past the fractures in her mind to realize that Zo was the predator.

The strange note split into two, then three, then more until it had grown into a song. The sound rose in volume, seeming to spiral upward higher and higher toward the climax of the song. I wanted to close my eyes; it sounded like a scream. But I couldn't move.

And then the sound was gone. Cut off as completely as if I had turned off a radio. The heavy, blocky drawings softened into thin lines; the sunlight lost its white-hot glow, returning to a more natural dusky yellow. The gray unrolled back into a stone floor and the trees melted back into three dimensions.

I was strangely aware of the space surrounding my body, of my own three-dimensionality.

"What did you do?"

"Valerie has such a fascinating mind. I'm sure she would want you to know what it's like for her, how she sees the world now that she's—"

I shot Zo a murderous look, and he paused.

"Well, let's just say she's more open to the possibilities around her than she used to be. You, on the other hand . . ."

"What? I'm what?" I demanded.

"You'll be a harder nut to crack," Zo said.

"That sounded like a threat."

"Did it?" Zo's eyebrows rose in feigned surprise. "I meant it as a promise."

I ground my teeth together. "I told you before: Stay away from me. Stay away from my friends."

"But Valerie wants me close to her," Zo said with an innocent smile. "And how can I deny her anything she wants?"

"She *wants* to be well," I countered. "If you can give her what she wants, why don't you give her that?"

"Do you always get what you want, Abby?"

I thought back to that terrible moment on the bank when I stood before the open hourglass door. I'd begged Dante not to go through it, even as I knew he had to. I thought of Emery College, of Jason, Valerie, Hannah—and then deliberately closed the door on those thoughts. I couldn't afford to be distracted right now.

"Life is all about balance," Zo said almost gently as he leaned the guitar on the floor by his feet. "You know that. Though Leo lied about many things, he told the truth about that. And sometimes, to maintain that balance, you have to make sacrifices. You know that too. Of course you want Valerie to be well—we all do, don't we?—but now isn't the time."

"Why not?"

"I need her this way," he said, the gentleness gone from his voice.

"What?" I snapped out a harsh laugh. "Broken?"

"Accessible."

A horrible word filled my mouth. I wished I could say it—I wanted to say it—but instead I clicked my teeth together, feeling a numbing tingle in the back of my jaw.

Zo smiled. He reached out his hand to my face, but I flinched back, avoiding his touch. "If you want to play this game, Abby, you really need to work on hiding your thoughts. You're worse than Valerie—and she welcomes me with open arms."

I remained silent, focusing on my breathing, on schooling my features into a flat mask of indifference. Inside, though, hot rivers of hate simmered.

"Better," Zo nodded, studying me with his dark shark's eyes. "Much better."

"Tell me how to heal Valerie," I said.

"No."

"Tell me where she is."

"No."

"Then we have nothing more to discuss." I stood up from the edge of the fountain and walked away from Zo without looking back.

Once outside the conservatory door, I leaned against the wall and wrapped my arms around myself. My mind wouldn't settle down enough for me to make sense of what had happened. I squeezed my eyes shut, hoping to find enough stability within myself to move forward.

Exhaustion climbed onto my back and draped its heavy weights over my shoulders and arms. Would this day never end? I'd had the best—Dante's kiss—and the worst—Zo's unexpected arrival—and everything in between. All I wanted to do now was go home and sleep for a week. But I knew I couldn't. There was still too much to do.

I pushed myself away from the wall and headed for the front door. On my way, I stopped by Dr. Blair's office. She sat upright in her chair behind her desk like a doll that had been placed there to simply wait for someone to come back and grant her life. I crept forward and grabbed my bag and my phone from the love seat. I half expected her to stop me or ask me what I was doing, but she kept her hands flat on the desk, and her unfocused eyes never moved toward me. I heard soft music coming from the hidden speakers and I immediately plugged my ears. If that was Zo's song, I didn't want to hear it. I didn't want to risk my memories.

I kept my hands over my ears until I was all the way out of the hospital and standing on the sidewalk. Only then did I exhale and lower my hands. I opened my phone and called Natalie's house. It was a lot later than I had thought. The sun was just a sliver on the horizon, and the night's shadows had already appeared around the parked cars and tall trees.

Natalie answered on the first ring. "Where are you?" she asked by way of greeting. "I've been calling you for the last twenty minutes."

"I'm still at the hospital," I said. "Dr. Blair confiscated my phone. I need a ride home. Is Dante still with you?"

"No, but—"

"He's not? Where is he?"

"He's actually on his way to get you, but—"

"But what, Nat?" I asked wearily, hearing and hating the bite in my voice.

"V and Valerie just showed up here."

I held the phone away from my ear and looked at it as though it had started transmitting in a foreign language. Natalie kept talking and I could hear her clearly.

"I don't know what to do, Abby. They just showed up at my house and V said that Zo was with you and then Dante ran out of here without saying anything and now they're in my room and—"

"Hold on, Natalie. Slow down." I pinched the bridge of my nose, trying to stop the headache before it crashed into my skull. "When did V show up?"

"I told you—like, twenty minutes ago."

"And Valerie was with him, right? And she's okay?"

"Well, she was with him, but she's not doing great. She locked herself in the bathroom and she keeps calling for somebody named the Pirate King."

I groaned. "Okay, listen. Keep V away from Valerie for now—" A car pulled into the lot. I recognized the growl of the engine and starting jogging across the lawn to meet it. "Oh good, Dante just showed up. Hang on. We'll be right there. And don't worry, Natalie. It'll be okay. I promise."

I flipped the phone shut and dropped it in my bag without breaking stride.

Dante stepped out of the car and ran toward me, his long legs covering the distance faster than I could. When he reached me, he swept me up in a hug that lifted me off my feet. "Abby, are you all right?" he asked, setting me back on the ground. He ran his hands over my shoulders, down my arms, and then back up to my neck. His eyes searched every inch of my face, his expression alternating between worry and relief.

Even in my present state of exhaustion and terror, I still felt that familiar tingle of electricity when Dante touched me. "I'm fine," I said, feeling myself already start to calm down now that we were together. "Zo didn't do anything to me."

"Are you sure you're all right? V said Zo had his guitar with him."

"Yeah, well, V didn't stick around very long once Zo showed

up." I continued toward the car, Dante walking with me. "You were right to be suspicious of V. Zo said he told V to tell me that story about how he'd turned on Zo and walked away. I shouldn't have trusted him."

Dante opened the car door for me and then slipped into the driver's seat. "Your mother called Natalie while you were gone," he said, pulling out of the parking lot. "You should call her back."

"And tell her what, exactly? That the former drummer of a rock band kidnapped my best friend from a mental hospital and I'll be home right after I do damage control?" I held my phone in my hand, but didn't move to call. I studied Dante's profile in the fading light. "You don't seem particularly surprised by the fact that V lied to me."

Dante glanced at me. "Call your mother. See if she'll let you stay at Natalie's tonight."

"What about V?"

Dante turned left at the corner. "Don't worry about V. I've taken care of it."

"What did you do? What are you not telling me?" I asked.

"I didn't hurt him. We simply came to an agreement about what needs to happen from this point on."

I waited one more moment to see if Dante would say anything else. When he didn't, I flipped open my phone and called home. "Hi, Mom? Yeah, I'm okay. Sorry I didn't call sooner. Um, is it okay if I stay at Natalie's tonight?"

CHAPTER 23

Natalie's room was chaos. When Dante and I walked in, Valerie was singing in the bathroom, V was sulking in the corner, and Natalie was in tears.

I had one moment to take in the scene before everyone started talking at once.

"You're back!" Natalie bounded off her bed and ran to me. "Thank goodness. I don't know what to do—"

V stood up at the same time and pointed at Natalie. "She won't let me near Valerie, and—"

Dante crossed the small room in two quick strides. "I told you to be quiet—"

"At least Valerie has stopped crying—" Natalie said, wiping away her own tears.

"You don't understand anything—" V said, shoving Dante in the shoulder.

Dante shoved him back. "I understand you deserted Abby at the first sign of trouble—"

"I knew Abby would be fine. Valerie was my first priority—"

"Who is this Pirate King she keeps talking about?" Natalie asked.

"Were you supposed to deliver Abby into Zo's hands?" Dante roared at V. "Was that your plan?"

V's face paled and he sat down under the force of Dante's anger. "No, I—"

I dropped my bag by the door and held up my hands. "Everybody just calm down." The headache I had tried to ward off earlier had ignored my efforts and now crouched behind my eyes. "Please. Just . . . be quiet for a minute."

"Abby, please, I can explain—" V started.

"No," I barked, pointing my finger at him. "I don't want to hear it. You stay there and don't say anything." I turned to Dante. "Make sure he doesn't go anywhere. And if he does, bring him back. I'm not done with him yet."

I turned to Natalie, who was still standing next to me, and gave her a hug. "I'm so sorry this mess ended up at your house. I know you didn't ask for this, but thank you for handling it."

Natalie hugged me back. "I'm just glad I was the one who found them on the doorstep. I don't know how I could explain this to anyone else."

"Tell me about it," I commiserated with a smile. Crossing the room, I knocked on the bathroom door. "Valerie, can I come in?"

"What's the password?" she said.

I looked to Natalie and Dante, who both shrugged. "She's been asking that all night, but I don't know what she wants to hear," Natalie said. "I've tried everything I can think of. She won't open the door."

I tested the doorknob. Locked.

"You can't come in without the password," Valerie sang out.

I suddenly had an idea. I wasn't sure it would work, but given the late hour and the high stress, I was willing to try anything. "Valerie?" I called through the door again.

"That's not the password," she said with a laugh.

"I know it's not. But I don't need a password."

"You don't?" She sounded surprised.

"No. I have something better. I have a key. Remember when you kept the key I threw away? You said you'd give it back to me when I asked for it. Well, I'm asking for it."

Silence from the bathroom.

"You do still have the key, right?" I asked.

"Of course I do," she said hotly. "It's right here in my pocket."

"That's good. Would you mind using it to unlock the door?"

The lock popped and the door slowly swung open. Valerie's eyes were wide and her mouth opened in an O of astonishment. "It worked," she breathed. She looked down at her empty hand, then held it out to me. "Here's your key back."

I lifted the invisible key from her palm and made a show of slipping it into my pocket. "Thank you for keeping it safe for me."

"I knew it was an important key," Valerie said, awed, "but I didn't know it could open *any* door. You better not lose it again."

I smiled at her like we were sharing a secret. "I won't let it out of my sight."

Valerie grinned and then rubbed at her eyes. "I'm tired. Can I go to sleep now?"

"Of course you can," I said. I handed her off to Natalie and caught Dante's eye. Jerking my head toward the hallway, I opened the door. Dante grabbed V's arm and hauled him to his feet, dragging him out of the bedroom.

Valerie took off her bathrobe and crawled into Natalie's bed. "Tell me a story?" she asked. "I don't want to have bad dreams tonight."

"Okay," Natalie said, sitting on the edge of the bed "Um, once upon a time . . ."

I closed the bedroom door behind me and then rounded on V. "What were you thinking? Where did you take her? And why did you come to Natalie's house, of all places?"

V tried to back up, but Dante was standing behind him and wouldn't let him move. "When Zo showed up, I panicked. I just . . . I didn't think. I jumped to the bank and I took Valerie with me."

"You took her to the bank?" I hissed. "Why? Because Zo told you to?"

"What? No!" V looked stricken. "I told you—I don't have anything to do with him anymore."

I folded my arms and stared at him until he shifted his gaze away from me.

"Yes, taking her to the bank was part of the plan, but it was *my* plan. Not Zo's. I thought . . . I thought if the shock of going there once was what cracked her, then maybe going there again would snap her back to herself."

"That was a dangerous risk," Dante said.

"I know. But I didn't know what else to do." He looked over my shoulder at the closed bedroom door. "It didn't work anyway."

"Why bring her to Natalie's?"

"Because I knew Dante would be here."

I met Dante's eyes over V's shoulder and raised my eyebrows.

"What do you want with me?" he asked, turning V's back to the wall so we could both face him.

"All I want is to help Valerie," he said in a low voice. "And if taking her to the bank didn't work, then maybe taking her through the door will."

"Is that why you agreed to build the door?" I asked. "So you could use it for your own purposes?"

"In part," V admitted, looking at me. "But only as a last resort. I built it because we had a deal, Abby. I did my part, and you did yours." His eyes flicked to Dante. "You got what you wanted. I just want the same thing."

"The door won't work for you," Dante said flatly.

"Why not? I built it according to your directions—"

"No, you didn't," Dante interrupted. "You built it wrong. If it hadn't been for Abby, I would never have made it out of that darkness."

V's face paled, his dark eyes the almost-purple shade of bruises. "Whatever it was I did wrong, it was an accident, I swear. You have to believe me."

"Why do you think taking Valerie through the door will heal her?" I asked. Information was coming at me too fast. It was hard to know who to believe, who to trust. My mind felt heavy with sleep, but I shook it off. I couldn't give in just yet.

"I don't know that it will," V said. "But both times she's been to the bank, someone else has taken her. Maybe that's part of the problem. Maybe if she can travel there like we did, it'll help her."

I looked to Dante. "What do you think? Is it possible?"

Dante brushed his hair out of his eyes. A stillness filled the hallway as he considered the questions.

"It's possible," he said finally. "It's not my first choice, though." His gray eyes turned to steel as he looked at V. "You were sent through the door against your will. You didn't choose this life. None of us chose this. Will you be the one to send Valerie through that same door against her will? What gives you the right to choose this life for her?"

"It's a better life than she has now," V said. "You've seen her. Who would want a life like that? Besides, what alternative does she have?"

I thought about my grand plan to wait for that split second when the true Valerie peeked through one of the cracks and then take her picture. It was as dangerous and fragile a plan as V's was, and it carried the same risks. I slumped against the wall, my memory filled with the vision Zo had shown me of Valerie's mind.

"She could stay in the hospital," I said slowly, "and grow old and die like a regular person."

"Exactly," V said. "If we don't at least try, then she'll be in that hospital for the rest of her life. She'll never get better."

"But if we do try, and it doesn't work, then she'll never get better—and she'll never die." I closed my eyes against the horrible thought of Valerie living for five hundred years or more in the state she was in.

"It's been a long day," Dante said, reaching out to me and drawing me close. "We don't have to decide anything tonight."

The weariness I'd been holding at bay for the last few hours broke through my defenses until my body felt like it was weighed down with sandbags. Now that my eyes were closed, I didn't think I had the energy to open them again.

I heard the bedroom door open and shut and then Natalie's voice say, "Let's put her on the couch in the living room."

I felt Dante's strong arms behind my knees as he lifted me off my feet.

And then the twin wings of exhaustion and sleep swept over me and carried me away into darkness.

For the first time in a long time, I didn't have any dreams. I slept in complete, unbroken darkness, and when I finally woke the next day, I felt more like myself. A quiet calm had replaced the turmoil from yesterday. My mind was clear. I still didn't have all the answers, but I felt like I could face the questions again.

I stretched my fingers and toes to their limits and yawned until my jaw cracked.

Footsteps thumped down the stairs. I quickly pulled the blanket up to my neck. I'd slept in my clothes, and they were rumpled and wrinkled. I wondered if I would have time for a shower, or at least a chance to change clothes, before I had to face the demands of the day.

Dante rounded the corner, carrying a plate of toast in one hand and a glass of orange juice in the other.

My stomach rumbled loudly and I looked up, embarrassed. "Sorry," I said.

Dante set the food down on the coffee table and sat on the couch by my feet. "Don't be. It's actually almost lunchtime. I thought you might be hungry."

I sat up and grabbed a triangle of toast and ate half of it in a single bite. "'Sgood," I mumbled around the crumbs. "Thanks."

"You did some amazing things yesterday," Dante said as I swallowed the juice. "We are all in your debt. Especially me."

I set the juice glass down. "It was a pretty hectic day. How is everyone else holding up?" I tilted my head, realizing just then how quiet the house was. "Where is everyone, anyway?"

"Natalie is upstairs with Valerie, who is surprisingly docile today. V and Leo are at the Dungeon waiting for us, but I wanted to let you sleep as long as possible."

I yawned again. "I could probably sleep longer if given the chance."

"I'm afraid you might not have that luxury."

I twisted on the couch until my back was against the armrest and my knees propped up under the blanket. "Why do you say that?"

Dante's eyes were as gray as ice. "Leo and I had a long talk last night about everything that's happened. We went to the bank. We looked into the river." He took a breath. "We had to make some hard decisions."

"And what did you decide?" I asked, afraid that I wasn't going to like the answer.

"We decided I need to restore the door to its proper working condition. We'll need it to open directly to the bank again."

"What?" My knees flattened as I sat straight up. "I thought we agreed it was too dangerous for V to take Valerie through the door."

Dante shrugged. "We did. And it is. But things have changed."

"Like what?" I asked, worried that Zo had been busy while I'd been asleep. "What's changed?"

"I have." Dante's mouth flattened into a grim line. "When Leo went to the bank, I went with him so I could study the river, see how the possibilities of V's idea would flow and change—I needed to see if there was even a chance that it might work—but all I saw were the ripples on the surface." He shook his head. "I can't see downstream anymore. I can't see down to the deeper currents of how events connect. I can't see where they lead. It's like I've gone blind."

I remembered Valerie's story about the Pirate King and the River Policeman and saw again in my memory the thin silver buttons in the palm of her hand. I didn't want that part of the story to be true. I leaned forward and gently touched the gold chains around Dante's wrists. His skin was cold under my fingers. "Do you think it's because of this?"

"I don't know. Maybe," Dante said. "Or maybe I lost my ability in the darkness between doors."

"Do you really need to see downstream?" I asked, trying to look on the bright side. "I mean, with Zo running free, isn't it more important to follow him through the past instead of the future?"

"Zo wasn't the only one I was watching in the river," Dante said, looking at me pointedly.

"Leo said I wasn't supposed to ask you what you saw about me in the river," I said, giving Dante my own pointed look in return.

"How am I supposed to keep you safe if I don't know what's waiting for you?" he asked.

"The same way everyone else does it. I mean, not every girl is lucky enough to have a boyfriend who can see the future and manipulate time." I shrugged with a smile. "It'll be okay, Dante. We'll stick together, and when trouble shows up, we'll face it together."

He was quiet, his eyes cloudy with thought.

"Just tell me what you need to tell me, Dante. I can take it." I covered his hand with mine. I could feel his swift heartbeat along his wrist. "I'm not afraid of the truth."

"I know," Dante said. "Sometimes I think you're not afraid of anything."

"Well, if you must know, I'm not such a big fan of spiders." I was glad to see Dante's smile widen into a grin and to hear his soft laugh.

Both faded away too quickly for my liking. "What is it? What's wrong?" I asked.

Dante clenched his jaw and kept his eyes fixed on the

empty space between us. "I tried to restore your family for you."

Hope flared into life inside me, releasing a flurry of questions. "You did? When? What happened?"

"It was the first thing I did after you fell asleep. I wanted you to wake up to good news."

I pushed back the blanket and moved to stand up. Natalie had a phone in her room; I could call home. I couldn't wait to hear my dad's voice again or talk to Hannah. "Why didn't you tell me that first?"

"Because it didn't work."

Dante's words cut through my excitement. I sat back down slowly, the blanket clutched in my fist. "It didn't?"

Dante shook his head. "I thought all I would have to do was find that moment when Zo interfered in your parents' life and then set things right. But it wasn't that easy."

"Why not? It seemed pretty easy for Zo to change whatever he wanted."

"I don't think it was that easy for Zo either. Since he couldn't touch your timeline directly, he had to follow the path of your life back to a point where he *could* intervene. He followed the links back to when your parents met, and then he changed something—I don't know what. And when Zo changed that single event, he set off a chain reaction that he hoped would result in your parents never meeting, thus erasing you from existence."

"But my parents *did* meet. They even got married. It was Hannah who was erased." Just saying it out loud made my heart ache with pain. I frowned. "Why didn't you just reverse the chain reaction?"

"No one's life follows a single, straight path. Events bend and twist, branching off into unexpected directions and forming unexpected connections."

Understanding dawned on me. "And since you couldn't see how events unfolded downstream . . ."

"I didn't know which connection was the right one to restore." He curled his hand into a fist. "I couldn't risk setting off another chain reaction. I didn't want to make it worse for you."

"Then, if you can't fix it, how will I get my family back?"

Dante was quiet, his attention focused on the crisscrossed pattern on the blanket crumpled in my fist. His fingers traced the path of my veins along the back of my hand. When he looked up at me again, his eyes were as serious as I'd ever seen them.

"When I gave you the plans for the door, did you find the note I left for you on the last page?"

"Yes." I remembered every word he'd written. "You asked me if I was willing to live without limits."

"And are you?"

"Of course," I answered, confused. "Isn't that what you wanted? Isn't that why you gave me the plans? So I could build the door?"

Dante tugged at my hand until he had pulled me close enough to kiss. But instead of touching my lips with his, he touched his finger to the locket around my neck. "I gave you the plans for the same reason I gave you the key inside this locket. So that when the time came, you would have everything you needed to make your choice."

My heart pounded so hard it felt on the edge of breaking. "Last time, I had to choose between you and Zo and it almost killed me. What choice are you asking me to make this time?"

"Whether or not you really are willing to live without limits. Whether or not you'll be brave enough to use the door once I fix it."

CHAPTER 24

If you go through the door," Dante said, "know that you'll be bound to the bank, just as I was. As Leo is. It's not an easy life. You'll have to find your own balance. You'll have to make sacrifices."

My body trembled at the implications of Dante's words. I'd been to the bank both in person and in my dreams and I'd hated everything about it. I'd seen what being exiled from time had done to Leo's life. I thought about Lizzy and how she had lost her father to the river and didn't even know it. If I did go through the door, I would have to leave behind everything, my entire life. And though I could return and visit my family and friends, it would only be for a short time.

Dante had said that no one had knowingly and willingly chosen that path. Would I?

"You think that if I go through the door, I'll be able to restore my family," I said as a half-statement, half-question.

He nodded. "You'll be able to see the connections that I can't because they are part of your family and thus part of your timeline. And once we know how the connections fit together, we can reverse what Zo did without fear of making it worse."

My true family was fractured—my parents divorced, my sister nonexistent. Did I dare walk into the darkness behind the door if I knew that when I came back, they would be whole?

"What happens if I don't go?" I asked, numbness prickling the pads of my fingers.

"I don't know," he said. "But I do know that the barriers between the bank and the river *are* weakening. We've both felt it. Even V and Leo have noticed it. Maybe, between the four of us, we can keep them from breaking." His eyes never wavered from mine. "I'm afraid that if the walls break, it may not be possible for you to use the door at all. Your family may be lost forever."

I sat back against the couch and pulled the blanket up to my chin as though it could protect me from the horrible possibility Dante had laid in front of me.

When Dante had given me the plans and asked me to join him, I hadn't thought much beyond the promise of being with him again. I had thought building the time machine would be an adventure and something I could do that would somehow help Dante protect the river from Zo. I had even imagined the moment when I would walk through the door and straight back into Dante's arms. But I'd forgotten the harsh truth of the time machine—it wouldn't take me anywhere I wanted to go, it would only take me to the bank.

The barren bank that could crush a soul and crack a mind.

I didn't know why I hadn't made that connection until now.

If I went through the door, I'd be stepping onto the bank, risking my life and my sanity. But if I didn't go, then Zo would break down the barriers and erase not only my family but the whole world, washing it away so he could remake it according to his will.

I blinked as tears started trickling down my face, quickly turning from a few drops to an endless stream.

"I know it's a hard choice," Dante said, wiping his thumb across my cheek as fast as the tears fell. "I'm sorry to have to ask you to make it. I wouldn't ask it of you at all if it weren't so important."

"I just want my family back." I felt a brittleness settle into my body, my skin as taut and sharp as glass. "Why do I have to make the choice?"

"Because only you can close this loop."

I huffed in frustration. "Leo said something about that too, but I didn't understand his explanation. What does that even mean?"

Dante gathered his stillness around him as effortlessly as he gathered me into his arms. "Maybe the best way for me to explain it is to tell you a story. Close your eyes and pretend we're under that tree on the hillside."

I did as he asked, relaxing into his embrace and nestling closer to his side. I folded my arms against my chest as though I could keep my heart from breaking. "What's the story about?"

"What all good stories are about: a boy and a girl and how they met."

I sniffled a little and wiped away a stray tear. "If this is about how you and I met, then I know this story."

"You know the story of how we met that day at school." Dante smoothed his hand over my hair and pressed a kiss to the top of my head. "This is the story of the first time I *saw* you."

I stilled as though I had turned to stone. "Isn't that the same story?"

"No," Dante said softly and tilted my face toward his. "It isn't."

I opened my eyes to see his gray eyes turn the silver-blue of the stars at dawn.

"This story begins in Italy, long ago. I was locked in a dungeon cell, fighting what I feared would be a losing battle for my sanity while I waited to learn my fate. And then, one day, I saw a girl standing in the doorway of the prison. She had the face of an angel." He gently traced his finger across my forehead, around the edge of my eye, down the slope of my cheek, and along my jaw before coming to rest on my chin. His thumb traced my lower lip. "She had *this* face."

I didn't dare breathe. His touch left fire tingling inside me.

"I'd never seen her before that moment. I didn't know her name or who she was or why she was there, but when her eyes met mine, I felt . . ." He closed his eyes, the memory moving across his face, smoothing away the lines of worry around his mouth and eyes. "It was like the roof had been ripped away and taken all the shadows with it. Like I'd been granted one last glimpse of the summer sun."

I felt a tremor start deep inside my body, rippling outward. I had seen that same moment in the river: a girl standing in a doorway, looking into a dungeon. Was it possible that girl had been looking for Dante? Was it possible that girl was me?

Dante opened his eyes. "The guards pulled her away and she was gone, but it didn't matter. I had caught a glimpse of heaven, and I held on to it all the way through the darkness, all the way through the door, and all the way to the bank. When Leo taught me about the river, it wasn't long before I started seeing that angel's face again in its liquid depths. This time, though, she wasn't looking for me, I was looking for her. And I finally found her one snowy January day at her school auditorium."

"You were covered with snowflakes that day," I said, my voice low, my memories spiraling back to the past.

"And you were as beautiful as I remembered you."

"But how could that girl you saw back then be me?"

"Because when faced with the choice you're facing right now, you chose to go back."

I blinked in surprise and then sat up, pushing away from Dante. "Wait a minute. So you're saying I've already made this decision? What about all that business about how you don't know what's going to happen downstream? If you already know what I'm going to do, then why should I bother making any choices at all?" My tears evaporated in a heat of rage. "I guess my life is already planned out, huh?"

"No, Abby, it's not like that. You still have your free will. Your choices still matter. In fact, yours might matter most of all." He ran his hands through his hair, his mouth a tight line of frustration. "In one sense that moment has already happened—I remember seeing you in the doorway of that prison—but in another sense it *hasn't* happened yet because you haven't yet gone back to the past to stand in that doorway. And it *won't* happen until you actually make your choice and do whatever it is you're going to do."

"So, if I decide *not* to go through the door, then you won't have seen me in the doorway?"

"That's right. But I will still be sent through the door, and I will still end up on the bank with Leo. It's just that if I don't see you in the doorway, then I won't go to the school that day to meet you."

My emotions ran as hot and wild as my words. "But if you'd never met me, then you'd never have taken me to the bank, and then Zo never would have known about the door and how he could go back. He wouldn't have gained the power to change the river." I barked a harsh laugh. "He wouldn't have changed my family at all—he wouldn't have had any reason to!" I pressed my fists against my eyes, squeezing until my knuckles ached. It was too much to process. There was too much to think about.

"I can't do this, Dante. I'm sorry. I'm just so tired. I just want my old life back," I muttered.

The room was silent. The stillness that had been centered around Dante shattered. I imagined it was the same sound as a heart breaking.

"If that's really what you want," Dante said softly, "I can arrange that. If that would make you happy."

My hot blood froze to ice in an instant. My memory flashed back to Zo sitting on a park bench, an impossible question on his lips: *If you truly wish we'd never met, why haven't you asked Dante to change things? He would do it; he'd do anything for you. Even if it meant endangering the river, or his own life.*

Here was my chance to change things. And I wouldn't even have to ask anyone to change anything for me. I could simply choose to go home, destroy the hinge buried in my sock drawer, and never look back. No door meant no Zo. Tomorrow I would wake up and I'd have my old life back. My parents. My sister, Hannah. Jason. The Valerie who lived with her parents and not in a mental hospital.

I would have everything.

Except Dante.

Zo's voice reached out to me across my memory again: *You can honestly say that you'd be happier without Dante in your life?*

I pulled my fists away from my eyes, blinking away the pressure spots. Zo hadn't given me a chance to answer that question, but I realized that the answer I would have given then was the same answer I felt now.

Without Dante in my life, whatever happiness I felt would be incomplete.

My family and Dante. I wanted both. I needed both.

If there was only one way it was possible to have both, then there was only one choice I could make.

Dante sat with his hands resting limply in his lap. "I understand, Abby, and I'll leave if you ask me to. If that is your choice, I'll go. I'm sorry for the pain I have caused you. Believe me, that was never my intention." He leaned his elbows on his knees and dropped his head in his hands, his dark hair falling over his face. "But there will always be a part of me that will miss you forever, even if we never meet."

Tears returned to my eyes, but this time they weren't from anger or fear. They were tears that came from understanding the truth about myself and from realizing that what I had was exactly what I had wanted all along.

"Dante?" I said, touching his shoulder, my heart fluttering in amazement at what I was about to do. "If I choose to go back, then everything happens just as it has happened, right? We meet, we fall in love. Everything. The good and the bad."

He nodded, but didn't look up.

"And if I go back, you think we can restore my family *and* stop Zo from breaking down the barriers between the river and the bank, right?"

He nodded again. "That's what I was trying to explain. If you go back and stand on that doorstep so I can see you before I go through the door, then everything unfolds along this path we've already traveled. But that moment is also what will close the loop and protect not only this part of the river but the past as well. And once the loop is closed, the river will be locked in place and protected all the way back to da Vinci. No one will be able to change it again. Not even Zo."

"That's why you said that our best chance of stopping him would be to let him go," I said. "Because if I let him go, then I would let you go as well, and I'd be more likely to build the door that would take me back to that crucial moment when you saw me on the doorstep of the prison."

Dante lifted his head and looked at me, admiration flickering in the depths of his eyes. "Exactly. Abby, seeing you then was what saved me during that long journey through the time machine. Having you in my life now is what has saved me here." He touched the locket at my neck before reaching for my hand. He kissed my fingers and then pressed my palm flat against his chest, covering my hand with his own. "My heart and my life have always been in your hands."

"I promised you I would keep them safe," I said, my heart beating hard and fast in my throat. "What would you like me to do?"

Dante shook his head. "I told V that it would be wrong for him to choose a life for Valerie without her fully understanding what was waiting for her on the other side," he said quietly. "You have all the information. You know the stakes. The black door changed everything about my life. It will change everything about yours, too. But I won't force you to make this decision. It must be your choice."

I pressed my palm against his cheek. "My life changed the moment I met you," I said simply. "I don't want to lose that moment. I want to have met you, Dante. I want you in my life. And if going through the door means I can save my family *and* stop Zo *and* be with you, then it's an easy choice. I choose you. I choose yes."

CHAPTER 25

Dante's kiss stole my breath away. He kept saying my name between kisses, his hands cupping my face. The nearness of his body ignited a fire within me, burning away whatever lingering doubts I might have had.

He swept his hands down my neck, resting them on my shoulders, his thumbs meeting in the hollow of my throat. His eyes were as bright as a sunrise. "I love you, Abby. I think I could live the rest of my life and never know the depths of you."

He kissed me one last time, at once so gentle and so deep that I saw stars in the darkness behind my eyes.

Some distant time later, I finally opened my eyes to see Dante smiling at me.

"I love you, too," I said, only then realizing how inadequate those small words were to express all the emotion I was carrying in my heart.

I slipped my hand into his, and together we went upstairs.

Natalie was making sandwiches in the kitchen and Valerie sat at the counter, coloring a picture with a fat crayon in her fist. A rainbow of discarded colors cluttered the countertop around her. She hummed a tune through her nose and dangled her bare feet from the tall stool where she sat.

"Oh, good, you're up," Natalie said, sliding one of two grilled cheese sandwiches onto a plate. "Are you guys hungry?"

"As long as it's quick," I said, my stomach rumbling. I picked up the sandwich and took a bite out of it. The hot cheese burned my mouth but it tasted delicious.

"Where are you going in such a hurry?" Natalie asked.

"She's going back home," Valerie chimed in, the tip of her tongue poking out of her mouth. "I hope she makes it okay, though, because it won't be as easy as she thinks. See, I drew a picture."

Valerie held up the sheet of paper proudly. The top third of the paper was filled with small golden stars linked together with thick yellow lines. The bottom third had been colored in bright blue until it looked like an ocean. A brown boat with a mast and a sail bobbed between the peaks of two waves. A crude skull and crossbones hovered above the boat. In the middle of the paper was a stick-figure girl with ragged brown hair standing in front of a door that had been colored solid black.

"Is that me?" I asked, pointing to the girl, unsettled.

"For now," Valerie said slyly. She turned the picture upside down and studied the image critically.

The three of us exchanged a heavy glance.

"Is that what I think it is?" Natalie asked, stepping closer to us. "Because it looks like Dante's description of the black door."

I nodded. "We're going to fix it so I can use it to save my family."

To Natalie's credit, she took that bit of information in stride. "So what's up with the pirate ship?"

"It's Zo," I said. "He's the Pirate King."

Valerie's head snapped up. "I told you not to say his name! I told you, but you did it anyway. Why did you do that?" She curled the edges of the picture in her hands, fretting and anxious. She tapped the boat with her finger. "The Pirate King knows where you are. He knows where you're going. He's on his way to meet you. You have to hurry."

Natalie dropped the pan on the stove with a clang. She scooped up the second sandwich and handed it to Dante. "Go."

"We'll be at the Dungeon. That's where the door is," I said to Natalie, giving her a quick hug. "Thank you for everything, Nat. You're the best friend I could have asked for." I held back the tears that appeared in my eyes. "If I don't see you again—"

"Don't talk like that. No good-byes. Just . . . do what you have to."

I nodded and gave her one more hug. Then I hurried after Dante, who had reached the front door in three strides and was holding it open for me.

"Yo, ho, yo, ho, a pirate's life for me," sang out Valerie as Dante closed the door.

We quickly stopped by my house to pick up the hinge. Dante would be able to work around V's mistakes, but there would be no point if we couldn't open the door.

As I exited my room with the brass machine heavy in my

hands, I couldn't help but peek into Hannah's room one last time. It was still perfectly presented, right down to the matching pillows on the bed, but the entire room was simply a shell, void of life. I curled my fingers around the three prongs of the hinge. With luck, I would be able to return this room to its rightful owner and fill it with the life I knew belonged there.

My heart twisted a little as I realized that, with Mom at work, I wouldn't be able to say good-bye to her. I held on to the thought that soon enough I'd be back home with my family and they would be whole, complete, and safe.

Coming down the stairs, I saw Dante waiting for me in the front room and I was hit with a peculiar déjà vu. I remembered the first time I had seen him standing at the bottom of the stairs waiting for me. So much had happened since that day when he had unexpectedly arrived to take me to breakfast. So many memories I didn't want to forget. So many memories I wanted to save.

"Are you ready?" he asked me.

I looked down at the hinge in my hands. My heart answered before my mouth did, and I was glad that they both said the same thing. "Yes," I replied. "I am."

The empty lot looked strangely ominous as Dante pulled up alongside the curb. I knew it was just my imagination, but I thought I saw a flicker of light shining up from the basement.

"How long will it take you to fix what you need to on the door?" I asked as Dante helped me out of the car.

"Not long," he said, moving to the back of the car and unlocking the trunk. "Luckily, none of the changes I need to make are time-sensitive ones. I should be able to restore the door to its proper working order—as well as fix the mistakes V made—by adding a few images and modifying the ones V misplaced."

I shaded my eyes and looked around the rubble. As far as I could tell, we were alone, but Valerie had said Zo was on his way. I hoped we had made it here first.

Dante lifted a toolbox from the trunk. "At least we know the hinge works, so that's good."

He took my hand and headed for the hole in the ground that led to the basement.

I didn't move, though, and Dante stopped only a few feet from me. He turned back to look at me. A light wind ruffled his dark hair, loosening that unruly lock so it fell across his eyes.

"Dante? Will . . . will it hurt, do you think?"

His eyes softened and he set down the toolbox. Returning to my side, he rubbed his hands over my arms. "No, love, no, it won't hurt. It will be dark. And cold. But whatever pain I felt from traveling through the door came from these"—he touched the chains on his wrist—"and you won't have them." He pulled me close to his chest. "It will be over before you know it. And I'll be waiting for you on the other side."

I closed my eyes briefly. I took a breath and exhaled it, forcing my fear to go with it. "Promise?"

"I promise."

"Okay," I said quietly.

Dante picked up the toolbox again but kept his arm around my shoulder while we walked to the basement.

The gaping hole still smelled oddly like smoke even though I knew the inferno that had devoured the Dungeon had happened weeks ago. A flurry of footprints were scattered around the opening, sharp heel prints and smudged toes alternating in the ash.

"Leo and V should be here already," Dante said, kicking the dirt off the first step. "I told them to wait for us."

I followed him down the curving steps to the basement floor, my heart seeming to skip a beat for every step I took. I counted them one through ten, and when I reached the bottom, my courage had returned. I smiled, thinking that Jason's counting trick had worked its magic again.

"Dante," Leo called, holding up his hand in greeting. "Is everything all right?"

Leo had cleaned the basement as best he could, clearing away as much of the debris and clutter as possible. His hands were black with soot and a line of it streaked across his cheek, another across his forehead.

"Abby agreed, so, yes, I think so." Dante set the toolbox down with a puff of dust. "But we don't have much time."

"Why not?" V asked, standing up from where he had been crouching next to the freestanding door frame.

"Valerie said Zo was on his way here," I said.

Leo frowned. "He's coming here? When? Now?"

V smiled, a strange gleam shining in his dark eyes. "Good. Then it's time to make him pay." He moved swiftly to my side, gripping my arm with a strong hand. He spoke in an undertone, so quietly that no one else heard him. "Remember—when he shows up, you hold him in place. I'll take care of the rest."

"Wait, I—" I stammered.

But before I could finish, V was already back at Dante's side, standing by the door, helping him lay out the tools Dante would need to fix and finish the black door.

Leo must have seen my worry from across the room because he gestured for me to come join him.

I stepped lightly around the door frame, skirting the blackened wood. For all that I was about to cross that threshold, I felt strangely reluctant to touch it before I had to.

I sat down next to Leo on a square of white-and-gold marble. I held the hinge on my lap, unwilling to let it out of my hands. "This is nice," I commented, tracing my fingers over one of the veins of gold running through the stone.

"It's one of the few things that survived the fire," Leo said. "I'm glad it did. It was a gift from an old friend. He tried to teach me the art of sculpture, but somehow my pieces never turned out quite right. I never seemed to end up with what I wanted. My friend made it look so easy. When I asked him what his secret was, he said, 'I saw the angel in the marble and carved until I set him free.'"

"Sometimes it's hard to see the ending from the beginning," I said, watching as Dante chose a thin blade from among his tools and pressed the tip to the dark wood.

"I know." Leo rested his hand next to mine on the stone. "And sometimes it's hard to keep your focus on the angel long enough for it to emerge from the stone. But when you do, and when it does, it's one of the most amazing things you can see.

I always thought that kind of creation was more like magic than art."

Dante deftly flicked his wrist, and a star-shaped spot appeared on what had once been a blank patch of wood. He brushed the edge of his hand over the wood, smoothing away any stray slivers. He touched the tool to the door again; this time, a swirl of petals appeared, a blooming flower caught in a breeze.

V hovered nearby, holding an array of tools, ready to hand over whichever one Dante required at a moment's notice.

Dante stood before the door and left his mark in all the far corners and intricate patterns that decorated the freestanding frame and the door. He moved with confidence, never lingering in one spot for very long. His hands seemed to automatically select and discard the tools that he needed to transform a simple door back into a passageway through time.

His dedication and artistry took my breath away.

Sweat slowly darkened his shirt as he focused all his energy on the task before him.

"I always knew he was talented," Leo said quietly, "but it's been a long time since I've seen him work at this level."

"You can tell that it makes him happy," I said. "I just wish he had more chances to use his art for something other than working on that door."

Under Dante's talented touch, constellations appeared and patterns formed. At his request, images came to life: scales and shells and stars. One by one, the grains of sand appeared in the hourglass in the center of the door.

I could almost hear the slippery sound of them rushing through the narrow neck of wood.

"This is a remarkable thing you have chosen to do," Leo said.

"Yeah, it's either the bravest thing or the craziest."

"I've seen what you are capable of, Abby, and I would say you are braver than you give yourself credit for."

"I suppose we'll see soon enough, won't we?" I tilted a smile in Leo's direction.

At that moment, Dante stepped back from the door, the thin knife still in his hand hanging by his side. He scrubbed away the sweat from his forehead with the back of his wrist.

"It's done," he said. His voice shook, though his hands were rock steady. "It's ready for you." He looked at me then, his eyes the same color as the marble. A hundred emotions flashed across his face, and I identified each and every one of them because I felt each and every one of them myself: excitement and anticipation, worry and fear, pride and love.

I stood up, cradling the brass hinge in my arms, and walked the few steps to Dante's side.

V slipped away from the door, moving to stand by Leo.

Dante smiled that small smile I loved so much and gestured for me to slide the hinge home.

As I had done twice before, I opened the hinge to its full length and lined up the three prongs with the three gaps in the wood. The soft click of completion sent a shiver down my spine. I felt as though the door had suddenly come alive, humming with power.

Heat rushed into my fingers as I moved my hand closer to

the door. My breath tasted of possibilities. I tried to tap into Dante's stillness and calm my racing heart. I pressed my palm flat against the black wood, but before I could push forward and take that first step that would lead me into the unknown, I heard a familiar voice ringing through the air.

"Oh, good," Zo said from the bottom of the stone steps. The light poured in around him like honey. His grin was as swift as a lightning strike. "The gang's all here."

CHAPTER 26

Everyone seemed to move at once. Dante stepped in front of me at the same moment Leo stood up from where he sat on the marble block. V spun around and charged toward Zo, his hands already balled into fists.

Zo, however, had moved as well. As fast as a thought, he was standing next to Dante instead of on the steps.

V looked around, confused by the sudden disappearance.

I gasped, stumbling backward. I didn't know anyone could move that fast.

Dante's eyes narrowed, his attention fixed on Zo's movements.

Zo didn't seem bothered by the sudden flurry of activity. He rocked back on his heels, his hands in his pockets. He looked up and down the wood and murmured appreciatively. "Very nice, Dante." He tossed a glance at Dante, who shifted his body as though to shield me from Zo's sight. "I'm assuming this is your work?" He strolled around the frame of the door as though he were examining a piece of art in a museum, debating whether or not to buy it. "You're quite talented. Perhaps I should commission you to do some work for me."

"Save your praise, Zo," Dante snapped, stepping away from Zo and taking me with him. "Why are you here?"

Zo ignored him, instead cocking his head back toward V. "Good to see you again, Vincenzio. You've done some nice work here as well." He offered up a small grin. "May I offer you my heartfelt congratulations on a job well done."

"What job?" I asked, looking from Zo to V with a cold stare. "What did you do for him?"

"Nothing," V said. "He wants you to think that I'm still on his side, but I'm not."

"Really? But you've helped me so much," Zo said. "And rescuing Valerie from that wretched hospital . . . that was a nice touch."

A ring of dark red appeared around V's neck. "I didn't do it for you."

"If you say so. And to be fair, you also have done quite a bit to help Abby, too," Zo said, his dark eyes as bright as polished stones. "You helped build this fine door like she requested, but—whoops, I guess you didn't do it right the first time because otherwise, why would Dante here have had to come in and fix your mistakes? They were honest mistakes, weren't they, V? I mean, you didn't deliberately sabotage the machine, did you?"

"Stop it, Zo," V said, the red flush creeping into his face.

"And then you've been here all day helping Leo like his own personal errand boy." Zo shook his head sadly. "You had so much potential, V, but you've let it go to waste trying to get people like this to trust you." He jerked his thumb over his shoulder at me, Dante, and Leo. "When you know very well that they don't."

With a roar, V lunged at Zo, his hands outstretched like talons.

But Zo was gone, sliding away in a blur of shadow only to reappear a few feet away; V's hands clutched at empty air.

I felt Dante grow still next to me, his concentration focusing on the spot where Zo had been and where he was now, as well as the space between.

"You should really work on controlling your emotions, V," Zo sighed. "Always acting first and thinking second. When you think at all." He turned his gaze to me, smiling his sharp white grin that made me shiver. "I think it's sweet that you thought V was still working with me. That you gave him enough credit that he could come up with a plausible lie and sell it so convincingly."

"I never lied to her!" V shouted.

"Oh, I know you didn't," Zo said without releasing my eyes. "But I did. And sweet Abby, you are so trusting, I almost felt bad about what I did to you."

I bit down hard on my lip, my anger tasting sweet in my mouth. "So you lied to me about V for no other reason than because you could?"

Zo lifted one shoulder in an elegant shrug. "You didn't have to believe me."

"I don't believe you," Dante spat. "You never do anything without expecting something in return. What is it you want from Abby? Why did you lie to her?"

Zo turned a dark eye to Dante. "I wanted to know how much she trusted me."

"I don't trust you," I said.

"But you did once," Zo said, shooting me a wicked grin. "And once was enough."

"We're done talking," Dante growled. He rolled up the sleeves of his shirt and shook out his fingers. The gold chains glinted like bracers on his wrists.

"Oh, are we finished with the banter now? Good. It was growing tiresome."

"I don't think that's a good idea, Dante," Leo said from across the room. "I don't trust him—"

"I can handle it," Dante said sharply, cutting his hand through Leo's words.

"Come, now—is that any way to talk to your brother?" Zo asked. His gold bands seemed to writhe around his wrists as he folded his arms across his chest.

I sucked in a breath and held it, fearful of what was coming next.

"No, Zo, don't—" Leo said, his tone halfway between a command and a plea.

"Brother?" Dante said at the same time, confused. He looked to Leo, who looked away.

Zo laughed in delight, leaning against the door frame and kicking his foot out so the point of his boot made a solid thump as it hit the floor. The wood frame creaked a little under his weight. "Oh, hasn't he told you?" Zo looked past Dante to Leo. "I'm sorry—was that supposed to stay a secret?"

Dante rounded on Leo, his face as pale as snow, his eyes as

still as ice. "What's he talking about?" When Leo didn't respond, Dante turned to me. "Abby? Do you know what's going on?"

I opened my mouth, but I didn't know what to say. The air was heavy in my lungs.

Leo licked his lips and swallowed hard. "Dante," he said, "please, I can explain."

"Yes, please do," Zo chimed in. "I can't wait to hear you tell the story of how you betrayed your country and your family and then dragged us all through the time machine after you."

"Be quiet, Zo," I snapped. "That's not what happened and you know it."

"It's close enough." Zo shrugged.

"Is that true?" Dante stepped closer to Leo. "Is that what happened?"

Leo slumped on the marble stone, the answer written in the curve of his shoulders.

"They said *I* was a traitor," Dante said slowly. "That's why they locked me in prison, why they sent me through the door—but it wasn't me. It was because of *you*."

"No," I said quickly. "It wasn't Leo's fault. Zo was the one who turned you in."

Dante was taken aback. "You knew about this too? Why didn't you tell me? I didn't think we had any secrets left between us."

"This wasn't my secret to tell," I said with a sad glance at Leo. It wasn't Zo's secret to tell either, and I felt a flare of hate burn in me that he had done it anyway.

"They had already punished me," Leo said, some strength

returning to his voice. "I didn't know they had plans to do the same thing to you. I swear, Dante, I didn't know."

"I knew," Zo said brightly, raising his hand as though volunteering information.

"You stay out of this," I said, hot tears burning my eyes.

"Why didn't you say something?" Dante asked Leo. The hurt was clear in his voice. "Why did you keep it a secret?"

Leo dragged a hand across his eyes. His fingers came away wet. "I don't know," he said heavily. "I wanted to—but your transition through the door was complicated. I didn't want to make it worse. And then . . . it never seemed like the right time. You always spoke so highly of your older brother. I knew how proud you were of him." He bowed his head. "I was afraid of what you would do once you knew the truth. I was afraid of what you would think of me."

"I thought you were dead," Dante said, his lips barely moving.

"I thought it would be easier that way."

"Easier for who?"

"Ah, Leo—a coward to his core," Zo said.

Dante turned away from Leo and walked back to stand beside me.

I think I was the only one who saw the old man draw a hand over his face.

"Dante?" I ventured, but he shook his head once without looking at me, and I let the subject drop. For the moment. Family was important, and now that the truth was out about Leo and Dante, I wanted it to bring them closer together, not drive them apart.

Zo clapped his hands together a single time. "As entertaining as this little family reunion has been, I actually did have another reason for coming here." He strode back to the door, looking it over one more time, before turning to me with a regretful sigh. "I'm afraid I can't let you go through this door, sweet Abby. It's not safe."

I shook my head. "I'm going through that door and you can't stop me."

Zo raised an eyebrow. "That sounded like a threat."

"Did it?" I said coolly. "I meant it as a promise."

"She's made her choice, Zo," Dante said, his fingers finding mine by my side and holding fast. "You should leave."

"And miss all the fun?" he said, slanting a grin at me. "I don't think so."

He turned on his heel, and between one step and the next he vanished, only the rippling air marking his passage.

Just as fast, though, he reappeared across the room, next to V.

V lashed out and tried to grab him, but Zo was gone again.

"What's he doing?" I asked Dante, clutching at his hand.

Dante focused on the patches of air. "He's traveling. But not far. Just fast. And I don't think he's changing anything. Yet." His body moved, automatically following Zo's flickering appearances.

"I don't understand. Why travel if you're not going to change something?"

"I don't know," Dante said, his eyes moving as fast as a bird in flight. "But there must be a reason." He let go of my hand and darted two paces to the left. "And I'm going to find out."

Dante pulled back his fist and swung just as Zo appeared in front of him.

The blow glanced off Zo's cheek, but it was enough to make him stumble and take a step back.

"Very good," Zo said, rubbing at the spot that was already turning red. "But not good enough." And then he was gone again.

This time Dante went with him.

I blinked in surprise as both of them disappeared into a flicker of rippling air.

I looked to Leo and V, who were standing off to one side.

"What's going on?" I demanded. I moved toward V until I was close enough to grab his wrist and leave a mark on his gold bands. "You've done this same trick—I've seen you. What are they doing?"

V didn't flinch at the harshness in my voice. "Dante was right. Zo is traveling along the river. But randomly. There's no pattern. Just there and back."

"Can you see them? Can you see where they are?"

V almost nodded. "They're so fast," he said, awed. "I knew I was no match for Zo, but this . . . this is beyond what I imagined he was capable of."

"Can you help Dante stop him?" I demanded, looking over my shoulder and only catching glimpses of dark hair and gold chains, only hearing the thump of boots hitting stone and the ragged breathing of exhaustion.

V hesitated, then shook his head. "I'm not skilled enough. I'd never be able to keep up with them."

Dante flickered into the room at the same time as Zo. "Stop!" he roared.

Zo laughed. "What, Dante—am I too fast for you?" And then he was gone again.

From across the room, Dante saw me with V. "Keep her here," he barked at V.

"We have to do something," I said.

"Sometimes all you can do is wait," Leo said, resting his hand on my shoulder.

I spun away from his touch. Between the blurs humming around me, I spied the door standing tall and untouched in the center of the room. "That's not true. I can put an end to this right now." I took a step forward.

"Abby, no!" V said, reaching out and grabbing my arm. He hauled me back and pinned me against his chest. "Dante said to stay here."

"Let me go! If I can go through the door, I can close the loop. I can stop this!" I struggled against V's grip, but he was stronger than I was, and I couldn't break away.

Zo rippled into the light, Dante hard on his heels. "I'm impressed, Dante. I didn't think you could keep up with me."

Dante's grin was as narrow and fierce as his eyes. "I didn't think you'd be so slow."

Zo's eyes lit up and his smile was all teeth. "You think you know what's going on, Dante. But you have no idea. Your confidence would be amusing, perhaps. If it weren't so pathetic instead."

My ears rang with Zo's words. I'd heard them before—when Natalie and I had met V in Helen's Café. Back then, I thought I was hearing snatches of a conversation that had already happened, or was happening elsewhere. But I was wrong. It was happening now.

"I'll just follow you wherever you go," Dante said, his chest heaving with the strain of maintaining his focus. "And eventually I'll stop you."

"No. You won't. Because I've already won. You just don't know it yet." Zo flickered one more time, his shadow a smear against the black wood of the door. Then, before Dante could react, he stepped forward out of the blur and grabbed one of the carving blades from the floor and slashed it across Dante's face.

The scream that started in my throat echoed back to me in Dante's deep voice and then echoed again from Leo until all three voices blended into one note of anguish and horror.

Dante staggered back, clutching at his face, his hands covering his eyes. Blood ran down his cheeks like red tears.

I broke free from V's grip and ran to his side, but Leo beat me there. He pulled Dante to his chest and turned him away from me.

"Abby, no, stay back."

"No, Leo, let me see. Let me help." I pressed my hands to Dante's back, his muscles twitching and quivering with each quick breath he took. "Dante? Can you hear me?" I circled around them, trying to catch a glimpse of Dante's face.

Dante panted in pain. Blood streaked through the gold chains and spiraled down his arm. "Leo, is that you? Where's Abby? I can't see." His whole body shuddered, and then he said it again, a moan of disbelief. "I can't see anything."

Two drops of blood fell from his elbow and made circles as small and thin as dimes on the dusty floor.

CHAPTER 27

I couldn't look away from those blood spots. I covered my mouth with my hands and shook my head. "No," I whispered. "Oh, please, no."

Zo threw the blade away, the clatter of the steel on stone sounding as sharp as a broken bone.

I turned on my heel, glad to have a focus for my rage. I felt my hand turn into a claw. Anger thumped in my heart; streams of fire poured out of my throat in a scream. This time, I would make Zo pay for what he had done. This time, nothing would stop me.

I rushed toward him, my hot blood burning like an inferno inside me. I reached Zo in three long strides and clamped my hand around his wrist, around the same hand he'd used to cut Dante.

He looked down in surprise, then back up to my face. His mouth curved in a small grin and I felt him start to flicker.

"No," I growled, squeezing his wrist hard enough that I felt his bones creak under the pressure. "You're not going anywhere."

Zo's grin faltered and his face twisted in confusion and anger. He tried to pull his arm away, but I held fast.

I could feel the edges of him thinning as he prepared to disappear, but I concentrated on keeping contact with him. I remembered how I had pulled Dante from the darkness between the doors. I did the same thing now, only this time I bent my will on keeping Zo from escaping. I forced myself to remember the first time I had seen him on the stage at the Dungeon. I chronicled the moments I had seen him with Valerie, the times he had hurt me or someone I loved. I pulled out of my memory each and every time he had said my name.

I wasn't surprised to feel tears washing over my face.

I *was* surprised to hear V's voice low in my ear. "Keep him locked in place, Abby," he said grimly. "I'll take care of the rest."

And then, out of the corner of my eye, I saw V flicker into shadow and reappear next to Zo.

That was when I saw the knife in V's hand, the blade still red with Dante's blood.

V clenched the hilt in his fist and drew his arm back, preparing to thrust down at Zo's chest in a killing stroke.

Shocked and surprised, I let go of Zo's arm almost reflexively—and V's blade swung down through empty air.

Zo flickered back into the room, this time behind V, who was off balance from Zo's unexpected departure. Almost casually, Zo reached out and pushed on V's arm, forcing him to follow through with his downward motion, forcing the blade to sink deep into V's upper left thigh.

Zo grasped V's hand and twisted the blade, cutting through

the main artery in V's leg. He pulled the knife out, let go of V, and stepped away.

V crumpled into a heap, blood pouring down his leg in sheets.

Zo grimaced as the blood stained his boots.

"No!" I cried and fell to my knees next to V. I pressed my hands to his leg, thinking I could stop the bleeding somehow, but he pushed me away.

"Too late," he managed, his face already turning pale.

"Oh, V, I'm sorry, I'm so sorry. I shouldn't have let go—" I didn't know what to do. There was so much blood.

"No, Abby," V said, his breathing fast and shallow. "It's all right. It's not your fault."

"Leo!" I called out over my shoulder, knowing that it was useless. He couldn't leave Dante to help me. I looked up at Zo with fury in my eyes. "Help him!"

"And why, exactly, would I do that?" he asked, his smile as pitiless as a shark.

"He was your friend," I said. V's body was cold to the touch.

"Was," Zo said shortly.

"Abby?" V said, clutching at my sleeve with a shaking hand. "Abby?"

I leaned forward, tears spilling over my cheeks. "Don't try to talk, V. Just hold on, okay? You'll be okay."

V's eyes were bright with pain and with the last light of his life. "Tell Valerie the truth for me. Tell her I loved her. Always."

He gulped down a jagged gasp.

"I will, V. I'll tell her. I promise," I said, squeezing his hand.

A faint smile appeared on his face. Then it faded, along with the light in his eyes.

"V?" I said, clutching at his limp hand, but he was gone. I bowed my head, my tears splashing onto his body.

The floor trembled beneath me, the stones creaking as they shifted on their foundation.

I looked up, startled. Leo caught my eye and we both looked up at Zo, who stood steady despite the uneven ground.

"That was faster than I thought," he said, pleased.

"What?" I asked, pushing myself to my feet. I wiped my hands on my jeans, leaving behind red handprints on the blue denim. "What have you done, Zo?"

"You know, Abby," Zo said thoughtfully, turning the blade over and over with his long fingers. "I've learned a lot since I've started traveling at will through the river. I've made some mistakes, sure, but I've tried to learn from them. One of the things that has fascinated me about the whole process of changing events is seeing how people's choices can change what happens to them. The chain reactions are fascinating. Sometimes things work out exactly as I planned." He nodded to Dante, sheltered in Leo's arms. "Sometimes I have to improvise." He knocked a toe against V's limp body.

"I've also learned that traveling *between* the bank and the river is easy. The barriers there are thin and flexible, but strong. But traveling *along* the river, as those of us with special passes can do"—he held up his wrists covered with gold chains for me to admire—"can ultimately weaken those barriers to their breaking point. And the more often we pass through them on our travels through time, the more strain we put on those barriers, and the easier they are to crack open."

"That's what you were doing with your disappearing act," I said, and the realization of Zo's plan made me catch my breath. "You were traveling along the river and making Dante follow you in order to weaken the barriers faster."

"I actually thought V might take the bait first, but it worked out better this way. V was becoming something of a problem." He sighed and slipped the knife through his belt. "Though it's too bad that Dante won't be able to see the fruits of his labors."

He turned his head to where Leo cradled Dante's body in the corner of the basement. Leo had ripped part of his shirt and tied it around Dante's eyes. The cloth was already soaked in blood.

I started heading in his direction when the ground rumbled again, louder and longer than before.

A crack appeared down the length of the basement floor, running directly toward Zo before stopping at his feet in front of the black door. Zo straddled the line, his head thrown back and his eyes closed.

"Abby?" Dante called out, his outstretched hand groping. "Abby? What's happening? Are you all right?"

I ran to his side and grabbed for his hand, holding on tight. I knelt next to Dante. My eyes met Leo's and he shook his head.

I didn't know what to do except hang on and hope. At least I was with Dante. Whatever happened, I knew I would be all right as long as we were together.

Zo lifted his arms as though he were conducting an orchestra, and for a moment the ground stopped groaning. The air seemed to be holding its breath. The sky outside the basement windows turned from blue to gray to black.

With a final, wrenching twist, Zo brought his hands together in a single, thunderous clap. The roof of the basement seemed to peel away to reveal the black sky over the bank. The darkness breathed like an approaching storm. The walls of the basement thinned to the point of transparency and through them, I could see the bank that held the river in place begin to crack and crumble. The air in the basement turned crystal as the dark cold from beyond the door seeped through into the here and now.

I felt the edges of myself thin. I heard music on the fringe of my awareness, right on the border between dreams and reality.

And then, beneath the music, I heard a roar in the distance, a husky cough like a beast on the prowl. The roaring drew closer, rushing high and fast.

The ground shifted, cracks appearing like a tightly networked web around my knees. They made a pattern I almost recognized. The sound of the destruction was a song I almost recalled. My memory suddenly bled into my present vision. I remembered standing on the bank as it dissolved and disappeared into a bottomless chasm. I remembered Zo redirecting the river to flow in new, uncharted passageways.

He was doing it again, only this time the changes weren't confined to the timeless bank. They were happening now. He was tearing down the walls that kept the river and the bank separate. They were never supposed to mix, and now that they were, there was no telling what would happen.

I remembered Zo's words from so long ago: *Something's got to give.*

I heard a tremendous rip, feeling the repercussions all the way up my legs to the base of my spine. I looked down, terrified to see water start to bubble up through the cracks in the basement floor.

The water wasn't a small puddle of rainwater, or the morning mist gathering into dewdrops. It wasn't even the cool, clear water of a mountain stream.

It was the wild, raging, silver-tipped river that carried within it all the past as it journeyed to the present and downstream into the future.

Released from the confines of the bank, the river of time suddenly crashed into the basement of Leo's Dungeon.

What had once been merely a representation of time had become an actual, physical river. Having overrun its banks, the river surged up through the ground like a whale cresting in the deep ocean. The river ran wild and fierce along the scorched stones and the ruined wreckage of the Dungeon. The curling waves washed away the ash and the dust like a baptism. The water seemed to have a strange sheen to it, an electric blue afterglow I knew I had seen somewhere before.

I struggled to stand against the rising tide; Leo helped me lift Dante to his feet. Together, the three of us waded through the water to the block of white-and-gold marble. Leo insisted I climb up out of the water and stand on top of the stone with Dante. The block wasn't big enough for all three of us, so Leo balanced carefully on a nearby filing cabinet that had tilted diagonally against the wall.

I wrapped my arms around Dante's chest and spread my feet apart on the marble to balance the extra weight.

"Abby?" Dante said, his hand finding my neck and touching my cheek. "Are you all right?"

"I'm fine," I said quickly, as though if I waited to say it, it wouldn't be true. "I'm worried about you, though."

Dante tilted his head. "What's happening? I hear water."

"Zo tore down the barriers, and now there's nothing separating the bank from the river or the river from us."

The river crashed up against the closed door of the time machine before parting around the edges and continuing to fill the room.

"Where is Zo?" Dante asked, his body trembling with fatigue and shock.

"I don't know," I said. "I can't see him anywhere." I wondered where he had gone, but it was hard to tell if the ripples I saw in the air were from Zo's disappearing trick or from the spray of the river.

"There!" Leo called out, pointing to the top of the stone stairway.

I followed his finger and saw Zo's boot heels step off the stairs and walk the perimeter of the hole that was the basement opening.

"You came!" Valerie's voice rose shrill and excited above the sound of rushing water. "I knew you'd come back for me. It's just like in the stories."

Dread filled me. What was Valerie doing here?

"I do love your pirate stores," Zo said. "I'm glad you got my message."

Valerie's laugh echoed down the stairs. "I did a good job, didn't I?"

"You were perfect. Would you be a darling and help me with this?"

"What's he doing?" I asked, craning my neck, trying to get a better view.

A slab of darkness landed over the square of sky with a hard metallic bang.

"He's trapping us in here," Leo said, his face hidden by the sudden shadows in the room.

"It just looks like he covered the opening with a board. We could still get out." I counted the paces off in my head. Five, maybe six to the door. Another seven or ten to the stairs. "I think I could do it," I called over to Leo. I could barely hear myself over the roaring water. If Valerie was here, maybe Natalie was too. If I could reach her, maybe we could get help.

Leo shook his head. "Crossing the river right now is too dangerous. I don't think any of us should touch the water unless we absolutely have to."

"Why not?"

"Look at it." Leo waved his hand over the water. "It's still full of time. Who knows what being exposed to that much of the river will do. Especially to those of us who have a different kind of relationship with time." He pointed at himself and Dante.

Then he pointed at V. The water had lifted his body as if on a pyre and the river turned ember red with his blood. V's hands, once so strong and swift, had relaxed in death, the waves lapping at his lax fingers.

The blue current that sparked through the water gathered around him, growing in intensity and brightness. V's body softened along the edges where water met skin. A silver-white shimmer appeared over his body, glittering like light, flickering like fire.

As the silver water washed over V, the outline of his body faded. Consumed from the outside in, V disappeared, washed away as completely as if he'd never been.

My heart ached to see him go. V and I had had our differences in the past, but he had turned out to be a true and loyal friend. He hadn't deserved what Zo had done to him. I hoped that he was finally at peace in the river of time.

I shifted my weight a little, trying to estimate how long before the river rose to swallow our marble perch. I could see images flowing past me in the river, but now the past and the present and the future were thrown together without any sense of how they were connected.

There was a glimpse of me with Hannah at Disneyland.

There was the same scene but without Hannah by my side.

There was a fragment of a moment where I saw Dante smiling at something I said.

There was a wisp of Leo standing on a hill, gray clouds gathering behind him.

The images ran into one seamless thread that was quickly

being twisted and knotted into a skein that might never be unraveled.

"You should go," I said suddenly to Dante. "You and Leo should go to the bank. That would be safer than being here."

Dante had started to shake his head before I even finished speaking. "I'm not leaving you," he said. "I'm sure that was what Zo was counting on when he dropped that board over the opening. He knew we couldn't wade through the river and we wouldn't leave you behind."

"Then take me with you," I said. "I've been to the bank before. I'll be okay to go again."

Again Dante shook his head. "It might be easy to go to the bank, but with the barriers down, it might not be as easy to leave. I don't dare risk it."

The water level crept closer to our toes. Leo had already started to edge up farther on the cabinet to avoid the spray and splash of the river.

I scanned the room again, desperate for a way out.

My eyes found the towering black door. Valerie's voice whispered in my ear: *How does anyone go from place to place? Through the door.*

"Dante, listen, I have an idea." I took a deep breath, trying to think it through before I said it out loud. "I'm going to open the door."

Dante opened his mouth, but I barreled on, and the more I explained it, the more certain I felt it was the right thing to do.

"It's the only way out. And I think it might be the *best* way out."

"I don't understand."

"I think if I can open the door, then the river will flow through it, right? And since the door opens to the bank, then the river will be directed back onto the bank as well. It will return to where it belongs. We can fix the barriers Zo pulled down before it gets any worse."

"You'll have to step into the river," Dante said, worried. "You heard what Leo said about how dangerous that could be."

I touched the cloth wrapped around Dante's eyes. I wanted more than anything to be able to look into his eyes right then. Not to see the quiet and constant belief that he had for me, but so Dante could see the strength and resolve in my own eyes. This was the right path, I could feel it. And I could fix this. I might be the only one who could.

I rose up on my toes and kissed Dante's mouth. I savored the taste of his lips against mine. I felt the familiar electricity running in my veins as he kissed me back.

"Abby—" he started.

"I remember the rules," I said quietly. "Do what I have to do. Change what needs to be changed."

"Come back when you can," he finished.

"I will always come home to you," I promised. I gave him one last kiss and then stepped off the stone into the river.

"Abby!" Leo called, panicked. "What are you doing?"

"What I have to," I called back. "Don't worry. I'll be okay."

The water was already past my ankles, past my calves, and inching toward my knees. My teeth started to chatter. I hadn't expected the water to be so cold. I would have to hurry.

I counted my steps to the door. One.

The electric blue aura crackled like broken ice around my legs. Two.

Numbness crept up my body, my fingers and toes the first to succumb to the unbearable cold. Three.

I could hear voices now along with the images swirling all around me. They sounded like my family—Mom, Dad, Hannah. They sounded close enough to touch. Four.

Music slowly enveloped me in a crescendo of sound. Five.

I was at the door. The water pushed against my knees, almost toppling me where I stood. I grabbed hold of the freestanding frame with hands that felt two sizes too big for my body. Struggling to keep my balance, I ran my fingers over the carved images on the door.

When I found the center point of the door, the spot where the two halves of the hourglass met in its timeless kiss, I placed my palm against the wood and pushed.

The door swung open on its silent hinge, revealing a yawning, gaping hole of darkness.

The river poured into the void.

I clung to the door frame as the churning, frothing water bubbling with images and sound funneled past me, threatening to wash me away with it as it flowed along the channel heading for its eventual destination: the bank.

The music in my head was loud and brassy. I couldn't hear myself think for the constant chimes that rang like church bells all around me.

I clung to the doorway as the level of the water slowly lowered from my knees, to my calves, to my ankles. The river swirled into the darkness of the door until finally there were only a few puddles of water still lingering in the crevices and holes of the basement floor.

I had no real way of knowing if my plan had worked, but I suspected it had. No new water was bubbling up from the cracked floor. The images were fading along with the voices. Even the music was settling down to silence again.

I almost dared to breathe again.

And then I remembered. My job wasn't finished. I had come to the Dungeon with one purpose in mind: to walk my own path through the time machine. I set one foot on the threshold of the door—and paused.

Turning around, I took one last look at Dante, standing as tall as an angel on the white-and-gold marble block, his body taut with tension, his face turned toward me even though he couldn't see me.

Leo climbed down off the cabinet and rushed to my side. "Are you all right, Abby?" he asked.

"It worked," I said with a grin. The numbness in my fingers and toes was fading, but slowly. "It really worked."

"Of course it did," Leo said. "It was a brilliant plan. Dangerous, but brilliant."

My grin faded. I couldn't make my eyes leave Dante's face. "I'm still going through the door, Leo. I have to. For Dante. For my family."

"I know," he said quietly.

"Will he be all right?" I asked, glad that Leo knew what I meant and didn't make me ask the terrible question that hung in the space between us: *Is he blind?*

"He will be fine," Leo assured me. "I'll make sure of it."

"Take care of him for me, okay?" I asked, placing my hand on his arm.

"Like he was my own brother," he said with a wry smile.

I laughed. "You'd better."

"Go," Leo said gently, his eyes both bright and sad. "And don't worry—you'll see Dante again soon enough."

I nodded, my heart taking hope in Leo's promise.

I lifted up on my toes, my hand clutching the door frame for balance, and called out to Dante, "I love you—always and forever!"

Dante raised his hand at the sound of my voice. "Abby!" he called out. "I'll be waiting for you."

Turning back to the door, I smiled one last time at Leo and then faced the unbroken black void in front of me.

I crossed the threshold in two steady steps.

I stood for a moment simply listening to my breathing, counting the beats of my heart. I thought about nautilus shells, and about stars that gleamed golden in the sky, and about travelers through time. I thought about angels who were trapped in stone and angels who wore gold chains around their wrists. I thought about spirals that needed to be closed into circles.

The music, which I thought had gone, returned in a series of beautiful notes lifting up in a rising scale.

I gathered my courage and held Dante's love like a diamond close to my heart. I stepped forward, ready to face the past that would become my future.

The door closed behind me, and then all was darkness.

ACKNOWLEDGMENTS

When I sat down to write this book, I thought, *No sweat. I've done this once before. I can do it again.*

Well, I should have known better. After all, no two books are the same—not in reading them, and not in writing them. I quickly learned that the methods and strategies that worked so well for me in *Hourglass Door* didn't work at all for *Golden Spiral.* It was its own book and it wasn't shy about letting me know who was boss this time around. (Hint: It wasn't me.)

So I'd like to take this opportunity to thank those people who were slaving away with me while this book took shape.

My family, who understood when I had to bail on yet another Sunday dinner and who never sighed or rolled their eyes (at least that I saw) when I wouldn't stop talking about my book.

A very special thanks goes to my brother, Dennis, who gave me a crash course in darkroom development one afternoon. Any technical details about the process I got wrong are clearly my fault and not his.

Thanks to my friends, fans, and fellow authors, whose

constant messages of support and enthusiasm via e-mail, Facebook, and in person did not go unnoticed.

Once again, my writing group rose to the occasion and read huge chunks of this book despite a tight deadline and still managed to give me valuable, useful, and indispensable advice. So thank you, Tony, Heidi, Crystal, Pam, Mary, and Kristen. You guys are the best!

Thanks to the team at Shadow Mountain—Chris Schoebinger, Emily Watts, Tonya Facemyer, and Richard Erickson, to name only a few—who care for me like family and who are always in my corner, looking out for me and my books.

Last, but never least, I must thank the love of my life, Tracy, for countless instances of making dinner, doing dishes, and running errands so I could stay chained to my laptop and find the words I needed to tell this story. There are no words, however, to express my deepest love and appreciation for his endless encouragement and support. I could not have done this without him.

Aside from learning to bend my will to the demands of the muse and working under her unrelenting whip of deadlines, I learned two very important lessons about writing:

First, write wherever you are. In addition to writing at home, I wrote sections of this book at the Spanish Fork Library, the Whitmore Library, in the waiting room of Presley Orthodontics and Family Cosmetic Dentistry, and on my daily commute on the UTA TRAX train.

Second, find inspiration wherever you can. One night I dreamed my friend James Dashner and Hannah Montana were doing the "Thriller" dance, complete with the zombie moves and the makeup. That dream saved the ending of this book. It's probably best if you don't ask too many questions. Trust me on that one.

Reading Guide

1. Was it a surprise to discover that the prologue was written from Zo's point of view? Did seeing the story through Zo's eyes change how you viewed V, Tony, or Dante? How did you feel about Zo's perception of his relationship with Abby?

2. Valerie tells Abby several stories of the Pirate King and the River Policeman. Why is it sometimes easier to speak the truth in the guise of a story? What stories have resonated with truth to you?

3. In *The Golden Spiral,* Abby learns more about photography and developing film in a darkroom and suspects she may have found a new way to express herself. What activities or hobbies do you enjoy that provide an outlet for your creative expression? What new activities have you always wanted to try?

4. At one point in the story, Abby realizes that Zo is working to isolate her from her friends and family. Why is it so important to have a support system around you during difficult times? Who helps you when times are tough?

5. V's loyalty is often in question during the course of the novel. Did you trust him? Did you suspect he was hiding something? Did he deserve his fate?

6. Zo asks Abby if there is a memory she would like to forget. Do you have memories you would rather forget? What events or feelings in your life do you want to remember forever?

7. Dante tells Abby the story of how he met Leonardo da Vinci and that da Vinci wanted an apprentice who could "leave the world a more beautiful place than he found it." In what ways have you left your mark on the world? Where do you find beauty in the world?

8. Dante and Abby are both striving to build a relationship that allows them to be their best selves with each other. What characteristics are important to you in your relationships? How would you describe the ideal relationship?

9. The book touches on the importance of making choices of your own free will, of shaping your own destiny and future. Are there choices you have made that have changed the course of your life?

THE STORY OF ABBY AND DANTE CONCLUDES IN

THE FORGOTTEN LOCKET